Darkly Sweet

Juliann Whicker

Copyright © 2018 by Juliann Whicker

All rights reserved. No part of this publication may be reproduced, stored in a retrieval system or transmitted by any other means, electronic, mechanical, photocopying, recording, or otherwise without prior written permission of the copyright owner.

Cover Illustration: Juliann Whicker
Graphic Design: John H. Whicker

The characters, places, and events portrayed in this book are fictitious. Any similarity to real persons, living or dead, places, or events are coincidental and not intended by the author.

For you, babe. Because no one else makes nonsense.

Witch

In the dim interior of my cavernous attic, I mixed ten ounces of helichrysm oil with four ounces of frankincense. I stirred rapidly with the glass mixer then divided it into the golden bottles labeled 'Darkly Sweet' before topping them off with the various other potions and lotions I carried in my shop.

As I worked, the best thing happened: time went by without me thinking or worse, feeling. I didn't notice that the candles had burned down or that my stomach rumbled until a solid, 'thunk, thunk' reverberated through my drafty attic. I sighed and capped the last bottles of my current batch and stood up, stretching. I shoved my hip-length black braids behind my shoulders and smoothed down the black dress with white collar, sharp points framing the mouse-skull brooch at my throat.

I took my time walking away from the quarter of the attic where I kept my lab. I straightened a stack of boxes, the dark background and poppy print with green vines my signature packaging. I'd have to order more in the small size this afternoon. With every step away from my lab, it grew darker until I could barely see the enormous fieldstone fireplace to my right or the body dangling on my left. I ran my fingers over the stone, the sloping shape and smooth texture soothing. My stomach tangled into knots the closer I got to the door.

I stood on the far end of the wide expanse of floor between the fireplace and the door, nothing besides the ropes tied to the rafter above me and dust. Lots of dust.

"Come in," I said in a low voice he shouldn't have been able to hear.

The door swung in slowly, revealing the dark silhouette of Revere, my step-father, backlit from the light on the landing.

He hesitated, flicking his fingers slightly, probably checking for booby traps before he entered in his black suit.

"Penny, this is your last chance."

I looked away from him towards the picture on the mantel. No, to where the picture used to be on the mantel. "What does that mean, chance? It's such a strange word, like dance or prance or glance, all kind of flirting. That's what I would be doing, flirting with the ultimate danger, the ultimate end."

He sighed and his fingers slipped into his suit pocket. "When is the last time you've eaten? You've been avoiding me. It doesn't matter. If you don't do what you must, everything you know will be torn apart whether you pretend it isn't happening or not." He took two steps into the room, his step soft and muted.

"I don't care. I've tried to care, but I don't. When she falls her screams will only echo the agony in my heart."

He sighed a dry sigh. "So melodramatic." He flipped the switch and I was left blinking in the sudden, horribly garish brightness. "How can you see through the haze of dust? You're acting like a child. You know perfectly well that the will explicitly states—"

"That I must marry a peer before my eighteenth birthday, but has it occurred to you that I am a child? Seventeen and to be fattened and sent to the seething hordes of the soulless elite with nothing to protect me from their diabolical devices." My lips curled as I glared at him, anger waking up inside my chest.

He stared me down, his black eyes and blacker hair gleaming in the light from the electric sconces that lined the walls. "You're hardly fat," he said drily. "You haven't eaten anything other than your emergency protein bars in days. You've been avoiding me, making me climb these stairs and enter your sanctum of dust. Penny, I know that you've wrapped yourself up like a spider in your own web, sucking the life out of yourself as you feed on nothing but memories, but it's going to end. You can't live like this anymore. You have to accept reality. Either you die and your mother with you, or you put your best foot forward and win the hand of a mage."

I rolled my eyes at him. He wasn't the only one who could be disgusted. "Someone like you, I suppose, someone clean and tidy, someone who knows how to do everything right."

"Someone who can cast a proper spell, hopefully, someone who knows the basics of defense. But most importantly, a peer, someone who knows that magic is only worth as much as the mind behind it."

"Mind? You mean money."

"Yes, Penny. You're going to Rosewood to find the most eligible male you can get to marry you. Either that, or this world, your world will be gone. Your mother, she'll be gone and so will every memory you ever made with…"

I held up a hand, a sharp move that silenced him. My heart pounded and darkness crept into the edges of my vision. I swallowed hard while I blinked it away. "Never. I'd rather die. I'd rather be burned alive and ripped limb from limb than talk to a stupid boy. You think I can make a man my slave, like mother did to you, but I don't have allurement. No. I'll find another house. I have my business even if it's not like the soulless beauty corporation great grandma founded, it's mine and it's enough."

He frowned at me. "Your mother didn't… You don't need allurement. You're a…" He stared at me with a consternated expression while he tried to think of something positive to say. "You're a special girl. You may not have all of your mother's talents, but you're clever. You have other gifts that are more rare and valuable than you know. I understand that you're afraid, but you can look at this as a business proposition."

"I'm not afraid."

He glanced at me skeptically and I shifted under that gaze. I hadn't left the house in months. Maybe I was getting as bad as my mother, the shut-in who could not leave without having a complete breakdown. The last time she'd left the house, I'd had to drag her back inside by her hair after I found her convulsing in the gravel road thirty feet from the front door.

I shook my head and wrapped the end of one of my braids around my hand. "It's a waste of time. You don't seriously think that I can trick a mage into marrying me, do you?"

He smiled slightly. "Mages are still half human. You can appeal to their humanity."

"Lust?"

He curled his lip. "The Darkness is full of lust, Penny. Be very cautious when wielding such a dangerous weapon."

I wound the braid around my wrist. "Charm?"

He hesitated as he looked at me. "Charm is what one makes others see rather than what one is. No, what you are…" He shook his head and stepped away from me towards the door. "Rosewood is full of vain, self-absorbed, bored children who have never wanted anything. All you need to be is what they want. Shall I take it that you're going?" He edged towards the door, his inner dust devil stirring. He hated mess but that didn't keep him away from my mother whose mind was a chaotic blur of madness mixed with insanity.

That's what this was about. Did I save my mother and sacrifice myself? She would stay here as the house was demolished around her. Would she mind dying very much? Probably not. Would I or would I rather leave here, find a place to live, deal with people, get on with my life? What life? I had my business and Señor Mort, but I wasn't happy. Had I ever been happy? Maybe a long time ago, before grandmama died, before Poppy…

"I'll go. For mother."

I stared at him and he stared back, both of us shocked at the words that had just come out of my mouth.

He smiled slightly. "If you had known her before…" His smile faded as he turned, heading down the stairs. "You need to have your trunks packed by tomorrow with whatever you want to take to the dormitory. I know that it's going to be a difficult transition for you, but I am certain you will find others who share your love of black and the skeletons of rodents."

I fingered the bleached skull at my throat and the others wound in my braids. "You're going to miss me, Revere. You're going to miss having a sane person in the old lady." I raised my voice as he disappeared from view down the curving stairs.

"Pushy, cantankerous old care taker." I slammed the door and turned to survey my kingdom. The attic covered most of the house, so for sheer square footage it gave me plenty of room for most of my everyday activities. The center was taken up by an enormous hearth and wide chimneys from the fireplaces downstairs. Candles and mirrors were sprinkled throughout the space and ropes hung from the rafters. To my right was a little alcove where a body dangled amidst the myriad dripping strands, Dandy's purple and black suit stuck through with hat pins. To my left was the bed, the armoire, and the wall that was an actual straight wall instead of the interior curves of the mansard roof. A French door led to a small patio and let in a little bit of natural light. Behind the chimney, past the body, was my lab.

My little business wasn't nearly so small and insignificant as Revere seemed to think. Darkly Sweet was a serious brand in indie beauty products. I'd seen several knock-offs that didn't have anything on my brand. Maybe it was small compared to the family business, the soulless beauty corporation Great Grandma had established, but it was mine in a way nothing else was.

I'd just agreed to go to school and catch a mage, one of those dreadful, monstrous beasties who would eat your heart out and make you love him while he did it. I was going to be sick.

I dragged two enormous trunks out of the shadows under the eaves, dust puffing off them when I flung back the lids. I packed away my vials and tubes with meticulous care, layers and layers of packing bubbles between until I was certain nothing would destroy my lab, my livelihood. That took up most of the trunk and the rest I packed with ingredients, herbs, oils, bottles and boxes.

The other trunk I stared at before opening the armoire, studying the rows of dresses, skirts, blouses, and the bulky capes made of impermeable rubber interfaced with a thin layer of lead. My fingers lingered on the golden yellow cape, the color Poppy's hair had been.

I whirled from the armoire and flung myself across the bed, muffling my scream in the mattress. After I had that out of my system, I didn't waste any time but reached under the bed and pulled out the laptop, booting up and checking the battery life. A quick search found Rosewood Academy, your generic preppy looking building, all marble pillars and leaded windows. So the insulation wouldn't be, and neither would the security. Great, that is.

I went back to the shadows and pulled out two more trunks. I filled them with quilts and tapestries, wooded scenes mostly. Grandmama had collected a wide assortment of tapestries on her travels through Europe. Most of them were quirky and had something odd about them, like the humans had chicken feet, or the trees had faces.

I flopped back on my bed and was surprised when my laptop chimed and then said, "Welcome to Rosewood, Penny Lane," in a pseudo-aristocratic New England accent. The screen had a scrollwork banner along the top, "Meet your peers," and faces of boys and girls I imagined I'd soon see in person.

An image slid onto the screen, a guy with dark eyes and a sneer, with red hair artfully messy in sharp contrast to his cravat and diamond stick pin. We had paintings in the gallery overlooking the hall of that kind of ridiculous tie, but they went with wigs and careful coifs, and not the diamond stud in his ear. Too quickly, the screen slid to another face, and I had to watch the whole thing around in a loop before it got back to him. This time, I clicked through to find professional looking shots of him—Drake Huntsman, apparently—in equestrian gear riding horses and hitting a ball with a stick (while creaming two other players) and dressed in a tux. I stared at the tux photo where he stood next to a dazzling brunette in a blue satin gown. Blue wasn't enough to capture the glamour. Peacock. Yes. Peacock that matched her eyes. He stood beside her looking indifferent, like the shot was taken before the moment of action unlike most of the other photos. He gave the impression of constant movement; even when he didn't move, his eyes seemed to show the action of his mind.

I sat back and closed my laptop. "Good-bye, Penny Lane."

Creepy. What kind of guy did I want to marry? I couldn't help but snort out loud. It was the most ridiculous thing in the world to try to seriously contemplate something that insane. Yes, I'd always known that was part of Grandmama's will, ever since the funeral when I was thirteen, but I'd done my best to pretend that it would all go away. Poppy…

I opened the laptop with a jerk and focused on the image of the Drake and … "Witley Penmore" at the "Annual Winter Musical Extravaganza." I opened a new window and typed Drake Huntsman in the search bar. That revealed a whole new dimension to his character. There were videos of him and his friends walking down a hall while girls bounced and squealed like rabbits that had been shot.

I watched video after video until I saw one titled, "Christmas Tree Suicide." I thought it would be something like a pathetic school play, but instead there was screaming in the background, dark night, snow, and this enormous Christmas tree in the middle of a courtyard, some kid at the top of it. The video zoomed in and I could see his face, see the way he clutched at his neck while he dangled there, hanging.

After a flurry of evergreen limbs, the camera refocused on Drake wading through the greenery of the now fallen tree. He hauled the guy out and then with this snarling smile punched him hard and fast in the face. Drake hit him until he staggered over, then Drake kneed him so that he jerked and sprawled onto the ground. Drake stopped for a second, staring at the other boy with his wild, crazy look in his eyes before he drew back his big black boot and started kicking.

That's when he started yelling, expletives that I wasn't very familiar with—being homeschooled and all—on and on until I closed my laptop with shaky fingers then pulled my knees up to my chest and started rocking.

Poppy. Cruel boys who ruined lives carelessly. It took me a long time before I could open the laptop and go back to Rosewood to find the boy who had been the tree ornament. When Drake's image passed, I pressed my thumb to his face.

"You're dead!"

Before much longer I found the other guy, Zachary Stoneburrow, brown-haired, nice looking enough, but not in sports or music, or anything else as far as I could find.

I searched the school photos and found him in the periphery: sitting in bleachers by himself, sitting at a table in the dining room by himself, a loner in a sea of guppies. He was a peer, though. He was eligible as my spouse. I hissed at the preposterous notion and leapt off the bed to open the armoire and dig through to the back, the lacy, frilly dress-up dresses I hadn't worn since Poppy... We'd had elaborate tea parties that lasted for days, combining drama, music and sparring with the consumption of tea and finger sandwiches.

If I wanted a nice guy, I had to be a nice girl. When I went somewhere where there were other people I felt less and less comfortable until I was snarling like Señor Mort. Who could snarl when they were cute and happy? I would be like those French candy sandwiches dyed unnatural colors. Macaroons. I used to love the macaroons Grandmama brought back after one of her long trips.

Remembering her, I left every single black thing in my closet and filled up the trunk with lace, pink, and florals. I went to close the trunk, hesitated then threw in the lead-lined black cloak. I could survive a nuclear blast in that thing.

After that was my sewing machine and fabrics in the school colors. I'd have to come up with my own elaborate uniform that somehow broke all barriers between myself and Zachary Stoneburrow, because I was going to marry him. Hopefully he liked legs more than breasts, although I could always buy a bigger pair if it came down to it.

I closed the lid of the last trunk with finality then shoved them to the door where they'd be taken in a very few hours.

Standing in front of the mirror propped above the mantel, I held up my two plaits before letting them slap down against my neck. I'd had "pitch" in my hair since Poppy tried to light it on fire when I was ten. The name 'pitch' was for irony. It wouldn't catch fire like actual pitch. It would take ages to get it all out. I pushed up my long black sleeves and got to work.

2
WITCH

I stood at the airport, hip length strawberry blond hair curling like crazy, as I waved goodbye to Revere, driving away in the nondescript gray sedan. I sucked on my lollipop, specially packed with caffeine and sugar so I'd be the bubbly macaroon I needed to be. It was either that or kill everyone.

I stood there beside Señor Mort's pink floral fabric covered cage and my pink carry-on, facing the road, waiting for the limo. I didn't look at the kids coming towards me, pretending not to hear the guy's, 'the driver's late,' or the girl's muttered response.

The white limo pulled up and the driver came around, took off his white cap at us and opened the back door. I stepped forward and bumped into the guy who happened to be Zachary Stoneburrow. Ha! Like that kind of accident happens. I'd gotten in contact with one of my few friends, friend is too strong a term, one of my clients who exchanged certain services for my less marketable goods in my Darkly Sweet shop. In other words, she wanted hurters, and I wanted hacking. It was an extremely satisfying relationship.

I pulled out my lollipop and gave him what I hoped was a sweet and shy smile. "Excuse me?"

"This is my limo," he said, his dark brows lowering over his troubled blue eyes, but he sounded uncertain.

I turned to the driver. "Do you know who ordered the limo?"

He nodded and pulled out his phone. "One limo from the airport to Rosewood Academy, ordered by Stoneburrow and Lane."

"I'm Lane," I offered but cocked my head, hesitating and widening my eyes at Zach adorably. "But who is Stoneburrow?"

"I'm Zachary Stoneburrow." He stared at me while he ran a hand through his brown hair, longish, like it needed a trim.

I beamed at him and grabbed his hand, shaking it while his eyes went big and he blinked at me in shock and mild terror, echoing how my own heart pounded. I'd never touched a mage before.

"I'm Penny Lane. It's so nice to meet you. Do you go to Rosewood? It's my school now and I'm so excited to get to know everyone."

He pulled away and nudged the girl who looked about half as scary and morbid as I had a week before. Her hair was dyed black, her eyes lined with layers of black eyeliner and smudged into her lashes over her high quality base that evened her skin tone. Her makeup was very subtle, giving the impression that she'd carelessly rolled out of bed looking like that. My makeup was more, of course, because I had color, pink cheeks with high gloss lips and sparkly eye shadow. So much sparkle and bubbly color.

I bounced and caught her hands. "Do you go to Rosewood too? I'm Penny Lane. It's so nice to meet you."

She glared at me, her lips curling while her nails would have cut my palms if they hadn't been bitten to the quick. I hadn't chewed on my thumb since I'd thrown myself into becoming Penny Lane resident macaroon, and therefore my nails were in better shape. When I accidentally squeezed her hands back she winced before jerking away.

"That's Viney," Zach said after a long pause. "So, you go to Rosewood?"

I nodded and sucked on my lollipop, trying to look seductively at him while also looking perky and cute. I'd practiced in my full-length mirror for hours, but it felt utterly ridiculous, particularly when I swished my super short skirt. His eyes widened as they darted down to my naked legs, tortuously waxed and polished with my best-selling lotion.

"Deal with it," Viney said shoving between us and climbing into the back seat of the limo.

Zach looked at me apologetically. "Don't mind Viney. She doesn't deal very well with surprises. I think she's a little stressed."

I blinked at him. Viney was perfectly fine as far as I could tell. I sucked on my lollipop before taking one last lick and cocking my head to study him. "Your girlfriend does seem a little bit tense. You should give her a back rub. I have the perfect lotion…"

He shook his blond hair and backed away. "Viney's not my girlfriend. We're friends. More or less."

"I'm sorry." I grimaced and bit my lower lip adorably. "This is kind of awkward. That is so strange that the same limo got scheduled for two different people, even if they are going to the same place… Why don't I take a taxi, or a bus? They have those here, don't they?"

He shrugged and frowned at me before he gave me a slight smile. "Don't worry about it. If you don't mind riding with Viney, it doesn't make sense for you to take the bus to Fairfield and then the shuttle up to the school." With that, he ducked inside the limo while the limo driver finished putting stacks of luggage into the enormous trunk.

I stood on the sidewalk pretending to think about it before I swished my skirt one last time in case he was watching me out the window, picked up my bag and my cage then ducked into the black interior.

"Black and white, like a checkerboard," I said as I settled across from Viney on the same bench Zach sat on.

She sneered at me before looking out the window.

Zach cleared his throat. "So, you're new at Rosewood? What year are you?"

"I'm a senior. I did homeschool and had private tutors, you know the whole crazy rich person thing, but for my last year I wanted to try something new, so here I am." Lie. "I'm so excited! It's going to be so fun to meet all the fabulous people." Double lie.

He gave me a tight smile and a small nod before he leaned over his knees and kind of studied the floor.

"What's the school like?"

"Don't worry, Penny, you'll fit in just right with all the crazy rich people." Viney glared at me, showing her teeth beneath her curled lips.

I beamed at her and leaned forward, brushing Zach's pants leg with my own bare knee while I covered Viney's hands in mine. "That is so sweet of you to say. Thank you, Viney. I'm so glad that I met you guys." I turned to Zach and gave him an enormous smile, close enough that I could smell his aftershave and he certainly smelled my subtle floral perfume that was a natural mood enhancer. I stayed there for the count of three before I slid back into my seat so my short skirt flipped up higher on my thighs before I smoothed it back down.

Did they notice my hands shaking? I was envious of Viney's black boots, so much like the boots I'd left behind. She wore them below her navy pants and a skull t-shirt with argyle vest and navy jacket, sleeves rolled up to show various bracelets with spikes and leather up her arm. The spikes went with her short hair that she'd moussed artfully.

"I love your hair, Viney. It's so authentic." I turned to Zach and put my hand on his knee. "Do you know if there's a pet store in Fairfield? I'm not sure how long my supplies will last for Señor Mort."

He blinked at me and I pulled away my hand before he could push it off.

"A pet store? I think so."

I bounced, flipping my skirt. I sucked on my lollipop because I needed a lot more sugar if I was going to keep this up for the entire ride to school. It should take forty-five minutes.

"Pets aren't allowed at Rosewood." That was Viney.

I felt the rock in my stomach I'd been trying to ignore get harder and bigger. "No pets?"

Zach nodded. "It's a school rule."

"But Señor is more of a... service animal than a pet." That was true. I had him sample suspicious goods to make sure that they weren't poisoned. Didn't that count?

"The dorm lady doesn't mind so long as it doesn't smell and doesn't make noise. They had to make the rule a few years ago when some senior decided she wanted to breed alligators."

I blinked at him and felt my actual real smile for a second before I replaced it with my macaroon face. "That's crazy. What happened?"

He spent a long time telling the story about the alligators getting out and causing a stampede while a few made it into the testing hall and disrupted the Chem exam. He took a break to talk about the horrors of exam week, and the dreadful Chem exam in particular before he went back to the story of the alligators.

It wasn't too much work to laugh a few times. He told a good story and after he forgot to be self-conscious and stopped looking at Viney where she sat with her phone, he actually showed some personality that had been impossible to see from the photos. All in all, not bad.

Finally, we got to a small town at the base of the hills, Fairfield, with a lot of cute shops, one with a dog bone under the sign. All the shops looked like they were from one of those happy movie sets, immaculate sidewalks, clear vibrant colors, and people who smiled as they went about their work.

It wasn't anything like the closest small town to the old lady. That had a ratty thrift store that made the big box store look high class in comparison. All the same, I'd loved that thrift store and the discount fabric store thirty miles away.

I shook my head and smiled at Zach. "This town is adorable. Does it have a candy shop?"

"You'd be right at home in the gum ball dispenser," Viney sneered.

I smiled back at her because she was trying to be edgy. It was cute.

"I do like lollipops too much. My mother is always trying to get me to stop sucking on them." Lie. Like my mother cared. "Do you want one?" I pulled two out of my jacket and held them out to Viney and Zach.

He took one while she sneered and turned away with her nose in the air. Her nose was really cute, kind of perky at the end. That nose would have helped my own look although it didn't do much for hers. I had the urge to offer to switch noses, but she wouldn't get it.

I unwrapped another lollipop and stuck it in my mouth.

He made a weird face. "Is this coffee flavored?" He took it out and studied the dark color.

"Tiramisu. It's my favorite dessert." Truth. "Is it too weird?"

He studied it for a few more seconds before he shrugged and stuck it back in his mouth before he turned to me and gave me a slight smile around his white lollipop stick.

He was nice. The rock in my stomach softened a little bit as we went to the base of the hills and through an elaborate arch over the road with Rosewood in ironwork over the top. The trees grew close to the road, woods that seemed to beckon me to come and play, to have a picnic. I forgot to chat for most of the trip until I got the first view of Rosewood. The online picture didn't show the enormous structure that I saw a flicker of through the trees.

"It's huge."

Viney made a rude sound. "What did you expect?"

I blinked at her and kind of stammered. "Not Pemberly. I shall expect to find Mr. Darcy in a place like this."

Her eyes widened and we stared at each other, kind of uncertain before I looked away and flashed a smile at Zach. He was studying me, his eyebrows slightly close together, almost concerned. "So, you've been homeschooled your whole life?"

I nodded.

"You've never been in the company of peers before?"

I cocked my head like I had to think about it before I shook my head.

He shifted uncomfortably. "They can be difficult to get along with, sometimes impossible. If you get on the wrong side of one of the popular kids you can have a really horrible experience."

He sounded so passive, not like 'they will torture you,' but like it was your fault somehow for other people being jerks, hanging you in a tree and then beating the crap out of you when you have the nerve to fall out. I shrugged. "I'm sure it'll be fine." Lie. "I mean, I already have two tentative friends so how bad could it be? Are you one of the popular kids at school, Zach?"

He looked horrified before he laughed and shook his head. "No. I'm not interested in that kind of thing. It's a balancing act. It takes a lot of concentration to stay on the top of a stack of volcanoes."

"Popularity is a waste of time. It turns people who would otherwise be worth something into worthless non-people."

I kind of winced at Viney before I forced a smile. It was just such a bad use of English. "That's so true. Those non-people are the worst. Are you sure you don't want a lolly Viney? I have some mulled cider ones that you might like."

"I want one of those," Zach said and I dug in my bag for one.

Viney studied me for a long time before she shrugged and rolled her eyes. "I don't hate tiramisu. I'll try one."

I handed her one and unwrapped my own special calming brew flavored like Lavender, St. John's wart, Melissa, and dirt. The rock reformed in my stomach as the limo pulled up in front of a brick building separated from the main structure by an enormous field where people milled around in their school uniforms holding bags and glittering with fancy jewelry.

I wanted to light the limo on fire as a diversion before I skulked to my room and hid there for the rest of the year. Instead, I took a deep, calming breath and smiled at Zach.

"I guess we're here. Do you know where Lilac dorm is?"

"You're kidding me." Viney's snarl practically dripped venom.

I gave her my most innocent and sweet look. Okay, it wasn't even my look; it was completely somebody else's, because I didn't have an innocent and sweet anything. "I'm in Lilac wing, room One-Oh-Eight."

"That's the haunted wing." Viney's eyes glinted with anticipation as she leaned forward. "No one lasts very long in Lilac Stories."

Zach cleared his throat. "That's where our rooms are, actually. Ghosts don't bother us very much."

I looked from him to her and then burst out laughing. "Very funny, guys. Are you serious about being in the Lilac wing? What a crazy coincidence! This is going to be so much fun!"

I opened the limo door and got out, stretching before I grabbed Señor Mort's cage and my bag. I smiled at Zach while he sat there, hesitating. "Would you show me the way to my room? I'm sorry if that's too much, I mean you were willing to share a ride, but..."

"Of course, we'll take you to the room." Viney slid over and I had to back up quickly to keep from being knocked over by her. She was shorter than me, but kind of like a cannonball.

I smiled and followed the two, Zach seeming to get more and more uncomfortable the closer we got to the building where more people stared at us. Zach didn't meet anyone's gaze but I was bubblegum, so I sucked on my lolly and waved and smiled at absolutely everyone who met my eyes, plus some who didn't. I was so busy smiling and waving that I didn't quite realize that I had broken an unspoken circle of popularity until the crowd became silent in an ominous way.

I glanced around, but Zach and Viney had stopped walking, letting me wander into the middle of the most beautiful and well-manicured set of people I'd ever seen. It was like they were all movie stars carefully prepped for the red carpet. I couldn't help but stare at them kind of fascinated, at the tall and muscular blond guy who had two girls hanging on his every word, but his words from what I could tell were eloquent and clever, if tinged with a touch of the sardonic.

He saw me staring at him and a flash of predator came over his features before he glanced down at the blond he'd been entertaining then walked over to me, the few steps before we were a foot apart, too close for a casual meeting, and the way he looked down his nose at me, the way he studied me, like he was analyzing every piece of me to see how well I'd been put together, well, I really wanted to light his perfectly tailored coat on fire and watch him run around the green screaming.

The image made me smile as I took out the lolly. "Hi, I'm Penny. Let me see if I can remember your name from the website. Drake?" Somehow I was certain that me comparing him to the incomparable would really irritate him. I have instincts like that sometimes.

His eyes narrowed while the blond girl tittered and then slapped her hand over her mouth while the guy studied me up and down like I was a pretty piece of pie. I returned the favor, glancing up and down his body the way he did mine. Was this normal? It felt weird.

"You have nice legs," he said moving a little bit closer.

I struggled to stand my ground without shoving the end of my lollipop through his eye socket. I licked my lips. "Thanks. They're super long. You have really nice hair. It's as yellow as dandelions." I stuck my lollipop back in my mouth and stared at him with my most charming look.

"How dare you!" The girl's hiss came right before someone shoved me from the side. It wasn't a docile girly push, but a serious rugby player shove and I went over while my back whiplashed. I hit someone's legs, bony knees and shins, and then I was lying on the ground, well he was on the ground and I was on his legs with my head on his thigh area pressed against his extremely nice wool pants, seasonless wool, you know, the good stuff. I blinked up past his crotch to the face beyond, an exquisite face of pale creamy skin, dark glittering green eyes framed by a crown of fire that fell over his forehead like a tumble of volcano stuff. Lava. Right. There were words for things. The rock in my stomach exploded and shattered my whole body with volcano shrapnel.

I froze there in that incredibly awkward position, staring at the most beautiful and evil mage in the entire universe. It took me a second to find words. "Hi. I'm Penny."

He quirked an arched eyebrow that he had to tweeze to get so perfect. "I'm Drake. Jackson doesn't like being mistaken for me. It's the red hair. He'd hate people to think that he had a temper." His voice was as beautiful as the rest of him, smooth and silky, like his skin and hair, but beneath the silk was a layer of steel, the kind used for medieval racks and other implements of torture. His voice was torture, all of him the most cruel trick played on women since the beginning of time. Someone that beautiful should be thrown into a lake of bubbling hot lava.

"Or a volcano." What? I'd said that out loud?

He blinked, narrowed his dark eyes then nodded. Oh, good, because he'd said something about having a temper, and that was practically like a volcano. Macaroons and bonbons. Truffles and pecan strudel. Lollipops and ding dongs.

"Or a volcano. You're new to our school." It wasn't a question and it wasn't an accusation, I wasn't sure what it was. A challenge?

No challenges. Ice cream cones, petit fours, not volcanoes or anything else explosive. I smiled and nodded while my heart pounded and fluttered and my stomach tried to recover from the shrapnel thing. While I tried to catch my breath I caught his scent, musk and grass with a dash of something sweet and dark.

"You're on top of me. Are you going to stay there all day?" His voice was amused and full of something mocking that sent a flush of pure unadulterated shame through me.

I gasped and scrambled off him while my cheeks burned. I was supposed to avoid Drake and every other mage like him. I was here to find a husband, not get involved with the king of wicked mages, the guy who tormented Zach who I was going to marry. I was still mixed up. I should want to stab his eye with the end of my lolly, not loiter on his trousers. I glanced down and there was my lollipop, fused to his trousers. I used my long arms to my advantage, quickly snagged the lolly, and stuck it in my mouth. He froze while I backed off, gave him as much of a smile as I could with something shoved in my face. It was supposed to calm me down, but if I didn't get out of there very, very soon, I was going to find out who had pushed me and I would rip off their face and terrify absolutely everyone, including Zach, who I was going to marry.

My heart pounded in my chest as I searched for the cage I'd dropped in the scuffle. Jackson had it, had Señor Mort, holding the cage high. I studied him and then glanced at Drake who was watching me intently. I hated him watching me, hated how aware I was of him, and (even though he wasn't my opponent in this battle) hated turning my back on him.

"Macaroon," I reminded myself as I swung around to Jackson. I jammed my lollipop in his mouth and leapt to snag the cage, landing without mishap in my heels with Señor Mort who was hopefully only shaken up and not completely unhinged. From the scuffling beneath the floral cover, unhinged was coming really fast.

"So nice to meet all of you," I sang as I broke out of the perfect circle with my cage swinging in a dangerous arc that kept back any other would-be rugby players.

Señor Mort wasn't the only one close to unhinged.

3 WITCH

I had to find my way to Lilac dorm on my own. Apparently, my encounter with the glossy high-maintenance clique took too much time for Viney and Zach. I knew that Viney had intentionally thrown me into the lion's den, probably to watch the ensuing hilarity, which if it hadn't been me would have been pretty awesome, watching me knock over the most beautifully vile creature in the world. Since it was me, not so great, in fact pretty much the most humiliating thing ever. What had that been? "I hate him," I muttered to myself as I walked around, aimlessly. I hung onto the manic smile while the caffeine made me bounce from one wall to another until I found the wing off a large hall with a small plaque, Lilac Stories. I was practically home.

I walked down the cream-pillared hall until I reached a large lilac room. All right, let's get right into how nauseating a room looks utterly swathed in lilac. There weren't any windows in the room, but that didn't stop someone from hanging velvet lilac drapes on the wall over pastoral scenes that were again lilac, lilac shrubs, lilac sheep with a splash or two of eggplant to keep things nauseating, I mean interesting. A TV screen hung over an amethyst studded purple granite fireplace on the far wall. My four enormous trunks were stacked outside of what must have been my room, and Viney stood with Zach, staring like they'd never seen nineteenth century shipping trunks before.

Lilac did not look good on me. "There you are! And here is my luggage. What time is dinner, do you know? Is this my key?"

I ripped off the key that was taped to the white painted door and held the large, old fashioned thing in my hands. I could unpick a lock that took this kind of key in the dark, blindfolded, with my hands tied behind my back while juggling octopuses. Well, weasels anyway.

I smiled as I spotted the package on top of one of the trunks. My real lock had come. Being the kind of person I was, and knowing that Viney was a little bit like me, there was no way I'd ever sleep anywhere close to her without making certain my person was completely inaccessible.

"These are all yours? What did you pack, a kitchen?" Viney's brilliance was wearing on my nerves.

I beamed brightly. "That's right. I'm going to go bake a batch of cookies right now. What kind of cookies do you like? Zach, can you help me with this end? Thanks, yeah, watch your fingers."

I got all the trunks in my room with very little space to spare even though the room was large. I wasn't in the same dorm as Zach on accident. Viney was suspicious, but if she wasn't his girlfriend then she shouldn't mind if I married him. If she did mind, I would bake her into cookies.

"When is dinner?" I asked Zach when he backed away from me, towards his own room.

"The dining room is open from five-thirty until seven."

"When are you going?"

He stared at me, kind of uncomfortable before he glanced at Viney who was studiously pretending like I didn't exist while she fiddled with her phone. "Maybe six."

"Great! I'll see you then. It was so nice to meet you!"

I headed to my room, closing my door firmly before I unwrapped the package and installed a security system that might even keep Poppy out. I barely finished up at five-fifty, but when I closed the door and looked around, no Zach and no Viney.

I knocked on their doors, nothing, so after pushing back my long, adorably curly hair, I stuck a lollypop in my mouth and headed down the hall toward the main building. It was easy enough to find the dining hall. First, all the students were flowing in that general direction, second, it smelled like food and I was hungry. Starving.

The dining room was a lot like my dining room at home times twenty with long tables and windows that looked out on a well-groomed garden.

As I walked in, Viney and Zach walked towards me on their way out. Viney smiled at me, apparently jubilant that she'd managed to eat in a half an hour so she could leave with Zach before I'd arrived.

Was this a challenge? I smiled at her sweetly. "Oh no, you guys are leaving already? Oh, well. I'll see you later. Maybe we can hang out after I finish unpacking."

I patted Zach's shoulder and waved at Viney before walking cheerfully over to the line where people waited to make their high-class selections.

"Hi! I'm Penny," I loudly introduced myself to the people in front of me.

They were a girl and a boy who were somewhere beneath the glossies in their grooming habits, but definitely above Zach. The girl rolled her eyes while the guy leaned towards me.

"Penny? Is that your regular fee, because the way you threw yourself at Drake…"

The girl elbowed him and turned, trying to ignore me and him.

I stared at him while I sucked on my lollipop—Lavender and dirt—before I smiled brightly. I was nice, super nice, and I didn't break people into pieces for looking at me wrong. "Oh no, Penny is my name," I said slowly so he could understand. "It's so horrible that I wrinkled his pants. They were really nice. I hope they didn't get grass stained. What's the best thing to eat here?"

The girl pointedly ignored me while the guy stared blatantly at my legs. I'd wanted to look cute and nice, but that look in his eyes wasn't nice at all. I sucked on my lollipop and swished my skirt so it went up even higher. His eyes widened for a second before he took a half step closer to me like a predator after a sweet bit of flesh. Suddenly the guy stopped snickering and turned around, his face blank. It was like he suddenly remembered that his mother was deathly ill in the hospital of something really gruesome and slow, like sepsis, or gangrene, or where all your guts spill out on the ground steaming.

"You could try the rosemary garlic lamb unless you're a vegetarian." A guy's voice pooled around me, low, hot and fragrant at the same time, not like evisceration except kind of exactly like that. His voice gutted me.

It took me a second to realize that I was holding my breath while my heart pounded and my skin kind of went all tight. I inhaled sharply before I slowly and cautiously turned around. Drake stood behind me, no closer or further from anyone else in line, but it seemed like he was far too close, too close and possibly even more beautiful than the first time I'd seen him. I stared at him stupidly, his supple mouth, strong jaw, straight nose, dark eyes flecked with green, with the red hair in a different mussy style, after I'd ruined his first one probably.

He opened his soft lips to say something brilliant. "The line has moved."

I nodded slowly until I realized what he'd said and then whirled around to find that indeed, the line had moved, and I had not.

"Haven't you ever stood in line before?" He sounded amused.

I was going to light him on fire and force him to eat a tray if he sounded amused again. I struggled to hang onto my smile as I nodded and quickly caught up with the end of the line. "Of course. I've gone to movies. There are lines at the movie usually, especially for popcorn. Do you like popcorn? I think it tastes like plastic, but I really like it.

I love the way they call it 'butter', like soy based mono-nitrates can possibly be related to actual butter. I'm sorry for earlier, for knocking you down. I always say I'm just like a ballerina without any grace." I inhaled deeply because it didn't seem like I could stop the mindless yammering otherwise. I gave him a quick smile while he stared back, face bored.

"I don't think you're anything like a ballerina."

I winced and then faced forward just in time to take a large clump of potatoes to the back of my head. My head jerked forward and kind of pulled my neck. It would take forever to wash potatoes out of my hair.

I sighed and rubbed it out, not bothering to turn around and see who had thrown it while I licked potatoes off my fingers. Potatoes assault was so much lovelier than trying to talk to the revoltingly droolworthy mage.

"Who knew that potatoes could have so much recoil splatter."

I glanced cautiously back at Drake and saw him dabbing at his school blazer with a handkerchief, a small rose embroidered in the corner of the white square.

I wanted to feel satisfied that potatoes dared touch the perfection that was Drake Huntsman, but he looked utterly delicious in potatoes. My traitorous mouth actually watered. "Oh, I'm so sorry. It should wash out, though, right? Potatoes don't really seem like something that would stain."

He glanced back up at me. "Why are you apologizing for being hit?"

Something about the way he said that reminded me of my mother, the way she asked me why I'd done something particularly stupid if she happened to notice me. I shrugged while I struggled to hang onto my vacuous smile. "It wouldn't have hit me if I weren't so tall. I know that you think I'm not much like a ballerina, but I have very long limbs, a long neck, and a long torso."

"So it's your fault for being too tall?" His lips curled deliciously. I wanted to touch his lips and see if they were as soft as they looked.

I shrugged again, while I forced myself to study his strong slender hands wiping off potatoes instead of staring at his lips. "Just because I'm sorry doesn't mean it's my fault, just that I'm sad for you. Responsibility should be something you accept, something you ask for. Empathy is free." Empathy for Drake Huntsman, ha! I felt bad for his jacket, though. That jacket was so beautifully cut, shaped perfectly to his exquisite shoulders. No, not his shoulders, his jacket. Penny, keep it together.

He narrowed his eyes at me. "Do you know what Harold meant?"

"Who?"

He nodded towards the guy whose leer had miraculously vanished once Drake came on the scene, like Drake was the big predator and all the other animals had to turn over the easy prey to him. I was prey? That was funny. I did want to give that impression, though. I needed a mage to think that he'd caught me. Not Drake Huntsman. I wasn't stupid enough to think I could play that game with him and come out of it heart and soul intact. Not with how stupid I was around him right off the bat.

"Fee, like for my stand-up routine?"

"More like your fall down routine." He smirked and leaned a little bit closer. He didn't stare at my legs, though. He seemed to only see my eyes, like he was searching for all of my secrets and inadequacies, those far more interesting to him than a pair of legs, however long and well-lotioned.

"Oh." I wracked my brain for something sweet and clever, but I was all out of dialogue, smart or otherwise. He was waiting for me to show my cards, to become one of the squealing rabbits who wanted to hang on every word and look, make it last forever. Was I doing that? I turned around just in time to move along with the line.

I tried not to notice him right behind me, but my heart was pounding in my chest not unlike a frightened little rabbit. He was just so beautiful. I wanted to gaze at him like an unearthly perfect piece of art. I should put my skirt on him so I could ogle his legs.

"I admit that I've very rarely been swept off my feet as thoroughly as this afternoon. What's your secret?" His voice was low, intimate, like this was a private conversation, not a few words exchanged in the middle of a moving line.

"Um, I guess when you fall down a lot, like me, the secret is to get back up again."

"How long does it usually take your partners to get back up again?"

The girl in front of me made a choking sound.

I wrinkled my nose and turned around. "I don't have a partner. I'm sorry if I gave the impression of intentionally falling on you or something, but I assure you that I had absolutely no intention knocking you down or touching you at all, ever. I really hope that your wool is okay. And you, of course. I hope that nothing's bruised."

He put a hand to his chest with a dramatic sweep. "You bruise my heart. I tell you that our encounter made an impression and you discount it as nothing." His eyes filled with tears while his lips quivered.

I rubbed the back of my neck when I really wanted to bite my thumbnail off, or his head. Macaroons. I was a macaroon. His eyes were really green when he gazed at me like that, filled with turbulent emotion like I'd actually hurt him.

I licked my lips. "I'm sorry. I don't mean to hurt your feelings. I'm sure you're very nice, but your shins were really bony."

He curled his mouth in a half smile while the moisture in his eyes vanished. "Everyone's shins are bony. Apparently you need to fall on a few more men so you can appreciate the wonderfulness of my shins.

I've had poems written about them. Reams and reams. The line has once more moved ahead without you my Pretty Penny."

I turned around and hurried to catch the end of the line, my emotions still whiplashed from his apparent ability to produce tears and emotions at will. Just as I suspected, more diabolical than anything I'd ever encountered. I had to stay far, far away from him.

He disturbed me on pretty much every level. He was the epitome of everything I'd sworn I would never fall for the way that Poppy… Thinking about her certainly made me stiffen up and stop trying to smell him. He had the most tantalizing scent, like musk and a hint of cherries. Black cherries. I focused on dinner, on the beautiful rosemary garlic lamb and the lovely potatoes that I intended to eat instead of getting pummeled with.

"Good choice," he murmured before he took his plate and walked off to a small table at the corner with only two chairs. I did not follow him even though it took me a few seconds to stop looking at him walk in that easy swagger that made his hips look particularly narrow and his shoulders perfectly strong and wide. I shook my head and took my plate to the middle of a long table where I could get knocked and bumped by everyone who walked by, picking up more delicious things in my hair. I would have to wash it, but later, after I'd unpacked. I had a lot of unpacking to do and I wouldn't be able to relax until I'd lit something on fire.

4
WITCH

Sunday afternoon, the day before classes started, I was finally finished with the forest bower that was my bedroom, except for the swing. Close enough. I stood back and admired my bed where it hung from the ceiling, draped in curtains and tapestries that hadn't fit on the walls. My Bunsen burners and tubes, jars, blender, and mortar and pestle were neatly arranged on shelves with enough head space I could actually use them there, while the table that took the place of the old desk was a charming drop leaf that I'd arranged between my swing bed and the chair that had come with the desk. I'd set the table with Grandmama's pink lace tablecloth and glass tea set, with beautiful pink rose china.

I checked my reflection in the elaborate mirror, the edges carved with branches and leaves and nodded at myself. I'd piled my hair up on my head in an elaborate updo, studded with red and pink roses and cupcakes suitable for a candy duchess while my dress, pink with red ruffles and trim had an even shorter skirt than my pleated school uniform. I looked ridiculous particularly with my bright red lips, rosy cheeks and fake eyelashes, but hopefully it would make an impression on Zach, you know, the good kind.

My heart pounded as I opened the door and clasped my hands in their little lace glovelets. I smiled at Zach and Viney where they sat on a couch, Zach holding a guitar and Viney a screen.

I cleared my throat and they both looked over at me. I beamed at them. "I would like to invite you to my tea party to celebrate the completion of my woodland boudoir!"

Viney choked on her laugh, staring at me like I'd sprouted an extra head, which my enormous hair admittedly might look like if you squinted. Zach's eyes widened, but he didn't seem disgusted. He looked at Viney, waiting for her reaction. That look was a problem. He waited for her to tell him what he thought. I'd have to displace her as the female he followed like a good little puppy. Would I have to kill her? No, that would be too easy.

It took her a minute for her sputtering shock to fully transform into contemptuous derision. "A tea party? Do you we look like five-year-olds? What are you wearing? You look like a bonbon."

I took a deep breath and beamed at her. "Oh, bonbons! I love bonbons but I didn't get any. Just macaroons and lady fingers. I don't really know any five-year-olds, but I think that they would be even shorter than you, Viney. So, do you guys want to come?"

Viney stood up and grabbed Zach, pulling him up with her. "No. We're playing video games. It's really important." She snickered again, not bothering to cover her mouth or pretend like she wasn't laughing at me.

I stood there and tried to compose a poem inside my head about macaroons so that I didn't break Zach's guitar over Viney's head and strangle her with the strings.

Macaroons could come in pink balloons
And you could eat them with a spoon
But the true joy of the macaroon
Is stuffing them in eye sockets after you've ripped out someone's eyeballs.

"What kind of tea are you having?"

I looked past Viney who had come to a sudden halt and saw Drake by the door wearing a black jacket that was way too gorgeous to be a school uniform. Whoever made his jackets was a master.

It took me a long time to realize he'd asked me a question as he walked into the common room, filling up the space with his dominant energy. Zach paled when he looked at Drake. The look on Zach's face, the memory of him dangling like an ornament before Drake beat the crap out of him spurred me to action.

I leapt between Zach and Drake, my arms outspread like a vulture about to strike. Not a vulture. I wasn't going to wait for Drake to die before I struck. "What are you doing here?"

My voice came out wrong. I expected angry, fierce, but instead it was breathy and high-pitched. Ew. Drake stared at me, withering me with that look because I was an idiot to think that he'd wear that jacket to beat the crap out of someone. I lowered my arms and edged away from Drake. He smelled good enough that I got confused about whether I wanted to bite him or light him on fire.

"That depends on the tea." His green eyes glinted as he smiled, his lips curling slowly, decadently while my stomach tightened for no rational reason.

Macaroons. Cupcakes. Cheesecake. I fixed the smile on my face and forced myself to focus. I had to be cute and nice, even if my heart pounded and adrenaline rushed through my body in fight or flight response, mostly fight. "The tea is Orange Bergamot. It's weird. Viney and Zach are going to play video games, so no tea party."

He glanced at Zach, arching an eyebrow before he shrugged. "I was going to have Zach teach me a guitar lesson. If he's going to be busy, then I'm willing to be the perfect guest at your little tea party."

I stared at him, at the way he gazed back at me evenly, like he was challenging me to not freak out and smash his face against a table. He'd noticed me leaping between him and Zach. He thought it was funny, called my tea party 'little' like I was a five-year-old or something. I'd left the door of my room open. While I tried to think of some reason he couldn't possibly come to my 'little' tea party, he walked languidly towards the door, like no girl in her right mind would ever turn down anything he offered. Luckily for me, I wasn't in my right mind, but I didn't want Zach to know that.

No. Drake couldn't come to the party I'd prepped so carefully for the guy I was going to marry, but I couldn't just scream at him to get out and never come back. "Wait... You're not wearing a hat. Your jacket is lovely, but what kind of tea party would it be if the gentlemen didn't wear hats?"

He smiled slightly as I walked over to him. He ran his fingers over the red ruffle on my bodice, a simple quick movement that completely paralyzed me.

His voice was low, mesmerizing while he leaned close, breath fanning across my parted lips. "I'm sure someone who created something this elaborate can make me a hat without any effort."

My heart pounded and black cherry scent overwhelmed everything. I backed away from him, stumbling into my open doorway. "I guess I could make you a hat." I stopped and held out my hand, palm on his chest. "There are rules. You can't grab anything."

He smiled slightly as he leaned closer, putting pressure on my wrist as I tried to hold him back. He wasn't really pushing, just letting his weight press against me so I could feel the muscular outline of his chest beneath his suit. "What kind of tea parties are you used to?" His voice was low and the way he said that made my skin prickle.

I chewed on my lip and tried to give him a stern look that wasn't a glare. I wasn't sure how well I pulled that off, because my whole body was doing this dancing rebelling thing from being so close to this decadent piece of pie. "I need you to promise. It's important."

He shrugged and gave me a devilish look, leaning even closer. "I promise that I won't grab anything until you beg me to."

I couldn't say anything as he brushed past me, into my glorious bower. I glanced at Viney and Zach hopeful for a moment before I let the door swing closed between us.

5
Witch

I stared at Drake while he looked around my room, walking over to examine all my tubes and jars, the tapestry between the glass and the window, the security system attached to that window, the greenery hanging all over, and then the bed. He spent a long time staring at the bed before he pushed it and sent it rocking gently back and forth.

I tried to feel something other than panic, anger, and the ridiculous awareness I had for him. Finally, he finished his circuit and came back to me where I stood trying not to frown. Macaroons, bonbons, truffles... He was such a delicious package of poison.

"Is this supposed to be a swing?" He bent down and held up one side of the rope that I hadn't been able to talk the maintenance guys into hanging. They were angry enough after they had to hang up some stupid princess's bed from the high ceiling; they weren't about to hang a swing too.

"Not at the moment. I'm trying to convince myself that a bed swing is enough, but I'm not sure I'm buying it."

He stood up on the chair and stretched up and up, tapping at the ceiling like he was doing Morse code. He wasn't. I was very adept at Morse and there was no way he was saying, 'horse nuts, horse nuts.' Unless he was. I giggled slightly and earned a sharp look from him.

"Aren't you going to make me a hat?"

The whole thing was beyond ridiculous. If I wasn't going to light him on fire, I'd have to pretend to be the sweet and slightly idiotic girl everyone would learn to love. If I wanted a nice mage, I had to be a nice witch. "Right!" I stopped staring at him and pulled a trunk out from under my bed with sewing and other makery things in it. I found some red felt, and some paperboard for the hat frame, and then I was ready but I needed to measure his head.

He'd taken off his jacket and his long, lean body stretched above me, chest outlined beneath his white shirt. He was using a pocket knife, a Swiss army knife to be exact, to screw my swing into the ceiling.

I swallowed before I could ask, "Can I measure your head?"

He looked down at me, giving me an arch look. "You expect me to allow such a double standard when you made it so clear that I can't touch you?" He glanced down at my bodice, reminding me of his fingers so close to my chest.

I blushed. I could feel my cheeks get hot, and my fair skin blushed beautifully. "Your head couldn't possibly be as large as it looks. For the sake of a well-fitting hat…" I flinched because saying he had a big head, while something I found funny, was definitely an insult, and I wasn't going to waste all this energy pretending to be delightful only to spoil it on weak slurs.

His lips twitched. "Fine." He stepped down off the chair and bent forward, but I lifted his chin, straightening his shoulders before I stood on my tiptoes and wrapped my tape around his crown. I didn't notice how strong and broad his shoulders were, how close I was to him with my elbows propped on his shoulders and my bodice brushing his suit coat. No, I focused on the feel of plastic inches in my fingers as I added the right amount of ease and pinched the tape before turning away only slightly breathless.

"Was that so bad?"

He cleared his throat before he shrugged and climbed back on the chair. "You smell different."

I glanced over my shoulder at him, but he wasn't looking at me. His focus was entirely on the ceiling and the effort needed to screw something in with a Swiss army knife.

I smelled like a subtle floral mixed with a slight aphrodisiac, because this whole thing was supposed to be a romantic tea party to get Zach to marry me. "Not everyone can smell like black cherries."

He cleared his throat but kept standing there with his arms up, working on my swing. "Who smells like black cherries?"

I stared at him, because I didn't understand what he was talking about, not because I liked looking at him. "Not Señor Mort. Do you like the way I smell because I can give you my lotion if you're tired of black cherry. In fact, I'll trade you. Black cherry is one of my favorites."

He flicked a glance in my direction, a look that made my stomach coil into a ball of something explosive. "You like the way I smell, Penny Lane? What else do you like about me?"

I blinked and blushed and wanted to hot glue the hat to his face. "Nothing. I mean, you seem perfectly nice," ha! "But you're not really my type. No offense. I like black cherry, not you."

He nodded with a smooth expression like that explained everything, but there was still a glimmer in his eyes that said it didn't explain anything, and that I was secretly completely aware of how incredibly delectable and delicious he was. At least he didn't fake tears again.

I shook my head and focused on stapling the base of his hat together then plugged in my glue gun while I knelt on the floor in my ridiculous dress. It was ridiculous and yet, I kind of liked it. It had been my favorite tea party dress back when Poppy...

He laughed and the sound wiped away everything dark in the world. I looked up at him where he stood, surrounded by dangling leaves I'd wrapped around the swing ropes. I stared at him and the knot in my stomach tightened like a corset so I couldn't breathe.

Then hot glue dripped on my fingers. I hissed and looked away from him, focusing on the hat. I put much more concentration into it than was strictly necessary for a one-time hat, but I needed to focus on my hands so I didn't focus on his.

The laugh apparently signified that he'd finished hanging the swing. He sat down on it, watching me until my hands shook, traitorous things, and I finally finished the hat, tying a pink ribbon around it with a few roses and cupcakes that matched the ones in my hair. He would look ridiculous in a red and pink hat.

I stood and placed it on his head. He swung forward and his knees brushed my bare legs. I stumbled back with that stupid blush again. When I glanced down I could see my entire chest had turned pink above the bodice. I should have worn something higher, not that I had a lot of décolletage or anything, but still, I did not need Drake to see the weird places he made me blush.

"Stay right there. I'll move over the tea table." I held my hands up, needing him to stay in place so I could get some distance, some space.

"I'll help." He ignored the whole 'stay there' thing and grabbed one side of the table, lifting it over to the swing so someone could swing and drink tea at the same time. He offered me the swing and I was tempted, but I couldn't be swinging when my most important guest hadn't arrived yet. I would have to swing and drink tea after he'd left, and after I'd lit something on fire.

On the table, I rearranged the plates and tea things, poured Drake a cup of Orange Bergamot, moved over the stacked serving tray full of delicious goodies and then got down my cage from where I'd hung it in the corner between the bed and the window. I put it on the table and untied the edges of the floral cover and opened the gate so that Señor Mort could slink out looking dignified and unamused. He sniffed the air and, with his beady brown eyes, studied Drake for a long moment. Finally, he scampered across the table between plates and saucers to the small chair where he curled up and lifted the small teacup in his little paws, opened his mouth, and took a sip.

I exhaled and took my own seat while Drake leaned forward to stare at my pet weasel. It was a little bit funny because Drake's hair was a lot like Señor's coat, and their eyes were both glistening dark and dangerous.

Drake whistled softly as I broke up a ladyfinger and slid the pieces carefully onto Señor Mort's little platter.

"Señor Mort, meet Mr. Huntsman."

Drake glanced at me then back at the weasel. "How do you do, Señor Mort? It's a pleasure to make your acquaintance." He turned to me and whispered, "Why isn't he wearing a hat? Doesn't he know that there's a dress code?"

I choked on my tea and took a second to answer after I cleared my throat. "Señor Mort is still a little bit testy after his recent adventures. He only puts up with his vest and hat when he's in a very good mood."

Drake grinned as he picked up his teacup, the tiny thing ridiculous and delicate in his large hands. "I see. Well, since he's not feeling well, I suppose we have to make allowances."

I smiled at him then buried my face in the scent of Bergamot and orange. It was fine to smile at him, but only to cover up a glare, not because he was funny.

"Do you have tea parties often?"

I looked up at him over my steaming cup of orange tea. "I used to. My grandmama loved them. She would dress up in pink feather boas and enormous hats." I took a slow sip, focusing on the color of the liquid, golden, deep and rich, like roasted orange peels. I missed her so much. She was the only one who didn't think it was stupid and infantile to have tea parties and wear elaborate gowns. I should have known that Zach wouldn't like tea parties. I was too weird.

"That's what your outfit needs, a feather boa." He shook his head and a soft smile fluttered across his face.

I took a bite of a cookie, chewing slowly while I stared at the table, my gaze drawn towards Drake, his fingers pinching a crumb before he carried it to his parted lips. I inhaled cookie and coughed for a minute before I smiled brightly. "What are you doing here?"

He raised an eyebrow. Well, yeah because my face expression didn't match the slight accusation in those words. "Zach was going to give me a guitar lesson. Didn't I say that?"

I took a deep sip of tea and then clinked my teacup back down in a hopefully ladylike expression of distaste. "I had a conversation with Mr. Stoneburrow explicitly about how he felt regarding the crowd with which you associate."

A sexy smile flitted over his lips before he licked them. "Do you always talk so elegantly at your tea parties?"

I gripped a butterknife tightly then picked up a scone and buttered it instead of shoving the curved end through his throat. "Always. Why would you want Zach to give you lessons if you aren't friends?"

He raised an eyebrow archly. "Zachary informed you that we weren't bosom friends? I'm shocked and appalled. What word would you use, flabbergasted or flummoxed?"

I exhaled slowly while I pressed the knife against the table. He was trying to be annoying. The trouble was, something about him made me want to smile, maybe even giggle. He was kind of funny, extremely charming and utterly irresistible. "So, you're saying that the two of you are friendly? Maybe he was talking about other extremely popular students that he didn't get along with."

He shrugged elegantly, looking seriously attractive instead of ridiculous beneath the brim of his red top hat. "It's possible."

"You take music lessons from your friends?"

"I may not be the finest musician in the world, but I am very good at practicing."

I stared at him, trying to make out something genuine in his expression. He looked beautiful, but something else, something wild and untamed, like Señor Mort, who I focused on instead of Drake. Was it possible for Drake Huntsman to actually think that hanging Zach from a tree and then beating him up when it didn't kill him was friendly? But Zach hadn't seemed terrified of him, had he? I'd forgotten to pay very much attention to Zach once I'd seen Drake. It wasn't my fault. I was genetically predisposed to be mindlessly attracted to the most dangerous, wicked, seductive and amoral man I could possibly find. The only way around it was to find another man who wasn't half as hypnotizing, and marry him instead. How much I liked looking at Drake, hearing him, smelling him, well, that told me everything I needed to know about him, as if I didn't know enough already.

The rest of the tea party went along as well as could be expected until Señor Mort knocked a macaroon off his plate and Drake thoughtfully, I mean thoughtlessly, reached out to put it back.

"No!" I said, but there was nothing to do besides what any good host would do, and that was cover his hand and the macaroon while Señor Mort sank his lovely teeth into me.

Drake froze while I held my hand still and picked up the cage with my other hand, setting it on the table for Señor Mort to scamper into. I dropped the door closed and set it on the floor before I looked up at Drake. He stared at my hand which was still over his while my blood trickled down between our fingers, staining both of us pink.

"I'm so glad I picked those colors. Pink and red are always a good idea." I pressed my lips in a thin line because the scent of blood went so beautifully with black cherry. He looked and smelled utterly edible, so much so that my mouth watered and my teeth ached to sink into his skin.

He took a handkerchief out of his pocket, the one with the rose on the corner, and wrapped it around my hand with his, still slick with my red blood. "Is it bad?"

I inhaled that intoxicating scent before I shifted my fingers to see if I could gauge the depth of the injury, rubbing against his skin in the process. "Probably a level four bite. I don't think it will need stitches, but it might leave a scar." I sounded distant, dreamy. I needed to focus on whipping up an incredible lotion and putting on a disinfectant, but with him leaning over the tea table, the glovelets and lace cloth specked with my blood, I couldn't seem to do anything other than stare at him with my heart pounding in my throat, mouth watering, and teeth aching.

He frowned at me, a sudden furious lowering of his eyebrows that made me sit back, pulling my hand away from his.

His frown lessened as he studied my hand while he slid his own to his lap. "That's what you meant about not grabbing."

I nodded. "It's my fault. I should have been more specific."

He shook his head. "I've never been to any party with a weasel. It's my fault for my lack of sophistication and inability to follow simple instructions."

I shrugged. "It's fine. Unless you'd like more tea, I kind of need to clean up and wash out the bite and..."

He stood up and started stacking plates. "Go ahead. I'll take care of things here."

I stood there with his handkerchief tied on my hand hesitating because I couldn't trust him not to destroy everything in my room. There was part of him that liked to needlessly destroy things. I knew that desire intimately and could recognize it in him as well as his need to create, to bring order and beauty to something. He'd hung my swing like someone who knew how to use his hands. He could build up and tear down. Which was he in the mood for right now?

I shook my head while I grabbed my little tin med kit out of my trunk and headed to the bathroom. I would take my chances because I needed to clean and dress my wound almost as much as I needed to get distance from his mouth-watering perfection.

I stared at my reflection in the mirror while pink water swirled down the sink drain. I couldn't tell if I looked pretty or not, I just looked strange, like cotton candy brought to life. Cotton candy was pretty, though, and so nice to taste as it dissolved on your tongue. I needed something on my tongue that did not taste like black cherry.

Finally, I turned off the water, dried my hand, put on a poultice and bandaged it up. When I opened the bathroom door to my bedroom, the dishes were washed and stacked in their space beside my brewing things, and the table was pushed back against the wall, the lace tablecloth the only thing missing, other than Drake of course.

Señor hung once more in his place and when I checked on him, he blinked at me sleepy from gorging on lady fingers and my flesh.

"Señor, I know you don't like strangers, but biting someone who is only trying to fetch your macaroon is a sign of bad breeding. Did you like him? I know you bite people you like, which is why you bite me so much."

I took him out of the cage and set him on my bed. He padded around and made a nice nest on my pillow while I undid my hair and got out of the ridiculous confection of a dress. As I hung it up in the largest trunk I was using for an armoire, I realized that the hat I'd made for him was missing. What on earth would he do with that?

MAGE

Sodium vapor would make my hair look good. It would piss Pete off, make him look pasty and sallow like a zombie. Definitely sodium vapor instead of scandium light for the first round in the Chemiss tourney on Saturday night.

I tipped my red top hat to a pretty little freshman girl who hadn't thrown herself at me yet. She gasped and went all wide-eyed like a proper female at Rosewood Academy. She was so charming, and I was in such an excellent mood, I pulled one of the roses off the hat and tossed it in her direction.

Penny Lane was not a proper female in Rosewood. For starters… One, two, three… The new girl, came after me, bounced off my personal shield and into a sophomore mage who held her up by the elbows, the expression on his face half disgust, half admiration as he watched me.

That was an appropriate reaction as well. The first time we'd met, Penny Lane should have bounced off the shield and knocked someone else over. Jackson maybe. She'd gone through it like it wasn't even there, tackled me like a polo player. I still couldn't decide if she'd done it intentionally or not. Nothing about her made sense. It wasn't like me to think about other people. They usually weren't particularly interesting, or at the very least I knew what to do with them and quickly did it.

What I wanted to do with Penny Lane would make her blush. I didn't need to tell her because she blushed anyway. Why I liked watching her pale skin go pink wasn't something I needed to dwell on. She was like an inexperienced freshman girl, exposed to mages for the first time. Except for the part where she stepped between Zach and myself, as though she were protecting him from me. Even an inexperienced witch knew better than to get between two mages.

I shrugged and nodded at Tony, an upcoming Junior who was going to be a solid backup man for this year's team. I walked through the doors of the lab, swinging them open then stood there smiling at every single person until the room cleared. It was so pleasant when everyone knew their place and there weren't any difficulties. Except that could get too boring.

I smiled at the last mage to leave. Lars, ponderously slow, moved away from his table, nodding at me before he left the room. I bolted the door and walked past the rows of tables equipped with Bunsen burners and sinks, nozzles dangling from the ceiling. I didn't stop until I was at the table nearest the large window that looked out on the garden. It was such a beautiful day, so many things growing.

I glanced around again before I took the red top hat off my head, placed it squarely on the table and pulled the blood-stained tablecloth out of its depths. What I was about to do wasn't strictly legal. It was also bad manners. Unfortunately for Miss Lane, I'd used up all my manners at her delightful tea party.

I hesitated, fingering the lace. She shouldn't have protected me from her guardian. She'd moved so quickly, her fingers sliding over my skin. I could still see her the moment she was bitten, her green-brown eyes widening until I could make out flecks of gold in them. She'd been surprised, irritated, like she'd been irritated with me the entire party, irritated that I was too stupid not to know better than to feed wild animals, irritated that I wasn't Zachary Stoneburrow.

Poor girl. If she had her sight set on that boy, she was in for a severe disappointment. Zach made me look practically accessible. Sooner or later, Penny would realize the way the world worked, and she'd set her sights on me, as nature and social status intended.

I curled my lips as I bent over the cloth, breathing lightly over the fibers before I took a bottle out of the cabinet behind me and sprinkled the contents over one corner. The blood rose up in fat, red drops. I rolled them into a glass vial with my fingertips until the lace was pristine and I had enough blood to find out all of Penny Lane's dirty little secrets.

I tested her blood five times. The results were consistent. The thing about Darksiders is they don't walk around in the sun beaming at strangers and offering them lollipops. Darkside is heavy with magic, with mystery and mayhem, which is why I love it so much, not heavy with tea parties and ruffled bodices. There was no possible way that the sweet, innocent, slightly intriguing female I'd encountered could be three-quarters Darksider.

Where else could I have gotten the blood if not from her? Could it have been contaminated in my hat? She'd made the ridiculous top hat on the spot, sucking on her fingers when she burned them with a hot glue gun like one of those crafty mom bloggers. Her sucking on her fingers after she'd gotten distracted watching me hang up her swing made me want to suck on her fingers for her, undo the pins that held up her ridiculously long hair and...

I blinked the glass vial and the lab back into focus. I heated up the blood and checked for a few more markers. I closed my eyes then opened them to see the swirls inside the deep red. Interesting. I closed my eyes again, but when I opened them, same result. I snapped my fingers, engulfing the blood, the vial and the Bunsen burner in green flame that singed my cheek as it roared to life.

I flipped the switch for the air filter that sucked the fire and smoke away then I folded the tablecloth before sticking it back into the depths of the top hat. Her genetic makeup was extremely interesting. Mythical even. Darksiders were a lot of extremely talented folk, but a few families really knew how to make an impression, also how to raise the dead or start a plague. Miss Lane's family was more subtle, but all the more horrifying for that.

I took two steps towards the exit, putting the top hat back on my head when the doors blew open. Zachary Stoneburrow. I smiled at him broadly.

"You look lively. Are we going to wrestle in the lab? Pewter would hate that."

He smiled slightly, a sweet smile at odds with the gleam in his eyes. I hadn't seen that gleam for a long time. It almost made me want to smile genuinely.

"What were you doing in my rooms?"

I fought the urge to say something irritating. I specifically wanted him in a good mood. "Are you going to do Chemiss this year?"

He studied me for a long time, long enough that I realized he wasn't thinking about what I'd said so much as he was sniffing the air, trying to gauge what I'd been up to.

"You have her blood? How did you get that?"

I tipped my hat at him. "I can't reveal my secrets. I know it's hard to believe that a female would willingly cut herself open for me..."

He frowned, brows lowering. "She wouldn't do that."

I stared at him. His reaction was too intense. Maybe she'd already ensnared my oldest friend. If that was the case, why hadn't she seduced me first? Not that I wanted to be a mindless slave to a witch, but if you were going to choose the most ideal mage to make your helpless minion, I was definitely the top pick.

"No, she didn't. Her pet weasel bit her and I offered to tidy up."

"And..."

"And the lace tablecloth is as good as new. Such a lovely pattern. I think I have a dozen or so like it in my sideboard at the grand manor."

His eyes glittered brightly. "You're not going to tell me?"

"Tell you what? Are you suggesting that an honorable, upright, law-abiding mage like myself would ever take the blood of a witch without her permission? Next you'll be saying that I intentionally break their dear little black hearts."

He grunted. "Speaking of Blackheart, did you manage to convince her honor to let them all come for Final's brawl?"

I nodded and grinned widely, slapping Zach on his shoulder. "I told you that I would. Are you in?"

He nodded but when he glanced up at the top hat, I noted the flicker of distaste. "Did she really make that for you?"

"Hm? Oh, yes. Who knew that a three-quarter Darkside female could wield a glue-gun so craftily?"

He raised an eyebrow, the expression on his face portentously blank. "And you're in one piece?"

"Mm. As far as I can tell."

"How did she get through your shield?"

I frowned at him, fingering my lapel, adjusting it like it wasn't already lying smoothly. "She didn't say."

"Did you ask?"

"I thought it would be rude."

"And you're never rude." His lips curled in a sneer.

I grinned back at him. "I'm probably completely misreading her, you know how little I know about females, but I don't think she has the slightest idea that I have a shield or that she broke through it."

He nodded. "You should ask Viney about it."

I pursed my lips. "I should, but as pleasant as Viney's charming company always is, I think I'll save that for a special occasion, when I want to have a truly inspiring day."

He grimaced. "You had to pick Viney."

I nodded soberly. "I did. Are you interested in her?"

"Never. Viney and I... Oh, the new girl." He frowned as he turned and walked out of the lab. I fell in beside him since we were conveniently headed in the same direction. He cleared his throat. "Interested is probably the right word. How about you? I never thought you'd agree to go to a tea party you weren't invited to."

"That's the only kind I would ever attend. On second thought, if Penny Lane invited me to another tea party I would consider it. I hope that she makes them a regular part of my schedule, Sunday tea parties after a frolicsome Chemiss tourney, could anything be more charming?"

"How long are you going to talk like that? You sound like you've been reading 19th Century literature again."

I raised an eyebrow and fingered the brim of the hat. "A man wearing a top hat must sound like a proper gentleman even if there's nothing proper about him." It wasn't the hat, it was Penny Lane, the way she spoke that rubbed off on me, like she was in a play and I was opposite her lead. How strange to let a female lead me anywhere. I would have to be very careful with this one.

Zach shook his head. "Have you finished with her?"

I raised my eyebrow. "She hasn't fallen in love with me yet. How can I be satisfied knowing that there is a female in this world who doesn't want Drake Huntsman?"

He snorted. "It used to be when you made a declaration like that, you were joking."

I shot him a hard look. "Don't suggest such things out loud. I've worked very hard for my reputation. I intend to keep it."

He made a rude sound, a ruder gesture, and took the next branch in the hall leading towards his room. No doubt to pick up Viney for dinner. Putting them together like I'd done was extremely risky, but he seemed to be doing much better. Perhaps this new girl, this incongruity would provide him with another distraction he could use.

I ignored the niggling discomfort at the thought of Zach playing with Penny Lane. He would do it all wrong.

7
WITCH

I sat in the dining room that evening while I nibbled on the roasted duck, not killing the idiots who walked by tugging on my hair. The duck was incredible. I was polishing off the last bite when blonde and beautiful Jackson sat down across from me, steepled his fingers, and leered. There was nothing terribly interesting about me after I had changed out of my candy duchess outfit. I chewed while I waited for something brilliant to fall from his luscious lips. His lips were poufier than Drake's, but didn't look as soft. Weird.

"Penny, isn't it? I heard that you had a tea party this afternoon."

I blinked my eyelashes at him. "I'm sorry. Did it hurt your feelings not to be invited?" How did he find out about it?

His smile deepened and took on an ominous tint while he covered my hand in his, the hand with the bandage. "It did. I'm also terribly worried about you being alone with the big bad wolf. Did he bite you?" He lifted my hand and turned it around so the whole dining room could see.

Macaroons, bonbons, petit fours. "Not the wolf, the weasel." I tried to stand and take my hand back, but he tightened his grip on my newly punctured wound, pulling me back down. He watched me with this smile, like he was waiting for me to react, to hurt him, like we could trade pain or something weird. I focused on the sensation, the sharp edges, the dull throbbing, the pressure, the feel of the gauze and herbs being ground into my wound. Something dark uncoiled inside my chest, something that chased all the panic and irritated frustration away.

"Now you're calling me a weasel? I'm flattered." Drake slid down beside me and smiled at Jackson.

Sitting so close to Drake, his jacket brushing my arm, buried the darkness with this other sensation, something that made me blush for absolutely no reason. He had made me blush more than enough times for one lifetime much less one day.

My heart pounded and I swallowed when he shifted closer to me.

Jackson snarled at him. "Drake, what brings you here? Nice jacket. It's very prince charming. Penny isn't stupid enough to think that you're a prince instead of the wolf."

Drake put his hand on Jackson's shoulder and grinned at him, looking in fact, very much like a perfectly dressed wolf in disguise. "Didn't we agree that I was a weasel and not a wolf? Jackson, I don't like it when you're so willfully obtuse. Makes me feel... frustrated."

Jackson finally dropped my hand and stayed where he was for a moment before Drake let go, still smiling at Jackson. My hand hurt much more after Jackson let off the pressure. It throbbed and I cradled it in my lap while my heart pounded. It was fine. I was not going to stand up and decapitate Jackson and Drake with the edge of my plate. Everything was perfectly lovely, just like me. I was nice, happy, cheerful and friendly. I cared about how other people felt and wanted to take care of them in some way that didn't involve cement shoes or sharp knives.

"So, what do you do here for community service?" My voice wavered, but it was the first thing that came into my head, my cute, fluffy, sweets stuffed head.

Jackson's eyes darted to my face while Drake turned slowly towards me. "It does seem like Jackson is a reprobate who serves time with community service, but I think he's managed to get out of it so far."

I took a deep breath and smiled at Drake, wishing I had a lollypop.

"Honestly, I want to get involved with the community. In the town, Fairfield, right? Do they have an animal shelter or anything like that?"

Drake stared at me. He sat so close, my hand looking like a white paw on his sleeve. How had my hand gotten there? I really needed a lollipop.

"There's the hospital. I'm going on Tuesday, five-thirty if you'd like to come."

I blinked at him. "The hospital? What do you do? You don't have to clean up throw-up, do you?"

Jackson laughed, but his voice was high pitched and wavering. "If he takes you to the hospital, you'll be in traction. Don't listen to him."

I stood up and edged away from the table while I tried to laugh instead of putting them in traction. "Jackson, you're so funny. I'll see you both later."

The rest of the evening I focused on brewing a whole slew of lotions to reduce scarring and added them to Darkly Sweet. I needed the trance-like state I achieved once I lit my burner and melted my first ingredient, swirling it around in the glass bulb before I added the drops of oil, the emulsifier, swirling them up with powdered beet to make it a nice pink color. After my batch I tasted it to make certain it was as delicious as it was functional. I sighed happily as I cleaned up my ingredients. Everything would fall into place. Zach was perfectly pleasant and would soon see how nice it would be to marry me. Somehow.

The next morning, I walked towards my class at six thirty in the morning like that wasn't an insane time to be awake. I probably shouldn't have stayed up quite so late with my potions. Everyone walked around buzzing with energy as they headed with purpose towards their class. Not one person bothered me. My English class was pretty boring, the next class, Chemistry was equally so, but the teacher, Professor Pewter was kind of cute and terrifying. My third class at nine was ballet. Ballet. I am not kidding. Ballet was a required class for girls all four years of high school. I'd been placed in beginner ballet with the freshmen girls who were still terrifyingly good. They danced circles around me. Literally, all these pirouettes and other types of spins like we needed that in our lives.

The teacher, Madame Torture had me plieing until I could barely stagger out of class in my pale pink leotard. She pursed her blood red lips and called after me. "Miss Lane, be certain your hair is secured. Tomorrow you will be dancing with a partner, and I don't want you to suffocate him."

"Thanks, Madame." I tried to curtsy and collapsed on the floor while freshmen girls with their perfect little hair buns walked over me out the door. I laid there for a few breaths before I got it together and went out to the locker room to change back into my school uniform. I would need a more secure lock. It was amazing that no one had stuck my clothes in a shredder while I'd been in torture.

My next class was language, which turned out as a kind of foreign language class where we were immersed in a variety of languages and had to be conversant in all of them. The only language I spoke fluently was mean girl, which was a little bit like Canadian English, but not enough to get by.

There were different language sessions and the instructor, a serious woman in serious glasses and serious blazers to offset how young and pretty she was, walked through the groups and corrected accents and added to the conversations.

I stood under the Chinese sign and smiled stupidly at the brown-haired guy across from me who stared back, twisting his hands awkwardly. Was he nervous? Most guys in the class were ridiculously self-assured. I edged closer to him.

"I don't even know basic greetings in Chinese, much less the necessary accusations."

He gave me a half smile. "Aligato." He bowed politely then straightened.

I copied him, bowing and greeting him like a genuine American who has no idea why she needs to learn another country's language when English is already too hard for us. After that I milled around until I found myself beneath the Spanish flag. I didn't realize it was the Spanish flag until I heard someone mention it.

It was the guy from earlier, the very polite guy from Chinese.

I moved closer to him. "Buenos Dias. Me nobre es Penny Lane. E tu?"

"Buenos Dias. Me nobre esta Barry."

I tried to smile demurely, but this was Spanish. "El gato esta gordo." The cat is fat.

He cocked his head. "El gato estas muy gordo." The cat is very fat.

I hesitated for a moment, but I couldn't seem to help myself. "Señor." I stepped forward and put my hand on his chest. I could feel his heart pound beneath my fingers and he smelled like pumpkin soup. Spanish was one real language I'd mastered. With the perfect quiver in my voice, I spoke from my Spanish heart. "¿Cómo pudiste dormer con mi hermana? ¿No sabe que estoy embarazada de tu hijo?" How could you sleep with my sister? Don't you know that I'm pregnant with your child?

He got the most fascinating expression on his face before he stammered, "No sé de qué estas hablando." I don't know what you're talking about.

I put the back of my hand on my forehead in a glorious sweeping movement. "Pero no, no lo harías porque tienes amnesia. Pensé que estabas muerto pero ahora deseo que lo estuviera yo!" But no, you have amnesia. I thought you were dead but now I wish I were!

I gripped his jacket and yanked him closer.

"Ahem. Miss Lane, excellent use of accent, but I think your conversation is a little more intimate than will be required for everyday use."

I exhaled heavily as I let go of his jacket then turned to the teacher and rallied my smile. "Sorry, Madame…"

"It's Miz."

My smile was brittle and I fought not to roll my eyes, holding them wide. "Sorry Miz. You mean more like, Donde esta el baño?"

She hmphed and walked off on her little heels, click clack, click clack.

Someone elbowed me and I glanced over. Zach was grinning at me. "Señorita Phillip needs to take a break to get the stick out of her…"

He was in my class? Oh. How had I not seen him? He'd definitely caught my scene with Barry. If he didn't like tea parties, what were the odds he liked impromptu outbreaks of telenovelas? At the same time, he was talking to me and being funny.

I smiled brightly "Well, hopefully she finds it soon. I didn't know you were in this class."

He shrugged. "Where did you learn Spanish?"

I hesitated before I admitted the scandalous truth. "Our cook used to watch telenovelas all day. It stuck with me."

"Spanish soap operas? That explains the amnesia." A slow smile spread over his lips and I noticed them for the first time. I'd seen his lips, but hadn't noticed that they looked soft and kind of pink before.

I stepped away from him even as I snickered. For the rest of the class I tried to not look like an idiot in French, German, Italian, or Japanese.

I was exhausted from listening with a polite smile on my mouth by the time class was over. Zach fell in beside me. "What's your next class?"

I gave him a super sweet and delighted smile, not a smile that was about to crash and burn. "Math. What about you?"

"Dressage."

I blinked at him. "How to get dressed or how to make dressers? That explains why everyone dresses so well."

He smiled again, a slight smirk. "Horse riding. Everyone has dressage. It's like ballet and fencing."

I checked my schedule. There after lunch was dressage, like he'd said. I thought it was a typo. I did not have fencing. A knot tangled in my stomach. If it was anything like riding in cars... "I see. I've never ridden a horse."

He raised his eyebrows. "Never?"

I shook my head and offered him a queasy smile. "How hard could it be?"

"What did you study in your homeschool?"

I thought about it for a long time before I admitted the shocking truth. "I learned how to make lollipops. I'm really good at most kinds of candy, anything you can do with a Bunsen burner, but no ovens. I learned how to speak Tolkien's elven pretty fluently. I noticed that there is a shocking emphasis on human languages instead of mythical ones at this school which I find speciesist."

He raised his eyebrows. "Wait, you made those tiramisu things? Viney loved them. She was searching all over the internet for more."

I smiled slightly and shrugged. How nice to talk about his not girlfriend. "I can give her more any time she wants some."

He quirked an eyebrow, giving me a slightly mischievous smile. "She'll be worried you poisoned it or something."

I smiled widely. "You shouldn't give me ideas. I think this is my math class. Have fun in dressage."

I ducked into my class which was boring but at least I didn't have to talk to anyone and smile idiotically. After that was lunch, and everyone was kind of focused on their assignments already, so much so that hardly anyone bothered me where I sat at the long table, enjoying every bite of the delectable clam chowder. Then it was out to the stables. Once more I was with the freshmen, and how awesome was that? Not very because the second I was on the back of this nice looking gray mare she started bucking and heaving like she was about to throw up.

I went up and came down in a pile of straw, but hit the hard flagstones with my knee. The instructor was furious, but still kept his voice low as he soothed the horse, searching her until he found these miserable looking hooked balls under the saddle.

"Who did this?" He held up the nasty little things that must have dug into the poor animal as soon as it took my weight.

I was still on my back trying to breathe as a girl got shoved forward out of the group. She swallowed hard and got pale while the instructor glowered, crossing his arms over his very fine physique.

"It was a joke. I'm sorry. I didn't realize that it would hurt Henrietta."

Henrietta was apparently the horse, and it was much more humane to hurt people than animals. I stood up, brushing off straw. "I'm fine." Like anyone cared. "Can we try this again?"

The instructor looked surprised before he nodded and held Henrietta still while I tried to mount. My heart pounded and my hands shook as I listened to all his instructions and poor Henrietta skittered across the stones with her head jerking, eyes rolling in spite of the instructor. It wasn't as bad as cars, but my heart wasn't pounding less when I finally slid off the horse. I fell down when my legs wouldn't hold me up.

The Freshmen tittered and the instructor sent me to my room to get cleaned up and changed because I'd sat down right in a lovely pile of manure.

The fragrant aroma filled the air as I walked to my room. What a lovely experience. To imagine that I'd put it off for three years. I changed back into my school uniform and made it to my next class with hardly any time to spare. Business management. When I walked in, I saw Drake immediately, like my eyes were pulled towards him where he sat at a desk typing on a laptop like he knew what he was doing. Not that I didn't know how to write on a laptop, but he just gave off that odious odor of competence and condescension.

I slid in to the seat furthest from him and pulled out my own laptop. The teacher slammed my lid closed as he walked briskly up to the board in his navy jacket and wrote in scrawling letters something I couldn't decipher.

"Welcome to the world of business. You may think that you understand the basics of shares and funds, but..."

My face was frozen part smiling, part snarling while I tried not to kill him. The professor. Also Drake. Either one would work. Apparently, it was fine for Drake to have his laptop open, but not me. I had a business. I understood a lot about advertising, tax breaks, and even bookkeeping. I was not some dim-witted-gumball-for-brains student. The first class that I thought had the possibility of being remotely relevant to my actual life, and the teacher was a complete...

I took a deep shaky breath and focused on smiling, breathing, not anything else. I didn't even notice that Drake didn't glance up for the rest of the class, his fingers moving as he shifted from one document to another, checking various graphs until the instructor dismissed us.

Drake had his laptop closed and in his briefcase before I could blink and then he was standing beside his desk, looking at me as if he'd just seen me. His expression was so interesting. It went from something cold with icy fury barely held in check to an indifferent expression with a vague smile resting on his lips as he walked over. I slid my computer in my bag and felt like a weakling with my trembling everything next to him and his raw strength. He wouldn't be bucked off a horse, a horse would be bucked off of him. Loser.

"How is your hand?"

I didn't have any idea what he was talking about until I followed his gaze down to my bandage. "It's fine. Thanks for asking." I sounded too angry. I cocked my head and batted my eyelashes to make up for it.

His eyebrow twitched like he knew what I was doing, which he couldn't possibly have known since I had no clue. "Since I'm responsible for it, do you need me to take you to the doctor? I'll drive you after polo practice."

I shook my head and edged away from him at the very idea of getting into a car with this beautiful monster. "It's fine. It's not the first time Señor Mort got a little too frisky."

He raised his eyebrow high for a moment before it lowered as if on its own. Revere's eyebrows did the same kind of thing, like a caterpillar crawling around on his face. If only Drake's dark red eyebrows weren't the sexiest caterpillars in the world. "If it's bothering you tomorrow, we'll have the doctor look at it while we're at the hospital."

"What?" I stared at him while he stared back. What hospital? Oh, no. He thought I was serious about doing community service. With him. "Um, the community service. Right." I smiled at him feeling like my mouth was numb from hanging onto that manic smile for the entire day. "To be perfectly honest, I didn't think that classes would be so challenging. I already have more homework and reading than I have time to finish after only one day, so…"

He inclined his head slightly while his lips curled, amused by my stupid little brain that couldn't keep up with all the other students. "Do you find yourself unequal to the task? Do you think that these other privileged and elite students are more capable than you are?" His voice mocked me along with his eyes.

I wanted to stuff his eyeballs down his throat and see how he sounded then, but instead I clenched my teeth as I laughed. "That must be it. Of course, community service is important but I probably shouldn't flunk out of classes in the first week. Maybe next time."

He shrugged as he walked with me to the door. "I'll help you with business on the drive down and back. It's more of an applied business class for me although sometimes professor Marsh helps me understand an obscure point of business law."

Because he was so super smart and above me in every way, so I definitely couldn't handle thinking tricky thoughts about profit margin and stocks. When he asked me what my next subject was, I held up my schedule silently. I couldn't open my mouth without screaming at him, or biting him. He still smelled ridiculously good and I was getting hungry. Very hungry. He walked with me to my class, smirked then disappeared around the corner. I stood in the doorway, trying to breathe and not scream while I checked the class number and found that it indeed was the right one. History.

The teacher didn't waste any time, and honestly when someone dances around in an Elizabethan costume, it's hard not to pay attention. The tension knotted in my shoulders loosened as I settled into my seat. Even Viney's constant glare didn't disturb the pleasure I got out of Professor Vale's performance. On my way out of class, I heard some girls muttering about how the teacher, Professor Vale, had the nerve to have worked at some other school I'd never heard of, Blackheart or something. Ooo. School rivalry.

On my way out, a brunette with thick glasses and a wrinkled blouse focused on me like a hungry cougar. "Hi. You're Penny. You seem to enjoy getting involved. Would you like to pass out some fliers for the Student Government club?"

I blinked at her. I'd rather light my hair on fire. "Sure. That sounds so fun!" I must be a masochist. That would explain so much about my life.

She dug into her backpack and gave them to me with an, "If you can get them handed out by Wednesday that would be great!"

Wouldn't it? Finally, I was able to stumble across campus to my dorm, plug in the code on my alarm with my hand print and DNA check before I collapsed on my bed to the scent of drying manure.

I stared at the ceiling with the glorious forest scene, deer leaping over a stream while some figures in the shadows were maybe embracing, maybe strangling one another.

"I must have done something terrible in a past life. Señor Mort, my face hurts from smiling so much, and my knee is going to be bruised. I need to make something for it, but I can't move."

I closed my eyes and had almost drifted off when someone knocked on my door. I groaned and made the ugliest face I possibly could before I rolled off the bed and smoothed down my now wrinkled uniform.

"Hold on."

I opened the door and Zach stood there awkwardly. I beamed at him even though I wanted to slam the door in his face.

"Hi. Viney and I were going to go over to polo practice and thought you might like to come."

I blinked at him. Wow, an invitation from the boy I was going to marry, and I wanted to say no in a very loud voice along with some pretty boring expletives.

"That sounds so fun! I think I have a lot of homework though."

He shrugged and gave me a slight smile, kind of bashful as he looked at me beneath his dark lashes. "I can help you with linguistics if you'd like. We can work on things while watching the players."

"Ooo, we could heckle in Chinese!"

He smiled broadly while his blue eyes twinkled. "I'm not sure how helpful that kind of lesson would be."

I sighed. "Apparently, I don't quite understand the purpose of conversational anything. All right, I'll go."

"Aren't you going to change first?"

"Change?" I looked down at my school uniform then noticed what Zach was wearing, which was a t-shirt and jeans. "Oh. Yeah. Give me a minute to put on something recreational."

After I closed the door, I pulled on a short floral skirt and a pink blouse with a scalloped peter pan collar then touched up my makeup and put on a spritz of some fabulous scent. I opened the door and smiled out at Zach and Viney, anticipation of some kind on her face. I should have worn my armored helmet. Oh darn, left that at home.

"Your knee looks really bad. What happened?" Viney's voice was only slightly sympathetic. She could have tried a little bit harder.

"I got thrown in dressage." I sighed and smiled at Zach ruefully. "Apparently riding horses is slightly trickier than it looks."

Viney sneered. "I heard that someone put cockles under Henrietta's saddle."

Zach looked suddenly concerned as he put a hand on my shoulder. "Is she okay?"

The horse. My smile tightened and I took that moment to unwrap a lollipop. "She seemed fine. Do you know her?"

He nodded soberly. "She's got an excellent temperament for a creature that has to deal with the brats at Rosewood."

I nodded like that made sense, which it did, but I was kind of limping and I really didn't know how I was supposed to handle an entire year of torture. The bullying was annoying enough, but the whole thing where I had to go to classes and smile leaving me with no time to do what was important, namely make potions for my shop, was so frustrating. Also, this guy that I was going to marry was nice enough, but he didn't seem to notice me at all. Maybe I should have stuck with the rodent skulls and found someone a little less nice than Zachary Stoneburrow. No. I could do nice. I could be a sweet little thing that needed a man like Zach.

After limping across fields until we got to the bleachers, we sat among other students who had their homework out, enjoying the sunshine after being crammed inside all day. I pulled out my linguistics sheet and Zach helped me fill it out. He was extremely good at languages. Apparently.

"You're in the same class as Zach? Are you that good?"

I blinked at Viney. "No. I'm not. I have no idea why I'm in any of the classes that I'm in, although they're all really fun!"

Zach smiled at me. "You're not terrible at Spanish."

I sucked on my lollipop and tried to look seductive. It was probably ruined by the growing bruise on my knee. And my legs had looked so nice. "Thanks. I'm sure Miz was impressed. What would happen if you had a French accent and a German accent at the same time?"

He said, "Merci borscht est gutt!" and I tittered attractively.

That's when Viney hit my shoulder and nodded out to the field where the polo players were emerging on their prancing steeds. Drake. He looked even better on a huge black horse in real life than he'd looked in his picture. There were two teams although both were from our school. Zach explained the rules generally, but I stopped paying attention once he started talking about points.

I kind of missed whatever else he said when Drake took that stick and whacked a ball, shooting it across the field with some serious velocity. I would hate to get in the way of that ball, or that stick. I'd been watching the practice for fifteen minutes, fascinated at these boys who somehow moved as one with their horses until the thing happened.

Drake was running down the field and Jackson came along to block him and then Drake and Jackson's horses got tangled up. Drake launched himself off his horse and into Jackson, tackling him off his horse. It happened so fast, if I hadn't been watching so closely, I wouldn't have seen the horrible angle of Jackson's arm or heard the crack as Drake intentionally broke it.

Viney gasped and looked pale yet excited and Zach looked away from the field, kind of sick and disgusted. I expected to feel the opposite of sick and disgusted since my hand still hurt from Jackson, but watching him writhe on the field in pain only reminded me of the way I'd felt after Poppy... I grabbed my papers, shoved them into my bag and left the bleachers without meeting Zach or Viney's eyes.

    I walked quickly back to my room, ignoring Zach calling after me, instead twirling my lollipop on my tongue over and over and over.

8
WITCH

It was a horrible enough day, I should have stayed in my room, but at five-thirty I was hungry, six starving, and by six forty-five desperate to the point of breaking people's skulls open and eating their brains. Just kidding. I wasn't that hungry.

I made it to the dining room, had almond chicken and steamed vegetables with an enormous salad that I'd have to somehow eat in fifteen minutes. It was pretty close, but my plate was almost clean when the bell rang and the navy suits started walking down the tables to chase out late eaters.

I headed back to my room and was in the middle of a large hall with a lovely inlaid marble floor and marble pillars holding up the arched ceiling when a girl stepped in front of me. She said, "Didn't you want some dessert?" before sending an ice cold slushy into my face, shirt, neck, and shoulders.

Macaroons. Petit fours. Lady fingers. Bon-bons. I wiped my eyes and when I opened them for some reason I really, really, really wanted to ruin that perfect smile permanently. Drake stood behind her, an impassive expression on his face. The girl glanced over at him like a good puppy who had fetched his slippers.

"You think you're good enough for Drake," another girl hissed before she pushed me, in his direction ironically enough.

I licked my fingers and studied the guy who stood there with that annoying smirk on his mouth. They didn't like me talking to him, falling on him, anything involving him. Was that what all the annoying things had been about? Did they think I was competing for Drake?

Fury made things sparkly and bright as I smoothed more shake off my face and licked my fingers, sucking on them hard while I studied him, the boy that all the girls would do anything for, would hurt anyone for.

His eyes widened slightly, just enough to make me realize that I was looking sexy. Right. I'd seen that on a music video somewhere, people licking fingers like that wasn't disgusting. I walked over to him, anger fueling my seductive walk, until I was close. I held out my fingers, dripping with melted ice cream shake.

"Do you want to taste?"

His eyebrow flickered before he bent his head and took my fingers in his mouth, sucking and licking like I was his ice cream. Oh no. The scent of black cherry swirled around my head the way his tongue swirled over my fingers. I gasped and tried to think about macaroons.

After he'd licked off all the shake he smiled lazily and leaned forward. "It would be a pity to waste it."

I nodded because, yeah, that made sense and then he took my shoulders and leaned down before licking my throat from my scalloped Peter Pan collar to my chin. I gasped and clung to his shoulders as my legs gave out.

He seemed to take that as encouragement because he kept licking my neck and face, holding me against his body until I'd moved past hyperventilating to completely not breathing. Finally, he pulled back and waited until I could stand up on my legs before he let me go.

He smiled, brushed my jaw with his fingers and licked them. His smile was dangerous and amused. I didn't like either of those. "Thank you so much for sharing, Penny Lane. You'd better get back to your room before I gobble up the rest of you."

I should have said something cool and clever, or at least bubbly and ridiculous, but all I did was spin around and get out of there as fast as my trembling legs could take me. So that was what it was like to be licked like a lollipop. Lollipops were so much more dangerous than I'd thought they were.

Lollipops. I unwrapped one as I went until I got to Lilac Stories and came up suddenly against Viney who glared at me like I'd just murdered her mother. I didn't have enough lollipops for this.

"Hi Viney! How's it going? I'd love to chat, but I have so much homework to do, so…"

She stepped closer to me, eyes narrowing wickedly. "You really are a piece of bubblegum, the kind without any flavor, just sugar and when he's tired of you he'll spit you out and people will walk all over you."

I blinked at her then at the video on her phone she held up for me so I could watch me being consumed by Drake like an ice cream cone. I didn't look like I minded. My eyes were droopy, lips parted while I let him do whatever he wanted to me without the slightest protestation. I should have done something, anything, but I'd lost my temper with stupid, insecure girls. I knew better. I'd been taught my whole life to control the anger, the frustration, been poked and prodded until I could recite any poem by Longfellow with the proper intonation. Revere liked Longfellow. My mother liked poking and prodding.

I shook my head and forced myself to focus. My mother's lessons must have been too long ago. I took a deep breath and focused on Viney instead of my vacuous face and Drake's bent head above me.

"There wasn't really any chewing and people already walk over me. Besides, gum sticks to people's feet, so there's vengeance in the seemingly pathetic gumball. Viney, if you don't move, I will lick you."

She stepped back with this grossed out face as I went straight to my room and my bathroom beyond. Being sticky wasn't fun. I showered, only washing the bits of my hair that were sticky, and made it fast because I somehow had to get my laundry done before lights out. I needed a lot more clothes if I was going to go through five outfits a day.

I grabbed all the dirty laundry in my room, including the bloody handkerchief Drake had given me. I held my head away from the pile in my arms as the aroma of horse feces filled the air.

The laundry room was abandoned besides one guy who stood at the sink, the stretch of his shoulders impressive beneath his t-shirt. I stopped and tried to edge backwards before he saw me.

Drake turned and glanced at me over his shoulder, stopping me in my tracks. He smiled at me showing sharp teeth. "I'm not going to ask what you're doing here. I got malt all over my suit. I can't imagine what shape yours is in."

I hesitated before I gave him a small smile and kind of edged over to the nearest machine. I opened the door and closed it before looking around for instructions.

"Usually you wash clothes before you dry them."

I spun around and fought the stupid blush on my face. "Yeah, thanks. I've never really washed clothes before."

He smirked like I was so funny and idiotic. "You're a spoiled rich brat, right?"

I nodded soberly. "Absolutely. This whole thing is really strange."

"Laundry?" I tried not to notice that he'd taken three steps towards me, all while working suds through a white shirt. His hands as he kneaded the fabric were hard not to stare at.

"And horse manure, pink leotards, conversational Chinese..." I exhaled and almost scowled at the machine that apparently dried instead of washed. Instead I smiled at him blindingly. "It's been a little overwhelming."

"You didn't mention being hit by potatoes, knocked into people, having your horse sabotaged..."

I laughed a little bit. "Oh, I expected that, it's the fact that I can't walk after doing ballet that is by far the biggest shock. I seriously can't walk. Ballet is supposed to be easy and effortless."

He raised his eyebrows from where he now stood only five steps from me. "It didn't bother you when Maureen dumped her malt on you?"

I winced because I did not want to think about that, not when my reaction had been so weak and pathetic. I licked my lips before I gave him a slight smile. "I need to apologize for that."

He smiled, showing his canines and reminding me how it felt to have that mouth around my fingers.

I quickly put said fingers behind my back. "It's not like me to ask some guy to suck on my fingers. I think I wanted revenge. I think that most of the girls have been sad because they like you and don't like you talking to me. I guess I got tired of it. I shouldn't have reacted like that. I'm sure it only made them feel worse." Was that it? Was it really the girls that bothered me, or was it something else, something darker, something to do with me wanting them to know that Drake Huntsman belonged to me? I inhaled sharply and shook my head. It wasn't possible for me to be that sick and twisted about some jerk guy that quickly. How long had it taken my mother to fall for my self-absorbed father, Poppy to fall...

I flinched away from him and gripped the nearest machine, my knuckles pale while I tried to erase those last words from my brain.

He whispered, close enough I could feel his breath on the side of my neck. "It's not how they feel that interests me."

I shivered and stepped sideways, away from him. I swallowed and was pleased when my voice came out firm. "I apologize for using you to act out my infantile aggression. I'll have to apologize to them, explain that I'm not interested in their crush."

He was quiet for a long time. Finally, I turned my head to see him where he stood, staring at me, his eyes penetrating while I stared back, forgetting to smile and feeling my breath catch while my fingers tingled as I once again felt his tongue and teeth...

"I don't think you need to apologize to anyone. I personally would reject your apology considering how much I got out of it." He turned and stalked back to the sink to drop the shirt into a basin with a splash. "Pissing off those females was most of why I did what I did. Not that you aren't extremely delicious, but I don't usually lick girls in public." The way he said that, 'not that you aren't extremely delicious,' was that no, I really wasn't delicious, and how could I be stupid enough to think that he liked licking me, that he liked anything about the idiotic gumball head that was Penny Lane?

I exhaled and lifted my chin. "Really? What a relief. I thought that maybe you thought… Anyway, is this a washing machine?" I finished with my most sweet and idiotic smile.

He glanced at me and nodded. I proceeded to stuff all my clothes inside of it and then closed the door and stared at the knob for a little while before I started twisting it around and around.

"First of all, you don't wash suits." He put a hand on my shoulder and I flinched away from him, startled and unnerved. He was supposed to be holding me in contempt from the other side of the room. He sighed loudly. "Can I help you? Apparently, I have compassion for wool that's about to be horribly mangled."

I glared and scowled at the washing machine, fighting the urge to scream and eviscerate this pretender good Samaritan, but instead I took a deep breath and forced a smile. It wasn't very bright, but it was all I had left.

I slid over to the next machine, gestured to the door and crossed my arms over my chest.

He opened the door and started sorting my stuff into different piles. "Silk, cotton, and here's the horse manure you were talking about, which is leather and drill, so dry-cleaning, but first you'll want to brush all the excess off." He did so, going to this special machine that he hooked my pants to and then these motorized brushes went up and down my pants, knocking off everything vile. He then took it to another machine, opened this door thing, hung them inside, closed the door, twisted a knob, and pushed a button.

The machine whirred satisfyingly while he came back to the pile and took out my beige suit, studying it closely. "It's not terribly soiled, so I'd just give it a good steam." He took it to another machine, and then he picked up the bloody handkerchief. He glanced at me. "It's best to soak blood out immediately. That reminds me, I have your tablecloth."

I nodded, still smiling. Of course. I did not want to think about the ruined tea party, the fact that I spent more time with this horribly tempting creature than the nice boy I was going to marry. I couldn't help it, I really loved blood and black cherry. Focus, Penny. "Is your handkerchief ruined? Sorry."

He shrugged. "I can get blood out of anything. It's one of my most useful skills." His smile was that thing that showed teeth and reminded me of the big bad wolf. It also made my stomach tighten and my fingers crave his tongue. "Do you need me to wash blood out of anything else?" He glanced at me in a way that made me blush.

I should not blush around him. I should save blushing and cuteness for Zach. Maybe Zach didn't like blushing girls. He hung out with Viney. I should have kept my rodent skulls in my hair and simply dragged him away with me to live in my attic. At the same time, he wasn't her boyfriend however much she led him around.

"No, thanks. So, how do you wash it out?" I sidled closer to him, keeping my hands behind my back against the counter. I watched the process of soaking and scrubbing, and found myself at his shoulder, smelling black cherries and vanilla. When he turned his head, I couldn't breathe, my heart pounded so hard. I couldn't look away for a moment as he leaned closer to me until I turned, wrapping my arms around my body.

"I hate chemistry."

That's what it was, right? He had so much chemistry, the right combination of hormones and pheromones that mixed up my head until I was doing things I knew were completely stupid, but couldn't help. Also, the way he looked and who he was didn't mesh with him handling my laundry. His hands were so comfortable doing laundry, brisk and efficient with none of that sultry seduction that made me want to stick something pointy into his soft bits.

He gave me a questioning glance. "Do you need help with your homework?"

I shook my head rapidly and eased away from him. "No, thanks. I'd just better get back to it. I brought my books, so I'll do that while the machines do what they do."

He smiled slightly and I took my books to the white desk on one wall where there weren't machines.

I sat down and stared at the chapter that I had to summarize when it was all so basic and simplistic, it seemed like a complete waste of time. I hastily wrote my paragraph and turned to English, the poem we were studying that was supposed to drip with meaning and wisdom. Macaroons, bon-bons, truffles... I wrote the most upbeat and unrealistic interpretation of the poem possible and then had the pleasure of my history class, which was a video I had to watch on my laptop, easily enough. I was nodding over my math when someone shook my shoulder.

"Revere, I'm going to sic Señor on you."

Revere laughed, but he didn't laugh like that. I sat bolt upright and stared at Drake whose lips were curled in the most fascinating way. I very nearly put my fingers on those lips, but instead I stumbled to my feet and then nearly fell when my legs gave out, muscles screaming. His hands wrapped around my waist, pulling me against his chest close enough that I could see the specks of green in his eyes. I broke eye contact and backed away, clinging to the edge of the desk.

"You really can't walk?"

I gave him an eighty-watt smile. "Ballet really beat me up today. I'm sure I'll feel better tomorrow. If I don't feel worse. Are there rules about staying in bed all day?"

He smiled sharply, cocking his head while his glance dropped from my eyes to my lips. "There are all sorts of rules. It all depends on how much you like breaking them."

I shook my head and turned towards the washing machine that had my laundry in it, but instead of me needing to change it he must have dried then folded it neatly in a basket I hadn't brought. He folded my laundry? My heart pounded and my stomach knotted. He must have done something to my clothes. I'd have to throw it all away or check every item for poisonous substances. That would take all night.

I gave him a sickly smile. "It's really hard to believe that I fell asleep. You should have woken me up. You don't need to worry about my laundry."

He shrugged. "You shouldn't sleep places where anyone can do what they want to you."

No kidding. I choked out a laugh. "Yeah, so, did anyone mess with me while I was sleeping?"

He smiled at me, his eyes greener the more I stared at him. "Are you worried that I grabbed you after what happened last time?"

I ran my fingers over the white gauze bandage. "That reminds me, I need to change my bandage. So much to do." I focused on smiling at him. "I'm sure that you're very busy. I'll try not to take any more of your time." I didn't look at him again while I carefully walked across the room with my school bag over my shoulder. My suit was on a hanger and looked better than it ever had.

"My pleasure, Penny. If you ever need help cleaning your clothes or your sweet flesh, don't hesitate to call."

I flinched then lifted the basket and the hanger, gave him a quick smile without quite looking at him, and closed the door on the weirdest if not the worst day of my life.

9
MAGE

Well, that had been interesting. I sat down on the chair she'd just abandoned, running like a scared little rabbit from the big bad wolf, as though she hadn't just been sleeping in my den.

She'd walked right in like she didn't notice the shield I'd put on the door to guarantee my privacy. I liked to do my laundry alone. I liked to do everything alone, but one could hardly do that while keeping up appearances. Appearances weren't much, but they were all I had to keep the ravaging anger and darkness at bay.

I wasn't in the mood for company, not even someone as delicious as Penny Lane. It was difficult not to snarl at her, throw her out of the room when she insulted me with her apology, but direct assault was absolutely out of the question. She was so utterly incompetent. I couldn't help but watch her in horror as she attempted to 'do laundry'. A witch shouldn't let a mage touch her personal property, but she did, blushing like a peach and having a difficult time meeting my eyes.

After I got her laundry started, I focused on hand washing another shirt. Did we have enough Selenium for the light projection I wanted at the tourney? I would have to talk to Pewter about it. The background sound of Penny scratching on her notebook with her pencil stopped and didn't resume for three minutes. I glanced at her and paused. I'd never seen a sleeping witch before. Her lips twitched and she murmured about flowers. Poppies. She sounded so sad. I stared at her for eight minutes until the washing machine buzzed loudly, startling me out of my fascinated reverie. She should have woken up from that sound, but she didn't even stir.

After standing there with nothing better to do, I changed her laundry, rotating her suit in the steamer before I walked back to stare at her. I stood there, seven feet away from her, four, two, until my fingers curled over the back of her chair, her strawberry blond curls covering her like a blanket.

I sat on the desk beside her head, but she didn't sense me on the base level of awareness every witch should have. A mage and his magic should have set off all kinds of alarms to a three-quarter Darkside witch. There was something wrong with her. I'd seen an aberration once. They'd fought a war over her, some female who was so deliciously vulnerable no mage could resist her. If that's what she was, she ought to be under lock and key, not thrown to the slavering wolves at Rosewood, wolves like myself.

"What are you?" Even my voice didn't wake her up as I moved my hand above her body, two inches of space between my skin and her hair, echoing the contours and shape of her head, her back. I sensed her easily enough. I could feel the warmth she gave off, the smell of her perfume, flowers and vanilla that couldn't hold a candle to the way she'd tasted.

My hand paused while my mouth watered. She'd wanted to irritate the petty little witches, and I loved to torment them. It seemed like a very straightforward, even noble, mutual cause, but somehow, I'd forgotten about our audience and simply tasted her. She'd run away from me when I showed my interest so clearly in gobbling her up. Maybe she took it as a literal warning rather than a euphemism. Maybe it had been. Either way, I did not enjoy watching her run away from me, not if I wasn't allowed to chase her.

I shook my head and refocused on the white and sterile laundry room where she slept. I sent a wave of magic against her that lapped over her skin then swirled around and around until there was nothing left of it. Fascinating. I spent twenty minutes pouring magic over her, harmless magic that would do things like help her study better. What I was doing, experimenting on a sleeping witch, was clearly outside the bounds of the covenant. Using magic on a witch without her permission was as forbidden as taking her blood.

I smiled slightly and touched her hair. It was practically its own person, a mess of shimmering red gold that would look so nice with mine. On my pillow. In my bed.

I shook my head and stepped away. I could never let down my guard with a witch. I'd seen the results of that too many times. Of course, I wouldn't sleep with her, not literally. Having her in my bed not sleeping, however...

The dryer buzzed and I waited to see if that would wake her, but apparently she'd had an exhausting first day of classes. It wasn't only classes. I'd seen her in the hall, tripped by a witch whose personal violence surprised me. I expected to see a full on witch battle, but Penny got up and kept walking as if she didn't notice falling on her face in front of twenty snickering students.

I shook my head as I got her laundry out and then, with another glance over at the pile of curls that was all I could see of her, I folded her things. It wasn't nearly as invasive as so many of our encounters, but I felt a little bit scandalized by my own nerve as I picked up a pair of silk polka dot pink panties in my rough, large hands.

It would make her blush when she saw how neatly I'd folded them. I shook my head and counted breaths, considered something desperately trivial like whether I should order a new green suit the exact shade of my eyes, and if so whether it should be straight or slim cut.

There were so many things to think about besides the witch sleeping behind me and her clothes in my hands. I'd held her very close after I'd tasted her, the warmth of her body seeping into me like a warm bath.

Another peculiarity. Awareness, desire, alarm, should all comingle. There shouldn't be any pleasantness. Euphoria, thrill, absolutely, but comfort? I finished folding her things, put her suit on a hanger and stood for a long moment, staring at where she still lay folded over her math book.

I should wake her up. My laundry was finished and it would be rude to leave her defenseless, where any witch could hurt her, or mage could take advantage of her. Normally, I would consider it my duty to seduce her, break her heart, and send her on her way, but it didn't seem sporting with her sleeping like some fairy tale princess, waiting for her prince to kiss her.

Her pink lips were slightly parted. I knew how her fingers tasted, but her lips, her mouth, it would be so easy… I shook my head and cleared my throat. She didn't stir. Either I kissed her, or I did more experiments on her. I held my palms over her back until they itched with energy. Not magic, just energy that we use to focus on things like fighting, killing, maiming, bringing the body and the mind together into one perfectly destructive whole.

I could heal a fellow mage with my energy while a witch would repel it. Oil and water, witches and mages, but when I sent the flow of energy into her, it sank like a stone in a slow river. I felt the pull of her, wanting more energy from me.

I exhaled and put my hand on her shoulder, one of the few places besides her face not covered by her hair. I pushed more energy at her, and she took it but then I felt a return current, her energy flowing into me. My hand jerked, shaking her shoulder roughly in the process and she frowned as she finally opened her eyes, the sleepy softness shifting into panicked horror as she realized that she'd slept with a mage.

Horrified panic described the rest of her behavior until she grabbed her laundry and fled to her room.

Very interesting. Also completely nerve-wracking. I'd sunk into the chair and wiped my sweaty palms on my pants. They were too casual to wear while spending time with a female of note. Penny Lane was that and more, the first and probably last witch to ever sleep with me.

10
WITCH

The next day was fine even if I was more exhausted than I should have been after one day in school. I hadn't found a trace of anything on my clothing other than a slight scent of black cherry. So annoying, also embarrassing because he'd apparently neatly folded two pairs of my silk polka dot panties while I'd been drooling on my math book.

The classes were no worse than they had been the day before other than ballet. Who teaches a beginner Pas de Deux anyway? Apparently Madame, because there I was in my pink leotard and tights when Drake walked in wearing soft black pants and ballet slippers with his white t-shirt. I stared at him while I clung to the wooden barre. He walked over to Madame, gave her a charming bow and then they chatted in French for a bit before she led him over to me.

She gave me a sharp look while she spoke to him. "Do you think you can manage with this flamingo?"

He gave me a sharp smile. "I shall do my very best."

I tried not to hyperventilate when he took position behind me and started warming up, his turn-out perfect along with everything else about him. I stared at him in the mirror and kind of forgot what I was supposed to be doing, his muscles stretching and clenching beneath the thin fabric. He met my eyes in the mirror and raised his eyebrows.

"You had no idea I was so versatile. You're thinking, 'What can't he do? Laundry and ballet? It's too much to believe!' In all humility, it's just the tip of the iceberg. I can also hang a swing and clean up spilled malts." He gave me a slow wink.

I looked down at my hand where it gripped the bar like it was holding me up. "Why do you keep bringing that up?"

"I think it's funny. Don't you?"

I shook my head and frowned down at my ballet slippers. My toes didn't point as well as the boy in front of me, or the girl in front of him who was glaring at me like I'd just defaced a work of art.

I turned around and came face to face with him who instead of turning put his hands on my shoulders, pushing them back and down. I inhaled and held my breath until I realized that he was fixing my posture. I stared to the side while he adjusted my arms and then obeyed when he told me to point my foot. He had me do that a million times until I was sliding along the floor just right, and then it was drawing circles on the floor, and his hands rested on my knees, pushing slightly, his fingers gripping my heel, pulling it forward. He crouched in front of me while I tried to ignore him, but it was a little bit difficult, particularly when I kept having flashbacks, his mouth on my fingers, sucking, while his green eyes mocked me in the most seductive way imaginable. And he'd folded my underwear.

Finally he stood up and I thought things were going to be better. Oh, no. We all moved into the center of the room, the freshman boys and girls and me and Drake. It was even more humiliating than the horse episode the day before. I was like a stork, a flamingo, completely ridiculous flopping around while this glorious graceful music played. Drake only laughed out loud once, but his green eyes mocked me the entire time.

What happened was fairly straightforward. He had his hands under my armpits and we were going to do a very, very basic lift, but as he raised me up in the air, I realized that I was ticklish.

"Put me down!" I squirmed and wiggled, but that only made his fingers tighten until I lost control. I squealed as my legs flailed and I kicked the girl next to us, and then kneed Drake in the stomach. We fell over, but I think it was from him laughing so hard instead of from me kneeing him. We came down kind of hard, but he took the force of the landing, other than my knee, the already bruised one.

"I told you to put me down." I scowled down at Drake while his body shook beneath me until I rolled off him. "I'm ticklish. I can't help it. Stop laughing." I pushed his shoulder and felt weird, like maybe I was going to cry from sheer frustration. I'd never been tickled before in my life. The idea of being helplessly ticklish was beyond humiliating.

He stopped laughing and sat up, his lips trembling while he tried to look serious. "I'm sorry. I've never tickled anyone before. Are you ticklish anywhere else I should know about?"

I shook my head and crossed my arms, although what did I know? I'd never done anything like this before, let a boy lift me up and walk around with me.

Madame didn't comment on our debacle, although the girl I kicked made certain to give me enough dirty looks to grow a garden. Drake didn't try anything hard after that, mostly led me around in a circle and had me imitate a dog at a fire hydrant, nothing more dangerous than one leg off the ground.

After we curtsied to Madame and left the studio, I put my hand on Drake's arm to hold him back. "What are you doing in my beginner's class?"

He quirked his eyebrow and gave me a look on the side of a leer. "I had to find some way to finally get my hands on you." At my shocked look he flat-out grinned. "As if I didn't have the chance last night. I'm joking, Penny Lane. Madame didn't think a freshman boy could handle you and asked me to come in. I'm not sure I did much better, but I'm not afraid to wrestle with a ticklish flamingo."

I almost hit him, but instead I whirled around and went into the locker room where I noticed that my new lock had been tampered with. Happily it had held and my clothes were intact.

After dressing and undoing my extremely messy bun so my long hair cascaded down my back, I pulled out a lollipop and bounced to language class. I had to flirt with Zach and that meant my real homework had been cute phrases in a multitude of languages.

I looked around before subtly edging over to the group Zach was in. By the way, not a good idea. My cute phrases couldn't keep up with his discussion about current affairs, politics, law, traditions and cultural symbolism. He was so good. I just sort of stared at him while he talked everyone's socks off. In Spanish I had to abandon my drama and instead tried to speak intelligently, which I discovered wasn't my forte.

Halfway through the class I edged away from the Chinese circle where four students and Zach were brilliant and rejoined Barry, the guy who got my imaginary sister pregnant.

"Buenos Dias." He said it seriously.

I smiled at him and used my cute phrase. It would be a shame to waste it. He looked kind of startled, but responded almost according to the possibilities I'd studied. We had a semi-flirtatious conversation which ended in me giving him a lollipop as class ended. I gathered up my books and was surprised when Zach fell in beside me.

"How is Barry's amnesia?"

I glanced over at him and smiled. "He remembers me, but alas, he's still going to marry my sister. Do you want a lollipop? Tiramisu."

He took one with a smile. "You should have stayed in my group. You would learn more about linguistics in five minutes with people who know what they're doing than an hour with someone like Barry."

I hesitated for a minute. Was that jealousy? I studied his blue eyes but he didn't look anything other than intent. "You really know what you're talking about, I mean you're really talented at languages. I didn't want to interrupt your conversation."

He shrugged. "It's a bit boring, to be honest. You're never dull."

Was that what I was going for? Weird? I gave him a wan smile and headed to my math class.

After lunch I went to the stables and when I got there, the instructor put his hand on my shoulder and led me over to Zach where he stood in his very flattering riding gear.

"Mr. Stoneburrow is going to teach you how to not fall off a horse. If you have any questions or problems, ask him. He knows his way around an animal."

With that I was left staring at Zach, feeling awkward. I hadn't tried to look cute and my hair was in a sensible braid over my shoulder. I couldn't flip it or twirl my skirt. I hadn't even brought lollipops to suck provocatively.

"Shall we start?" He didn't smile, and his tone was really flat. Maybe he didn't want to be there.

"Of course."

He went slowly. That was the largest difference between him and the real instructor, the fact that he didn't skip anything. He explained all the little stupid things I should already know but didn't, like not walking behind a horse, and how to get a horse to like you, and how to check under the saddle for burrs or other foreign objects. I forgot that I was supposed to be flirting with him and just listened intently and learned. When he slipped into Spanish, I gave him a questioning glance, but he didn't act like he noticed, and then when he repeated a phrase in three languages, I shook my head.

"So you're teaching me languages and dressage? You're very efficient."

He smiled at me, the first time since I'd seen him in the stable with Henrietta. "You'll catch on quickly. It's satisfying to have an intelligent student."

I raised my eyebrows. "So, I'm your student now? I'll have to start bringing you and Henrietta apples."

He shook his head. "Stick with lollipops, at least for me." He smiled one last time and then it was time for me to mount up. I wanted to hurry up and get it over with, but he had me take my time, his hands over mine as I held the reins, his hands holding the stirrup for me, and then giving me a boost up to the saddle, his hands on my waist.

I sat there on top of Henrietta feeling too high off the ground because I was almost certain she was going to start dancing around. She snorted and tossed her head once before she settled down and let Zach lead her out of the stables and onto a field. We walked around, well, he and Henrietta walked while I sat upright on the horse trying to remember how to hold my knees, my ankles, my hands and my shoulders. My stomach was aching by the time we got back to the stables, golden strands of hay floating through sunbeams in the old stone and wood building as Henrietta trotted in.

"Dismount," Zach said, putting a hand on my leg. I kind of jumped at that touch and Henrietta took that moment to help me off. I hit Zach kind of hard but he didn't fall over backwards, instead he wrapped his arms around me and I slid down him to the ground like he was used to catching inept horse riders. I stared at him while he held me and the horse at the same time. Henrietta stood stolidly, apparently satisfied once she had me off her, even if I was pinned between her and Zach.

"Sorry about that." I winced and tried to edge away from him.

He cleared his throat and stepped back, giving me a slight smile before turning to the horse, stroking her dark gray nose. "Henrietta, you need to be nice or Penny isn't going to give you any lollipops."

I smiled slightly and took another step away from them. I hadn't relaxed since the moment I'd gotten on the horse's back. "Or apples. We can't keep meeting like this."

"You mean parting." Zach glanced at me with a slight smile.

I sighed. "You linguists are so particular. But... thanks Zach. Thank you for being my private horse tutor. Apparently, I need special help."

"It's the least I can do after yesterday."

I froze. Was he talking about the licking the shake off me thing? "Yesterday?"

He focused on Henrietta, stroking her face with his steady hands. "Viney asked me to invite you to polo practice. Drake always does something like that at the first one. He's methodical about his madness, likes to set the tone for the new year. I don't know why Viney wanted you to see his vicious streak, but I didn't mean to upset you."

I exhaled and beamed at him. "It's fine. Don't worry about it unless that means you'll have to give me more special lessons, because in that case, I was completely traumatized."

He laughed. His voice was soft and gentle, like his hands on the horse. "I'll come again on Thursday."

"It will be my reward for Pas de Deux."

He looked at me and raised his eyebrow. "You're in Pas de Deux already? That's right, we did that as Freshmen. How is your partner doing?" He looked like he was fighting a grin.

"Well, I think I bruised his tailbone when I knocked him over, but I think that Drake can take a fall."

His eyes widened. "Drake? He's your Pas de Deux partner?"

I sighed and nodded. "It's pretty terrible. I feel almost as bad for him as I do for you. At least I didn't knock you over."

He smiled slightly. "Maybe I'm just a better catch. Listen, Penny, I saw the show last night Drake put on for his audience."

I stiffened and felt my cheeks heat up. "Oh. It wasn't how it looked."

He put a gentle hand on my shoulder, like I was a horse he was taming or something. I wanted to bite his hand, sink my teeth really deep until he stopped looking at me with pity in his eyes. Horror and fear would have been so much better. "Penny, a lot of girls really like Drake, but he only messes with them. What he did, that's going to make them crazy, and they're already crazy. He likes them to be jealous and cruel to each other. He likes it."

I nodded slowly, pulling out a lollipop. I stared at it, the shiny cellophane wrapper. There was something so therapeutic about ripping cellophane that crinkled so nice. "Are you warning me not to be jealous when he licks another girl? I'm pretty sure I'll just be relieved that it's not me. I didn't mean for any of that…"

He cut me off. "I know. I saw the footage and the way he grabbed you, the way you looked, paralyzed with shock, I don't think it would make anyone jealous, but I think you should be careful. Be really careful."

I laughed. "You don't need to worry about me. I'm tougher than I look."

He nodded, still staring at Henrietta. "I just wish that Drake would leave you alone. People are saying that Drake broke Jackson's arm because that's the one he used to hurt you."

"What?"

He waved his hand. "It's not like Drake to have deep motives, he just likes to hurt people, and Jackson has been irritating him for a long time, but you know how people talk."

Not really. "Thanks for your help with riding. I'll see you later. I've got to get changed before class." Business. Drake was in that one with me. Hopefully he would ignore me like the last class.

I waved at Zach and hurried to change in my room. I flopped on my bed for a minute, and swung while I stared at those mysterious figures in the trees. Zach had seen the video of the malted thing? I screwed up my face and put my pillow over my head so I could scream.

I couldn't go to class with Drake. Something horrible was going to happen.

I gritted my teeth and rolled out of bed. I was acting ridiculous. I smoothed down my suit and put my hair in a high ponytail so I looked less cute and flirty. I should have pants to wear to business class. Why didn't I have pants?

I went to class sucking on a calming lollipop, but all my nervousness was unnecessary because Drake wasn't there. I took careful notes, and after that I had my favorite class, History, with the devine Professor Vale. She wore leather pants that day with a spiked leather jacket. She did this rap sequence of Shakespeare that completely blew me away. Even Viney looked impressed.

After that, Viney grabbed my arm and glared at me.

I licked my lips. Macaroons and parfait. "Hey, Viney! I'm sorry about yesterday. I was pretty tired and kind of upset. I'm sure you understand. It was too cruel of him to use me just to make some girl jealous."

Her eyes widened. "Who, Drake?"

I nodded, looking mournful and all kicked puppy. "I thought he kind of liked me, but he told me there's this other girl that he likes and she's the one who that whole performance was for. He's so cruel. I wonder who she is. Do you know who Drake might like?"

She shook her head violently and dropped my arm before spinning away to march purposefully into the distance.

Good enough. Apparently, my dramatic flair was useful for something. Real world skillz.

I walked slowly back to my dorm, dodging a few times from errant missiles and 'accidentally' kicking a girl who tried to trip me. If only I had my boots. When I got to my room I took off my suit, hanging it neatly before I put on a floral dress and my apron. I hummed as I got all my tubes filled, smelling beeswax and shea butter along with lavender and peppermint. I needed to make a nice bruise cream for my knee because it was really ugly. At least I'd been wearing the riding pants when Zach had walked beside me.

11
Witch

I was happily pouring lotion into hot bottles to cool and was on the last bottle of that batch when someone knocked. I checked the time and saw five-thirty. Maybe Zach wanted to go to dinner with me.

I pulled off my apron, undid my hair and fluffed it before I opened the door with my sweetest smile. My smile froze and so did I. Drake stood there looking dangerous and blatantly beautiful. My fingers immediately began to tingle.

I fought the urge to slam the door. "Drake. What are you doing here?"

He raised his eyebrows. "Aren't you going to invite me in?"

I glanced over my shoulder at my room and then stepped out into the common room. "I don't think that's a good idea. Señor Mort is having his nap. He gets cranky if someone disturbs him."

"Are you ready to go?"

"Where?"

"Community service." He smirked at me. "Don't tell me that you forgot about it. That would be a pity. I told the head doctor that you were coming, and he was so excited. He has something special planned for you."

Something special sounded horrifying. "Are you serious?"

He nodded. "Don't make me cancel. He would cry. He's a very emotional guy."

"I thought that we already talked about this. I'm sorry, Drake, but I have a lot of homework to do."

"I'm going to help you with Business."

I shook my head. "You weren't in class today."

He grinned. "Did you miss me?"

I tightened my lips. "I really don't think that's a good idea. I mean, it will give people the wrong impression."

"That we care about people?"

"That you like me."

He cocked his head, teeth sharp on his full bottom lip. "I hate to break it to you, but that's not what people will think."

I crossed my arms and tried not to notice his mouth, focusing instead on his eyes. "What will they think?"

"That I'm bored and you're weird and I'll amuse myself at your expense until you get boring too."

I froze and fought the urge to knee him in his kidneys. "If that's how you feel about it then I'm sure you won't mind going without me."

He put his arm around my shoulder, and a few things happened. I couldn't quite breathe right. He smelled so incredibly rich like a black cherry chocolate truffle. The other thing was that Zach came out of his room.

I tried to duck away from Drake, but he tightened his hold and I couldn't get away from him unless I did something violent.

"What are you up to, Drake?" Zach studied Drake then me, his mouth thinning when he saw the way Drake gripped me. Would this kind of thing make him jealous in a good way?

"Penny asked me to take her to the hospital to do some community service. Isn't that like her, so compassionate and caring, she's even rubbing off on me? Why don't you come along, Zach? We can mop some floors or read books to people in comas…"

Zach shook his head, forcing a smile. "Maybe next time. See you later." He stood there and I couldn't do anything besides smile at him while Drake hauled me out of the room.

He dropped his arm once we were in the hall and I took a deep breath and tried to think happy thoughts. This would be good. Drake would only want to do this once. I had to be really brilliant if I wanted to deal with him without screaming and pelting him with acid bombs. What I needed to do and be was boring, insipid, and it would help if I could throw myself at him like all the other girls, you know, without losing it completely and sinking my teeth in his skin or setting him on fire.

I glanced up at him and tried to visualize behaving like those other girls, the ones he didn't bother, but it was impossible. If I tried to kiss him I'd end up biting him instead, and liking it.

"Thanks for agreeing to do this, Drake. It's going to be good to take a break from thinking about school for a little while."

He glanced at me with his eyebrows raised. "Weren't you just saying that you didn't want to come?"

I chewed on my bottom lip before smiling brightly. "It seemed almost like you didn't hear me. Of course I want to, it's just difficult for me to hang around you when you're so attractive and dangerous, and how many girls like you."

Blegh. That had been the worst come on line ever.

He patted my shoulder. "Hang in there, you're doing all right."

It was so hard not to slam his face against a marble pillar until his lips were a little less perfect. Instead, I studied the floor of the hall until we got to a covered walkway that led to the garage.

"Why are you doing this, Drake? It doesn't make sense that you'd spend your time..."

"Penny, you think too much. A girl like you just needs to look cute. Don't try to understand someone as complicated as me."

I smiled sweetly while I visualized shoving a fork into his eyeball. Bonbons. Macaroons. "That's so true. Thank you for reminding me of the broad distance between the two of us. You are so deep and anguished, like a complex baked Alaska, while I'm nothing but a creamy truffle, one of those with lots of sugar and milk. And sprinkles."

He stared at me, kind of frozen expression before he grinned. "Who is he?"

I stared at him. "Excuse me?"

"Who is the guy that you like so much that you can resist my charm?"

I raised my eyebrows skeptically. He was supposed to be charming? I tried to look vaguely confused. "Was I resisting? That would only make you more... I mean how can I resist someone who smells like black cherries?"

"And acts like Baked Alaska, but you must know that if you flat out reject me that will only make me pursue you more vigorously. I'm contrary like that. I'm waiting for you to throw yourself at me in an effort to get rid of me."

I stared at him with my mouth open while he smiled smugly and walked a few steps away from me before he glanced at me over his shoulder.

"Aren't you coming, Penny Lane?"

After that we walked in silence beneath the covered walkway to the garage where he stopped in front of his large, dark green suburban.

"You drive a soccer mom car."

He glanced at me, green eyes the color of his car. "Don't worry, I don't drive like a soccer mom at all. You shouldn't say things like that, Penny, it makes it very difficult for me not to flirt with you."

I glanced at him skeptically while he opened the passenger door for me and after hesitating, I scrambled up, showing a lot of thigh from my short skirt. I really, really needed to find some pants somewhere.

"How is your knee?" he asked as he settled in beside me, buckling up.

I looked around, trying to gauge how many people were going to gossip about me driving around with Drake Huntsman, but I didn't see anyone. I kind of ducked down anyway.

"What?" I said when I realized he was looking at me like I was supposed to say something.

He nodded down to my knee where I'd wrapped it with a poultice. "Oh, it's good."

"How about your hand?" He nodded to my still gauze wrapped hand.

I laughed and pulled out a lollipop. "Doesn't it seem like I have a lot of injuries for the first two days at school?"

He frowned and his hands tightened on the steering wheel. "As a matter of fact, I think you do. Don't you ever want to get some real vengeance, not just let some guy drink malted off you, but actually hurt someone?"

"Honestly? It's a little bit therapeutic to plan someone's demise, and the tears in their eyes as they beg you for mercy, but then I get stuck on logistics."

"Logistics? Do you need help planning a good revenge?"

I shook my head and dug my fingers into the edge of the leather seat as he accelerated down the steep road through the trees. "I don't stop daydreaming at that point, but always end up where I become the person I hate, where the best things about who I am are destroyed by my hatred for someone else. There is no way to hurt someone else without it hurting you more in the end."

He raised his eyebrows skeptically. "Who told you that?"

I cocked my head and smiled at him. "You did. Your focus on fear and violence robs you of satisfaction from all the amazing things you accomplish with your talents. Instead of doing something hard, like making friends out of enemies or forgiving, you hurt people. Instead of truly challenging yourself, you settle into what comes easily to your nature, and what's the fun in that?" Wow. I'd really said all of that with a straight face. Where had I picked that up from? Passiones, probably.

He exhaled and then laughed, but it sounded different than his usual hard and dangerously edgy laugh. "Enough, Sensei. I told you I'd help you with business. Let's start with basics. How do you make certain you have a high enough profit threshold to maintain stability?"

I pretended to have no idea, and he explained in great detail all the way to the hospital. While he talked, I couldn't ignore the panic that built inside my chest as I stared at the road then glanced at him, his eyes focused on the road while he talked, gesturing instead of keeping both hands on the wheel at all times.

I tugged on the seatbelt, checking its strength while I nodded at Drake and tried not to throw open the door and jump out into the woods.

He glanced at me more often the closer we got to town, and it seemed like the closer we got, the faster he drove, and the wilder he careened around curves until I was hyperventilating.

Finally, we were in town and he had to slow down, jerking to a stop before he revved the engine, throwing me back against the seat while he drove around the hospital to the parking lot. He slammed on the brake while I unlatched my seatbelt and threw open the door. I slammed it closed behind me and leaned against it, breathing hard, like a wolf was chasing me.

Drake came around until he stood in front of me, but I didn't look at him because I couldn't quite smile and I thought I might throw up. I was supposed to be bubblegum, not vomit. After a second, Drake shoved me back against the car then grabbed my wrists, putting them above my head while he loomed over me, only not that looming since I was quite tall, thank you very much.

I stared at him, his eyes glinting green, fury flashing through them like I'd insulted his grandmother.

"Do you have a grandmother?" My voice barely shook, so that was something. I still wanted to throw up. I hadn't felt like this for years and years, well, not from riding in a car anyway.

He leaned harder against me, the lines of his chest pressing into me. "No."

I swallowed and inhaled deeply, ignoring the knotted panic twisting inside my stomach and chest, like a twining pile of worms, eels, something with sharp teeth and slimy squirming. No, forget about that, think about something else, something like Drake so I don't throw up on him. Black cherry. He smelled like black cherry, right? Not really. He smelled more like lava and angry burning. "I like your new aftershave. Very volcano. Matches your hair. I wonder what they use for that, musk maybe with a hint of charcoal and sulphur. Not an everyday kind of scent but very distinctive."

He growled at me, like a big bad wolf. The growl cut through the panic until I could really focus on him, and me, and us, him holding me against the passenger door of his car with my hands above my head. Why were my hands above my head, held in his strong fingers, and his body pressed against me?

"What are you doing?" I stared at him, the way the afternoon light played on his hair, gold and russet, eyes burning emerald into me while his lips pursed into a bud. Angry lips. I wanted that anger. Anger would push back the panic, the mindless fear that left me a spineless cuttlefish.

I leaned my head down against his shoulder, pressing my cheek against the warm skin of his neck, not warm, hot, volcanic. I inhaled deeply while I trembled, my nose brushing against his throat. Black cherry bloomed from his skin until I was dizzy from it.

He stiffened up and pushed away from me, dropping my hands and crossing his arms over his chest. He cleared his throat. "What's your problem?"

My arms slid down the car door until they were limp at my sides. "Problem? What problem?"

He raised an eyebrow, cocking his head. "I would have to be very oblivious not to notice how..." He blinked and something shifted across his face. "I have a temper. Seeing you so afraid of me when I've put so much effort into reining in my less gentlemanly impulses doesn't agree with me. I apologize for grabbing you like that."

I cocked my head while I studied him. I really wanted to close the distance between us so I could focus on his skin, his scent instead of the growing tangle in my stomach. It should be easing by now. I wasn't in the car anymore, but apparently the fear wasn't in any hurry to move along. "That was your temper? Really? That's kind of disappointing."

He stared at me steadily. "How so? You want me to ravage you against a car?"

I smiled a shaky trembling smile because that's the only kind I had. "Is that what being ravaged is like? I don't think you're very good at it. Not to insult you, but you didn't even kiss me."

His mouth twitched, but that was the only reaction. "You want me to kiss you?"

"Oh, no! I'd probably throw up in your mouth, and no one deserves that. Do you mind... would you... can I..." I closed my eyes tight and then took the two steps until I'd bumped into him. He stood there while I leaned against him, inhaling deeply while my heart pounded and the nausea clawed at my throat. He smelled of volcano again and then black cherry, and then a weird mix before he grabbed my shoulders and held me away from him.

"What is wrong with you?"

I blinked at him while involuntary and disgusting tears filled my eyes. "I'm afraid of cars. Sorry. I should have mentioned it before I rode with you, but it hasn't been so bad for a really long time, and I just sort of hoped it was over. I can sit in the back without having such a pathetic and disgusting reaction but the front turns me into a sniveling wreck. I'm sorry I wanted to touch you. You smell like really interesting things and your skin is hot so it's distracting from the nausea and the eels swimming around my intestines, unless my guts are eels, and that's the problem."

He stared at me, his eyebrows coming together while his fingers dug into my shoulders until he jerked me back against him. I inhaled deeply and pressed my face against his skin.

"I'll take this as you begging me to grab you. It's not quite the scenario I imagined, but maybe I should get used to being surprised where you're concerned." He pulled me closer making my stomach lurch.

"Be gentle or I'll surprise you with vomit."

"How am I supposed to be surprised if you warn me?" He gave me another only slightly gentler squeeze.

"No one likes puke surprises."

"I do. I like all kinds of surprises, particularly about you. Do you prefer me to hold you closer to me, or further away, and where should I put my hands for maximum distraction, that's what we're doing, right? Distracting you from your fear? I could tickle you."

"I'd definitely throw up."

"I could kiss you."

I tried to pull away, but when fear gripped me I was about as strong as a dishrag. "I told you, I'd probably vomit in your mouth."

"That's a risk I'm willing to take."

I snorted and smiled against his neck. "You really know how to live on the edge."

He leaned his cheek against my hair and relaxed his hands, sliding them around my shoulders to my back. "You have no idea. Do you want me to talk about my edges? I have so many. The edge of my nose, my shins, although you already know my shins intimately. I like going fast in cars, on horses, anything really. Speed, the thrill of almost dying, it's one of the things I live for."

"You live to feel like you're dying? That makes sense." I hesitated before I added in a pathetic, mewl, "Talking helps."

His hands smoothed across my back sending a shiver over my skin in spite of the nausea knotting my stomach. "Your hands are still gripping your skirt like you're trying to strangle it. I've seen a lot of people vulnerable, terrified, but you're the first one who asked about my grandmother. You have ridiculously good manners for a petrified person."

I shuddered while a wave of terror swept through me. I gasped while my stomach knotted tighter and bile coated my throat. I twisted to the side right before I threw up. Drake kept one arm around me and pulled my hair back with the other hand so I wouldn't have to wash out puke. Really, it was the sweetest thing anyone had ever done for me. What was wrong with him? I retched until my stomach was horribly empty and then I kind of dangled from Drake, his arm wrapped around my ribs, his hand spread over my side so there wasn't any pressure on my stomach.

I stayed like that, with trails of spit dripping from my lips until I straightened and wiped my mouth with the back of my hand.

I stared at the hospital with him behind me, still holding onto me. I waited for him to hurt me, to say the words I deserved for being so weak, so pathetic and disgusting. I counted the windows of the two-story gray building while I concentrated on breathing in and out.

"You're missing two ribs."

I covered his hand with mine, the strong fingers wrapped around my side, the position perfect for burying into my vulnerable side and squeezing my internal organs. "Car accident. Five years old. Six weeks in the ICU. It's stupid. I should be over it."

He didn't squeeze anything, but held still, very still like he was holding my organs in place, protecting me. "You lost two ribs in a car accident when you were five? It must have been horrible."

I shrugged. "I don't remember. It's disgusting to be afraid of something I can't even remember."

He let go of my hair and wrapped his other arm around me, brushing his fingers along my jaw. "You keep saying that. I'm not sure what's so disgusting about fear. Terrifying, yes, disgusting, no."

"You don't think being thrown up on is disgusting?"

He tightened his arms only slightly, pulling my back closer to his chest. "Not particularly. You can't live on the edge without encountering things like blood, broken bones poking out of your skin, vomit, urine, you didn't even piss yourself. It's impressive."

I ground my teeth and stiffened up as the fear loosed its hold on me and I had the delayed realization of who exactly had seen my core, my true self. I had the genetic disposition to be nothing more than a spineless coward and now Drake Huntsman knew it.

"You're feeling better. That means I should let go of you. For some reason, I don't want to. You must hate me having my hand here, right where you're most vulnerable. I could hurt you so easily."

"So, hurt me."

"That wouldn't bother you as much as seeing you throw up. No, I think I've tortured you enough for one day. Have to save something for next time."

He let go of me and I whirled around, staring at him wildly. He wasn't smiling, frowning, anything really. He watched, waiting to see what I'd do next. Right. I was Penny Macaroon Lane, human gumball. How did that work? I inhaled shudderingly and licked my lips. I needed a lollipop.

I took a step towards him and gave him a weak smile. "Will you please move? You're blocking the door. I left my bag in your car."

He raised an eyebrow before he turned and got my bag out then held it up in front of me, strap dangling from his hand.

I held out my hand and waited incredibly patiently until he lowered it, his fingers brushing mine, sending awareness through me that I hadn't had to deal with when I was scared stupid. So there was one perk to being scared. I smiled at him brightly while I fished through my bag until I found the right kind of lollipop. I unwrapped the cellophane with trembling fingers.

I walked towards the hospital, my legs weak and not only from ballet. He walked beside me, blatantly staring at me.

"What are you looking at?" I turned my head and saw his slight smile, eyes narrowing seductively as he took a step closer to me until his arm brushed mine.

"I'm starting to feel things I've never felt before. Confusion mostly. Penny, are you really so afraid of something that irrational?"

"It's not irrational. People die in car crashes all the time." It was irrational. I couldn't even remember it, but it still haunted me, controlled me.

"But it is disgusting, right?"

I inhaled sharply, feeling my shoulders tighten. Yes. It was.

"It's not, but someone's worked very hard to convince you that it is, that you are. Your mother?"

I laughed. "My mother?" How did he think I knew about how disgusting fear was? I'd seen her a sniveling wreck when she tried to leave the house. She'd made it down the steps and across the dirt drive. I had to drag her back inside by her hair because she was out of her mind at that point and couldn't find the house through her hysterical tears while Revere was off getting groceries or something.

"Not your mother. Father?"

I shook my head tightly. "Revere is the only father-figure I have. Everything about me disgusts him."

"Particularly your tea party outfits?"

I shrugged. "Not particularly. My mother hates them the most." The walk to the hospital was taking forever. Why didn't he stop talking? He should be tired of me at this point. The novelty couldn't possibly be there after I'd thrown up, whatever annoying thing he said.

"Is it the pink or the ruffles she finds objectionable?"

I stopped walking and turned to stare at him. "Either, both? What does it matter? Why are you doing this?"

"Community service is good for the soul and my soul is pretty sick."

I sucked on my lollipop while I stared at him, his eyes glinting with amusement. He found this whole thing amusing, me scared, me pathetic, me out of control. He was genuinely enjoying himself.

"Why did you want to drag me out of my room when I'm tired and hungry and need to do so much that I just can't do? I can't even ride in a car without breaking down. You're Drake flaming Huntsman. Why don't you find someone who would appreciate the whole rapturous experience and not throw up on you? I know that school is probably pretty boring, and I'm a new thing, but it's not fun for me. You should drag someone to the edge who likes it there instead of someone whose only glorious accomplishment is making lollipops."

He raised an eyebrow as he kept walking towards the building. "When are you going to let me have one? They're supposed to be incredible."

I scowled but it was okay because he wasn't looking at me. Still, I should control myself, the parts I could control. I forced a sweet smile to my mouth. "Are they?"

"Barry told me all about it. I think he has a little crush on you. He's only a junior though, so I'd take it easy on him."

I blew out noisily. "No, you'd see his weakness and pounce on it. You are the big bad wolf."

He glanced at me grinning before he started muttering under his breath.

"What are you saying?"

"Foreign language. Don't worry about it." He continued his muttering like a crazy person all the way to the revolving door. "Shall we?" He finally stopped the muttering and gestured me through.

I gave him a polite smile I reserved for crazy people like my mother and headed into the hospital lobby.

12
Witch

It smelled weird, like pine tree air fresheners and rubber. He led me past the front desk and down a hall. When he opened a door at the end of the hall, a woman wearing blue scrubs smiled at him.

"The doctor is on his way. Would either of you like a lollipop?"

Drake glanced at me and raised an eyebrow before he took a sucker from the nurse. "Thanks. She's already got one so I'll take hers too." He winked at the woman and she blushed and shook her head, tutting at him.

"Drake, and Penny isn't it?"

I turned and smiled at the young doctor who held a clipboard in his steady hands. He was kind of cute.

I gave him a little wave. "Hi. Thanks for letting us come by."

Drake gave me a quick look before turning towards the doctor. "That's right. There's nothing more uplifting than community service."

The doctor spoke to the nurse. "Dottie, take Penny to visit our young princesses. Drake, you come with me."

I felt practically normal, as though I hadn't had a complete breakdown in the parking lot, as I followed Dottie out the door and down the hall towards a room full of kids, many of them without any hair. I froze in the doorway while they all looked at me, eyes large and their little bodies so small. It smelled like pain and fear, the horrible feeling I'd been paralyzed by so recently. I swallowed and forced a fabulously happy smile to my lips.

"Hi!"

One little girl came up and stared at me, standing right in front of me with the most enormous brown eyes in her sweet face. "Are you Rapunzel?"

I hesitated as the other little girls gathered around me before I nodded. "That's right, I'm Rapunzel. I was trapped in my tower by my wicked witch of a mother."

Another girl gasped and reached out to touch my long, strawberry gold curls. "How did you escape? Did a prince rescue you?"

I knelt down on the floor, and the girls all gathered around, leaning forward, anxious to hear every word about my exciting escape. I made it good, embellishing the story about the bored princess in her tower, giving her a magic cloak and mirror that she could travel to alternate dimensions with, and then how she met her prince in one of these worlds, but he couldn't see her face beneath the cloak or her mother would know and curse her to never leave her tower again.

I used to tell stories to my pets, the vermin I collected and dressed up for tea parties. The kids were a much better audience. None of them bit me and they gasped at all the best parts.

"Even though he could never see my face, he loved me because I was smart, funny, kind and stubborn. He liked stubbornness in women. In his small village, many people were afraid of the unknown. Someone raised the cry of witch, and wanted to burn me, accusing me of being a monster beneath the hood. To save me, the prince pulled back my hood, revealing my face and brilliant eyes, but alas, the moment he saw me, I was pulled back through the mirror to the tower where my wicked witch of a mother waited."

They gasped and I sighed dramatically as I tried to think how to make this story have a happy ending with me looking cute in a hospital. The kids leaned forward, eyes rapt as they waited, breathless to find out what happened to their princess.

"Finally, after searching through all the different worlds for thousands of years using the magic cloak, the man found my world, the birds I'd described, the color of the sky, everything exactly as I'd named it. He searched for me for years until he finally came to my tower. Rapunzel, Rapunzel, let down your hair, that I may climb the golden stair."

I frowned at them. "Having someone climb up your hair isn't any fun. Even though I loved my prince very much, I insisted that he had to find a different way up to my tower. He tried catching a flock of birds and having them carry him to the top, but he picked sparrows, and we all know how bird-brained they are. Next, he tried lassoing the top of the tower to climb up, but of course every time he got his lasso around the building, the rope slid down to the ground. Finally, gathering his courage, he scaled the tower, fingers gripping the stones as he clung to his love and his hope. By the time he reached the top, he was really tired, so I gave him a nice cup of tea, and then we captured a flock of ravens, which are very intelligent birds, and flew far away where the wicked witch could never find us again."

I smiled while they sighed happily. One girl with a shiny bare head reached out to stroke my hair. Another girl did the same. I thought I'd mind, feel poked and prodded, but instead I felt kind of aching. I couldn't imagine losing my hair. All the other things I'd lost, all the pain, fear, I'd always had my hair to hide me from the rest of the world.

"Do you guys want to fix my hair? I have a comb in my bag."

They cheered and scrambled all over me, tugging and wrestling until each girl had her own strand of hair to do whatever she liked with. I learned their names while they braided and knotted my hair, learned what they liked, how long they'd been in the hospital, what they liked about it, what they didn't like, which ones missed their families, which ones missed their pets. I told them funny stories about Señor Mort and they clapped their hands in delight when I described him in his hat and vest, drinking tea like a gentleman.

When Drake came to find me, my hair tangled into knots with all sorts of garish hair bows, ribbons, and clips, I didn't want to leave. Not just because I'd have to ride in the car with Drake, double shudder, but because for a long time I'd forgotten that I was supposed to be something else, someone else.

I waved goodbye over and over, promising that I'd come back while Drake stood in the doorway, waiting, watching, his eyes kind of dangerous. Was he the kind of person who would mindlessly search for something for a thousand years? No, he wouldn't waste his time. He'd wrap things up much more quickly.

I should make the kids lollipops. Peppermint for nausea, something for the pain, and of course, something to make them happy.

"What are you thinking about?"

I glanced over at him. Why did he watch me like that? There was nothing to see. "Lollipops. What?" I added when he smiled like that meant something.

"That's what you want for dinner?"

I shook my head. "Who eats lollipops for dinner? I'm going to make them. Colt's foot, I think for the pain and borage to help with their homesickness."

He stared at me for a moment before he nodded unsmiling. "Of course. What do you want to eat?" His shoes squeaked against the tiled floor and his voice was brisk and no-nonsense.

"Food?"

He nudged me. "I'm going to feed you before I take you back to school. You threw up lunch so you must be starving. I'm surprised that you didn't gobble up a child or two. We can stop at a restaurant or go to the cafeteria here. I should warn you that hospital food is terrible."

I stopped and stared at him. He wanted to take me to dinner? That sounded suspiciously like a date. I wasn't on a date with Drake

Huntsman, was I? Of course not. Community service was not a date, and people didn't throw up on dates or pin them to cars. I was almost positive about that.

He smiled slightly and reached up to flick a hot pink bow in my hair. "I know it's a difficult and important decision, but try to make it quickly before I get too hungry and nibble on you."

"What kind of food is in the cafeteria? That seems like the most efficient choice. That way we wouldn't have to drive anywhere else."

"It's delicious if you like reconstituted freeze-dried potatoes, slimy green beans, soggy cheese toast, and cardboard meatloaf. I mean, cardloaf, and we can't forget about the coleslaw." He screwed up his face horribly.

I laughed and tried to smother it. I cleared my throat and smoothed my skirt down. "I might throw up again and the idea of tasting slimy green beans twice...maybe we should go somewhere else."

He smiled and we walked out of the doors into the evening air, a little cooler than before. I slowed down as we got closer to his big car truck thing.

"Do you want me to knock you unconscious? I'd have to grab you, for purely transportational purposes, naturally."

I shook my head and pressed my lips together. "I'm fine. Just... can we take it slow?" I looked up at him and couldn't help the weakness, the vulnerability.

He grinned. "If you're worried that I'll be bored with you too quickly if we move fast, that's fine with me."

I pulled out a lollipop and undid the cellophane. I sucked on it, Lavender and St. John's Wart, until he put his hands on my shoulders, pulling me closer. I struggled not to bite him. I did not need him to touch me anymore, couldn't handle it and maintain my macaroon persona.

His voice was a low growl, his eyes dark and intent. "I'll go slow if you let me have your lollipop."

I took it out of my mouth and he bent down, covering it with his mouth quickly.

"Hey! I'll get you a new one, not this kind. This isn't the nice kind and I haven't brushed my teeth since the last time I threw up. That's really gross."

He pulled his head back, pulling the stick out of my hand. He tongued it into the side of his mouth and smiled at me. "Do I look as sexy as you do when I suck on this?" He bent his head down, making his eyes go all soft and sweet, green beneath the fall of auburn hair.

"You have freckles on your nose that make you look like a five-year-old. No wonder you like tea parties." I shook my head, walking faster. "Let's get this over with. Drive fast."

I climbed in the passenger door and put on my seatbelt while he walked around to the driver's side. I noticed him take out the lollipop, frown at it and then put it back in his mouth before getting in.

He reached forward, turning on the stereo so that loud music filled the car. I covered my ears at the sudden sound while he started the engine and pulled out, driving smoothly this time, not jerking to a stop and accelerating. After driving through town, he pulled up outside a little Chinese restaurant that lacked the gleam of cleanliness the shops closer to town had.

He turned off the engine and it was suddenly quiet. "How do you want to do this?" Drake put the lollipop back in his mouth while I inhaled deeply.

"I think that this time you shouldn't pin me against the car although… can I hold your hand?" I was such an idiot, but that short of a ride left me weak and my stomach knotted.

He raised his eyebrows as he extended his hand towards me, palm up. "Who's the five-year-old now?"

I grinned at him as I gripped his hand with both of mine. "I love tea parties." I squeezed his fingers and felt an almost immediate dimming of the nausea along with the growing scent of black cherry.

He rolled his eyes. "I meant how do you want to get food? This place isn't that popular with kids from our school, but I can't guarantee there won't be someone who might report the shocking scene to everyone else. I know you're concerned with your reputation so that guy you're angling for doesn't think you're unavailable. I wondered if you'd like to put my shirt over your face, like a disguise, or if you'd rather I ordered and got everything and we could eat out here."

I stared at his hand, my fingers white from hanging onto him so hard while his own skin might wear my imprint after I let go. I had to let go of him. In a minute. What were we talking about? How to order? He made it seem so complicated. "Okay. What do you want me to get you?"

He frowned. "What do you mean?" His hand gripped me back easing the panic.

"I can go in and order while you wait in your car. Didn't you say that we shouldn't be seen together?"

He pulled his hand away until I reluctantly let go. He shook it and smiled slightly. "You have a good grip. No, I said that you don't want to be seen with me because you like someone else. I'm giving you the opportunity to deny that you could ever want someone without freckles."

"How do you know that he doesn't have freckles?"

He raised an eyebrow while his lips curled. "So, there is someone else."

I laughed and turned to open the door. "There are a lot of other people. You do realize that you aren't the only person in the world, don't you?"

He followed me over the blacktop towards the low-slung Chinese place. "I don't take girls to restaurants."

I paused for a moment before I nodded. "Then you didn't take me. We'll just go in, order separately and eat separately. You're making this more complicated than it needs to be."

"You want to eat alone?"

I hesitated. I was supposed to be a macaroon. I turned and batted my eyelashes at him. "It seems to be the most logical solution, don't you think?"

I gazed up at Drake sort of shyly. He looked uncomfortable, possibly nauseous then walked into the restaurant ahead of me. I followed after a minute or so and ordered my food. I sat on the other side of the restaurant from the bar where he leaned, looking irritated. I ordered plates of dizzying variety. I ate until I couldn't eat anymore, and then I got up and noticed that Drake wasn't in the restaurant. Maybe he got bored and left me there. It would be hard to find my way back to the school, but maybe walking up a mountain through the woods in the dark would be less stressful than riding with Drake. Yeah, not really a maybe there.

I shrugged as I went up to the counter to pay for my meal. The host refused my money, explaining in only slightly accented English that 'my man' had insisted on paying for my dinner as well as his. I tried, but I couldn't be a bon-bon and still push people around.

I took the fortune cookie he gave me, thanked him, and left the restaurant. Drake was sitting on the hood of his soccer mom car, leaning back on the windshield to look at the stars.

"You didn't have to pay."

"You're welcome." He still had the lollipop stick in his mouth and didn't look at me.

I stood there for a minute before I went closer. "Aren't we going?"

"You eat a lot."

I exhaled and crossed my arms instead of hitting his leg, gently, you know, cutesy, not breaking bones or anything. "That's not polite to say to a girl. It's true though; I'm always starving. After the cook left, it's been kind of horrible eating at home. There are lots of cans of food and salad and fruit, but not actual cooking very often. Revere can cook, don't get me wrong, but he's more into dusting and laundry than cooking."

He swung his legs off the hood and slid down, landing with an ominous thump beside me. He took my shoulders in his strong hands and looked at me intently. "That is the most heart-wrenching poor little rich girl story I have ever heard. What can I do to console you?"

"You can take your hands off me."

He raised an eyebrow at the tone of my voice, but he did let go of me and stepped back, crossing his arms over his chest. "I see. Sometimes you like me to grab you and sometimes you don't. You're very complex. I'll have to learn how to read mixed signals. Do you want to get a malted in a cup before we head back?"

"Yes." My mouth watered as I remembered the taste of the shake the girl had dumped on me. Maybe it watered from something else, something to do with Drake licking it off me. I did not want to spend more time with Drake and I definitely didn't want to be in his car more than necessary. Yes was not the right answer, but I'd said it so certainly that I couldn't take it back without sounding crazy.

He studied me for a long drawn out moment, his eyes falling to my mouth for some reason. Maybe I had soy sauce on it, nothing to do with shake and him wanting to taste me. Finally, he stepped away and opened the back door, gesturing inside.

"Drive through. Let's go, princess. Your chariot and driver await."

13
WITCH

The next day I rolled out of bed feeling strangely okay. I should feel worn out from my panic attack the day before, but instead I felt relaxed while I dressed slowly, weaving a few small braids with ribbons that mingled with my curls. I wanted to take a walk in the woods. No, I wanted to run and feel the wind rush through my hair, spinning the ribbons behind me while I spread my arms and flew.

I fed Señor Mort, scratched behind his ears and headed to the cafeteria for a muffin and juice or something. I ignored the scathing looks of basically everyone before ducking out and heading to my class. I felt so strange, happy or something. When someone opened a locker into my face before ballet, I just rubbed my nose and didn't apologize because I didn't feel angry or vengeful, just fine.

Drake wasn't going to be in my class. I knew that, but I still searched the room for his green gaze before I focused on my own reflection, my own hazel eyes. They looked different, slightly less focused, softer. I shook my head and remembered Drake's hand on my knee, his voice coaxing my body into the correct position. I pushed myself until I was shiny with perspiration at the end of class. The freshman girl I'd accidentally kicked bumped me on my way through the door, her elbow digging into my ribs while she gave me a nasty smile. I smiled back at her, but I didn't feel anything close to anger.

In my linguistics class I tried to participate as well as I could in Zach's group, having something to say about how to ride horses when Zach carefully led the conversation in that direction. I gave him a grateful smile and he nodded slightly before the conversation once more veered into foreign territory. Barry wasn't in class. Why did Drake know that I gave Barry lollipops?

During lunch I wasn't as hungry as usual. I took a sandwich and an apple before sliding into a seat on the edge of the room where I wouldn't get bumped so much. It was too distracting, and I had to think. Drake. I had to figure out what exactly I'd revealed about myself the evening before so I could cover for it. If Drake and Zach were friends instead of enemies, which still seemed impossible, then Drake would tell Zach what an idiotic and pathetic person I was. Zach would never marry a spineless puke-face. Who would? I ate quickly and slid to the side as a girl 'accidentally' tripped and dumped her plate of noodles where my head had been.

I smiled at her and handed her a lollipop before I turned and walked away. In dressage, the instructor nodded his head into the annex to the main building where Zach had helped me the day before. Again, Zach was there, standing with Henrietta. I hesitated in the doorway before I straightened up and smiled at him brightly.

"Are you here again? That's so nice, but don't you have other classes you need to take?"

He gave me a slight smile while he rubbed Henrietta's nose. "Marcus is giving me extra credit for keeping you out of the regular class. Come on, let's get started. You have a lot to learn."

I smiled at him and by the end of the class was riding short distances without Zach holding the bridle.

"How are you liking linguistics?"

I glanced at him and smiled brightly. "I'm so bad. It's really nice of you to be so patient with me. Barry wasn't in class, so I'm worried that he's in a coma or having a sex change, or had an affair with a mob bosses' wife and gotten run over by a car."

He smiled slightly, an odd smile that I wasn't used to. There was something kind of crazy in his nice blue eyes. "That would be terrible, particularly if it was Drake's car. It's a tank."

"I thought it was more of a soccer mom car."

His smile grew slightly. "Did you tell Drake that?"

I shrugged and winced. "Maybe."

"How did last night go?" He didn't look at me while he asked me the question, walking beside me back to the barn.

I inhaled then blurted out, "I threw up. It was awesome."

He looked up, his blue eyes large before he grinned and his eyes crinkled really adorably. "Did you throw up on Drake?"

I shook my head.

"Too bad. Maybe next time."

I sighed. "I get carsick sometimes. It wasn't very…"

"How was he?"

I studied him. He didn't seem all that interested in me throwing up, either way. How was Drake? "Weird. He didn't seem to mind the puke nearly as much as…" Why had he pushed me up against the car, eyes shining green with rage? Did he really hate people being afraid of him so much? He probably shouldn't break people's arms then.

"Wow." He walked silently for a few steps. "I've heard a lot of descriptions of Drake Huntsman, and weird hasn't ever been one of them. What did he do to earn that title?"

I shifted and tightened my grip on the reins too much. "I don't know, just the whole thing was really strange. He stole my lollipop, the one in my mouth, which is gross, and then he was muttering like a crazy person, said it was a foreign language and I should mind my own business, like he had every right to mutter to himself in the parking lot."

He made a sound like that was interesting. "What flavor of lollipop?"

"Lavender. Not the good kind, but what I use to help with car sickness. Also, he stole it after I threw up, which is so disgusting. I don't have the slightest idea why he'd do that."

"What did you do for dinner?"

Why were we talking about this? At least if Drake told Zach about the whole sordid affair, he'd already have heard it from me, well, a version of it. "Szechuan chicken and Pot-stickers. And sweet and sour soup, and broccoli chow mein, and sesame chicken along with porcini mushroom stir-fry. Also a side of fried rice and some hot and spicy soup. And egg rolls. The Szechuan Chicken was amazing."

He laughed. "You guys ate all that, or do you have leftovers?"

I frowned at him. "Leftovers? I don't know what that is. We didn't share it. It's not like we were on a date, or anything. We just happened to arrive at the same restaurant in the same car at the same time."

He grinned at me. "You didn't eat together?"

I shrugged. "It's not interesting enough to talk about."

He gave me that slightly wild smile again. "I think it's safe to say that ninety percent of the student population would love to hear all about it."

I flinched. "Right, Drake is big news, but I'm not. You won't talk to people about it, will you?"

We reached the barn and he didn't answer, just helped me dismount and unsaddle the horse.

Before my business class, I smoothed my skirt down and fluffed up my hair. I walked in, finding a seat without looking around for Drake. When I heard his voice, I looked over to find him leaning against a girl's desk. He was talking to her, low with this sinfully seductive smirk then he walked up to his normal seat in the middle, barely glancing at me as he passed my desk. He opened his computer and stayed focused on his work except for one time close to the end of class when he raised his hand and interrupted the teacher, asking about a complicated point of business law that distracted the teacher from the lesson.

I read my textbook and jotted notes in the margins about how I might be able to apply some of the concepts to my own business. I had to get a handle on classes or I'd never be able to regain my equilibrium with my shop. By the end of class my happy state had shifted to some kind of foot twitching, lollipop craving, nail-biting monster. I gripped my book and focused on it, refusing to look up at Drake. He'd paid so much attention to me the day before, but apparently he was over whatever wild hare had him chasing Penny Lane.

I got up and swept out of the class without looking backwards, desperate to spend some time alone in my room. Of course, I had to make it through History first. Viney stared at me suspiciously, but I only beamed back at her and took a seat beside her.

"How are you doing? Did you like reading that assignment? This is my favorite class."

She curled her lip, her dark eyeliner looking more ominous than usual. "How dare you talk to me?"

I cocked my head to study her. "What do you mean, dare?"

The teacher, Professor Vale called class to order and I didn't get to hear her fabulous response. I took notes feverishly and by the end of class was ready for solitude. That's when a vaguely familiar brunette blocked my exit, her eyes serious and stern behind her sensible glasses.

"Did you get the flyers passed out?"

It took me a minute before I remembered stupidly agreeing to help her with something. I let my eyes go all big. "Oh! I haven't really had time."

She stared at me. I stared back.

I pressed my lips together tightly before I smiled brightly. "I'll do it right now."

She grunted. "A lot of kids are on the Green right now."

I nodded. "Right. I can go to the Green and hand out flyers to all the lovely students at Rosewood. I'll see you later."

She gave me another stern glance before she turned and marched off in her sensible Mary Jane's. I walked slowly out of class trying to rally my strength. I leaned against a wall and unwrapped a lollipop, Tiramisu with lots of caffeine and sugar in it, which I sucked on until I could bounce and skirt swish with the best of them.

I pulled the flyers out of my bag where I'd shoved them on Monday, and headed out to the green where I'd first met Drake and the rest of the school. In a half hour I'd been rejected 46 times. I wanted to hurl the flyers into the air, but that wouldn't be responsible and kind. Someone knocked into me from behind and I fell, the flyers dropping out of my hand. A guy I didn't know dashed by, grabbing the flyers and running off while I watched him. He ran very fast and headed across the green and into the bushes. I started clapping because he was very fast.

"He should be on the track team."

"Rosewood doesn't have a track team."

I turned to stare up at Jackson who'd crouched down beside me, a ridiculously attractive smile on his extremely puffy lips. "That explains it. I can hardly blame someone for racing off with my papers when he has no other possible outlet." I stood up and brushed of my knees. Grass stains, but probably not a bruise.

"So, you threw up on Drake."

I froze, hands on my knees. Slowly I stood, staring at Jackson for a long time, the satisfied smirk something I was going to rip off with my perfect nails and stuff up his... Bonbons. Macaroons. Cheesecake.

"What goes down, must come up." I shook my head. "Are you fascinated with vomit? Maybe if you come closer, I can throw up on you too."

His smile widened, but he backed away. "Do you need help with your fliers? It's almost like no one likes you."

Who besides Zach or Drake could have told Jackson about me?

Why would either of them? Drake wasn't friends with Jackson, even after he broke his arm, was he? If Zach and Drake were friends, why not Jackson? They could all laugh at me together. I clenched and unclenched my fists while I stared at him.

"I guess it's hard to make friends in a new place. I'm sure that eventually..."

He sneered at me. "You don't belong here." He took a step closer and I could smell something revolting rolling off his skin, like nasty socks, garlic and mouse urine. "You belong in a cage where freaks like you can be laughed at from a safe distance."

I stared at him. Instead of edging towards the violent, angry abyss, I felt a wave of vague amusement. Did he seriously think that was an insult? I smiled brightly and tucked my chin so I could give him my enormous-eyed innocent look. "What kind of cage did you have in mind? Chains? Whips? Leather and steel?" I sounded like Marietta, the most notorious seductress in the history of the telenovela.

He cleared his throat and the scent of mouse urine faded. "I don't..." He cleared his throat and his eyes narrowed. "I'm not interested in you like that. You're disgusting."

I cocked my head and reached out to stroke his clammy cheek with my fingers. I'd made him sweat. "Do you know what is disgusting to me? People who make promises of pain and anguish, and never follow through. I thought you were going to really hurt me, Jackson, but the next thing I know, you have a broken arm and don't seem interested in me at all."

Yes, this was sick. Also weird. I clearly shouldn't have followed the S&M plotline of the cook's show so closely. On the other hand, Jackson looked ready to faint or throw up, and that was definitely a good thing. He stood there, while I curled my fingers, trying to get the feel of his skin off before I smiled brightly and swished my skirt.

"I'd better go find that extremely fast runner. Wish me luck." I twirled away and fluttered off after the flyers like I ever wanted to see them again. I left the green and found myself in the garden. It was very formal, all box hedges and rose arbors with fountains and benches here and there. It was nice, lovely, but I had a headache and my fingers still felt icky from touching Jackson. The nice thing about someone like him was that he could tell everyone I was a crazy S&M girl and people would believe it the same whether it was a truth or a lie. That is to say, he was a liar, and a cruel idiot who would say things just to hurt someone. Even I could see that and I'd only talked to him twice. Three times. Whatever.

I walked further and further from the school towards the woods. The birds called louder and freer the closer I got. As I approached the dark and deep greenery, I stopped and stared at a four-story tower, slender gray stone like an oversize tombstone. A trail of fliers led to the base of the tower and the ladder propped against the side.

This was quite the elaborate prank. So, I was supposed to stupidly climb the ladder to get my precious fliers, which no one would take from me even if I got them, and then someone would take the ladder away leaving me stuck up there, definitely overnight, possibly through classes the next day which would break rules and maybe even get me expelled. I should know the rules a little bit better.

I shrugged and walked towards the ladder, spreading my arms and swaying so the wind could blow through my hair. It seemed to whisper to me, "You'll be hungry if you miss dinner," and I whispered back, "If I don't spend some time in isolation I'm going to eat one of the lovely students here instead."

I danced up the ladder all dainty and carefree then swung over the stone lip at the top. "There you are, cheeky fliers. And all covered in bird poop. I will have much more fun handing out bird crap coated fliers to the immaculate students of Rosewood."

I heard the slight rustle as someone pulled down the ladder, but

I didn't bother getting up to see it happen. If worst came to worst, as in, if I got tired of being up on the tower, alone, I could always make a rope out of fliers and bungee down. No, I'd get paper cuts. Much better to train the birds to carry me away. I could make tethers with woven strands of my hair.

I folded a sheet of paper in half absently. I felt weird. Ever since I'd woken up I'd felt different, a little less gloomy and a little more energetic. This is how I felt before I came up with a brilliant scheme. My schemes always ended disastrously, but the important thing was that they weren't boring. The last scheme I'd had was probably starting my business, because I'd thought that if great grandmother could start a global beauty corporation, how hard could it be? She was dead, after all, and I was not.

I threw my excellently folded airplane and watched it soar and swoop around, caught in the breeze until it stuck into a fuzzy bush. What I really wanted to do was sing, like I'd used to sing with Poppy, up in the top of trees while we drank tea and juggled whatever we had on hand, spoons, teacups, sugar cubes, all very polite things. No knives until after the singing. Would Drake like that kind of tea party? Could he juggle?

I grabbed a flyer and scraped an area along one side of the wall then spread out more papers so I could lie down inside the small balcony. The sun shone down and the leaves rustled all around while birds twittered happily. The sun slanted over my legs, warm and golden. I wanted to scoop up the sunshine and drink it until I felt golden, happy, okay. Sometimes it was so hard to be okay.

I hummed the tune of a song we'd used to sing at the top of our lungs. 'I'm bad, I'm bad, you know it, you know…" I only whispered the tune at first, but when the birds continued twittering and the wind kept whispering I took that as encouragement and sang a little louder. I wasn't a particularly good singer, in fact, I was probably completely tone deaf, but that had never stopped me or Poppy from filling the world with our song. I sang louder, trying to drown out the memories of her, wrinkling her nose before she shoved me over, trying to knock me off my branch, or when she made me a lumpy lotion for a bruise she'd given me.

I was singing really, really, really loud by the time a head appeared over the edge, green eyes staring at me beneath his tousled red hair.

I stopped singing and sat up, smoothing down my skirt while Drake swung over the edge of the platform then hesitated when he saw all the bird crap.

"Penny, can you fly or are you an excellent climber?"

I stared at him before I shook my head. "What are you doing here?"

He shrugged and squatted down, kind of careful to keep his clothes from coming in contact with the sparrow guano. He hadn't even said hi to me in Business class. I pushed him over before I could rethink it and he fell backwards, sitting down in the goop. He narrowed his eyes before he shrugged and leaned back, apparently giving up on keeping his clothes clean.

"I'm sorry. I didn't mean to push you over."

He smiled slightly. "No, I could tell it was an accident. How did you get up here, Penny, and what was that noise?"

"Noise? Nothing. I may have been singing a little bit to keep myself company. I didn't think anyone would climb over the wall. I don't know why you would come all this way just to see who was stuck in the tower." No. It was the story, the one I'd told the girls about my prince scaling the tower. I stood up hurriedly and peered down, but there was no ladder. I whirled around at Drake.

"Did you climb up here?"

He shrugged. "I like to live on the edge. I'm so irrational and inconsistent, like bullying you into coming with me last night, and then not even saying hello to you in class today. You looked like you were getting some good reading done."

I nodded. "It was good. I think I learned a few things that I can use."

He raised his eyebrows. "You sound like you're actually interested in business."

I shrugged. "Crazy rich people have money or they'll just be crazy people, and that's not nearly as fun."

He pulled out his phone and nodded to me while he pushed a button and talked into the speaker. "Hi. Would you mind bringing a ladder to the tower? I thought her hair would be long enough, but I was woefully wrong. That's right. Take your time; it's quite cozy up here."

He put away his phone and frowned at me. "Weren't you singing this?" He proceeded to howl in the loudest and most discordant way, but somehow in that awful sound, I could make out the words and maybe something like the tune I'd been singing.

I nodded and with a sigh joined in, closing my eyes and singing loudly, but still drowned out by Drake's voice. I was giggling by the last verse, and he stopped singing to frown at me.

"What are you laughing at? I may not be the best singer, but I make up for it in enthusiasm. Do you know this song?"

He launched into another song I knew, which was amazing because I only knew a dozen or so. We were singing when I heard a vague holler from below. I started to get up, but Drake grabbed my wrist, the sudden silence stretching taut between us, his hand warm on my skin, reminding me of the night before, of the fear he'd pushed back with his simple presence.

"I had fun last night."

I inhaled sharply while my stomach twisted. "I really liked the little kids. They were sweet."

He smiled slightly and let go of my wrist. "You're sweet, Penny. So sweet and delicious, starting with your lollipops and ending with your weasel."

I blushed and scrambled to my feet. I looked over the edge and saw a stranger at the bottom of the ladder, not smiling when he saw me. Would he hold it still or knock it down? I looked over at Drake where he watched me with those sharp white teeth and that soft smooth mouth. My fingers tingled and I scrambled over the side, down the ladder so quickly, the guy barely had time to get out of the way.

"Are you all right?" he asked.

I nodded while he pulled down the ladder, shortened it, and put it on his shoulder.

"What are you doing? Doesn't Drake..." I glanced back and saw Drake scaling down the wall, his movements sure and easy, like he climbed it every day. I watched him until I realized what I was doing and turned to smile at the stranger. "Thanks for the ladder. I'm sorry Drake had to bother you."

He shrugged. "It was worth it hearing him sing. You have to admit that he's very loud."

I shook my head and glanced back, hesitating for a moment when Drake caught my eye at the base of the tower, something wild and untamed that made me want to run in the woods with him. Fun. I'd had genuine fun with him at the top, forgetting who I was supposed to be for at least fifteen minutes, but I shouldn't forget, couldn't ever forget.

14
Mage

I bent over the mould while I shaped it carefully with the chisel. I'd never attempted Selenium conductors in a tourney, but I wanted more than a simple image in the air, a flash of light. Selenium would hold the image as long as the static particles stayed aloft. I wanted something like Blackheart would do. Since they were coming for the winter break, we all had to push ourselves if we didn't want to be humiliated.

"Drake, do you have a minute?"

I continued smoothing down the side until it was good enough to hold a bond then straightened up. Not a lot of witches visited the workshop, but Viney went where she liked. I turned to Viney with a smile as I grabbed a rag to wipe off my hands.

"What can I do for you?"

She went pale as she stared back, her dark eyes getting larger and larger until she looked away and started breathing again. The effect I had on most females still seemed strange, particularly after I spent time in a tower with Penny Lane, or in a parking lot with Penny Lane, or anywhere doing anything with Penny Lane. She wanted me or she wouldn't like how I smelled, but she wasn't like Viney and the rest of the females who could barely bask in my presence without becoming stunned and dazed. It was hard not to take personally, but I knew that Ian and Theodore had the exact same effect. It had to do with what we were, not who we were, or some other distinction.

"Zach is acting strange. You said you wanted me to tell you if I noticed any changes."

I nodded and smiled. The smile made her stop breathing again. I sighed instead and spoke in an intentionally harsh tone. "What changes?"

She licked her lips and frowned fiercely. She didn't like being an idiot about me any more than I did. "He's smiling."

"I'm shocked. Is that all the sordid gossip you have for me?"

She shook her head. "He's taken over Penny's riding instruction. He goes every day to teach her one-on-one." She chewed on her bottom lip. "He didn't tell me about it, but since he's my responsibility, one of the girls saw them in the pasture, her riding, him walking beside her, and reported to me."

I raised an eyebrow as I walked from the table which held my two-by-two-foot mould to the sink and started scrubbing my hands, front and back, methodically. "I heard about poor Henrietta. No doubt Zach is protecting the horse. Not to be disparaging, but Miss Lane can be accident prone."

She ran her knuckles over her navy pants, the spikes on her wrists glinting in the fluorescent lighting. "If he hurt her things would go badly for him. I know that you're used to having your way with any female, but the law still applies. You can't force a witch, hurt her without serious repercussions, even if you're a Huntsman."

"I thought we were talking about Stoneburrow."

She glanced away, shifting uneasily. "I don't know if the two of you are playing a game with her, seeing which of you can crush her first, but you should know that whatever my personal feelings towards her, she's still a witch, and you're still a mage."

I smiled blandly. "Drawing battle lines, Viney?"

"I saw the footage of the laundry room."

"I did nothing to her."

She glanced up with a glare. "Just because I couldn't see what you did, doesn't mean you didn't do anything."

I smiled broadly and stepped towards her. She held her ground even though her eyes widened and she stopped breathing. "I didn't hurt her. I've just never seen a sleeping witch before."

She swallowed hard while she clenched her fists, struggling against the ridiculous pull I had on her. "And the spell you used on Tuesday? You were muttering to her in a foreign language. Don't tell me you were practicing German conjugations."

Hm. Penny had told her about that? Were they actually on speaking terms? I wouldn't think so, no, but if Zach was seeing Penny every day while bonding over horses, she probably had mentioned it to him, and of course Zach would tell Viney anything about me. "She didn't feel very well. I was soothing her nausea."

"Without her permission?" Her eyebrows rose alarmingly.

"If you are looking for technical request and assent, she requested assistance and I gave it to her. Doesn't it seem strange that she didn't go to you with a complaint? It's almost as if she doesn't mind whatever I do to her."

Her face tightened. "I'm not going to overlook the law, even for you."

I cocked my head. "Really?" I stared at her until she looked away.

She'd ignored the law enough times for me without my asking, what bothered her was not that part, not really. It should bother her. Someone should try and protect Penny Lane. Maybe I felt inclined to step between her and Jackson, or her and her terror, but who was going to save her from me? And Zach, of course.

"She's different." Viney's voice was low, angry. "She completely terrified Jackson. I don't know what she said to him, what she did, but there's something not right about her. You should stay away and let me handle it."

I smiled. "What you should handle is the way that the females of this school torment her. If you're so worried that she's a danger, I would be careful not to push her too far. If she kills someone after being tortured and bullied past her breaking point, the blood will be on your hands."

She glared at me openly. "You sound like Zach. It's my responsibility to protect our kind from you, not to step in the middle of a personal feud."

I raised an eyebrow. "I see. In that case, I hope she finds a powerful mage to bind so she has someone between herself and your kind."

I stared at her evenly while she stared back. I wasn't seriously offering to bind myself to Penny Lane just so that I'd have the technical right to fight a witch on her behalf, but I liked the way Viney took that threat, far more alarmed at the prospect of Penny Lane owning me than me fighting Viney. I glanced over her, quite short, but crackling with power that wrapped around her. It would be exhilarating to fight her, but not even Viney would stand very long against me.

She saw the gleam in my eyes and inhaled sharply. "I appreciate the warning. I will do more to bring peace and good feeling back to the honorable halls of dear Rosewood." She scowled and rolled her eyes before she spun on her heels and stalked off.

After such a charged conversation, I felt exhausted. It was a little bit funny that Zach decided to take over Penny's riding lessons the way I'd taken over her ballet. Even though I only got her twice a week and he got her five times, when she was with me, she only wore a leotard, and her hair was up so I could smell her long neck. She was built like a ballerina, but she moved like something else.

I should talk to Jackson, torture him until he told me something interesting about the conversation Viney brought up. What would Viney have done if I'd touched Penny while she was sleeping? I should have. It was a once in a lifetime opportunity. For me to pass it up made me look like a gentleman. Not that I hadn't experimented on her.

I leaned my hands against either side of the sink and stared out the paned window to the grass outside. Everything was so green and glowing, like it didn't know that summer was ending and it was time for gold, strawberry gold like her hair.

I'd insisted that she come to the hospital with me because I wanted to test her, see what she was really made of, but it didn't work out quite like I intended. For starters, her fear was a curse. I was almost positive of it, and the annulling of magic was tied into that curse, as an antidote or side-effect. When I thought she feared me, I'd lost my temper. I had no idea what I would have done if she hadn't rested her cheek against my neck, pulling my energy into her until she could breathe. Stupid. I'd never hurt a female and wasn't about to start now, unless you counted Creagh. I'd killed a few of those, but things that happened in Darkside didn't seem real.

Penny was like that, a bit unreal. I felt like I'd entered a different world, a dream world where people sang at the top of their lungs from the tower as though no one could hear, a place where you went to a restaurant with someone and ate separately, a world where witches sat on the floor telling stories to children, making them laugh and smile, chasing their pain and fear away with her sweetness.

I'd watched her for an hour, waiting for her to snap, to scream at one of the children who pulled her hair too hard, but instead of getting wound tighter and tighter, she unfurled and relaxed. They were like Señor Mort to her, pets, creatures she could tame and love.

She did not look at me like that. Maybe she wasn't paralyzed with debilitating terror in my presence the way she was riding in my car, but her eyes were wary, and she refused to eat with me.

When she was stuck in the tower singing so horrendously, I couldn't help but scale it, like the prince from her story. Is that what she wanted? She'd taken comfort from my presence, as in she'd pulled that energy from me without seeming to realize it. Did she actually admire heroic acts, kindness, goodness? Witches didn't. That's why Zach put on his act of shy and sweet intellect, because it didn't make them froth at the mouth the way my blatant disregard for human life did. The fact that Zach's nature was more diabolical and cruel than mine was one of the ironies we both enjoyed.

What would I have done to her if she hadn't sought my strength? I would have to watch myself. Viney was right about that. Penny Lane left me unbalanced, dangerous to us both. I would have to leave her to Zach. What if that's what she saw in him, sweetness, and that's what she wanted, not his name, Stoneburrow, a mage with power?

What was his name, the kid I saw talking to a lollipop? Barry? He was one of the weakest mages in school, but still bright, an excellent Chemist and not a terrible fighter. If he had the right friends, he could do well enough. It would be nice if someone found love in Rosewood. Love wasn't possible for myself or Zach. For different reasons. Very different reasons.

I shrugged and turned back to my work. I would focus on doing what I did best, being Drake Huntsman, the mage without a heart. I'd learned as much as I could about Penny Lane without using a scalpel. The curse was a mystery, but not mine.

15
WITCH

My days fell into a pattern, waking up early to put together some potions, running to class, seeing Drake in Pas de Deux and Business, Zach in Linguistics and Dressage, and Viney in History.

I put the whole tower thing out of my head and didn't spend any more time trying to understand Drake. What did I care if he seemed conflicted, like he was several different personalities? The big bad wolf walked around the halls, saying something cruel and cutting then he'd smile at someone and be really nice for no apparent reason. It didn't matter if he had a real personality disorder, or if he just liked messing with people. Either way, at the end of the week I hadn't talked to him since the tower and was ecstatic that he no longer invaded my personal space.

At the end of Business class on Friday, I was putting away my books and not looking at him, completely unaware of the way his jacket formed over his broad shoulders and strong back. He always ignored me in that class for mysterious reasons I couldn't possibly fathom with my cute little bubblegum brains.

"Penny Lane, what are you doing over the weekend?"

I inhaled sharply before I looked up at him. I didn't have to force a brilliant smile. "Nothing. I'm going to stay in my room all weekend, order pizza and not see anyone. What about you?" I stood up and got my books organized.

His lips lifted in a snarl. "You're hiding?" He moved closer, brushing my leg with his as he pressed me back against the edge of my desk.

He was so close; I could feel the warmth of him against my bare legs and my skirt felt very short. I swallowed hard and found my smile slipping.

"I have things to do." I put my hands against his chest and pushed, but he only leaned his fascinating contours into my palms.

He spoke in a low voice. "You're not going to invite me to a tea party?"

I swallowed and shook my head while my fingers curled around his lapels instead of pushing him away. "You're developing a reputation for doing things without thinking."

He raised an eyebrow while his focus shifted from my eyes to my lips. "It's balanced more or less by all the things I think about that I don't do."

He stepped back ripping his jacket out of my fingers before he left the room, moving so quickly, it almost seemed like he was running.

I unwrapped a dirt tasting lollipop while I headed to History. I was jostled and knocked into walls, had my books pulled out of my hands to the ground, my hair pulled and my arms pinched before I made it to class, heart still pounding although it had nothing to do with Drake's thighs pressed against mine.

I slid into a seat and didn't notice Viney until she said something stupid about how gross those people were to live with fleas, like it was an issue of intelligence instead of circumstance. In spite of Professor Vale's excellent lesson, I had no idea what it had been about when after class, Viney passed me a note. I ignored it, leaving it behind me on the desk. I'd waited until everyone else had left the class, staring at that white slip of paper before I stood, packed up my books, smiled brightly at Professor Vale and headed to my room.

Halfway there, I saw a guy hobbling along on crutches, a guy who looked remarkably like my missing Linguistics partner.

"Barry? What happened? Did you really get involved with the mob bosses' wife? Oh, you must have taken out a loan from the loan shark to pay for your mother's funeral…"

He glanced up at me, and his face was swollen, his brown eyes nearly closed over. I walked a few steps closer to him before I stopped again.

"Penny," he said through split lips, "I hope you're having all sorts of sordid affairs in linguistics without me." He winced when he smiled.

I shook my head and took another step closer to him. "What happened?" I held my lip between my teeth while I waited for an explanation.

He shrugged, hanging onto his crutches. "I was involved in a mafia war between two rival gangs. There were multiple women I was trafficking black market furs for, and while it was strictly business, their husbands were convinced that I was actually seducing them." He cocked his head slightly. "There may have been a little bit of that. I fought them off, you know, but when my ex-lover Russian assassin spy discovered that I'd been having an affair with multiple women, she hit me with her…" He pursed his lips for a moment. "Tank. Yes, her pink tank, stole all my furs, decimated both mafia lords and left me like this."

I exhaled and reached out to touch his shoulder. "Are you coming back to linguistics? There are so many missing details that could only be justified in the Spanish language."

He gave me a half smile before he shook his head, looking away.

I stood there for a moment before I let my hand drop. "A tank? A green tank?"

He looked at me, his eyes sharp. "No. Pink. Didn't I say that?"

I nodded and licked my lips. I pulled a lollipop out of my bag and stared at it. "Can I give you a lollipop? I'll unwrap it for you."

He stared at me for a long time before he shook his head, a slight movement that sent a spike of pure fury through me. "I don't think it's a good idea for me to be addicted to your drug-laced lollipops. I'll see you around, Penny Lane."

I stood there and watched him hobble away. Someone had to do something about his Russian Spy mistress and her green tank, aka soccer mom car. I'd seen Drake break Jackson's arm. Who else would hurt Barry for absolutely no reason?

By the time I made it to my room, I could barely keep from screaming. I entered the common room of Lilac Stories and froze. My door was gone. Not open, not ajar but gone including the doorframe, black scorch marks on the lilac colored wall around it.

I dropped my bag and ran into the room, crunching over the broken glass that littered the floor along with shredded clothing. Zach was in the middle of the room and swung around with a bat ready on his shoulder before he came up short.

"What are you doing here? Didn't Viney tell you not to come?" He stepped towards me, his expression intense and body language dangerous instead of his usual relaxed, lazy.

I stood there staring at him until I heard a little scuffling in the corner behind my trunks.

"Señor," I called, stepping around Zach, but he grabbed my wrist, and then I twisted, shoved his arm backward and would have dislocated his elbow if he hadn't gotten out of my way quickly.

I tugged on the trunk, sliding on the glass while I crouched down. "Come on, Mort. It's okay. I know you're scared, but it's going to be all right. Come here."

A flash of russet and a pair of beady eyes were all I saw before it scrambled along my arm and hid itself in my hair, curling around my shoulders and nudging my neck with his cold nose. I stood slowly then turned to Zach. I couldn't smile, so I looked away, at the walls spray painted nasty words I didn't know very well, at all my tubes and vials shattered, at my bed ripped out of the ceiling and broken up, at the only thing left standing: the trunks.

"I chased them out before they could get into your trunks." Zach lowered the bat and crossed one well-muscled arm over his stomach. "I asked Viney to keep you away until I got maintenance in here."

I tried for a smile but my lips were trembling. "Thanks. I should... I can't..."

I looked around for a lollipop, but my latest batch was nothing but shattered red bits ground into the floor.

"Why don't you wait in my room? Come on."

I shook my head and stumbled away from him, rubbing my arms. "I'm fine. I mean, everything will have to be replaced, but it's just stuff. Señor Mort is fine. I think I'll take a walk. He hasn't been able to get out since we've come here. The woods are so beautiful."

I turned and left the room, picking up my bag on the way through the pale lilac commons while Señor Mort dug his little claws into my skin. I walked through the pillared halls and out onto the Green, past all the students who watched me with terrible anticipation on their faces. They knew about my room. They wanted to see me react, see me break and shatter into a million pieces. I stopped and stood there for a moment, clenching and unclenching my fists while a few students close to me edged away, fear tingeing their faces. I dug through my bag and found a bright pink lollipop I'd been saving for a special occasion just like this.

I unwrapped it slowly, the edges of the cellophane sliding against my fingertips until I put the lollipop on my tongue, swirling it around until my heart sped up, blood pumping while I continued walking across the grass, swishing my skirt as I walked, eyeing every guy I saw with my most seductive lollipop look.

I gave girls the same glance because it didn't make any difference. None of them mattered. Nothing mattered in this stupid little world. I kept walking through the garden until I came to an iron fence, eight feet high. I didn't hesitate but scaled it, glad it wasn't electric before I jumped off the top and landed in my stupid shoes.

I slipped them off, tucked them in my bag, shifted it on my shoulder, stroked Señor Mort a few times and then started running. There were narrow deer trails that wove through the woods and I followed them, running in my socks over the spongy earth. While my heart pounded, the concoction in my mouth entered my bloodstream. I ran faster and faster, pushing my body until my mind couldn't process, until all the pain inside was replaced by the pain in my muscles, my legs screaming. I ran until my legs collapsed and I fell forward, spread fingers catching on layers of moldy leaves, but gladly not on top of Señor Mort.

I lay there on my face, hands outstretched, legs askew until I felt Señor's little nose on my ear, then my cheek. I curled up on my side, wrapping my arms around my little weasel, and pressed my forehead against his while the pain I'd been trying to outrun pounced and devoured me.

Poppy had died on a day like this: sunshine, running through the woods, coming back to the house and seeing her motorcycle in the driveway. I'd run inside, eager to tell her what an idiot she'd been to leave with some uncouth blackguard, and seen her perched on the edge of the balcony, three stories up. She'd looked at me and smiled, like she'd been waiting for me, and then she leaned forward like she was going to fly away, and fell instead.

I hadn't even had time to scream while she tumbled through the air, her long golden hair rippling before she came to a sudden jerk, on top of the unknown soldier's spear.

The bronze statue had always been in the hall, but I'd never really noticed it until the mounted soldier carried my cousin on his shoulder, blood running over the aged bronze and dripping to the floor.

I curled into a tighter ball while I hurt and the pain didn't seem to have anywhere to go. I ached with a fullness of the grief, the agony, the loneliness, all the emotions I'd never felt, not like this. I hadn't cried at the small service we'd had for my cousin, just me, Revere, and the priest, before we buried her in the backyard.

"Why were you so stupid?" I muttered, my lips gritty and specked with leaves. "Why would you trust someone on the outside? Why would you give your heart to someone like that? Why?" I smashed my fist against the earth, the pain rushing up my arm and dulling some of the ache in my chest. I slammed my fist again, and again and again and again until someone grabbed it.

I shuddered, trying to control myself, to keep the panic and anger in check. If it was Zach, I couldn't dislocate his elbow or break his neck, or light him on fire and hope the whole world burned. He was a nice boy and I was going to marry him.

"Penny?"

I sat up and stared at Drake in the dim light of the deep woods. "What are you doing here?" Seriously, the last person in the world I wanted to see, and he dared look like that, dangerously delectable in the shadowed woods with that hair and his green eyes dripping with faux concern.

He shrugged and glanced away and then back at me. "I was in Chemistry club when I heard some yelling, so I thought I'd find out if we had a new banshee in the woods. Turns out it was just you."

I opened my mouth to say something, but only a sob came out.

His mouth twisted in disgust. Finally, he could see how revolting I was. Fine. Good. I didn't want Drake to see anything other than vomit when he looked at me. I wiped my nose on my arm and left a long line of snot. My makeup would be streaked with leaves and dirt in it. Fine. I wanted him to see vomit, snot, and dirt when he looked at me. I caught my trembling lower lip in my teeth while I stared down at the leaves. "Now you know it's just me so you can go back to Chemistry club. Sounds super fun. Run along."

He put his hand on my shoulder. I'd completely forgotten about Señor Mort. Drake pulled back with a gasp, pressing his now bleeding hand with his other one.

The smell of blood and black cherry filled the air. I closed my eyes and clenched my fists. "When are you going to learn your lesson about grabbing girls?"

He laughed, low, the sound a caress to my senses. I opened my eyes wide to stare at him. He watched the red blood well from his hand before he bent his head and covered it with his lips.

I turned away, rubbing my chest. He made it look good, like a wolf licking his wounds, which reminded me of him licking my fingers. I never should have let that happen. My fingers tingled even though I knew perfectly well that he'd be just as happy licking me as he would be breaking a bone.

"Here." He held a handkerchief over my shoulder, like he wasn't worried about being bitten again. I stared at the fluttering white fabric, at the embroidered heart slashed through the center. A broken heart. He was giving me a broken heart. I wiped off my face with his handkerchief, smearing it with my subtle and natural looking makeup along with the dirt and leaves. And the snot. I had a lot of snot and blew my nose shamelessly. Loudly and repeatedly.

"Is this yours?"

I turned my head to glare at him over my swollen nose.

He picked up my lollipop covered in leaves and dirt, rolled the stick in his fingers, and stuck it in his mouth.

I gasped. "That's filthy."

He shrugged and tongued it into his cheek while he smiled at me, showing his teeth. "Not as filthy as you are. This one isn't as bad as the last one I stole from you. Why don't you eat the delicious ones? Are you afraid that you'll get so sweet I won't be able to resist sinking my teeth into you?"

I reached out and snagged the lollipop out of his mouth and stuck it into mine. It tasted strange.

He smiled a sharp smile at me while my eyes widened because I hadn't quite thought it through, his taste on my tongue, a hint of blood and black cherry. He tasted so good.

I pulled out the lollipop and stared at it like it had betrayed me. "You even taste like black cherry."

"Did I ruin the flavor for you? You prefer bitter herbs and dirt?"

I sighed and put the lollipop back in my mouth while I slumped over my knees. "You should go."

He leaned forward mimicking me, and I noticed that his hand had stopped bleeding and seemed to have a much smaller cut than I'd expected. "Do you know which direction school is? You're halfway to town and it's going to be dinnertime soon. Something hungry is going to eat you if you don't gobble him up first."

I shrugged. "I'll be fine."

"Maybe you will. You don't exactly seem fine, but I'm sure that's just the dirt smeared across your face and your ripped jacket. Where are your shoes?"

I nodded at the bag and he grabbed it before I could stop him. Not like I tried. I felt kind of numb and kind of horrible in spite of the lollipop. He stood up and slung the bag over his shoulder. I half expected him to leave me there, but he put out a hand expectantly, his green eyes gazing at me until I put my hand in his and let him pull me to my feet.

I stood there, past numbness while he brushed leaves off me, kind of careful, pulling his hands back any time he saw a flash of Señor Mort. When he bent down to brush off my legs, hands sliding over my bare skin, I stepped back quickly.

"It's okay."

"I think you scraped your knee, and it was looking so good."

"Do you think so?" I sounded more skeptical than flirtatious. I couldn't remember what I was supposed to sound like.

He looked up at me, for a moment caught his bottom lip in his teeth before he flashed his toothy white grin. "Your legs are the first thing I noticed about you, or maybe your hair. You know that you have incredible legs. That's why you wear such short skirts and bounce so it flips up just enough to drive every male here insane."

I blinked at him. "You're blaming your insanity on my legs? You should break them, smash my face in, make me a little less attractive so you don't notice me so much." Like he'd smashed Barry.

He raised an eyebrow like I'd suggested something seductive. "Yeah? Unfortunately, I'm not into hurting girls, at least not physically. I'm perverted that way, sexist too. You do make it sound fun."

I shook my head and ran a hand through my hair, pulling out leaves and sticks. "Fun, fun!" I smiled brightly at him and flipped my skirt. "What else is there besides fun?" I sounded completely hysterical. I didn't care.

He raised an eyebrow. "Rolling around in the woods with a weasel? Screaming at ghosts? Who is Poppy?"

I stepped away from him but he took a step closer and his legs were longer. "Poppy?" I could barely whisper her name and my stomach twisted into a knot.

His green eyes narrowed and he studied me with that look, the one that saw too much I was trying to hide. "You were saying that name. You don't remember?"

I nodded while my head spun and I twirled the lollipop over my tongue. Finally, I pulled it out and smiled at him. "Poppy was my cat. She was my best friend but then she died. I'm still super sad about it. This is the anniversary of her death so I came to the woods to have a good cry."

He stared at me for a long time before he cocked his head. "You're pretty passionate about a cat."

I pulled my hair back so he could see Señor Mort's nose behind my neck. "Animals make more sense to me than people. If you think that I'm attached to Señor Mort, you should have met Poppy. We used to have tea parties in trees and sing. Did you know that cats can sing? They can dance, too." I turned, looking around me in the woods for the first time. "Where are we? Where is the school?"

"This way." He grabbed my hand and started pulling me around.

I winced when I stepped on a sharp stick that poked through my sock.

He glanced at me his eyes gleaming. "I'm not going to carry you, so don't ask."

I said through gritted teeth, "my hand is too heavy for you too."

He grinned at me. "It's not your weight that would bother me, but your red-headed guardian who would probably bite me on my nose. I'm very attached to the pattern of freckles I already have."

I should have killed him for what he did to Barry. I wanted to, but I also wanted to sit down in the dirt and cry some more, and I wanted to hold his hand because in spite of how horrible he was, how much I hated him, my heart hurt a little bit less with his hand around mine.

We kept walking until we stepped around a tree, and I pulled up short. The sun was sinking but in that evening light, rays shone across a small clearing, hitting a waterfall and turning the spray into drops of gold. Two enormous trees stood guard on the end of the clearing, arms twined together over the waterfall while green jewels of rich moss dripped from their brown and silver branches.

It looked like a fairy tale and I half expected fairies to dart around us, or a talking wolf or something. I glanced at Drake with a slight smile I couldn't repress. He was my talking wolf.

He raised an eyebrow, waiting.

I couldn't stop myself. I wanted to fall into the fantasy, talk to Drake like he was one of my imaginary forest friends, wanted to hear him say something clever and slightly cutting. I should have sucked on my lollipop and gotten back to Rosewood as fast as possible, but the evening in the clearing was too much for my stupidly overwhelmed self to ignore.

"This is an enchanted forest, and you are the wolf. I need to build my gingerbread cottage with lollipop windows and gumdrop roof to keep you out."

His eyebrow quirked. "This wolf only nibbles on witches. I can see you living in a candy house, but not gobbling up children."

I smiled sweetly. "You haven't seen me when I'm really hungry."

He widened his eyes in pretended horror before he shook his head. "Are you so hungry now? Am I in terrible danger?"

I stepped close to him until I was standing on his boots. He was wearing kind of sturdy clothing, leather jacket and pants. I felt very underdressed and tried to step away from him, but he slid his hand over my back, holding me in place, my sock covered feet balanced on his steel covered toes.

I stared at him and my breath caught. His eyes sparked green in the light from the setting sun while his burning hair tumbled over his pale forehead. I reached up and brushed his hair back, the silken strands in my fingers feeling like fire, the strands burning into me.

I stared into his eyes while his hand tightened against my back and I swayed against him. It would be the easiest thing in the world to fall into him and never resurface. Fall like Poppy…

I twisted out of his grip and walked quickly in the direction we'd been headed. He hadn't been looking at me like he really saw me, saw everything about me and liked me, not covered in leaves and smeared makeup from my tantrum. My tantrum. If there was anything worse than throwing up in front of him, it was crying, screaming, completely losing it.

Drake kept up with me easily, and when I glanced at him had a slight smile, no sign of blatant disgust. "You're running away like you're afraid, but of what? You're not afraid of a wolf, are you? I promise, I'm very well mannered. I wear hats to tea parties and everything. If you make friends with weasels, you should be perfectly comfortable around wolves."

I swallowed. "I'm afraid that you're going to tell Jackson all about how pathetic I am, crying like a little girl in the woods, like you told him about me throwing up in the parking lot."

"Jackson?" He laughed, derisive, cruel laughter. "I don't talk to Jackson. Is that what you were talking about on the green before you sealed yourself into the tower? Throwing up? He really has no idea what to do with a woman. And you're trying to impress him? Why would you ever care what he thinks?"

I gritted my teeth and kept pushing forward in spite of the fact that every step made my whole body ache. "I don't care what Jackson thinks. He's possibly the most vile creature I've ever met, like you without any charm."

He barked a short laugh. "You think I'm charming? More charming than Jackson anyway. That's practically a compliment. Jackson has charm when he uses it. Something about you rubs him all wrong. I wonder what that is. Maybe because you don't need anyone or anything else. Maybe because you don't look at him and want him. Maybe because you don't need anyone's approval and he'll never have enough."

I shrugged. "I haven't wasted any time thinking about what his issues are. I'm not his therapist."

He laughed. "I see. What about me, have you wasted any time trying to figure me out?"

I glanced at him and then stared straight ahead. His hand

tightened on mine and I chewed on my bottom lip. "You've made it impossible to ignore you."

"I've left you alone for two whole days. Have you thought about me since the tower when I rescued you so heroically?"

I sucked hard on my lollipop. I didn't want to think about that, to think about how easy it was to be with him, to forget what he was. Barry. Yeah. I tried to hold the image of Barry's pain-filled smile, but Drake was right at the end of my hand and I couldn't think about anything besides him.

"I have thought about you."

He looked surprised for a moment and then smug. "Of course you have. You've been wondering if I taste as good as your weasel says I do. Am I in danger? Are you going to grab me and taste me, finally settling the question once and for all?"

I laughed; I couldn't help it. Sometimes it seemed like he was as ridiculous as I could be. "Of course, you're in danger. If I were to kiss you right now, Señor Mort would probably sink his teeth into your ceratoid artery until you bled to death. Jealousy, you know."

His laugh rumbled low as he smiled and swung my hand. "You have no idea how tempting that is. Death by weasel? Can you imagine my epitaph?"

I rolled my eyes and turned away from him. "You are so confusing."

"Am I? I'm not the one with a weasel boyfriend she likes to roll around in the woods with."

"I have a thing for redheads."

"Really?" He drew the word out like he was tasting it on his tongue.

"And beady eyes."

He laughed. "And sharp teeth?"

"Of course." I shook my head. "I'm not sure what I'm supposed to do with you."

"I'm sure you'd figure it out after some experimentation." He waggled his eyebrows and I giggled.

"You're ridiculous. Are you really in Chemistry club?"

He lifted his chin and said in a snobbish voice. "I'll have you know that I'm the captain of the Chemistry Club. If you wanted to join you'd have to either blackmail or bribe me to let you in."

"I can't see you responding very positively to blackmail, and what kind of bribe would sway you? All I have to offer is death by weasel. It's just as well that I can't stand Chemistry."

I stepped away from him, but he just followed me until he was walking very close, my hand in his. "What don't you like about Chemistry?"

My heart pounded in ridiculous awareness of him, our chemistry. Of course it was nice to feel something besides the sadness, except that was exactly what had ruined Poppy. I shook my head. "The names are so hard to remember, all those poly…"

"Mono-nitrates like fake popcorn butter?"

I licked my lips while I tried to remember what I had or hadn't said to him about it on my first ramble. "Exactly." I tried so hard not to notice him walking beside me, his hand still in mine, strong, slightly calloused, warm. When we stepped out of the woods beside a road, I didn't even notice the thinning trees or hear the sound of cars until we were beside the pavement.

A long black limo was parked in the grass, the driver standing beside the open back door as if waiting for us.

I turned to Drake. "This isn't the school."

He smirked at me. "The Captain of the Chemistry club can't just abandon his subjects. There should be food in the limo. Drink a lot of water because you're dehydrated from all your crying. Also wash your face before you get to school. Not everyone finds dirt and leaves as attractive as I do."

He lifted my hand to his lips, kissed it and then turned, heading back into the woods. I took one step after him before I shook my head and watched him disappear beneath the branches.

"Miss Lane? Mr. Huntsman gave me specific instructions. If you feel nauseous let me know and I'll pull over at once."

I walked over to the driver, studied him for a minute then ducked inside.

When I got back to school, I felt better. I was fine riding in the back of the limo, and after eating way too much food, I felt a lot more stable. I washed my face with a napkin in a bottle of water after I drank three of them. I fed Señor Mort samples of all the dishes and he didn't drop dead, so I probably wouldn't either, at least not from the food. The shame on the other hand might very well kill me.

Of all the people I wanted to find me curled in a ball in the woods sniveling, Drake was the last one on earth. And what in the world did the Captain of the Chemistry club do? He must have seen me having my breakdown, called the limo, and then taken me to it.

It had been really nice. He must be setting me up for an elaborately cruel and humiliating joke. I shrugged as I stepped out of the car. I walked slowly to my room, stroking Señor Mort as I walked beneath the pillars of the school until I got to Lilac Stories.

Professor Vale stood in her black leather clothing, nostril pierced and hair spiked a lot like Viney's, but she didn't wear any makeup. "Penny, have you eaten?"

I blinked at her then glanced to the side where Viney and Zach stood, Viney's arms crossed and a petulant scowl on her face.

"I did. What's going on?"

My room was still without a door, but it was empty now, cleaned out and a handful of maintenance workers were painting the room white. I was supposed to work all weekend, catch up with my orders, but with everything destroyed, there would be no way. I kind of slumped down while Professor Vale gestured to a room two doors down from my former domain.

"You'll stay there until your room is repaired. The wall has to be reinforced after the mysterious felons blew the door." She glared at Zach for some reason while he shifted uncomfortably but managed to give me a slight smile.

"Are you okay?"

I smiled back and nodded. "I'm fine."

Professor Vale snorted loudly and scowled at me. "You'll lie better after you've gotten a good night's sleep. I'm the new dorm mother. Apparently, you need one. Take a bath and get to bed. I've bothered to fill the tub for you."

She whirled around, a flurry of energy as she went to my room, barking orders at the men who flinched at her voice. I edged over to Viney and Zach before I whispered, "What does that mean, that she's going to be the dorm mother?"

Viney fairly spat. "It means that she's settling in here permanently so she can spy on us for Blackheart. This is all your fault!"

Zach nudged Viney and glanced over where Professor Vale stood. "It's not her fault. If you'd been watching out for her then we wouldn't need a dorm mother. I agree, though. People can't do this and get away with it."

"People?" Viney leaned forward, poking Zach with her bony finger. "Do you know who did it?"

He shrugged and stepped away from her. "No. Do you?"

She scowled at him before whirling around and went into her room, slamming the door behind her.

Zach sighed then shook his head slightly while he looked after her. I stared at him for a few seconds before I turned and went to my temporary room. I nearly fell asleep in the tub after I washed my hair.

I got out, wrapped my hair in a towel and curled up in the spare bed, piling the white bedding on top of me. I barely noticed Señor Mort snuggling into my neck before I was dreaming.

16
Mage

After I left Penny Lane with the limo, I rejoined my fellow Chemists in the woods where we played long games of steal the flag and not get blown up. I headed back to the school in the dark, fingering my soot stained chin before I threw back my head and howled.

Laughter shadowed me along with echoing howls. I did so love running with the wolves. Being interrupted by some insignificant witch having a fit in the woods was not something I loved, particularly when I was trying so hard to ignore said witch and leave her to another fate. I'd seen enough witch fits, I didn't have any desire to see another one, but someone had to go and make certain the witch's meltdown wouldn't actually melt down the entire forest.

I ran faster, pushing myself through the trees cloaked in shadows, completely dark before the moon came out. I didn't activate any night vision. I liked running in the darkness, the risk of killing myself on a tree was so much more invigorating than your usual jog.

"Drake, you left this behind."

I turned and slowed down to see a gasping Pete holding out Penny's bag. I'd taken it off and forgotten about it, forgotten about her while I played. All right, I hadn't forgotten about it or her. I couldn't forget about someone who demanded to know when I'd stop grabbing girls right after her weasel bit me. I grabbed the bag and slung the strap over my shoulder while Pete fell in beside me. He hadn't played with as much intensity and focus as I had, sliding through the trees with explosives going off around us, no, he'd played at captain while I'd gotten all that irritation out of my system. Not all of it, but some. A little. Not enough.

She shouldn't come into my woods with her large, tear-filled eyes, cuddling her weasel like he was her teddy bear and she was some ridiculous child who needed to hold onto something. That was not the sort of witch freak-out I expected, particularly the lack of anger, so much grief instead that it hung in the air like it would at a funeral.

It wasn't my problem. She wasn't my problem. So why did I hold her hand? Why did I give her another handkerchief? Why did I care who Poppy was and whether Penny made it safely back to school? Viney had promised that she'd do better, take care of her. Viney should be friends with her, be someone she could cry with and talk about things to instead of a mage in the woods when she was vulnerable, sweet, smiling at me even when she accused me of wanting to hurt her. I would never hurt her that way, break her legs, smash her face, where was she getting these ideas about me?

I reached the school too soon. I wanted to run more, wanted to smash something. I settled for joining the other mages in the showers beneath the Chemiss tourney stadium.

"Are you going to Makiss tonight?"

I glanced at the guy, Pete, who had asked Oscar the question who stood, rubbing his black hair with a towel. Oscar was mostly dressed while Pete only wore a towel. Pete came from a family who felt that clothing was more optional than required.

Oscar grinned. "I wouldn't miss it for anything. Viney's going to be in fine form tonight. Didn't you hear what happened?"

I didn't. I pulled off my shirt and tossed it into a hamper.

"What's got Viney upset? Is it the new girl?" Pete asked.

Oscar laughed, a wicked sound that filled the shower room beautifully. He had very good tone. "Maybe Viney blames her for getting a dorm mother, but I don't think that's very fair considering that the poor girl got her room completely smashed, door blown off, clothing, Chemistry set, everything completely destroyed."

I froze with my hands on the top button of my leather pants. Penny's room was destroyed? That's what set her off in the woods like a crazed weasel lady?

"Who did it?" Pete asked.

Yes, who did it?

Oscar shrugged. "Zachary said that he scared off a few guys in masks, but wasn't sure if they were female or male. He's not saying whether or not they were male or female, anyway."

"Was it Barry?" Another kid joined the conversation, stark naked and blond.

Oscar frowned at the newcomer and handed him a towel. He was only a Junior and shouldn't interrupt seniors particularly without a towel. "How would that be possible?"

The kid shrugged. "Otherwise, why did Zach beat him up so bad?"

"How bad?" I stepped forward, remembering to smile at the last minute when the kid saw the look on my face.

"Broken legs, smashed face, really colorful, and what's more, Zach did something to him to keep Barry from healing."

Oscar shook his head. "It happened before the room. They were arguing over a lollipop. Apparently, Zach tried to take Barry's away from him." He rolled his eyes. He wouldn't be stupid enough to keep a lollipop that Zach wanted. Or maybe he would if the lollipop in question was Miss Penny Lane.

Who had cried. Because someone had gone to her room, her beautiful woodland boudoir and smashed it up. Someone had wrecked the swing I'd worked so hard to hang from her ceiling. No wonder Señor Mort bit me. No wonder Penny had been so angry at me, angry and then hysterical, before shifting to sad, resigned, and then strangely enough, somewhat content.

Of course she was content, after all, why should she be upset when someone went into her private space and destroyed everything she loved? If someone dared do that to me... I grimaced and pulled my shirt back on. I'd shower later. I wasn't in the mood to be pretty for anyone, not tonight.

I headed to the Makiss tourney. It had already started when I arrived, climbing the bleachers up to the top where fewer seats were taken. I sat down and other men from Chemiss filled in around me, blocking out the females who were watching me rabidly. If I dressed well and had impeccable grooming at least I could pretend that my looks had something to do with their attention.

"You're in a good mood," Pete commented.

I grunted. "Such a good mood. Remind me what a good mood I'm in later when I'm trying not to strangle a witch."

He raised his eyebrows. "You're not serious."

"Of course I am. When am I ever trying to not strangle a witch?"

He laughed. "True enough."

We stopped talking, instead focusing on the scene unfolding below us on the Tourney field. Famiss had a stage, but the witches needed more space. I watched the two figures down on the field throwing hurters at each other, at the pop and crackle before the flash of bright light and shower of shrapnel. It was fine. The two witches were young, and this wasn't supposed to impress anyone. They wore their black cloaks and simply took each hit that got close to them, not bothering to duck and dodge. Their hurters weren't terribly impressive either.

I shifted impatiently. Our tourney would be much more entertaining. At least we'd have music. Why didn't Makiss have music?

Finally, one of the witches fell over and the other was declared the winner. People cheered half-heartedly, but then Viney stalked out in her white mask with black cloak, a skull burning on the back.

The guys around me perked up while I swallowed and clenched my fists. She'd said that she would do something about Penny. Letting her be assaulted was not what I'd had in mind.

Viney took her place on one side of the field while three other witches gathered across from her. Interesting. They began with magic, throwing spells and curses at Viney that she countered with her own spells. After they got tired of that, although who got tired of hearing a witch scream in agony, they moved on to hurters. Viney's delivery was very good, the quality of her hurters unmistakably fine, and she put some effort into moving around so it wasn't as terribly dull to watch. She split the three other witches apart, moving between them so they couldn't strike her without hitting one of their own, and she beat them deftly with beautiful strikes and thrusts that dropped two of them in one magnificent sweep.

Someone to my left grunted appreciatively and I turned to glance at Oscar. He watched the scene riveted, clearly fixated on Viney and her lovely violence. The other mages weren't quite as focused, but still, she put on a good show and all of them would enjoy spending a little more quality time with her. If only she wanted one of them.

The last witch held her own for a long time, their final exchange a flurry of volleys that filled the night with crackles and smoke from the hurters. Finally, Viney lobbed a large ball and dropped down, pulling her hood low over her face as an enormous explosion wrapped around the witch.

After a very long period spent listening to witch screams mixed with popping, crackling snaps, Viney stood, and the crowd with her, roaring their approval. She swept off the field without glancing around, completely confident in her superiority. Excellent.

I stood and stepped out of time and into Darkside. I saw a black dog silhouetted against a red sky before I took another step and came out in the hall beneath the stadium. I stood there, arms crossed over my chest until she turned the corner and stopped, her face hidden by the white mask, but I could see the eyes, the bright anger in them.

"What do you want?"

I smiled. "What I always want when faced with a tempting witch. Pizza. This time I also crave justice."

She walked towards me quickly, stepping around me and continuing down the hall. "What are you talking about?"

I followed her into a room, closing the door behind her while she took off the white mask with shaking fingers and unfastened the heavy cloak from her shoulders. She smoothed it out reverently and laid it in its own box, like a coffin.

"You allowed someone to destroy a room in your dorm."

She glared at me, crossing her arms. "I didn't allow anything. Anyway, what happens in my dorm isn't your concern."

I smiled. "No? Did a mage or a witch destroy Penny Lane's property?"

She sneered. "Zach won't say."

I stepped closer, looming over her although I kept my voice low. "You told me that you'd take care of it. I listened to your warning, stayed away from her like a good little mage and trusted that you would do your part. You put up no precautions, no spells, no wards, nothing."

Her eyes glittered at me. "I think that Jackson did it. You know the girls that follow him, what they're like. If it was a mage with witches working with him, how could I possibly prevent that?"

I quirked an eyebrow as I studied her. I should leave her alone, let her get some rest after her exhausting battle. "You're saying that you need help?"

She snarled at me. "No. I mean, I can't control everyone in school. I don't cultivate a following of mindless drones who do everything I say. I'm not like Witley."

I narrowed my eyes at her. "I see. Fortunately, I do have a following of mindless drones who will happily do as I ask. Apparently, you are helpless and require rescuing. You're welcome."

I turned to the door.

"Wait. What are you going to do?"

I hesitated, my hand tightening on the knob. I was leaving before I strangled her. "I'm going to be involved, close enough to not only discover and punish the culprit, but to keep her from harm."

"How close?"

I glanced over at her. Her face was tight, the question a subtle cry from her obsession for me. She wanted to know if I'd be close to her, Viney. "As close as Miss Lane will let me be. Closer than she'll be comfortable with, close enough that everyone will assume I'm desperately in love with her. Who knows. Maybe I am. Excellent tourney, Vineldra. I'll see you tomorrow, and the next day, and the next."

I stepped out of that world, into Darkside and the same black dog with the same red sky. I howled at it before I once again stepped back into our world.

17
WITCH

I was chased by wolves, all of them Drake, his eyes gleaming, teeth sharp and cruel as he finally caught me. I sat up in bed, heart pounding, but not afraid. My mouth was watering while I rubbed my head, trying to get rid of the sensation of his tongue on my neck. It must have been Señor Mort. I needed to get him another cage.

I lay back down and had closed my eyes when a howl came from right outside my window.

I sat up, rubbing Señor Mort's head where he curled on my pillow and went to the window. There were bars criss-crossing the glass in a diamond pattern that was sort of beautiful, but also very strong. I wouldn't be going out of that window and nothing would be coming in. Unless it got blown off like my door. What had they used? I should examine the wall for traces of powder, take samples then track down who had access to it and… What? Chop them up in bits and send them to their parents? So, someone had trashed my room. That didn't change anything. It didn't matter who had done it. What I needed to focus on were ways to protect myself and Señor Mort in the future, ways to get Zach to fall in love with me and marry me, and ways to get time to do what was important, namely, my business. I had a loyal following, but they wouldn't wait forever if I couldn't get them their potions and lotions, their healers and hurters.

Out in the darkness I saw a flash of something. I heard another howl and shivered. I pulled on the long lace robe too elaborate and ruffled for anything other than dress-up and opened the door. I'd taken two steps when two other doors opened, Zach's, and another door beside my temporary room. Professor Vale, wearing dark soft clothing with her bare feet, toenails painted pink, glared at me. I smiled at those toenails before smiling at her.

She did not smile back. "What are you doing out of bed?"

"I thought I heard howling."

"You did." That was Zach. Both Professor Vale and I looked at him. He cleared his throat. "The sorority group, the Makiss, are hazing their Freshman recruits tonight. I don't know if you were warned about it, Professor Vale, but it's kind of an institution around here. Are you all right, Penny? Do you need anything?"

"Aren't you considerate? Weren't you the only one at the scene of the crime?"

I frowned at Professor Vale. "Zach would never hurt anyone or do anything cruel. Please apologize to him."

Professor Vale lifted a thin eyebrow. "I see. You trust him so much? I suppose you trust the girl as well."

I hesitated before I gave her a weak smile.

She took two steps closer to me before she leaned over, her expression stern. "He is not free from her influence. Try not to forget that. Now, back to bed."

I went, but it took me a long time to fall asleep with the howling and the memory of the big bad wolf's gleaming green eyes staring at me.

In the morning, I woke up late and felt groggy, weird, disoriented. All my clothes that I hadn't left in my trunk were ruined, shredded up, so that meant I had to find an entire wardrobe that weekend as well as order all the equipment for my personal lab. Luckily, I'd had my laptop with me in my bag so I could order stuff. I sat up and stared at the empty white room. I threw myself back down on my pillow, buried my face in its depths while I screamed. He still had my bag. Drake. The wolf.

It took me a long time to get out of bed when I knew what I had to do that day. I did not want to see Drake any time soon. I couldn't see him soon or I might freak out completely. How had I forgotten to take my bag with me? What was wrong with me? I was supposed to be cautious to the point of paranoia, particularly with someone like him, someone who broke arms and legs and hearts for the fun of it, someone who gives a girl a handkerchief with a broken heart embroidered on it just for irony.

I opened my trunks and found a lot of fabric, some interesting costume pieces, and that was about it. My sewing machine had been ruined as well. I pulled my lacy dress-up robe over my rose print bustier and ruffled panties. My hair would take hours to comb out after drying in my bed. Of course, I didn't have a comb, so I didn't have to worry about it.

I opened my door and saw Drake walk into the common room. I gasped and tried to step back into my room, but then his face, filled with fury that he directed at Zach, made me hesitate. Was Drake going to break Zach's leg for no apparent reason? Drake moved through the room towards Zach too quickly.

I licked my lips. "Drake! It's so nice to see you!" I was going to die of shame, but at least Zach wouldn't die of Drake.

Drake stopped and turned towards me, the anger in his eyes melting into something else, something even more dangerous. I fumbled with the edges of my ridiculous robe.

"Penny Lane, are you still in bed at this hour? I hope I didn't disturb you."

His eyes disturbed me as he raked over me, like my robe was completely sheer. It wasn't, I was almost certain of it. He kept staring at me, which was good because then he wasn't about to kill Zach, but my knees were getting weak and I had this idea I was blushing in weird places because I felt kind of hot and melty.

"Of course not. I hope you brought my bag. I need to order a lot of things and..." I looked at his body, his t-shirt, his soft pants, no bag. "Are you in your pajamas?"

He smiled at me. "Are you interested in what I wear when I'm sleeping? You're welcome to find out any time."

Zach made a sound. "Penny, are you going to breakfast like that?"

I glanced down at my robe and saw that the lace had slid off my shoulders revealing the top of my rose print bustier. I yanked it up while I blushed. "No, of course not. I actually thought I might borrow some clothes from Viney. Is she awake?"

Zach's eyes got large while Drake choked.

"No need," Professor Vale said, sweeping in the doorway. She prodded Drake on the shoulder while she passed him. "The lady is not ready to receive suitors. Be on your way." She walked over to me without waiting to see if he backed out.

He glanced at Zach, and then back at me before he grinned. "Penny, I'll get your bag and see you at breakfast. I'll be waiting for you." With that he left and Professor Vale stared at me with amusement. She pushed a few large shopping bags at me.

"Get dressed. You shouldn't stand around in that kind of negligee unless you're trying to seduce the other residents. You're quite the temptress."

I yanked the robe back up before taking the bags into my room. It seemed like the robe had a will of its own, which was possible. My grandmother had worn it on her honeymoon with my mysterious grandfather.

In the bags were three school uniforms complete with vests, skirts, blouses, pants, black Mary-Janes, knee high socks, and two riding uniforms with boots. In a small bag was a toothbrush, hair brush, and some hair clips and hair bands. It wasn't a lot, and I didn't have makeup, but I wouldn't have to wear elaborate gowns until my express deliveries came.

I got dressed in a sensible uniform, fixed my hair, and headed to breakfast, taking Señor Mort along, riding on my shoulder under my enormous hair. I needed my own conditioner to keep it from the unkempt, wild curls of an eighteenth-century peasant.

Drake was sitting at a table in the corner, but stood when he saw me. He gestured to me to come then lifted the straps of my bag. I went directly to him, ignoring the looks and the whispers as I walked. I licked my lips while I stood there, hesitating until he pushed the other chair out with his foot, now wearing boots that were a little equestrian to match his jacket.

"Sit down. Eat. I got everything so you can eat what you want."

I looked at the table, the eggs benedict, crepes, soufflé, plates of hash browns, scrambled eggs and waffles.

I sank down in the seat and proceeded to eat. I fed bits to Señor Mort when he poked his nose out of my hair.

"You brought your boyfriend."

I shrugged because my mouth was full. I ate until I felt a little bit less hollow. "Thanks for bringing my bag." I held out my hand for it.

He handed it over but held onto the strap when I tried to stand up, pulling me back down. "The thing is, I'm kind of curious, Penny, why you would rather that I think you're emotionally overwrought about a cat more than being vandalized and victimized."

I stared at him, desperate for a lollipop that was in my bag. I also felt slightly nauseous while he stared at me with his eyes narrowing, and I started to get angry.

I forced a bright smile. "I'm so sorry that I ruined the story. It would be much better to talk about the shocking attack, but I am much sadder about Poppy than I am about my room. It's incredibly frustrating that I'll lose some time, but that's all it is, stuff, time. As for what you think about me, you don't owe me your good thoughts and while they would be nice, I don't expect them. I wish you hadn't found me like that." I stared down at the mess of mostly empty dishes. I should have plucked out his eyes and thrown them to the wild weasels. "I'm not usually so emotional."

"It must be PMS. You're a woman. As the weaker sex, you can't help it."

I sucked in a breath and glared at him, yanking my bag out of his hand so hard that the strap broke. His lips twitched and some lollipops fell out onto the floor. I bent down to retrieve them while he watched me, his eyes full of something dangerous while he struggled not to laugh at me. It was like he wanted me to eviscerate him, like he was intentionally goading me.

I took a shaky breath and stood, clutching the lollipops in my hand. "That must be it. Thank you for enlightening me. If you'll excuse me, I have tears to cry and men to hate."

I held out my hand for the bag that he still held. He stood up and slung it over his shoulder with the remaining strap.

"I'll walk with you. I'm very easy to hate if you need a handsome, irresistible target."

I exhaled, ignoring the way that people looked at me, girls, guys, everyone watching me with Drake so closely. "What are they looking at?" I murmured.

"Maybe they want another show like the time with the malt. Or maybe they're waiting for you to go crazy and attack me with your beady-eyed friend."

I glanced at him. "Why are you walking with me again?"

"Maybe I want to look at you and imagine you in that robe from earlier. It's easier to visualize when you're right in front of me."

I stiffened and at the same time my stomach tightened. "Why do you say that?"

"Why not?"

"If your purpose is to shock and revolt me, that's fine, but you're calling me good looking which I might find complimentary, so are you trying to attract me or repel me? Both? Maybe you don't know. Maybe you have no purpose other than shock value. I just don't understand you."

Silence spread between us for a few heartbeats until he finally spoke. "Do you want to understand me?"

I glanced over at him and then away. "What I want isn't important."

"Why not, Penny? Maybe it's the most important thing of all."

I stopped for a moment. What did I want? I wanted to run away from here and my family and never have to deal with any of them ever again. I wanted to hide from the memories of Poppy and the knowledge that if I didn't marry somebody, anybody, my mother certainly wasn't particular, I'd be responsible for at best, making my mother homeless, at worst, killing her if she still refused to leave the house. I wanted to scream and scream and scream until the sound had shattered all the things in my life that didn't make sense.

Most importantly, I didn't want to become worse than my mother, someone who had sacrificed her life for mine. If I couldn't do that, marry a perfectly nice boy in order to save her, I may as well light this school on fire and watch everyone and me burn, because there wouldn't be anything inside of me worth saving, worth redemption.

I gave him my brightest smile. "Thank you for reminding me, Drake. It's important to remember what you want, isn't it? I hope that you'll always be my friend."

I smiled for the rest of the walk, swishing my skirt and looking up at him sweetly with my lollipop in my mouth. Lavender and dirt. I had to get moving on Zach, and Drake needed a different girl to play with.

18
Witch

How to get Zach to marry me. I thought about that while I sewed a new wardrobe, sewing machine courtesy of Professor Vale. It's not that I didn't appreciate the standard school uniform, except that I didn't. What did Zach like? Languages. Horses. Video games. All things I knew nothing about. Well, I could appreciate what he did know and cultivate some new skills in the process, like video gaming. It wouldn't be that bad, except that it was a complete waste of time when my time was already so precious.

If I lost my business during this ridiculous mission I would have a lot to say to dearly departed Grandmama in the afterlife. Señor Mort perched on my shoulder while I hemmed my third identical school skirt, just a shade paler than the usual beige, a little more creamsicle than blah.

It was Sunday afternoon and I was still waiting for my express deliveries to arrive that would restore order and peace to my life. Ha. Like anything in my life would ever be peaceful again. I stood up, stretched, tucked Señor into his makeshift cage and smoothed down my flippy skirt and simple top that were still fairly cute. At least I had my cute shoes and I hadn't ruined them during my woodland walk. Freak out. I flinched at the memory, me looking like... I couldn't even think about it, and Drake rescuing me like a romance hero from some novel. Poppy used to read those. No wonder she made such poor choices in her life. Telenovelas were so much more inspiring.

I stuck one of my last lollipops in my mouth and left my room, ready to sacrifice some precious hours learning the art of the video game.

I sucked. I was worse at it than at horse riding, and that was saying something. It was worse than boring, humiliating, while Viney and Zach smirked at me while I sat there, dead for the thirty-seventh time and they were still fighting each other and zombies and aliens or whatever. Who cared?

"Thanks for letting me play. I'm going to dinner now." Or else I'm killing you like a zombie alien bonbon you did not see coming.

Zach bothered to look at me for a half second before he turned back to his thrilling game.

Awesome. He was like a zombie. Boring. Why wasn't he running around in the woods rescuing females? He could ride up on his horse all gorgeous and stuff... Not that he hadn't been truly great with my whole room mess, but this was ridiculous.

In the dining room, everyone was whispering and the whole hum was very excited, my name mixing with Jackson, Drake, and someone else, Wit? I kept hearing it, 'Jackson and wit' like he was trying to have wit but had failed, but Jackson was definitely bringing wit back to school, and he might speak mean boy fluently, but wit, probably not.

"Sit with me."

I froze while Drake grabbed my elbow, steering me to the side table. He pushed me down on one side and sat on the other. "I think Jackson did it."

I stared at him. He was talking about my room. It made sense, but didn't seem to match his personality. "I don't think he has enough clever dialogue to be considered a wit." I stood up and he pulled me back down, impatient. He wasn't the only one. I did not need to think about Jackson or whoever had messed with my stuff, not when I didn't have enough lollipops to take me through another homicide free week.

"Witley. Jackson is bringing her to school because he knows that I know that he did it."

I stared at him. "That's nice. I'm so glad you told me."

He frowned. "Don't you want to know who trashed your room?"

I smiled. "It would be nice if whoever did it was caught so they couldn't do it to anyone else, but it's not my job."

He leaned forward. "But whoever did that won't do that to another person but something else to you. You're not serious about letting people walk all over you, are you? Because, I can't do that."

I stood up quickly, moving far enough away that he couldn't grab me and drag me back over to him. "No one asked you to do anything, Drake. I appreciate your interest in the mystery of the bedroom debacle, but I have a lot of other things to worry about, mostly stupid things like how to play video games."

He raised his eyebrows. "You want to play video games? With who?"

I shook my head. "Zach and Viney and I think everyone else at school. I think I stand out too much, but at the same time, I'm cute, aren't I?"

He smirked. "Very cute. So does the guy you like like cute or something a little more…"

A silence descended on the dining room other than a slight rustling and then a laugh, the kind of throaty chuckle a woman on Telenovelas made before she declared that she'd stolen your husband and made him hers. I turned and saw a girl who could have stepped straight from a drama, oodles of black hair in luscious waves, perfect oval face with a tiny pointed chin, and a luscious mouth that matched her large and luminous eyes. Her makeup was perfectly vixen without being quite too ho. Jackson walked beside her, a smirk on his annoying face.

Drake cursed behind me, a series of colorful profanities that I tried to remember. This must be Witley, the mysterious girl who had caused such a furor. She walked right up to me, glancing from me where I stood to Drake where he still sat, sprawled back like he didn't care one way or another who had arrived be it the pope or a green alien.

"Hi, I'm Penny." I smiled at her, but I didn't have my lollipop, so I wasn't quite as bubbly as usual. Maybe that was a good thing. Maybe Zach didn't like bubbly. I needed a friend, a girl type friend who knew what guys liked. The way that guys looked at this girl, she certainly knew, but the way that she looked at me, she wouldn't be sharing any helpful advice, unless it was how to light myself on fire. I already knew how to do that.

"Penny. I've heard so much about you. You're the girl Drake broke Jackson's arm for, right?"

Jackson glared at Drake and his supple lips twisted, soft lips that looked a lot like hers. Did he botox them?

I laughed. "That's so funny. I'm sure Drake would like to give that impression. He's too cruel sometimes, isn't he? I'm afraid I didn't catch your name."

"Witley Penmore. You look like you're on your way out. By all means." She made little shooing motions with her hand, and it took all my strength not to grab those fingers and snap them one by one.

"I'm going to go and get my food, but I'm eating here. Why don't you two pull up chairs. It will be so nice to get to know Jackson's girlfriend."

I left the three staring at me, feeling Drake's eyes burn into my back, or maybe I was imagining things. Probably. I swished my skirt big time as I left Jackson and Witley with Drake. Drake had better be looking at my legs, not some perfectly made up hot thing. Not that I cared.

I got everything carbs and rich sauce and decadent meat plus a lot of salad and vegetables and… okay. I got a lot of food, but I'd skipped lunch trying to get my homework done and my stuff ordered and my uniforms sewn along with current cute if not quite as cute as usual outfit.

When I got back to the table, there was an empty chair right next to Drake. I should have found a different seat, but I'd announced I was sitting there like a lunatic, thanks to Witley's aggressive femme fatale vibes, so I may as well learn something from the experience.

"Did you eat yet?" I asked as I settled next to Drake, noticing that he had no food. Would I have to share?

He seemed to see the fear in my eyes and a slight smile flicked over his mouth. "I ate earlier. I was just sitting here, waiting for you to come in." He put an arm over the back of my chair, leaning over to give me a smoldering glance that made my idiotic heart pound.

I gave a choking laugh and then started eating. I realized that they weren't talking and glanced up to see all three of them staring at me. I chewed what was in my mouth then gave a nervous smile.

"You're so thin and hungry. Did they starve you at home?"

I stared at Witley, the barely veiled mockery in her eyes. "Yes. They did. It was completely cruel. In fact my last dinner home was herbed chicken, five servings of cheese, two soufflés, a beef stew along with the usual courses. How is a girl supposed to live on that? I've put in complaints with the local authorities, but minors have so few rights."

I sighed heavily while Drake choked on a laugh and coughed, trying to clear his throat. I gave him a few solid thumps on his back for putting his arm on the back of my chair. He only leered at me. I restrained myself from kicking him under the table.

Whitley laughed, that same throaty laugh that put up my hackles. She put her hand on my arm and I smiled at her sweetly instead of stabbing her with my tightly clutched fork.

"You are adorable. I can see why Drake is so fascinated with you."

I blinked at her then glanced at Drake before I gave her a particularly sweet smile. "It's the legs. Apparently Drake is a legs kind of guy. Who knew, right? I mean you'd think he'd prefer someone with a perfect hour-glass body, immaculately beautiful face and hair that just fell off the pages of a two spread shampoo ad, but no, he likes legs. Isn't that crazy? Particularly if you look at this hair." I shook my head vigorously and my hair kind of fluffed out like an untrimmed poodle. "Who can possibly predict what a guy's going to like? It's so bewildering. And there's the issue of if you want a guy who likes you as you are, or if you'd rather get the guy that you like how he is, and change yourself to fit him. Which is more important, being yourself, or having the one you want? I don't know. This whole experience is completely alien to me. I'm used to hiding in my garret and making miniature clothing for the rodents."

Whitley inhaled sharply while Jackson glowered and Drake's expression went perfectly smooth. I shrugged and focused back on my food, ignoring the rest of the table until I was sated. Not quite sated. I wanted a chunk out of Witley's perfect face for dessert.

I wiped my mouth on a napkin and stood. "It's been such a pleasure to meet you. I hope I have you in all my classes."

I turned to go, but Drake stood with me, sliding his arm in mine. "So nice to see you two. Congrats on your new relationship. I hope you find it as satisfying as he does, Wit." He thunked Jackson on the shoulder before he walked off with me.

I looked up at him, sighed, and shook my head. I should not let him walk around like he was my male escort, but that girl made me want to do crazy things, like walk with Drake.

He quirked an eyebrow. "What kind of girl does the guy you want like?"

"I have no idea. Maybe he doesn't like girls. I hadn't thought of that, but a gender switch for me wouldn't be too difficult. I would probably miss the hair, but the jackets for boys are much more interesting, and the vests and the sensible shoes..."

"So you admit that you like someone."

I giggled. "Of course. I like lots of people. I'm sorry about that back there. I think my cruel vengeful streak came out again. It's a lucky thing she didn't dump something on me that you were allergic to. I know you don't really like me or my legs."

His arm tightened on me. "Everyone likes your legs, even Jackson who otherwise thinks you're an evil harpy."

"A bit redundant since all harpies are evil, aren't they?" I sighed. "I'm not nearly as good at language roots as I should be. Why are people so talented at this school?"

He glanced at me and smiled. "You've been here one week. Put these people in your world and what would they do?"

I cocked my head at him. "Oh, dear. That wouldn't be very good."

My mother would kill them all. Yes, yes she would. Even Revere who was technically polite had a streak of cruelty a mile long. I would never leave Señor Mort with him. He'd probably roast him for my first dinner back or something.

"No? What was the hardest thing about living at home?"

I shook my head. That was easy, walking past the waiting soldier every time I went to dinner. "Probably just being lonely. Not that Señor Mort isn't great, but tea parties are kind of fun with real people."

He nudged me, his side brushing mine and sending completely unnecessary shocks of awareness through me. "I think that was almost a compliment, Penny Lane. I'll take it."

19
WITCH

I researched, 'how to get a guy to like you' and came up with a few promising ideas, very few. First, I had to do research, find out his secret weakness, the one thing that was their key to affection, their love key. Did he like physical affection, visual attraction, acts of love, gifts, attention or appreciation? It was definitely a different way to look at attraction. The basic keys were a pretty face, kind words, thoughtful acts, small gifts, and gentle touches. I rolled my eyes and closed my computer. I would have to craft the key to Zach's heart over the next week. He'd shown interest in lollipops. That was either acts of love or gifts.

He'd kind of ignored me during the video game thing, maybe I hadn't given him enough affection or kind words or something like that. I hadn't apologized for almost breaking his elbow. I slid into the white, boring twin bed and hoped that it was the last night I'd spend there.

The next morning was lovely. I wore my cute customized uniform with a pink ribbon beneath my peter pan collar that matched my shoes. I skipped down the hall, smiling and greeting all my wonderful friends, giving them sincere compliments, validation, friendly touches, and beautiful smiles.

They gave me mutters, snarls, flinches and glares. Honestly, I loved it. I had no idea it could be so fun to be nice. When I walked into my English class, Witley sat looking glamorous and glorious.

"Witley, you are in my class. I can't wait to hear what you think about Pre-Raphaelite poetry." I patted her shoulder and skipped to my seat on the other side of the classroom, my back to the wall. She glanced at me a few times that I noticed, saying things in a low voice to the students gathered around her, evenly split between girls who wanted to be her and guys who wanted her.

I concentrated on my work because I had no idea about Pre-Raphaelite poetry. At the end of class I hurried out, but Wit was already standing, waiting for me. She hooked her arm in mine and pulled me against her.

"You must tell me how you caught Drake. He's such a difficult fish."

I glanced at her before I kind of laughed. "He is difficult. The truth is that he's only using me so that people don't know that he's actually gay." I gasped and covered my mouth with my hand. "I shouldn't tell you this. I should never reveal the shocking fact that Drake broke Jackson's arm because he likes him so much and can't bear him to touch another woman." I sighed dramatically, using the movement to take my arm out of hers and pat my chest woefully. "The path of love never did run smooth."

With that, I gave her a small wave and skipped off to my next class. After two more classes, I was on my way to Linguistics when Drake sidelined me into a wall. He had his arms on either side of me, his green eyes dark and brooding beneath his lowered eyebrows, his sensitive lips in a hard line before he leaned close, brushing my cheek with his and whispering in my ear.

"I can't thank you enough for agreeing to be my decoy so no one knows how I really feel about Jackson." He leaned closer, his body pressing against mine, his breath on my skin making me shiver while my body tightened in the weirdest places. "You're so generous, allowing me to use your body this way." He slid his hand down the wall until his palm was flat beside my hip. "I had no idea you read between the lines so intuitively."

I shivered and then when he put his hand on my leg, right below the edge of my skirt, I shuddered, a wave of awareness shooting through me. His hand slid a little bit higher over my skin and I gasped. He stuck a lollipop in my mouth while my lips were parted, stepping away from me, crossing his arms while he scowled.

I sucked on it helplessly, trying to breathe like normal, but my heart was racing and I still felt his hand on my leg and smelled black cherry. I shouldn't eat anything that someone I couldn't trust gave me, but it was already in my mouth and it tasted like lavender and dirt. I pulled it out, stared at it for a second then looked up at him.

"Thoughtful gift, or kind act? Did you make this?"

His mouth tightened as he leaned forward, but his dangerous hands were still tucked against his chest, the chest that had been pressed against mine so very recently. "I am the captain of the Chemistry club. I think I can tell what's in a lollipop, even one as weird as yours. You need that kind of lollipop even without cars?"

I put the lollipop back in my mouth and stared at him, letting my eyes get big and puppy-dog before I took it out and gave him a wincing smile. "I'm sorry about the Jackson thing. I think Wit is bad for me. She starts talking and then I start talking and I have no idea what's going to come out of my mouth. I mean I'm responsible for everything I say, don't get me wrong, it's just that I feel kind of like I want to..."

"Jackson does like boys."

I stopped talking and stared at him.

He shrugged. "He likes girls too. I personally don't like anyone, but you knew that." He slid a handful of lollipops in my bag. "Be careful what you say, Penny, because it might come back to bite you." He gave me a sharp smile showing his teeth before he turned away, leaving me a shaky-kneed lollipop sucking fool as I stumbled to class.

20
WITCH

In linguistics, I edged over to Zach where he was beside the Chinese flag in the little Chinese alcove, where some girl was pouring green tea in these really ugly mud cups. When everyone's attention was on the girl I used the phrase I'd learned particularly, with just the right accent, something like, "Thank you for your help with my room. I'm sorry if I hurt your elbow."

He smiled slightly and shrugged. His response didn't have any of the words I'd looked up for, 'no problem,' or whatever. I bit my lip and studied him until he shook his head and leaned forward to whisper the translation in English. "It's a relief to know that you're not entirely defenseless. You probably shouldn't use ju-jitsu against someone with a bat, though."

I blinked at him and nodded as I remembered the words he'd used. I'd definitely heard ju-jitsu. I accepted a cup of tea from the girl, giving her the traditional thank-you I'd learned the week before and then nodded and smiled mostly while she talked about her sick cat. Or her sick grandmother, or something.

Zach wasn't in Dressage and Drake wasn't in Business class. Riding wasn't as bad as the first day I'd been in class with the girls. I didn't fall off Henrietta, but I made the teacher come back and fix absolutely everything I did over and over while the rest of the class glared at me.

In Business, I struggled not to notice that Drake wasn't there, like he didn't have to show up if he didn't feel like it, and apparently didn't. What a jerk. I thumped my leg where it still tingled traitorously from where he'd touched me. Stupid chemistry, stupid Chemistry captain and stupid me for wanting something so bad for me. Maybe it was the lollipops. Every time I pulled one out my leg started tingling along with my fingers while I saw his eyes in my head, daring me to want him. Jerk.

In History, I looked over, surprised when I saw Viney next to me. She glared at me for a second before it softened into a more neutral expression.

"What are you doing after class?"

I shrugged. "Homework?"

She took a deep breath and gave me a tiny smile, the first one I'd ever seen and it was terrifying. I flinched before I beamed back at her, my smile chasing away hers.

"Anyway, there's a really effective study lab that you might want to try. I can take you after class and introduce you to the brainy bunch."

"Brainy bunch? Is that like the Chemistry Club?"

She snorted. "No. It's like the anti-Chemistry Club."

That sounded promising. I'd had enough chemistry for one lifetime. After that, Professor Vale came in and spread her hand, capturing my attention like a magician. I loved her class so much. Learning seemed so effortless. Afterwards, I went with Viney out of the classroom, feeling kind of nervous because why would she be helping me? It made no sense, then again, maybe she was anti-Witley and therefore on my side. I wasn't sure why I was anti-Wit, she hadn't done anything besides look much better than I did, but of course I didn't look good, I didn't have my life back yet. I could look as good as Wit if I had the right makeup and hair conditioner. Wishful thinking.

I sighed as we walked up marble stairs, then more stairs, then more stairs in the enormous building that was apparently the library, and the study area must be at the top. I sucked on a lollipop as we went, our steps echoing on the wide halls with cavernous ceilings, dim chandeliers lighting the passageways.

Finally, we stepped out into a large room with tables and computers. Papers rustled and people talked in low voices, an all-over buzz that seemed to stop when Viney's boots thudded across the marble, me following in her wake. She walked right up to a large desk that took up the middle of one wall and slammed her hands on top.

The sound reverberated through the room. I wanted to offer her a lollipop to calm her down, but I wasn't about to give her something Drake had given me. It wasn't safe. Surely one of them would be poisoned or have a laxative. It had nothing to do with the fact that no one else got to touch something Drake gave me.

A tall guy with very black hair that could use more shampooing came up to the desk, his shoulder twitching like he was waiting for Viney to hit him or cut off his head.

"Oscar, this is Penny Lane. She needs help with her studies. I want you to set her up with your best tutors. I want her to try out all of the top ten to see which one she likes best. Okay?"

She gave me another small smile that made me lean away from her before she turned and stomped out, her exit eliciting a breakout of hushed exclamations. I turned back to Oscar who was scowling at me as darkly as Viney ever did. Maybe it was the only way to deal with brainy types, sheer overwhelming domination.

"Hi, I'm Penny Lane. It's so nice to meet you!" I grabbed his hand, over the desk and shook it vigorously.

"I know who you are. Everyone knows who you are." He was sneering at me. Drake's sneer was somehow attractive, but this guy's was just annoying.

I smiled brightly. "Great. Well, as fun as it is to chat, I hate to waste your precious time. Let's get started."

"Fine!" He turned around, searching the room before he swung over the desk in a not half-clumsy way and stalked across the room, his long legs still not as fast as Viney's vigorous stride. This guy and her would make kind of a cute couple, a study of opposites, Viney short and roundish, him tall and angular, but both of them scowling at the world adorably.

"Lars, Viney wants tutors for Penny Lane. Don't screw it up."

Lars, a large blonde with blue eyes that looked rather vacuous, blinked at me, then after Oscar where he walked off before looking back at me. "Um, hi, I'm Lars."

I waved at him and slid into the seat beside him. I took out my books and went right to linguistics. "I don't understand the basic structure of Chinese. Every time I think I have a grasp on it…"

Soon Lars showed that he was indeed as sharp as the proverbial tack. I didn't have to look cute, and I didn't have to be polite, and it really helped when trying to understand something. He pulled out a little music player and went through it until he'd downloaded something he handed to me with a little headphone set.

"Listen to this when you're not doing anything else. It will help settle it in your head. I'd focus on one language at a time, for a week or so. I can't imagine jumping into advanced conversational studies as a beginner. Hopefully the instructor grades you on improvement."

He gave me a large smile, because he was large, his face large, his whole body kind of enormous, not just his blue eyes.

I stood up. "Thank you. I appreciate your help."

He stood up and started walking with me. "It's my pleasure. I'll be here on Wednesday if you'd like to study with me again."

"Wednesday she'll be with Dude, tomorrow Orc." Oscar glowered at Lars who looked vaguely confused instead of threatened.

I left the two guys and the room where everyone seemed absorbed by their studies, but I caught a few quick glances.

Maybe I should marry someone like Lars or Oscar. Zach seemed easy-going, he had to be to hang out with Viney, but he hadn't opened up to me about anything, even in our horse lessons. Not that he'd been at my last one. Why did that feel like a betrayal?

I bit my lip and unwrapped another lollipop Drake had made. Maybe he'd put something addictive into it because I couldn't stop eating them in spite of the risk of eating strange lollipops. I went downstairs, out the doors of the library, down the covered pillared walkway over to Lilac Stories.

I should have come right back to work on my room. The maintenance guys had been working in there all day Saturday and Sunday. I expected piles of boxes, my new bed and brewing supplies, but instead I stopped in the doorway to the Commons and stared at Viney who was wearing a skirt. It was really cute and she had great legs, if short, nice and curvy above her black boots. She had her arms crossed over her black vest and skull t-shirt.

"Viney, you look really cute."

"Doesn't she?" That was Drake, seated at a table wearing a creamy cravat with a diamond pin with his black suit and black top hat. His green eyes glittered dangerously and my idiotic knees went weak.

"You don't. Here, change and then we can get started." Viney gestured at Zach who I hadn't noticed until then stood in the doorway of his room wearing a black suit that was pants and vest over a t-shirt, without a jacket, but he also had a black top hat. He handed me a bag and nudged me across the floor towards my temporary room.

I gripped the handle and turned to survey the group. "What are you guys dressed like that for? Is there a funeral?"

Viney rolled her eyes. "I might wear a skirt, but I'm not wearing pink. Come on already."

She shoved me into my room. When I closed the door, I opened the bag and pulled out an outfit a lot like Viney's, only the skirt looked suspiciously shorter. My shoes were platform Mary-Jane's instead of boots, and I had fish-net stockings and a vest with little skull buttons. It was so cute. A white slip went under the skirt, and the lace at the bottom of the floofy thing was also skulls, to match the buttons.

I dressed hurriedly, my fingers shaking from excitement mixed with fear. What were they planning to do to me?

I opened the door.

"Finally. Can we get this over with?" That was Viney.

I walked slowly in my platform Mary-Janes, feeling really weird in so much black without my black hair. "Get what over with?"

Zach gestured towards my old room. "We're having a tea party to celebrate your room being finished."

I stared at him, his nice smile and then at Drake, his smirk and eyes gleaming with wicked anticipation. I shook my head. "You don't like tea parties."

"It's not really a tea party, although there will be tea, but I know that you need to eat about five pounds of food at each meal, so the catering will be a little heavier than your usual tea." Drake opened the door and gestured me in.

Somehow the maintenance guys had managed to salvage some of my tapestries, and everything looked perfect, better than perfect. The shelf on the side holding my assortment of glass vials was curved like a tree branch, carved with leaves and small flowers in a way that wouldn't catch on my clothes. Everything was like that, carved intricately, like my bed, hanging from the ceiling had an elaborately carved headboard of roses that matched the backs of the three chairs around the table. The swing on the far side had incredible silk roses that looked real and felt real when I touched them. Sounds played in the background, wind rustling and water falling, exactly how it sounded in the grove between the trees and the waterfall where I was going to build...

On the table, on my grandmother's lace tablecloth, a gingerbread house rested on a plate with roses carved into the pale ceramic edges.

I turned and shoved Drake against the wall, covered in the tapestry with the mysterious figures that were either kissing or killing.

I stared at him, my fingers curling in the lapel of his coat until they turned white and I struggled with my own kiss or kill impulses.

Finally, Drake pulled my fingers down, and dragged me over to the swing where he wrapped my fingers around the rose twined ropes and then pushed me onto the bench before taking his seat across from me.

"She's in shock. I never thought Penny Lane would be shocked into silence." Drake grinned at Zack. "We should have a tea party every week."

Zack shrugged and sat down, pulling a tea cart closer that was heavily laden with food. He put a plate in front of me while Viney sat at my right and held out her hand impatiently for hers. I didn't eat right away because my heart was pounding and I felt so sick and panicked I wasn't sure whether I was going to scream or cry.

I bit my trembling bottom lip, trying to control my reactions. This didn't mean anything, it was just... I stared at Zach, his smile a little bit shy before he nodded at my plate. "Do you need a poison tester?"

I didn't say anything but Viney grabbed a chunk of meat off my plate and shoved it into her mouth then Zach speared some vegetables with his fork before chewing on them.

Drake winked at me when I looked at him. I quickly looked away, gripping my fork before I forced myself to take that first bite, which was always the hardest. The first meal I'd had after Poppy died... I blinked rapidly while my chest rose and fell.

"You should have worn a shirt under your vest. I can almost see cleavage." Viney pointed down at my chest which made me look down, and then up to grin at her.

"I think you're right. Might need to get out a magnifying glass, but definitely a small trace of cleavage." I put a hand on my chest and felt my heart race, but I didn't look up at Drake. "This is really a lot."

Zach leaned over, resting his hand on my shoulder for a second. "You haven't even finished the first course. There is a lot more."

I smiled at him and tried to really see Zach, nice, brown haired, lazy smile, sweet, easy-going guy I was going to marry, but my eyes craved Drake, and Zach's hand felt heavy until he pulled it away.

The tea party went in kind of a hazy blur of clinking dishes, hot tea spilled on my skirt, Viney making inappropriate comments that were sometimes almost funny, and the gingerbread house in the middle of the table that I stared at instead of Drake.

After we'd all eaten until we weren't hungry and I'd stopped feeling nauseous, Drake gestured towards the house, the movement forcing my eyes up to meet his for a moment before I locked my gaze back down.

"Who wants to smash it?"

"No!" I grabbed the house and pulled it to me, protecting it with my body.

Zach scooted back while Viney rolled her eyes, and Drake, who I glared at grinned at me.

"It's for eating, Gretel. Don't you want to nibble on the roof?"

I shook my head tightly.

"You're so weird," Viney muttered, standing up. "I'm getting out of this crap. Are we still watching a horror movie?"

I tried to relax my grip on the house but couldn't do it even as I turned to look at her. "Horror movie?"

Drake stood up too. "Good idea. We'll eat the house while we watch the movie. Zach, is it all set up?"

Zach nodded and I caught him looking at my legs which were over-exposed in my position leaning on the gingerbread house. I bit my lip and tried to not act crazy. What had changed? Why would they do all this stuff, fix my room and throw me a tea party? They couldn't really like me, not Viney, definitely not Drake. What were they setting me up for?

I reluctantly pulled away, noticing that I had white frosting on my skull buttons and the chimney looked a little bit crooked from my embrace. I stood there, staring at the house while Viney and Drake left my room, leaving me and Zach.

"Are you okay?"

I smiled up at him automatically but as I looked at him it kind of faded. "I'm kind of freaked out, to be honest. I didn't expect all of this. I didn't expect any of this. Thank you." I put my hand out, slowly and kind of patted his arm before I turned back to the house. "It's perfect. Everything is better than perfect, just strange."

He cleared his throat. "If you don't want to eat the house, you don't have to."

"Yes, you do," Drake called from outside my room.

Zach rolled his eyes and I smiled at him.

"It's okay. I will let the children gobble up my house and I won't even cook you in the oven this time, but only because I'm already so full."

21
WITCH

I carried the gingerbread house out of my room carefully. I put it on the elaborately carved coffee table across from the large screen where they played video games opposite the big lilac floral couch. I fiddled with the house, running my fingers over the roof, the swirls of white frosting, the gumdrops along the edge before I finally stood with a sigh.

Viney came out of her room at that moment wearing black pants, slouchy, comfy looking, and an over-size t-shirt of a skull wrapped in flames beneath a long black sweater. She looked really comfortable. She stared at me dully.

"Aren't you getting changed? The tea party is over."

I sighed. "I have my school uniform and dirty laundry. I'm still a little short on clothes. I've never owned a t-shirt and my only pants are my riding ones."

Her lips curled in disgust. "You don't own a t-shirt? Why not?"

Why didn't I? They were too loose, caught on things, were flammable and my grandmama disapproved of them? I shrugged. "I don't know. No one I know wears t-shirts, at least not until now."

"What?" That was Zach as he came out of his room wearing a t-shirt and soft pants, like the pants Drake wore the other morning. Where was Drake?

Viney turned to him with a shake of her small head. "She doesn't own a t-shirt."

"Really?" He pulled out his phone and stared at it, typing in it while I shifted awkwardly beneath Viney's contemptuous stare.

"Drake's going to bring something."

"No. It's ridiculous. Is there a horror movie rule about wearing t-shirts? I am just fine in this outfit. I'm perfectly comfortable and just great."

Viney narrowed her eyes at me. "If I had to wear that skirt and vest, you have to wear a t-shirt and pants. You don't want someone to accidentally put his hand on your leg during the movie, do you? I'd offer you some of mine, but you're way too flat and tall."

I blinked at her. "Thanks?"

Zach made a rude sound. "Viney doesn't let people touch her stuff. If she actually let you wear her clothes, that would mean she was possessed by a demonic force and we should call in a specialist."

Viney sneered at him. "As if I'm not already possessed by a demonic force."

I giggled and they both looked at me. "You guys are cute. Are you sure you're not dating?"

Zach shook his head decidedly while Viney scowled at me. "Zach and I have no chemistry. None. I could kiss him for five hours and only notice how chapped my lips are. He's like a piece of broccoli to me." She shrugged.

I glanced at Zach waiting for him to chime in on it. He shrugged. "I've only been attracted to one female before."

"One? Really?"

Zach smiled slightly, blue eyes crinkling sweetly.

"Are we talking about who we like, because I do not want to miss this conversation?" Drake came in wearing a soft looking dark green long sleeved t-shirt with a v-neckline low enough I could see his clavicles. Not that I was looking. He threw a bundle of clothing at me that I caught, dark clothes soft in my hands.

Viney glared at me. "Don't argue, just change. I'm making popcorn and I don't want it to be cold when we start the movie." Viney gave me a scowl just in case I thought I should argue, but I didn't, instead I went into my room, my temporary one, fed Señor Mort, and changed into the knit top and pants that were rather large on me. The v-neck dipped much lower than my clavicles and smelled like black cherry when I pulled it over my head, not that I noticed or buried my face in it for a second while I thought about gingerbread houses.

"Señor Mort, he is not being nice to me, he's just messing with me. That's what he does. He gave me the gingerbread house just so that we could smash it, and helped fix my room just because..."

What was I supposed to do with the weird feeling in my stomach, like butterflies? I came out of my room, tugging on the hem of the shirt. I felt strangely indecent in such soft fabric. I felt much less naked in my lace robe. Maybe I just wasn't used to it.

"Sit down." Viney gestured over where she sat on the couch.

Zach sat down beside her and then I sat by him while I ignored Drake where he stood by the screen, fiddling with cords for a second before he turned off the lights. The screen glowed green as he came over to the couch, but there wasn't enough room for anyone else. He sat down anyway. On me.

"What are you doing?" I gasped as his weight pressed me down into the lilac floral couch. I was going to die smothered in the most ugly upholstery known to man. Death by couch. It would be a good epitaph.

I put my hands on his waist, trying to get him off me, but instead of pushing him off, my hands slid around his stomach, over the soft fabric that barely hid his hard muscles. He shifted and I could breathe a little bit better, but his weight on me still made me dizzy, the scent of black cherry making my mouth water.

Drake hit Zach lightly on the shoulder. "Move over, Zach. Viney won't bite, probably, and if she does, you might like it. If I sit on Penny much longer, I think she's going to take advantage of me."

He put his hand over mine where they rested on his stomach, right above the waistband of his pants.

My heart pounded against his back where he pressed me into the couch. "I'm going to bite you if you don't move. You weigh too much. You need to go on a diet."

Viney snorted. "Drake is always going on diets to try and gain weight. He's the lightest guy in his weight class."

I groaned and tightened my arms around him before I heaved and ended up falling over with Drake onto Zach's lap.

Zach jumped, his thigh under my cheek. "Hey! Are we wrestling or watching a movie?"

"Sorry," I muttered while Drake finally got off me, but instead of him going and sitting in a chair like a normal human, he sat down in my place and pulled me off Zach and onto his lap.

I stared at him in the green flickering light of the TV, my heart pounding in my chest. I swallowed hard. "I'm heavy."

He slid his hands around my waist, like I'd done just a moment earlier. I couldn't breathe, and I couldn't blame it on his weight. He pulled me back against him, lifted his chin and whispered in my ear, "You smell like black cherries. Do I really smell that good? How can you possibly resist me?"

Zach yanked on Drake's arm and I escaped making my way to the chair beside the couch with trembling hands. I pulled up my knees and frowned at the TV. "Now I can't reach the popcorn."

Viney passed it over, her gaze on the screen which I also focused on instead of looking at Drake. Stupid teenagers were drinking and laughing loudly while they walked along a dark country road. The music built up kind of horribly, and a truck was coming along, faster and faster as it got to the teens. I flinched and gasped even though the teens somehow got out of the road, narrowly missed by the truck.

I shivered and took a handful of popcorn from the bowl Drake held out to me, the green tint of the screen making his eyes look alien. I studied the popcorn kernels and ate them one at a time, the weird crunch not entirely unappetizing with all the butter on it.

"Haven't you had popcorn before?"

I glanced over at Drake who was apparently still watching me. "Of course I have. Haven't we had this conversation before? I go to movies in the movie theater all the time. I mean, I have gone a few times. Not a lot. Twice. Aren't you going to watch the movie?"

He left his hand on the edge of the armrest through the film, kind of close to me. I leaned away from him, huddled on the far side of the chair while the music got more intense. I wrapped my arms around my knees while I stared at the screen, my chin going lower and lower until I could barely see the screen above my knees.

When the girl was standing in the woods, calling her boyfriend, she turned and screamed while this guy in a mask swung an enormous chainsaw at her face.

I gasped and grabbed Drake's hand, dragging his arm against my chest where my heart pounded, holding on tight while blood splattered the screen. I held his arm like that for the rest of the movie, probably uncomfortable for him, but I didn't think about that until the movie was over.

I sat there in the credits with a pounding heart until I let go of his hand and straightened up. "So that's a horror movie. I'm going to have nightmares."

"You're welcome to spend the night in my bed, Penny Lane. You can hold onto me as tight as you like."

I glared at Drake, but I had clung to him through the entire movie. I glanced over at the gingerbread house and knelt down in front of the coffee table.

"I almost forgot." I hesitated for a moment then broke a chunk off the roof. I ate the gingerbread, and it was really nice gingerbread even if there was too much frosting. The gumdrops didn't hurt. Viney and Zach broke off chunks and ate while they discussed the movie, talking about bad directing, like who hadn't seen that chainsaw guy coming a mile away? Drake grinned at me so I shoved a large chunk of roof in his mouth.

He grabbed my hand and licked frosting off my fingers before I could pull away. My heart pounded ridiculously hard before he let me go. I shook my head and ate gingerbread until I really needed some nice tea to go with it.

When the roof was gone and half a wall devoured, I stopped and stared inside. Written in swirling frosting were the words, "Come to the fairy-tale dance with me. I'll wear Lederhosen if you'll be my Gretel."

I stared at those words while my head got dizzy and everything grew fuzzy around the edges.

I woke up on the couch, Viney sitting next to me while behind her Drake paced and Zach sat on the edge of the table, grinning and eating gingerbread. I squeezed my eyes closed while my head hurt.

Viney yelled at Drake. "What did you put in the gingerbread? Are we all going to die?"

He scowled back at her. "It's fine. She's just tired."

Zach grinned at me. "Sleeping beauty is waking up. Are you all right?"

I sat up slowly while Viney quickly moved away from me. I put my hand on my forehead where a bump was rising.

"You hit your head on the corner of the coffee table." Viney scowled at me like I'd done it on purpose.

"That makes sense. I had this weird hallucination that Hansel asked me to a dance. Wait, maybe it was a mistake. Where did the gingerbread come from?"

I looked from Viney's blank face to Zach who tried hard not to smile and Drake who stared at me intently.

"I made it." Drake sounded almost casual.

I stared at him. "You made it? You made the gingerbread and the frosting parts particularly the..."

He rolled his eyes and sat down on the couch beside me, too close so I couldn't breathe very well. "Why not? It's not for another month, but girls have already started asking me. If I have a date, it's easier."

I shook my head and winced because it hurt and my head was aching. "Drake, as my Pas de Deux partner, you know that I can't dance. You should ask Viney who probably dances really well. Or Zach, he'd be a great partner. You're even taller than him."

Drake leaned closer to me, his eyes going wide and soft. He smelled so ridiculously delicious, my mouth started watering. "I know it's sudden, and I know that you like someone else, it's just that I thought we were friends and if you're not going with someone else by then it would be convenient. You don't have to agree just because I made you gingerbread and frosted all of those little roof pieces, or that I hung your new bed and..."

"Stop it!" Viney grabbed his hair and pulled him off the couch.

His eyes widened in surprise as she rounded on him, a small ball of fury that was pretty terrifying.

"She's just had a concussion. You can't guilt her into going out with you just because she's the only girl you know who doesn't melt at the sound of your voice. You asked her. Fine. I'm not going to let you stand there and try to seduce her into going with you if she actually likes someone else. And as for you!" She rounded on me.

I pressed into the back of the couch and smoothed down my hair to make it harder for her to grab.

"Don't you ever wear a bra?"

I blinked at her. That wasn't where I'd been going. "Um..."

"Do you even know what a bra is?"

I gestured at her. "It's for girls with voluptuous curves. I'm fine without one."

She scowled at me. "Do you think Zach and Drake don't notice your nipples in that shirt?"

I felt my face get hot while Zach choked then burst out laughing.

Drake stared at me, his gaze dropping to my shirt while his lips twisted into a smirk. "You say that like it's a bad thing."

Viney whirled on him which gave me slight breathing room. "You should have gotten a shirt from the same kid you stole the pants from. Your shirt, hanging off her shoulder and no bra…"

Zach put a hand on Viney's shoulder and didn't take it off when she turned her snarl on him. "I think it's time for all of us to go to bed. Professor Vale is going to turn off the lights at ten, and Drake's got to clean up the tea party while Penny collects her things for her room. I know it's weird to see Drake acting like this, but you should probably stop screaming at people."

She stiffened up and shook off his hand. "I'm going to bed." With that, she marched off leaving me alone with Zach and Drake. I stood hurriedly then grabbed the arm of the couch while the world spun again. Drake moved like he was going to grab me then held back while Zach put an arm around my shoulders.

"You got it?"

I nodded and carefully took his hand off my bare skin. Viney was right. Drake's shirt hung off me. Of course, Viney was the one who insisted I wear a t-shirt. Drake spun around and I heard the click of stacking dishes while I headed to my room.

Alone in my room, I stood in front of the floor length mirror holding Señor Mort's floral covered cage and staring at my reflection. My forehead was red, my shoulder was bare and Viney was right about the whole nipples thing. The knit fabric clung to absolutely everything, and my femininity was glaring. Weird.

I put the cage down and pulled off the knit clothing, throwing them violently to the ground before I rustled up my temptress robe and rose bustier. Fine, if knit clothes were too provocative, I'd stick to my grandmother's negligee and call it good. I folded up the clothes, burying my face in the shirt and inhaling deeply of black cherry before I picked up Señor Mort's cage and stalked into the common room.

"Drake, I'm putting your clothes on the couch. Zach, could you help me move my trunks into my room? I didn't see what kind of security system it had. Could I speak to the maintenance team that fixed my room?" Drake came out of my room and I nodded at him. "Will you help Zach get my trunks? Thanks so much."

I stood back, lifting my chin and not quite looking at his narrowing green eyes as he stood there, hands clenching and unclenching.

He leaned close as he passed me. "You can't think that you look less enticing in your practically sheer lace robe and that contraption. You must be trying to tease me into giving you a better offer. Fine. I'll wear Lederhosen without a shirt."

I gasped and shivered, but that wasn't from his arm brushing across my body, sending a flare of bewildering heat through me. I didn't say anything, just hung onto my cage and tried not to faint again.

22
WITCH

After everyone was gone, I sat cross-legged on my bed with my phone. I took a deep breath and pushed the call button.

"Penny."

"Revere."

Silence stretched on the line for a long time before I finally sighed and muttered, "I fainted."

"Details."

My upper lip curled. "After I watched a movie with two males and one female, I ate gingerbread and fainted."

"What movie?"

I shrugged even though he couldn't see me. "It was a horror movie."

"Cars?"

I scratched my chin. "A truck."

"Lots of blood?"

I took a deep breath. "Yes."

"Two mages and a witch?"

I wrinkled my nose. "You would say that."

There was silence on his side of the line for a long time while he contemplated the mysteries of the universe. "Any surprises?"

I hesitated. "Yes."

"Letting your guard down?"

"Probably." I scowled at the swing and the exquisite silk roses above the wooden carved seat.

"How do you feel now?"

"Hungry."

He sighed.

"I'm angry. Confused. Frustrated. Also a little bit..." The word was hopeful, that somehow these people were my friends for real. I knew it wasn't possible for that kind of thing, so much change so fast, but I hoped.

"Rosewood brats have ingenious ways of tormenting each other. It seems to me that your natural distrust for the mage was exacerbated during this intimate gathering. I advise you to keep physical distance from the opposite sex until you've secured a marriage."

"How am I supposed to do that, secure a marriage without getting close to anyone? It's not as easy as it sounds."

He inhaled long, loud, his sigh ringing with the exhaustion he always felt when dealing with me. "You clearly announce your intention to marry a peer, and select one of those who come forward."

"And if I don't like any of those who come forward?" If anyone did come forward.

"What does liking have to do with anything? You've romanticized marriage too much."

I threw myself back on my bed and sent it swinging back and forth. "Thank you so much for your help, Revere. What would I do without you?"

He made a rude sound that made me smile. "Your mother asks if you've killed anyone yet."

I scowled at the ceiling. "I'm pretty sure if I killed someone you would have heard about it."

He sniffed. "If you couldn't get away with murder, you'd better not do it."

I rolled my eyes and almost giggled. "That is so true. Thank you for this truly inspiring conversation."

He made another disapproving sound. "Your mother says that the fainting is most likely from..."

I waited. "What does she say?"

He cleared his throat. "Attraction."

"Attraction?"

"Not only attraction, mindless response to physical chemistry, otherwise known as love."

I clicked off the phone and dropped it from my limp fingers. Macaroons, bonbons, petit fours, ho-ho's, ding dongs, eclairs…

23
WITCH

The next day was great if you call Pas de Deux with Drake great. His hand seemed to drift towards the top of my leg, although his hand was supposed to be at the top of my leg, and right beneath my breast, and his hands on my body while I was concentrating on turnout and not kicking the girl behind me, and holding my arms in a beautiful curve instead of like frog legs, it was too much.

My conversation with Revere kept playing in my head. If I were going to murder someone, I should start with Drake. His eyes glinted green as his lips curved showing sharp teeth. My fingers knew his mouth far too well. My heart pounded from being so close to him, from his scent and the feel of his strong hands holding me steady.

He wasn't just the wolf who wanted to rip me to pieces, he'd hung my bed, made me gingerbread, and installed a top-notch security system with camera outside the room so if someone blasted off the door again, I'd know who did it. Every time he touched me I felt an electric current go through me that made the rest of the world disappear besides his touch, his scent, his wicked smile. I was falling for him after only one week.

After class, he grabbed my hand for a second. "You're getting better."

I gave him a sickly smile before I took off for Linguistics. I went to the Chinese corner and stayed there the entire time, listening for patterns in language, the best way to respond, and in general trying to get a grasp on the structure. Zach spoke to me a little bit, but I felt awkward about it after the night before. How was I supposed to be enticing him when Drake acted like that, making me a gingerbread house and asking me to a dance? Had Zach noticed me holding Drake's hand through the movie?

I still had no idea what Zach liked. He just treated everyone kind of normal, and people treated him a little bit like… To be honest, they kind of treated him with watchful respect. Of course, because he was such a brilliant linguist. After class, I followed him, watching him and while he didn't exactly interact with anyone, people gave him space and looked at him with that same kind of watchful respect. People threw their bubblegum in my hair, tripped me, called me a slut, a whore, and a lady of the night, which I really liked, while I spread love and cheer like a crazy person.

After lunch Zach was once more petting Henrietta's dark nose when I came in the stable. He smiled at me slightly while I beamed back.

"How is Miss Henrietta today?"

He handed me a sugar cube to feed her. "She's jealous that she didn't get invited to the party. I told her about Drake's hat."

I held out my hand and tried not to remember Drake, dressed in that insanely attractive black suit with the hat perched rakishly over his eyebrows. "It was a wonderful party. Thank you Zach. Is that why you weren't here yesterday, because you were helping maintenance with it?"

He shrugged. "I was keeping an eye on Drake. He can go overboard sometimes. He sourced all your rose themed stuff, sent back the things you ordered, and found a custom woodcarver to do the shelf. Maybe he has a secret fetish about interior decorating. His room is nothing like yours."

I licked my lips and glanced over at him. "What is his room like?"

He shrugged. "Black mostly, some silver and white but mostly black."

"Do you know how to stop the woodland sounds? I had really scary dreams last night and only Señor Mort kept me from climbing into bed with Professor Vale."

Zach smiled at me, and led me around to Henrietta's left side. He held the stirrup for me as I mounted. "Drake installed the sound system. You'll have to ask him. His room has an incredible sound system. If we watched a horror movie in there, it would be even scarier." His eyes lit up while he smiled at me.

I swallowed and held the reins in my hands lightly. "Happy thought. Zach?" I hesitated while I got up my nerve. "Last night you said that you've only liked one female. What was she like?"

He grinned at me while he led me out into the sun. "To tell the truth, I've liked a few girls, but I don't like to tell that to Viney. I don't want her to feel bad that she's not one of them."

"But why? She's cute and kind of funny, besides that she's really good at video games."

"Yeah, Viney's fine, but she's not my type."

"What is your type?"

His eyebrows lowered. "It's hard to describe. Maybe more confident and feminine while being strong yet warm?"

Like that helped. "Do you like Wit?"

He laughed. "It's hard not to like Wit, at least from a distance, but up close she's incredibly cold. Viney has a tough shell, but she's not that bad once you get to know her."

I exhaled in relief. If he wanted Wit it was over for me. "I like her."

His eyes widened. "You like Viney? She's the one you're trying to...?"

I shook my head too enthusiastically and Henrietta side-stepped, tugging on the bit warningly. "I like her as a friend. She's fun. I feel like she noticed my chest way more than either of you, though. Why doesn't she have a boyfriend?"

"Viney likes a guy. She's liked him for a long time, forever practically, but it's not mutual. What about this guy that you like? Are you just making him up to drive Drake crazy?"

I wrinkled my nose and tightened my knees too much on Henrietta's back. "I think that Drake made him up. I do kind of like someone, but I don't know him very well. It's hard to get to know people at this school. Everyone is so busy."

His face went kind of still before he smiled and nodded. "So, there is someone besides Drake? Good for you. Let me guess, someone you don't know very well, someone busy, could it be Barry even though he's already gotten your sister pregnant?"

I laughed before the laugh died as I thought of his smashed and swollen face, the crutches. "Linguistics isn't nearly as fun without him. Do you think he'll come back?"

He cocked his head before he shook it. "I talked to him about it. He's not the greatest linguist. He only took that class because the one he really wanted to take was full. The other class had an opening so he transferred."

I nodded slowly. "I guess that makes sense. What class is it? I'm not the greatest linguist either."

He pursed his lips. He had very nice lips. I blushed and glanced away. He put his hand on my knee, his touch warm and careful. He was good with skittish animals, calm, patient, so nice.

"Advanced chemistry. This school is full of eager chemists."

I nodded and held very still, half afraid he'd move his hand, half afraid that he wouldn't. He finally pulled his hand off my knee and I exhaled.

"What about your tutors?"

I stared at Zach. "My tutors?"

He smiled sweetly. "I think that Viney is trying to set you up with one or all of them."

I pursed my lips. "I've only met Lars so far. He's brilliant."

"Lars is. Does he like you?"

I shrugged. "He was nice."

He smiled. "The last girl Lars dated was Marilynn Schroeder. She's a really great dancer, singer, and does a lot of plays. Very vivacious and fun. You're a lot like that. You'd probably be a good match."

I nodded and tried not to frown. If Zach was so easy-going about me liking someone else, that probably meant that he didn't like me at all. "Good to know. Except if he liked that, why did he break up with her?"

He raised his eyebrows. "That, I don't know. Marilynn isn't the brightest girl so Lars might have gotten tired of her, you know, it can get irritating to try and have conversations with people who only understand life on a superficial level."

Ouch. That explained why Zach didn't like to talk to me that much. My stomach churned and I struggled not to kick Henrietta into a gallop and kill both of us on the nearest fence. I licked my lips and smiled brightly.

"That must be why you don't talk to people very often. Do you geniuses ever get lonely with all your deep and brilliant thoughts?"

He frowned. "I wasn't talking about…"

"It doesn't matter. Why did Drake ask me to the dance? Is it a prank?"

He cleared his throat. "No, I mean, maybe, but I don't think it's about you. I think that he's just doing it to irritate the other girls. That's what he usually does. He wasn't always like this. He used to be really quiet, kind of shy before he became captain of the Chemistry Club." He glanced up at me. "He told you that, right?"

I nodded and giggled adorably. "He did. Drake tells me so many things that completely confuse me. To me it makes sense that smart guys would be the same as science guys, but apparently, the brainy bunch are completely different from the Science club."

"Chemistry, not science."

I smiled brightly. "Either way, I'm so excited to go back to the study hall every day and interact with all those bright minds. Some of them might rub off on me."

He grabbed Henrietta's bridle and pulled me up short. He looked me in the eye, his blue eyes intent, serious, kind of scary. "You aren't stupid. Sometimes you're ignorant, but that isn't the same thing. I know that you pretend to be happy and cheerful when you'd rather burn something, but I like that. You make happiness seem possible."

I licked my lips and let my smile fade. "Is it?" I shook my head and smiled brightly. "Today I'm going to study with Orc. I can't wait to see what he's like."

He gave me a sudden fierce smile. "You're studying with Orc today? You'll like him."

I raised my eyebrows. "If you say so. What do you know about Oscar? I think Viney should date him. Wouldn't they be cute together?"

He cleared his throat. "Very cute. You're not going to study with Oscar? He's the perfect blend of chemistry and philosophy."

I shook my head. "Viney likes him. There's no way she'd stomp her boots so loud or slam her fists on the counter so emphatically. I couldn't possibly like someone Viney liked."

He spent a long time looking thoughtful while I rode around on Henrietta and managed to stay on her back.

In Business, Drake sat up near the front and I sat near the back, and then when I looked up from unpacking my books, he'd moved to sit beside me. I stared at him and he gave me a sharp smile while he gripped the edge of the desk with his hand. He had a ring on his middle finger, a gold band that slithered around like a snake or a dragon.

"I like your ring."

He raised his eyebrows. "Do you want it?"

I leaned my chin on my hand. "Desperately. Forget the fact that it wouldn't even fit me and that it would look ridiculous with all my outfits. Is that why you don't compliment my skirts, because that would mean you want to wear them?"

He smiled at me slowly while he glanced down at my legs. "It's not your skirt I admire." When he glanced back up to my face I looked away. He stayed staring at me for a long time.

"What do you want?" I asked finally staring at him back.

"You." He grinned widely while I squirmed. "I thought I should sit beside you in case you get scared during today's film and need someone to cling to."

I bit my lip. "Why are we watching a horror film in Business class?"

He leaned closer. "It's the horror of bankruptcy. Prepare to be terrified."

I shook my head and focused on my own desk, my own books, but he kept shifting beside me, his foot stretched out in the aisle between us, brown loafer scuffed and comfortable looking beneath the edge of his navy pants. I stopped staring at his shoe and forced myself to pay attention to the teacher and then the video, but he was so close, and I could smell him, black cherry and vanilla, but I wanted to smell more, wanted to press my face into his skin and inhale until I passed out in his arms.

When the lights came back on, I took a shaky breath and smoothed down my vest. It was wool and there didn't seem to be any show-through, but maybe Viney was right. I shook my head because I did not need thoughts like that in my head, not when I turned and could imagine Drake without a shirt. He should wear a bra. And five sweaters. What was with the double standard? Why was it okay for guys to have nipples but not girls?

I stood up and left the room, class over, but Drake fell in beside me as we walked down the broad marble hall.

"I'll see you at five-thirty tonight."

I spun around to stare at him. "What?"

"Community service. Did you forget?" His green eyes sparkled, mischief and something else in them.

"What? Community service? Drake?" Witley stared at the two of us like we'd just turned into dodo birds.

I edged closer to Drake, automatically ready to say something stupid.

He beat me to it. "Wit, you're invited if you'd like to come. It would be great for the whole community to be involved with our local hospital. It's always terribly understaffed, and cleaning up vomit isn't bad once you get used to it."

I beamed brightly while he nudged me with his elbow. "Oh, Wit, do you think you'd like to come with Jackson? I had such a great time last week, and the hospital even has a cafeteria so you can get dinner without having to go anywhere. They have these amazing mashed potatoes that are freeze dried and then reconstituted. Isn't that amazing?"

She gave Drake a large smile before she patted my shoulder with her strangely sensibly short nails. I kind of expected long and red, vampy like a real Telenovela star would have.

"You know how many girls would be throwing up in the halls of the hospital if they knew that Drake was the one cleaning it up? I'll do you the favor of keeping it quiet. Have fun, you two."

She edged out of sight and he raised his eyebrows at me. "I'll see you at five thirty for some community service and doubly amazing mashed potatoes. Don't argue. Just stand there and look pretty."

What? He was laughing as he turned away from me, his voice kind of low and reverberating through me in a completely ridiculous way. I rolled my eyes at myself and smiled brightly at the next girl I saw walking in the same direction I was going.

"Hi, I'm Penny Lane!"

In History, I sat down and unwrapped a lollipop. Viney sat beside me, pulling out her history book. She scowled at the teacher and then turned her scowl on me.

"Did you give Drake your answer?"

I stared at her. "What?"

She rolled her eyes. "Are you really that stupid? Sometimes you don't seem quite as stupid as usual, but then other times you're twice as stupid as seems humanly possible. The dance," she hissed, leaning close so no one else could hear.

"Oh, I..." I shook my head. "Didn't I answer him yesterday?"

She raised her eyebrows and crossed her arms over her chest. "If you are going to say no to him, you have to be a little more clear than fainting. He's not the kind of person who hears no very often. You should say no, just for all the pathetic girls who want him and can't have him."

"But they would say yes. I mean, if I'm going to represent the girls who like him, I would be excited about it and less nauseous."

She studied me thoughtfully. "You kind of like him, but he makes you nervous."

I shook my head. "Terrified. He's terrifying." I nodded my head as I stared at my desk. It wasn't like the car fear. It was something else, something even worse. I should have control over it, should be able to not want someone, but I couldn't help it. My whole body and mind rebelled against my mandate against falling in love with some guy who was going to ruin my life when that guy was tall, lean, red-haired Drake.

She sort of laughed, sort of snorted. "So, you don't want to go to the dance with him?"

I shook my head, still staring at the desk. "I can't."

"You are so weird. Do you know how completely crazy you are not to jump all over this? I get that he's completely overwhelming you, but you like him. I can tell."

I winced. If Viney could see that I liked him then so could Zach. "I'm not used to guys at all much less ones like Drake who made me a gingerbread house."

She exhaled. "I get that. He's freaking me out and I'm not the one he's flirting with. There are so few competent flirts in this world. Have you ever dated before?"

I shook my head. "Not unless you count pets."

She snorted again. "Pets do not count. We are going on a date."

I widened my eyes at her. "Really? You want to go on a date with me?"

She glared at me. "A double date. I will get the guys, and you will wear pants, and a bra, and have a normal date in town with people who aren't Drake or Zach. He's been acting weird lately, probably because of Drake. Are you sure you don't want to go with Drake to the dance? It might make things easier for you to be 'Drake Huntsman's girlfriend'. People might not put gum in your hair quite as often."

She wrinkled her nose and picked a chunk of pink gum out of my hair with her nails.

"I'd rather have the gum."

She yanked out a chunk of hair before she rolled the pink hairball up and threw it in the garbage across the classroom. She smirked at me. "I can't wait to see what Drake does after you let him down."

I rubbed my head and gave her a slight smile.

24
Witch

After that, Viney walked with me to the study hall, and her encounter with Oscar was just as fist-slamming, ordering-the-tall-guy-around as the day before. They would make a cute couple. Orc was five foot three inches and wore glasses with lenses the size of golf balls.

"Penny Lane, let's get started." His voice sent a shiver through me it was so low and deep and frankly delicious. I smiled at Viney as he led me away and then spent the next hour and a half on Chemistry even though I kept telling him I wanted to do languages. Apparently, he was really into Chemistry even if he wasn't in the Chemistry club.

I shook my head. "I'm actually struggling more with languages right now. I'm not exactly on the short list for the Chemistry club. I'm okay flunking it, actually."

He stared at me, his gray eyes getting kind of cold looking and hard. "Girls aren't allowed in the Chemiss Club."

"Ooookay. Good to know. Do you not know any languages?"

That set him off and he regaled me in Swedish for ten minutes. Swedish. Ten minutes of my life I could not get back. Bon-bons and truffles, although his voice was pretty amazing. After a few minutes, I leaned my head on my hand and just stared at him while he talked until finally, it was time to go.

I took my time because apparently I was going to do Community Service, take a ride in a car with Drake, and somehow make it stick that I did not want to go to a dance with him however many ginger-bread houses he made for me. The idea of going to a dance, of dancing with him like just standing and kind of moving to music without him having his hand on my thigh, holding me above his head while I tried not to flap my flamingo wings, well, it had some appeal. Of course it had appeal. The boy was absolutely delicious, his whole scent and body and voice and everything. That was the point. If he was just the voice or just the body or just the scent then maybe I could go with him and not end up killing myself or ruining my life over him.

I shook my head furiously and noticed a guy staring at me like I was crazy. "I am kind of crazy," I told him which made him back off. I sighed and kept walking until I got to the green Suburban where Drake wasn't. Were we going to meet in my room?

I took my phone out of my bag, but I didn't actually have his number in it. I didn't have anyone's at school. No numbers besides Revere and Poppy's. I hit her contact number and saw her face, a close-up of her eyes, all big and manga looking.

"There you are. Are you ready to go?"

I fumbled, clicking off the picture before I smiled up at Drake. "Yeah. Were we supposed to meet here? I couldn't remember and I don't have your number."

"What's yours?"

I shrugged. "I don't know."

He touched his phone to mine, there was a little beep and he grinned at me. "You do now. Or rather, I have yours, and I will call you..." He pressed a button and my phone beeped. I stared at my phone for a little while before I pushed the phone icon.

"Hello?"

He put his phone to his ear and I got to hear him in stereo. "Hello. This is Drake Huntsman, of the Huntsmans, what can I do for you?"

"Do you think it's weird that the phone icon looks nothing like phones look anymore?"

"I had not thought about that. How long are you going to stare at me and talk on your phone?"

I shrugged. "It's kind of fun."

"I hate talking on the phone."

I smiled at him. "Really? So, this bothers you?"

His eyebrow flickered and he leaned closer to me. "It's ridiculous. Only you could make something I hate so interesting." He hung up, tossed his phone in his bag and got in the Suburban. "Are you going to ride in the back?"

I shook my head and went around to the passenger's side, sliding my phone in my bag and getting in. I acted fine and calm while I adjusted my chair, pulling on my seatbelt, but when he held out his hand, I grabbed his arm, hanging onto it like we were watching a horror movie.

He smiled shaking his head as he shifted into gear and pulled out. He drove quickly, but much more smoothly, almost like he was trying not to freak me out or something.

"You grab onto me like you like me."

I pressed my lips together as he turned the steering wheel, following the curves of the road. The force sent me into the door and I clung to him tighter. "Drake, I do like you as a friend, but I'm not comfortable going to the dance with you. I don't like you like that." Bon-bons, truffles, peanut brittle. It would be clearer if I slammed his face against the steering wheel and leapt out of the car. That would give him the message much better than me clinging to him desperately.

"Mmm. All right, although I already ordered the costumes."

"Costumes?"

"You think I would joke about something like lederhosen? Never. Have you ever been to a dance? Have you ever kissed a guy? Held a hand because you liked someone, not because you were scared to death?"

I shook my head and swallowed down nausea. He was driving so fast. "No. I did like this guy once. He was Italian and really ugly, but he'd call me Caramia when he asked me to sign for packages."

"Sign for packages? You had a crush on the delivery guy?"

I nodded. "I used to wait on the porch roof to see the dust of his truck on the road. I'd give him a glass of whiskey and he'd tell me a story about goblins or ghosts. And he winked at me."

"How long did that last?"

I shrugged. "A different delivery guy started coming, a woman who couldn't get my name right. Penny Lane isn't exactly hard to pronounce and she wasn't from a different country, so what was her excuse?"

"So you like to sit around drinking whiskey and telling stories with Italian delivery guys. Good to know."

"And what about you? Who was your first crush?"

He wrinkled his forehead. "Marta. She was the housekeeper's daughter. She wasn't supposed to come to the house. Sometimes when my dad was away on long trips, Heloise would bring her and we'd get into trouble. We colored an entire wall with permanent markers one day when we were old enough to know better. She didn't come after that and neither did Heloise."

I gripped the seat while this weird feeling descended on my intestines. I swallowed down the double nausea. "Do you remember her last name?"

He gave me a suspicious glance. "Why?"

I squeezed his hand tighter. I should let him drive with both hands, but I couldn't. "That's so romantic! You can be like prince charming, only you'll need to use a different car because this isn't a prince charming car, and you can swoop her off her feet and carry her to a castle far, far away from her dreary life sweeping floors! Let's find her and…"

"No." He pulled his hand out of my grip, holding his palm in front of my face before I recaptured it.

"You can say, 'Marta, it's been too long but you still have the eyes of the girl I first loved! And she can say, 'I never thought you noticed me, but I always loved you from afar.'"

"She told me she hated me and kicked my shins until I agreed to color the walls with her."

"And then you can sweep her into your arms and gaze into her eyes. 'Oh, Marta, you are the stars twinkling in the sky and the rose petals strewn across my bed,' and then she'll say…"

"Rose petals strewn across my bed? You mean like chopping her up and spreading her around on my blankets? Like that?"

I ignored his interruption. "She'll say, 'Antonio, you light my way through the darkness. Let us be one tonight!'"

"Who is Antonio?"

"And then you'll clasp her to your breast. 'Martina you are my flower, but there was an accident in Guatemala and I am only half a man. You must be gentle with me.' And then she'll say…"

"What do you mean I'm only half a man? You'd better be talking about Antonio."

By that time we were swinging into the hospital parking lot and I managed not to bolt out of the car before he braked. I let go of his hand and shot out of the door, slamming it behind me and leaning against it while my heart pounded. I slid down until I wrapped my arms around my bare knees. I should have changed, but I didn't have a lot of clothes. Yeah, I should think about what I was going to sew. I should order some cute pink and floral fabric along with more shoes and forget about the churning in my stomach.

Drake leaned against the car beside me. "Aren't you going to have a lollipop?"

I took a deep trembling breath. "You put something weird in them. I should be home making lollipops. Viney wants tiramisu."

"Are you taking orders? I haven't actually had anything like tiramisu or mulled cider, just the weird ones you eat for anxiety. Are you saying that you don't like my lollipops?"

I turned my head to look up at him. I stood slowly until I could look in his eyes. "For your first batch of lollipops, it's incredible. It's typical that you're so disgustingly talented. Gingerbread houses, lollipops, laundry, even ballet, there really isn't anything you can't do."

"I can't sew."

I smiled at him. "You'll have to work on that. Are you going to stand here all night or are we going to go clean up vomit?"

After we spent our time in the hospital, I rode in the backseat to the Chinese place, eating in separate booths again, and then going back to get a malt and drive home.

I sat behind him, spooning cookie-dough malt into my face and staring at the back of Drake's head and his ear.

"We need to learn sign language." His voice was low, kind of growly.

"You don't know something besides Sewing? Stop, Drake. You're really bending my whole conception of reality."

"Don't you think the waiter gave us weird looks when we went in together and sat at different booths again?"

"Not at all. When you tried to pay, did the guy tell you that your woman paid for it? That was the highlight of last week's trip, 'your man paid'."

He grunted. "If I was your man I wouldn't sit in a separate booth. At opposite ends of the restaurant. Don't you think that you should sit in front and cling to me, you know, for the sake of exposure to fears so that you can overcome them?"

I almost put my hand on his shoulder just for a second before I pulled back and ate another bite of malted, concentrating on the deliciousness, but unfortunately that was the flavor that Drake had licked off me. I put the spoon in the cup and put it in the cup holder in the door. I took a deep breath and took my headphones out of my bag. I put them on and listened to Chinese. Drake glanced back at me frowning while I gave him a mild smile.

I didn't want to think about holding onto his hand, or gingerbread houses, or knit shirts and tea parties.

When we pulled up at school, Drake got out quickly, opening the back door and grabbing my bag so I had to move fast since I was connected via headphones.

He pulled off my headphones put them on his head and then scowled at me before he shook his head.

"Really? This is what you listen to?"

I sighed. "I know, Spanish dramas are so much better, but the teacher isn't impressed with my conversational skills if I'm not talking about something boring, so..."

He pulled out the device and flipped through it, pushing little buttons on it until he seemed satisfied, listening until he took off the headphones and put them on my head. I smiled when a man and woman started screaming at each other in Chinese about...

"She caught him cheating on her with her cousin. The wedding is next week and she already sent out invitations. Come on, Penny, I'll walk you to your room while you immerse yourself in something you can appreciate."

The next morning, I got out of bed and felt kind of bouncy without any lollipops, without anything besides the headphones I'd fallen asleep to, racy, scenes in Chinese that I had no idea where Drake found. I wore the headphones through the halls, listening while people bumped me, knocked me, pulled my hair. In English, I took them off at the door, tucking them in my bag as I went to my seat.

"Penny, how was the hospital?"

I smiled at Witley and her ravishing hair. "It's always really satisfying to serve the community. How was your evening?"

"Well, I did shots with a few friends and watched some movies. You should come party some time when you're not off doing good."

I sighed sadly. "I'm afraid I'm always off doing good."

She smiled widely, her perfect teeth straight beneath her lush lips. "You're an inspiration, Penny Lane. I imagine you're so busy doing good to Drake. Lucky boy."

I inhaled and licked my lips. "Some would say I'm the one who's lucky."

Her lips twisted in a parody of a smile. "I always wanted a lucky Penny. Have fun with Drake, but be careful. The boy has sharp teeth."

I opened my mouth to say something about how I liked his teeth and instead turned and marched to my seat against the wall. Talking to that girl got me into trouble. I didn't want bon-bons, I wanted fireballs, the kind that would leave an ashy green residue on her perfect skin. What compounds would it take to create something with the perfect balance between flame and ash?

I hadn't thought about that kind of hurter for a long time, not since Poppy...

I shook my head and concentrated on my English but at the same time, I was thinking about ratios of Phosphorous to Magnesium.

In linguistics I got to see Zach's shock when I confronted him in Chinese about impregnating my grandmother and demanded five hundred tulips for repayment. His answer was a little too complicated for me, something about how he'd thought it was me in the dark and he would marry me if I would raise the child as my own and start a flower business together, named after dear grandma. The girl who was pouring tea had a scandalized expression on her face through our conversation, but I thought it went well.

"Miss Lane, your accent has improved," was all the instructor, Miz had to say.

The day progressed without anything out of the ordinary happening, and in Business, Drake sat beside me when he came in class and even though he spent the whole time on his computer, he looked at me and raised an eyebrow once which made my stomach do the butterfly thing and me want to kick myself for staring at him so blatantly.

In History, I sat by Viney and turned to her immediately. "Let's go shopping on Saturday. I need help. I've never really worn a bra before. And jeans. Is it hard to buy jeans?"

She rolled her eyes before she leaned her chin on her fist. "Jeans are the worst. Actually bras are terrible too. Fine. We'll go because if you order something it will turn out wrong and then our date will be completely messed up. I have a few guys selected, upperclassmen that seemed vaguely interesting. We'll go play pool and eat. Low pressure kind of thing for your first date."

"I don't swim."

She rolled her eyes and patted my head like I was an idiot. At least she didn't yank out some more of my hair. "Not that kind of pool. Billiards, cue, eight ball, are those familiar terms in your bizarre vocabulary?"

"Aaaaah. We're going to shoot some pool? I've never done that before. Do you think there will be a bar fight?"

"Only if Drake is there."

"We should bring him, then. I've never been to a bar fight."

She snorted. "You can go bar fighting with Drake some other time. This is a date. No bar fights on dates."

"Page forty-seven," Professor Vale said, her eyes shooting daggers at the two of us. Viney glared back at her but I gave her a meek smile and opened my book.

25

MAGE

I was in business class with Penny when I got the email. I opened it, scanned the contents and quickly closed it. She didn't notice anything. She was frowning at the book we were reading for class, marking up the text with a pink marker.

What was she thinking about? She never said what she actually thought, keeping everything close to her like I would steal her thoughts and leave her empty. Could I do that? Probably, but that wouldn't leave room in my head for my own. Not that my thoughts were very interesting lately. I kept going round and round with the room thing.

Everything pointed to the obvious conclusion, Jackson destroying Penny's room, but it made no sense. Rather, it made all the sense and Jackson wasn't that rational. For him to plan to break into Penny's room, there had to be something he wanted. Her trunks were impervious to violence and force, so heavily spelled that no one without her family's blood could open them. I'd seen inside two of them, and there hadn't been anything noticeably precious other than hat making supplies and elaborate tea party costumes. The tapestries were priceless, several mangled beyond even my ability to repair them. That made me angry. Also confused. Jackson would know their value and steal them, not destroy them.

He knew that I wouldn't allow him to touch Penny Lane. Neither of us knew why, but my reaction in the cafeteria when he'd grabbed her hand made it pretty clear to both of us. If he hadn't gotten Wit, he would be in traction for a very long time. Jackson didn't like traction.

Why would he risk that?

I shook my head and smiled at Penny before leaving her behind and heading towards the stables. This assignment would be good for me, help clear my head, or fill it with noxious fumes. I grinned as I donned my leather riding outfit and heavy cloak then stepped from this world into Darkside.

After I took care of business in the military camp at the base of the mountain, I took one step back into Dayside then returned to the ash filled air of the mountain city above the camp. I stepped out from the dark alley and walked down the narrow street that tilted so I walked like a drunken man. Darksiders sulked around me, heavy cloaks covering their heads and large shoulders. It was a witch city, but with the war going on, there was heavy traffic of all kinds.

I raised my head to look at the fortress carved into the protruding rock above the city. That's where he'd be. I didn't have any business in that fortress, but when I'd stumbled on his location, I couldn't pass up the occasion for a good chat.

I walked up the streets closer and closer to the fortress until I found a wizard's square. In other words, gold was embedded in the stone, patterns of stars within stars, twined together, framed by five gnarled trees at each point between streets. I stepped into the exact center of those stars and cast a spell. My body flared green, star shapes coming to life over my skin in a neon flash before I vanished and reappeared inside a room.

I took two steps in the dim light, barely lit from glowing coals in the hearth, tripped over a body, and caught myself on the edge of a table.

"Light, please."

At my words, candles flashed bright all around then dimmed as they began burning according to nature, at least nature in Darkside. Instead of gray stone, it was a charming collection of gold and burgundy veneer with heavy drapes and thick rugs behind the scroll-footed chesterfield couch. On every flat surface, graceful glass bottles rested with large glasses. I didn't need to see the bottles. I could smell a drunken spree as well as anyone.

I ignored the body and went to the table, picked up a bottle of cobalt blue and maroon with swirls of gold, uncapped it then poured the contents into a glass, bubbles spinning around like a little whirlpool as I recapped the lid and carried the glass to the couch.

I sat down, leaned back, sniffed the contents then shook my head. "Music."

It took some concentration, but soon the trumpets of a big band filled the room, followed by a crooning voice that soothed even more than the burnished gold in my glass.

I took a sip and winced. Ian certainly liked to brew his elixirs strong. Speaking of Ian, he stirred, raising up two inches and turning his head, face covered in long, golden, filthy strands of hair.

"Nice boots."

"They're yours if you want them. I don't remember if my feet are larger than yours."

"They were the same size last time I checked."

I undid my laces and kicked them off revealing my socks in the Rosewood argyle pattern. Green and Gold.

Ian sat up, leaning one arm on a knee and squinted at me. "Dim." The candles all responded to his command, leaving us in shadowy darkness. "What is this? Frank Sinatra?" His voice was raspy.

"Sammy Davis Jr. Don't tell me you drink in silence. It's not healthy. How are you supposed to drown out the demons without music?"

He snorted and grabbed the glass out of my hand. He threw it back, gasped and choked. His eyes watered while he stared at me, face turning an interesting shade of purple while I tapped my fingers on the arm of the couch, raising the light level to somewhere between bright and dim.

"What was that poison," he gasped.

I'd changed the liquid while he complimented my boots. He would never mention something personal if he wasn't in desperate need of sobriety. "Jasper makes it for me. I believe he calls it natural consequences, but there's not very much nature in it."

He breathed shallowly, in and out, before he sprang to his feet and dashed to the closet where he kept the plumbing. He threw up for a long time, getting the alcohol out of his system. Good. He might be coherent in a few minutes.

While I waited for him, I went to the table and poured myself another glass of golden death. When Ian came out, his hair was damp, his face washed along with his hands. His clothing was still stained and frankly revolting. He'd been having a very good time.

"How did you find me?"

I raised an eyebrow as I leaned back, enjoying the crackling fire in the hearth mixed with the music. "I had to release someone."

"That explains the blood."

I frowned then followed his glance down to the glass where I'd left faintly pink fingerprints. I put down the glass and pulled out a handkerchief, the one with a rose embroidered in the corner. I hesitated before I wiped my fingers on the white fabric.

"You still have some of those left?" Ian smiled slightly as he went to a large carafe and poured himself some water. He leaned on the edge of the sturdy table, sipping and watching me over the rim.

I smirked at him. He looked like a Darksider but he remembered the hours we'd spent in detention embroidering handkerchiefs. "Yes. I have three remaining, two. One isn't currently in my possession."

He raised an eyebrow. "But you intend to retrieve it?"

I shrugged. "Eventually. How are things?"

He laughed, a short bark that made me a little more wary than I already was. I sank deeper into the couch and crossed my legs.

"Are you here to interfere?"

I smiled at him, showing my teeth. "I told you why I'm here."

He raised an eyebrow. "Really? You just dropped by for a chat?"

I nodded. "Yes, actually. I thought I'd invite you back. We're having Blackheart for midfest tourney and we could use you, but probably not in your current condition."

He growled at me. I smiled back until he turned and gripped the table with his fingers. Finally, he gulped down an enormous container of water. He slammed it down on the table and I tossed him an apple. He caught it, rolled it around in his hands before he gave me a flat glare and took a large bite out of it.

I exhaled while he chewed. I'd been patient with Ian for a long time. I was getting bored. He strode to the fire and stirred it with the poker before turning towards me. He'd put the poker down, also boring.

"What did you release him for?"

I shrugged. "It was time. One hundred and thirty-eight years of service is a long while, even for Huntsman inc, to keep a Darksider sane. He turned on his companions, took out an even dozen before he was neutralized."

"A rager?"

I nodded.

"Did you personally 'release' him?"

I smiled, showing my teeth. "I did."

I could still smell the reeking Darksider, the blood, sweat and death that clung to him like an already rotting corpse. Two enormous men held him up between them, the soldier's eyes empty of reason, humanity, oozing blood and something else, puss probably.

"Is Jasper here with you?" Ian's voice was careful, eyes wary.

I smiled. "No one is here with me."

"You ended a Rager without any assistance? Do you have any injuries?"

I sighed. It had been far too long since I'd seen Ian. He was acting like he didn't know me at all.

I took a long, slow sip of the golden liquid in the cup while I closed my eyes, reliving my most recent release.

I'd pulled out the printout from inside my shirt, ran my fingers around the edges of the still mostly white paper with a name and number on it.

"Horace Bellbody?"

The creature between the two men stared at me, oozing. I could hear his breath, rattling through him like an old air conditioner.

"I release you from the service of Huntsman incorporated. Thank you for your noble service." I ripped the paper in half down the middle, a fast tear that went through the creature like I'd just ripped him.

He threw his head back and screamed, throwing off the two men like they were bowling pins and rushed me, breaking through the chains like paper. Sparks filled my vision before he struck me, magic filling the air and my throat with a pungent aroma of jasmine.

With one half of the torn paper, I decapitated him using the side with his name printed in neat black letters, well, now smeared red. The other side of the paper I expanded into an explosion of white confetti attached to strands of green, shielding me from the furious magic before I folded it out and over the specks of wild magic until it was contained in one neat package. I'd always been good with origami.

Ian cleared his throat and I opened my eyes. He still stood at the table, frowning from beneath his stringy hair.

"I love what you've done with your hair. It reminds me of Lester. He's left the Chemiss to join the Philosophia."

Ian gave me a tiny nod.

"I don't remember you being such a good listener. If you continue with your charming silence I'll be forced to regale you with tales of Rosewood."

He cocked his head and he smiled slightly before he took a deep, even breath of the noxious Darkside air. "It's the pull. It's unbearable when I'm conscious. She doesn't want me in Darkside."

I winced and curled my lips. "Ah, the divine Witley misses her golden dragon."

"Golden Goose."

I shook my head. "She would never kill you. She's far too practical for that."

He scowled at me then laughed and dropped down on the couch beside me, a boneless flop that left him staring at the ceiling. "True enough. How did you find me?"

"I heard that my mercenaries are fighting a war over a pretty dragonlord. I have to thank you for the business. I expected you to be wrapped in the arms of a witch."

He closed his eyes. "She's leading the charge against Helystia. I haven't seen a witch for days. I think that they've forgotten all about me."

"Poor Ian, nothing to do but drink by yourself. I'm so glad I dropped by. I love being useful."

He opened his eyes and stared at me, his head still lolled back before his nostrils flared and he sniffed, deeply.

"What flavor of witch are you wearing? She's lovely."

I growled before I remembered that I was supposed to be a human or something. "Nothing. That is, there are so many females how can I know which scent you're catching?"

He raised a golden eyebrow, the most seductive look in his repertoire. I should feel flattered that he was using it on me, but he wasn't. He was aiming it at the female he'd caught scent of. Ian was like that, couldn't help it. "Sugar and blood. Semi-sweet chocolate, no, chocolate is all wrong. Sweet and fluffy, candy canes? No, not peppermint."

I threw myself off the couch and away from him, taking my place at the table where he'd been not long before. "It's lollipops not candy canes, and strawberries, not chocolate. Also, she's mine and I will kill you if you touch her."

His eyes flickered gold at that challenge but he only raised his eyebrows for a moment before smirking. "You've fallen for a witch? The mighty Drake Huntsman who swore that he would never be a pathetic slave like his friends has finally tasted the poison of love?"

I gripped the edge of the table and scowled at my boots where they were strewn over the floor. "I wouldn't call it love."

He laughed a wild delightful sound that was like golden bells. He'd definitely been in Darkside too long if he sounded like that. "She has your handkerchief. Which one?"

I scowled at him before I went to the fireplace and jabbed it a few times with the poker. Flames roared from my energy more than the poker, swirling orange and gold mixing with green flames and sparks.

"It's not like that. I am protecting her from the other witches. It's my hatred for them which brings us together, not my attraction towards her."

"But there is attraction? No, she's probably hideously ugly, cruel, a true beast."

"Strawberry golden curls past her waist, legs like a sylph, hands…" I snarled at him. I'd actually fallen for his baiting like a completely instinct-controlled imbecile.

He laughed again and leaned forward over his knees, eyes bright and burning. "Do you want me to kill her for you? She doesn't possess you yet, does she?"

I swallowed and held very still. Was this why I'd come to Ian, to help me escape my growing fascination for Penny Lane? "No. Never."

"Never possess you, or never kill her?"

I poured myself a drink with shaking hands. I should say both. I had to say both, but the idea of owned by Penny Lane had been slithering around the back of my mind ever since I'd threatened to bind myself to her. There were distinct advantages to it. She could challenge Witley, I could fight for her, and then we could free Ian. Would she ever agree to that? She hated Wit, instinctively and at first sight.

Wit had tried to be charming, friendly, but Penny barely kept from snarling at every encounter. If Penny saw Ian as a poor wounded animal that she had to nurse back to health... I scowled at Ian. His reputation was even worse than mine, which was saying something. It wasn't only his reputation. He tried to seduce every virgin he'd ever met. It wasn't his fault, not entirely but that didn't change the reality. If he seduced Penny, I would break him.

"No one is going to hurt Penny."

He curled his lips in a delighted smile. "I'll drink to that. I'm so glad you stopped by."

26
WITCH

Saturday came quickly. My life was a blur of studying, mixing potions, making lollipops and going to classes.

I got up, dressed in my cute freshly sewn pink blouse with little heart cut-outs beneath the neckband. The floral skirt was a little bit longer than usual, because I was hanging out with Viney, not Zach whose love key I still hadn't cracked.

When I came out, Viney was sitting at a table, slumped over looking haggard, even her glare at me lackluster. She sipped from her steaming cup of coffee.

"You look great, but a little bit tired. Oh, you must have been up all night with the sorority club. What was it called, Famiss?"

"Makiss. Who told you about that?" She snarled at me and had a bit more energy as I plopped down beside her.

"Zach. Last Friday you were howling like wolves. I thought we were under attack."

"She almost went out to see, wearing her stunning lace robe."

Zach smiled at me, his eyes twinkling a little bit as he sat down with his own cup of coffee. I fiddled with my skirt hem. Coffee was not food and that much caffeine on an empty stomach would turn me into a homicidal weasel.

"I'll go get some breakfast and be right back."

"I brought food, enough even for you, hungry girl." Drake's voice wafted around me almost as delicious as the scent of bacon.

I inhaled deeply, clasping my hands to my heart. "Drake, I nominate you for a promotion."

"What's his current position?" Zach looked up at me from his cup of coffee.

"By the door." I patted the chair beside me. "How did you know that I was craving bacon?"

Drake grinned at me, his green eyes glimmering beneath the fall of his auburn hair that looked genuinely mussed and not very stylish. "It's my job to know and give you everything you crave."

My stomach tightened and those butterflies fluttered around but maybe that was just because I was starving. I resisted the urge to grab his arm and pull him down as he laid out breakfast from the bags he carried.

"Are you trying to be slow?"

He turned his head and his mouth was inches from mine. "It's also my job to drive you crazy before I give you satisfaction."

I sighed breathily, leaning even closer to him until I was dizzy with his black cherry scent. "If only I wasn't crazy already. Oh, that reminds me!"

I got up and went to my room, flipping my skirt kind of ridiculously in hopes that someone was looking at my legs. Besides Viney. I came back with a bag I'd sewn a russet weasel to the front of and held it out for Drake.

He was sitting at the table at that point and took it with a puzzled glance. "What is this?"

I handed a bag to Viney, black with skulls, and Zach, an applique of his favorite video game bad guy.

"I made lollipops. I know it's not much, but it's my thank you for all your help with my room. The red ones are raspberry, the dark brown tiramisu, light brown mulled cider, and the dark purple ones are…" I gave Drake a sidelong glance before I beamed at Zach and Viney. "Anyway, that's what's in the bags."

They all looked in the bags and Viney immediately unwrapped one of the dozen of tiramisu ones and popped it in her mouth. She sucked on it and drank her coffee at the same time. The girl was going to have a heart attack.

Drake pulled me down on my chair. "Enough, lollipop girl. Eat before your eggs get cold."

I beamed at him. "You sound like a grumpy grandpa. Drake, you would be such a cute grumpy grandpa. I hope that you have fifty grandkids and they all have your red hair and green eyes." I focused on eating and didn't notice everyone staring at me for a long time. I shook my head and gave Drake a pointed look. "See, so uncomfortable when people stare at me while I eat."

Zach laughed. "I think we're staring at you because you just offered to give Drake ten children."

I cocked my head while I analyzed my last sentence. "I did not."

"Who else has the right genetics to give Drake red-headed kids? Your hair is light red."

I felt suddenly sick. I gripped the edge of the table and stared at the half-eaten muffin crumbling across my plate.

"Zach, you're such an idiot. You're going to make her faint again. You know that Drake freaks her out. She can't even go to a dance with him without losing it."

I smiled at Viney. "It's fine. I just ate too quickly or Drake poisoned the food, or the thought of having ten kids kind of…"

Drake put a hand on my shoulder, gripping it tightly. "I don't want any kids. My parents sucked and I'll probably be even worse than they were. If you have ten kids, it won't be with me."

I nodded, but I'd lost my appetite.

After that, I left Lilac Stories with Viney and climbed into the back of a limo to go shopping. Wow. Bon-bons and truffles, ding-dongs and ho-hos. Not that I'd ever had ding dongs or ho-ho's. I tried on a hundred pairs of jeans to find two that were perfect, both of them so close in style I couldn't tell the difference. Bras were worse.

Viney sat outside the changing room and had me model various bras like a general, ordering me to turn and bend over and jump up and down. I ended up with a dozen bras, one of which she insisted I wear right away, but it made my clothes fit wrong. It kind of pushed everything out and up and who knew I had anything to push out and up.

The bra lady measured me, not like that wasn't ridiculously awkward. I sucked on a dirt-flavored lollipop desperately while the stranger wrapped her measuring tape around my chest and said how lucky I was not to have to get a serious jogging bra.

Viney kept eating Tiramisu lollipops. She was going through those at a crazy speed. It made me smile to see her walking around with her black skull bag that I'd made for her. When she dragged me into the salon, I kind of freaked out because I was not chopping off all my hair however loud Viney got.

I agreed to one inch off the bottom, and then they straightened my hair, not permanently, but it still took forty-five minutes while Viney sucked on lollies and read magazines. I listened to my Chinese while the poor woman given the task to tame my mane struggled with the beast.

By the time we climbed into the back of the limo that would take us to school, I looked a lot more like the other mall shoppers than when I'd gone in. We only had a few hours before the guys Viney was setting us up with arrived to take us to Fairfield and the cool hang-out I'd never been to.

Back at Lilac Stories, Zach and Drake were sitting on the couch playing guitars.

"Aren't you losers doing anything today?" Viney walked past them with her shopping bags while I inhaled deeply and my pushed up breasts shoved against my blouse. No breathing.

"What happened to your hair?" Zach stared at me while Drake kept strumming, keeping his attention on his fingers while they plucked strings. He was incredibly good. Zach had not taught him to play that quickly.

"Do you like it?" I swished my hair and it actually swished across my arms, not just poufing out like normal.

He stared at me for a little while before he nudged Drake. Drake glanced up at me, his green gaze catching mine like a tractor beam.

"It's nice. I personally prefer tangled with leaves, but I have eclectic tastes. Black cherry?"

He stuck his tongue out and I saw the color stained on it. Apparently he'd eaten a few of those. I bit my lower lip and edged away from him. "It's not quite right. I think it needs a little bit of blood or something. Anyway, I've got to get changed."

I hurried to my room and flung myself on my bed, sending it rocking while my head spun and I unwrapped a black cherry lollipop. I closed my eyes and enjoyed being alone until Viney pounded on my door.

"Put on the uncomfortable bra and jeans. And one of the t-shirts. Don't forget your heels."

Like I wasn't tall enough. "Bon-bons and eclairs," I muttered as I rolled off my bed. I changed quickly, pausing in front of the full-length mirror to check out the new and improved me. My hair swished, really, really long without any curl, almost to my knees like it had been coated in pitch. Maybe I should chop it all off. Poppy and I had sworn that we'd never cut our hair. I shook my head and put on another coat of pink lipstick and dark brown mascara before I grabbed my new denim jacket and walked out of my room.

Viney scowled at me. "You took long enough, but at least you look normal. Doesn't she?" She turned to glare at Zach and Drake.

Drake still sat on the couch plucking strings faster and faster, his fingers mesmerizing before he looked up and flashed me a smile that froze as he really looked at me in my skin tight jeans, and perfect t-shirt that showed off how my breasts were now unnaturally round and stick outty. The t-shirt had a character from Zach's favorite video game. Was he paying attention? I turned around and beamed at him.

"I am not going to tell you how many pairs of pants Viney made me try on. She has more stamina than I imagined possible."

Viney snorted. "You're the one who kept me hopped up on lollipops. That reminds me, I need more. Zach, say something positive. Hard to believe, but Penny is nervous about wearing pants."

Zach blinked and nodded before giving me a slight smile. "Your jeans are nice. Your legs look nice, too."

Drake slugged his shoulder. "Not nice, Zach, edible, tantalizing, exquisite, desirable, sensual…"

Zach's linguist brain kicked in. "Libidinous, alluring, provocative, arousing, tempting, titillating…"

I giggled a little bit. The jeans were working! "Thanks, Zach."

"You look practically normal," Drake said, giving me a wink before focusing back on the strings.

Something about the way he said that made me feel kind of stupid. Viney was shooting for normal, but he was saying even with a complete makeover, I still didn't make the cut. "Thanks. I guess I'll see you guys later."

"Call if there's a problem." Drake didn't look up, but his lips tightened.

I nodded, staring at him, his hair falling over his face while he stared at the strings. He'd brought me breakfast. Maybe I should have picked up something for him at the mall. Probably not a bra. Viney grabbed my arm and we were off.

A silver car waited in front of the pillars at the bottom of the steps, and two guys stood looking drop dead everything. They both smiled at Viney and kind of knocked over themselves opening the front and back door like she needed options. She nodded at them and slid into the backseat. I bumped past the black-haired guy, sliding in beside her instead of ending up in front. Not a chance.

Viney gave me a weird look and I smiled back at her. "This is going to be so fun."

"That's right. We're so excited that you called, Vineldra." The black-haired guy spoke in a well-modulated voice that could have oiled a car.

"And that you brought your friend." The blonde one looked at me with a gorgeous smile that didn't touch his eyes, and that was the last time anyone looked or talked to me for the rest of the night.

The two jumped over themselves to open doors for Viney, or Vineldra, complimented her, made interesting conversation about fascinating topics that were sure to interest her but didn't, and in short, dated her while I got to go along for the ride. I couldn't really complain because it was seriously amusing to watch Viney's suitors vie for her reluctant hand.

27
WITCH

We were in booths, the guy across from me trying to subtly put his arm behind Viney, and the guy next to me leaning across the table, gazing into her eyes, or at least he would be if she bothered looking away from her phone.

I ate, but then they were talking and talking, and I said that I was going to the restroom, and Viney glanced up and nodded, but the two guys didn't seem to hear me, so I went, and as I came out for some reason I wasn't drawn compulsively back to my fabulous date. I didn't even know which guy was supposed to be my date. I was wearing jeans, and that meant I should play pool or basketball or something. In my heels? Whatever.

I wandered over to the pool table, stood back and watched them play. There were more guys than girls, and the girls were kind of cool messy hair, jeans and t-shirt girls who teased the guys, leaning provocatively over the pool table.

I had a favorite girl, a red-head in black boots who flirted and sassed. I clapped along with everyone else when she made a spectacular shot.

"Do you want to play?"

I glanced over at the guy who had come to stand next to me, a bottle of golden liquor in his fist. His eyes were brown with golden flecks like his bottle, his hair very short which showed the sculpted perfection of his head. He was so pretty. His lips weren't too big, but perfectly balanced beneath his straight nose. He was taller than me even though he slouched in his t-shirt and jeans.

I smiled at him and shrugged, focusing back on the players. I was aware that he was watching me, not looking at me like a weird thing but like guys looked at Witley.

He cleared his throat. "I like your t-shirt. Do you play that game? Stupid question. Do you come here often?"

I glanced over and raised my eyebrow. "Are you flirting with me?"

He smiled slightly. "I am. Badly. You make me nervous." He gave me a half shy, half teasing smile.

I really wished for a lollipop, but it didn't really go with the jeans and t-shirt thing. I settled for smiling down at my hands and wishing I had a bottle in them to hold, or a hand, a Drake shaped hand. This guy was really nice looking, no better than nice, much better.

"Come on." He handed me a pool cue and turned to an empty table, taking off the black triangle around the balls.

I held the cue awkwardly, as I slowly eased closer to him. I really did want to play. I wanted to be that cool girl who knew how to make other people laugh. "I've never played before."

He glanced at me with a raised eyebrow and I licked my lips because something about the way he looked at me reminded me of black cherry. I wanted to smell black cherry not his scent, something sandalwood and citrus.

He moved slowly over to me, put his bottle on the edge of the table and rested his hand on the cue above mine. "You hold your hands like this. Can I show you?"

I nodded and expected him to demonstrate with his cue, not to step behind me and put his arms on either side of me, his hands on my hands and his chest against my back. I swallowed down my innate urge to slam my elbow back into his body when he leaned forward, bending me over the table with the slightest pressure.

"You slide it through your fingers like this, then strike through your shoulder, like so." His voice was low, silk, and his scent more sandalwood than citrus as he shoved the cue forward and it hit the white ball, sending it into the triangle of balls which shot out in every direction with a resounding crack.

He stepped away from me, giving me a toothy smile before he took a long drink revealing the perfect column of his throat above his t-shirt, the movement showing the sculpted muscles of his chest beneath the fabric. I blinked away from him, tightening my grip on the stick before I bent over and hit a ball, knocking it a few inches, not the satisfying thud that this guy had done.

"Your turn." Did I sound flirty and cool or homicidal and terrified?

I forced a smile at him and he half smiled before he turned to the table and did a shot that knocked three balls into holes. Pockets. Or was that a billiards term? His arm had a muscle on the back center that flexed as he made the perfect shot. What would Drake's arms look like if he was the one leaning over the pool table, the wooden shaft in his capable hands?

My mouth watered as I bent over and focused on making my fingers slidable before I pushed the cue and hit a ball, sending it flying off the table with way too much velocity. The guy moved fast, reaching out to snag the ball before it could hit the cool redhead. He held the ball and studied me, his eyes strangely emotionless.

I swallowed held the pool cue like a weapon. "Sorry. Am I disqualified?"

He glanced down at my fingers, like he could tell exactly what they were doing. "Excellent trajectory, but I think you're breaking a few rules. You're supposed to keep the balls on the table."

"Oops. Nice catch."

He smiled slowly as he took one step towards me, then another. He put the ball in my hand, pressing my fingers around the sphere. "This is just a warm-up. Do you want a drink? What do you like?"

"Whiskey." Why did I say that?

He raised an eyebrow and his smile widened while I tried to look calm and not like I wanted to light something on fire and run as fast as I could out of this place. I did not like whiskey. I did not drink whiskey. Drinking, me, in public was quite possibly the worst idea in the entire world. But he was so pretty, and maybe he wasn't a mage. Maybe he was a normal guy who wanted to talk to a normal girl in jeans.

"There you are. I thought you were flushed down the toilet." Viney came up to me, glaring.

I glanced from her to the guy. "I'm sorry. I should have told you where I was but I got sucked into watching them play. After that, this guy showed me how to hold a stick."

"I bet." She whirled around, the whip before the lash, but the guy didn't flinch away from her attack, instead he smiled like he found her amusing. "Listen, jerk face, before you hit on someone, you should probably..." Her voice trailed off as she stared at him and her expression went from somewhat angry to white and bugged out furious.

He smiled at her widely. "Have we met? We must have. I get that look a lot."

She swelled with visible rage until I took her hand and tugged her away from him. "Hey, Viney, let's go get coffee, okay? I saw this cute little shop a few buildings down that I've been meaning to try."

The guy's eyes snapped from my face back to hers. "Viney, right. It's been a long time. How are things?"

So he was a mage. No wonder I found him so good looking. He was probably completely evil, too. Viney swallowed like she was trying to choke down a sack of poodle poop. "Ian. It hasn't been long enough."

"I'm sorry you feel that way. I have nothing but the fondest memories of you. Are you going to introduce me to your friend?"

The words were a challenge and Viney was going to accept it with the pool cue, him at the end of it.

I wrapped my arm around her shoulder and kind of tugged her away from him. "Hey, I bet they have tiramisu. My treat."

They guy's expression changed as he eyed my arm around her. "You're together?"

Viney inhaled sharply and then bared her teeth at him. "Obviously. That's right. We're here on a date."

I stared at Viney while her eyes plead with me. Okay. Um. "Right. We ate and I was distracted watching the cool girl, but enough of that. We should get dessert."

Viney dragged me away from Ian who watched us looking amused. He clearly was far less upset at seeing Viney than she was to see him. After we were out the door Viney shrugged my arm off her shoulder. "From all the dressing up you do, I expected more."

"Wow. I'm sorry to disappoint you, Viney, but that was my first date ever. I kind of got thrown at the end. So, he's a mage. That explains it."

"What?"

"Don't you think that mages have that glowing kind of attractiveness about them?"

"Ian, alluring? You mean like Drake. Yeah, they're the same kind of mage, but Ian is so far beneath Drake, I can't even..." She sputtered and glared at me like I'd talked to Ian on purpose.

I took a deep breath. I didn't know how to smooth things over with people. Pets, sure. You just gave them food and spoke in a calm voice. "What happened to the guys? Will they notice that we took off? Also, if the point of pretending to be with me was so you wouldn't look stupid for not having a date, wouldn't it be better to show off those two very nice males instead of me?"

Viney sighed and pulled out her phone, texting rapidly. I put my hands in my pockets and tried to walk normally in the heels. They were stupid and I was already tall enough.

"Come on." She hurried me along, her own sensible boots way better for walking than my heels. We stood in line at the café, a glass case full of the most delectable desserts, even tiramisu, which made us both exchange glances and smiles. All right, I smiled. Viney looked a little less grim. After we'd ordered hot chocolate for me, coffee for her, and an entire pan of tiramisu, we settled in a corner.

Viney took a big drink of her coffee before scowling at me. "Ian is vile."

"Okay."

She frowned at me. "He's like Drake only less particular. That makes him so much worse. You're right about the allurement. He looks at a girl and she gets stupid. It's like his superpower. I thought if he knew I was with a girl he wouldn't use it on me."

I studied her while I blew on my hot chocolate. She crouched over her cup of coffee with her eyeliner smudged messily beneath her poky hair. She wasn't pretty like Wit. Why were guys fighting over her? Why was she afraid of Ian? "Okay. In that case, I'm glad you were there. He was really smooth."

Her lips tightened, her dark eyes intense as she gazed at me. "He used to go to school with us at Rosewood, left in the middle of his Sophomore year. He messed around with a lot of girls. He'd make you feel special and beautiful and then after he got bored with you, just move on."

I stared at her, this mysterious Ian guy taking on new depths. "So the problem with him is that he made you think that he liked you when he really only liked the conquest? Sounds like Enrique."

She frowned at me. "Who?"

"From Passiones. He's a character in a TV show. Never mind. Just not a good guy to date, but the characters really got addicted to him."

She wrinkled her cute nose. "Yeah, he made you feel like the only girl in the world for ten minutes, but no one could keep him, not even Wit."

I sighed. "So, he broke her heart? Maybe that's why she's so…"

"Wit's always been that kind of witch, but yeah, after Ian she did go kind of bats. Eat. This tiramisu isn't going to eat itself."

She didn't have to tell me twice. She did have to tell me to slow down and save her some.

"Right after Wit broke up with Ian, she dated Drake for a little while." Her lips tightened and I put a hand over hers while my own jaw clenched. Wit and Drake? I couldn't even…

"Forget about him. You don't need a man. You are strong and intelligent and beautiful, and cool. Besides that, you're more interested in guys who look a little less like an alien. I mean, that kind of symmetry is completely abnormal. I think we should capture him and skin him to make sure he's human."

She snickered. "Now that's something I can agree with."

"How are we going to get back?"

She shrugged. "I texted Zach. I'm sorry that this date ended like this. I wanted you to have a normal experience so you could feel more comfortable if you ever were in the position of dating someone real."

I stared at her. "Thanks for trying. I appreciate the effort."

She sighed. "Yeah. I didn't think the guys would be so lame. Sorry about that."

I held up my hands. "No more apologies. It was a fantastic experience. Even if there wasn't a bar fight, there was a sordid affair, a secret identity, a near-seduction and tiramisu."

She rolled her eyes. "I'm going to use the restroom before Zach gets here. Watch out for him, okay?"

I nodded and sat there, eating tiramisu and pretending that all was right with the world when Zach stepped in looking a little bit nervous, not nearly as beautiful as Ian which I desperately appreciated. I stood up and waved him over.

"Zach, come here before I eat all the tiramisu. My jeans aren't going to fit at this rate."

I was too loud and lots of people looked at me and then did a double take when they realized that sleek haired jeans and t-shirt girl was Penny Lane, resident weird girl. I wasn't sure how I'd ended up weird when I'd been trying to be adorable and irresistibly cute so Zach would marry me. Weird was much easier for me than cute.

He smiled and nodded, edging through the tables until he got to me. When he reached the table, I held out my fork full of tiramisu, and he opened his mouth, his eyes kind of big and I realized that I hadn't let him say anything. It was just so nice to see someone who I knew that wasn't so impossibly attractive and evil.

He chewed, swallowed, licked the cream off his lips and smiled at me. "Where is Viney?"

I thumbed over my shoulder. "My date is in the toilet. I don't mean in the toilet, just... Do you know Ian?"

His eyes widened and he leaned forward, his hands on the table. "Ian..."

I frowned. "Left middle of Sophomore year after breaking all the girl's hearts?"

He spoke in a flat voice. "Yeah. Ian Featherwell. He was one of the guys you went out with?"

I shook my head. "No, he taught me how to shoot pool while our dates flirted with Viney. Apparently she's really popular with the silver car crowd. Ian is so smooth, I actually bought that whole, 'I'm shy and awkward, and you're a cute girl I'm not sure how to talk to' thing. It's a little bit disappointing. I thought my jeans and t-shirt would be more of a hit real guys."

He stared at me. "You don't think he was real?"

"No, I mean like non mages. I've never met any of those. I kind of thought…" I shook my head and held out another fork full of tiramisu.

Viney came back while he was still chewing. "Let's go."

I wrapped the last of the tiramisu in a napkin while Viney stared at me. "For later."

She sighed and glared at Zach. "Don't ask."

"I don't have to. Heard Ian's in town. Is he coming back to school? That would be a riot." Zach did not sound like it would be a fun kind of riot, more of a violence and death thing.

Viney made a rude sound as we walked out of the café and crossed the street to where this tiny little red sports car was parked. I stopped, staring at the large windshield and the teeny seats while Zach opened the door and Viney went around to the other side.

"How many seats are there?"

Zach smiled at me while he slid into the driver's seat. "It has a back seat. Not a big one, but Viney will fit okay."

"I get sick if I sit in the front."

Zach frowned. "Like motion sickness? Isn't that usually the opposite, that people in the back get more sick…"

I climbed over him and into the back where Viney already sat.

"Get off me. Your legs are too long to be back here. What is wrong with you?"

I gave her a demure smile and tried to keep my knees to myself. I looked up and saw Ian standing on the sidewalk, watching our whole thing. He nodded when he noticed me, gave me a slight smile then turned away.

He smiled like a wolf, like Drake.

28 WITCH

When we got home, I climbed over Zach to get out. He kind of 'oomphed' when I accidentally kneed him in the stomach then I was safely on my own two feet, in my heels and jeans. I pulled out a lollipop and unwrapped it slowly while Zach and Viney got out.

"Are you okay?" Zach frowned, studying me. "Did the date or Ian bother you?"

I smiled brightly. "I just want to get out of these crazy pants. I tried, but normal isn't really me. Apparently."

Viney climbed out and glared at me. "You looked fine. It's not the jean's fault that Ian showed up. That he hit on you shows that they make you look good."

"Good isn't my thing, either." I stumbled ahead Viney and Zach in my heels so I didn't hear what else they said. I really needed some time to be alone and light something on fire.

I got to my room, changed into a cute skirt and then flopped on my bed with Señor Mort.

I gazed into his eyes and stroked his fur. "It's been such a long week. And short. So busy. I still haven't found Zach's love key." I groaned and rolled over. Señor Mort padded over my shoulder and nibbled on my sleek hair, apparently finding it deliciously weird. "I need to thank him for driving us back. And apologize for kneeing him." I still had no idea what kind of girl he liked. He needed to show me pictures. Or I could go for Lars. Out of all the brainy bunch he was by far the least irritating.

Viney pounded on my door. "What are you doing?"

Bon-bons and macaroons, I was going to decapitate her with a pool cue. I made a face at Señor Mort and put him back in his cage with a snack before I padded to the door in my brand new polka dot socks. I opened the door and smiled brightly at Viney.

"What's up?"

"Can I come in?"

I exhaled slowly before I nodded and stepped back. She walked over to the swing and sat down, having to stretch out her tiptoes to reach the floor. Apparently Drake had hung it to my height. My stomach contracted at the thought of Drake standing with his arms above his head, screwing in my swing with his miniature screw driver.

"You like a guy, right?"

I stared at her. "What?"

"If it's not another guy, how do you hang around with Drake and Ian and not get crazy? After that first time, with the shake, you should be as obsessed with Drake as every other girl."

I stared at her. "I think Drake's evil. I want a nice guy."

She frowned at me. "A nice guy? What does that even mean?"

I shrugged. "You know, someone you can trust."

She made a sound of disgust. "You can't trust a mage. Maybe a human guy, I don't know, but never a mage. I figure if you're going to have one, may as well get one of the ones who are honest about what he is. Drake's a jerk, yeah, but he doesn't pretend to be anything else."

"So, you think that Drake's an honest evil mage?"

She shrugged and leaned forward then back, swinging higher. "I don't know. I thought I knew everything about him, but lately I've been confused."

I nodded as I climbed on my bed, sitting cross-legged. "He's really confusing, but they all are. Like there is kind of a guy, but I don't think he even notices me. And then with the way Drake is, he probably thinks I'm into Drake instead of him."

She frowned at me. "I just find it inconceivable that you can think about another guy when you have Drake licking malted off you. I've seen the way you look at Drake, staring at him like he's the most beautiful piece of cake at the tea party. The way that you blush, the way you act when Witley is around him. You do like him, but somehow you can control it. Is it a spell you use? A potion?"

I shifted uncomfortably. How I was with Drake was considered controlled? "I guess I'm looking for something else."

"Someone nice," she said skeptically.

I sighed. "It's pretty stupid, but yeah. I want a nice mage."

She hopped off the swing, graceful for someone so short. "I'd be bored with a mage who wasn't at least a little bit wicked. I'm running to the kitchen for a snack."

She left and I stared at my bed for a long time before turning towards the door. I needed to talk to Zach and find his love key. Viney didn't even think of Zach like that, look at him because he wasn't like Drake or Ian.

I walked across the lilac room and held up my hand for a long time before I let my fist hit the wood of Zach's door. I glanced over at the couch where Drake had been playing guitar earlier. He'd been far too good to be Zach's student, so he'd lied on that day he'd come here, saying it was for guitar lessons. What was Drake's wicked game?

Zach opened the door and I whirled around, beaming at him, but my smile faltered when I noticed what he was wearing, what he wasn't wearing, which was a shirt. He had really nice muscles and silky looking skin.

"I'm sorry. I didn't realize that you'd be half naked. Never mind." I edged away from him trying not to notice so much skin.

He lifted his lips in a half smile. "It's fine. It doesn't bother me if it doesn't bother you."

I held up my hand so I could only see his face above it. "It really bothers me. Zach you are so beautiful."

He kind of blushed and I bit my lip. Bon-bons and macaroons this was going well.

"Penny, did you need something?"

"Ah. Yes, I wanted to thank you for coming to town to pick us up after we had that weird tangent on our date. Also, I'm sorry I kept climbing over you in the car."

He grinned widely. "Are you really going to hold your hand up like that until I put on a shirt?"

I lowered it slowly, caught a glimpse of his chest and brought my hand back up. "It's weird, isn't it? Okay. I can handle it." I put my hand down and kept my eyes firmly closed. "So thanks for the ride and..."

Zach laughed and grabbed my hand, pulling me into his room. I stumbled and saw a whirl of black and white before I landed on a soft bed. Zach pulled a shirt over his head, crossed his arms and shook his head. "You're a funny girl."

I gave a strangled laugh. "Who doesn't love to laugh? I want you to show me pictures of all the girls you've ever liked."

So subtle, Penny. As if this couldn't get more awkward. He just shrugged and flopped on the bed beside me, making me bounce while his arm brushed my hip. He lay back, arms behind his head and pointed at the wall opposite the bed. I stared at him for a second, that fascinating muscle on the back of his arm like Ian had, a little longer, not quite as defined but somehow so interesting.

I turned my head quickly and then froze when I saw the poster hanging on his wall. The girl was in an action shot, body suit glistening and bumpy, black like the rest of her clothes and hair. She stared at the camera, eyes black as pitch, skin painted white with black mouth, eyes shaped with black kohl. A cape rippled around her, black. She must have just spun around and started walking forward. I glanced to the right and saw part of an arm that had been cut off. I could see her hand, though, the thumbnail bitten to the quick and painted white.

"Do you know who that is?" he asked.

I swallowed. "I had a cousin who was into all that stuff. I never saw any of the performances, fights, I'm not sure what you call them." I couldn't stop staring at that white thumbnail.

"Sometimes tourney, or competition, duel, challenge…" The bed bounced while he shrugged.

I was sitting on Zach's bed with him, and all I could think about was that jagged thumbnail. My heart pounded.

He cleared his throat. "Maybe it seems stupid, but if you'd ever seen her fight, you'd know why I'm transfixed with her."

I turned my head to stare at him. "Transfixed with…That's the female that you like? Wow. She's really cool. How many dates have you gone on?"

His face froze kind of and he shook his head. "I haven't actually dated her."

"Oh, but you're friends? Maybe you guys hang out a lot online." My stomach churned with anxiety and something else I hadn't felt for a long time. I stared at Zach and tried to look interested instead of homicidal.

"I don't actually know her, but I know everything about her."

"Wow. So, you like someone you've never met?"

His eyes narrowed at me. I expected denial, not, "I love her. There isn't anyone else in the world that will ever compare to Pitch."

I closed my eyes for a long time before I got off the bed and walked over to the poster, brushing my fingers over that white nail and the sliver of arm. "So, if Pitch came up to you and told you that she wanted to marry you…"

"I'd be the happiest person in the world."

"What would you do together? Play video games?" My voice

sounded strangely emotionless.

"We'd fight in tourneys together."

I laughed and glanced over my shoulder at him. "So you're a fighter, Zach? Do you have a cloak and a body-con suit?"

He nodded, still dead serious. I stared at him, seeming so nice and sensible, but this was absolute insanity. He was in love with someone he'd never met? How did that make any sense? It didn't. It absolutely did not. And I was supposed to marry him, but this, this wouldn't work. Would it? Could I possibly get Zach to marry me when he was in love with someone else? Maybe I could tell him I was Pitch. No.

I smiled brightly instead of screaming and screaming and screaming. "Well, I wish you the best with that. Is she fighting somewhere I can go see her? If you fell in love with her just by that, it's got to be incredible."

He got this horrible melancholy look on his face. "She hasn't fought in over a year. She just disappeared. I don't know what happened to her, but she's not dead!" He swallowed hard and the veins in his neck stood out before he took a deep breath. "Some people say that she goes to school in Blackheart, others say that she went to school here, but that she's already graduated and gone to Darkside. One girl in Blackheart claimed to be Pitch, but she broke both legs doing Pitch's signature 'Twist-Jet' so it clearly wasn't her."

"That's terrible. Is the girl okay?"

He blinked at me. "Who cares? She lied about being Pitch. She deserves to be gutted."

I stared at Zach and nodded slowly. He was the epitome of a rabid fan, and he'd seemed so nice. Nice, a mage? I was too stupid to live. "So, no one knows what she looks like?"

He shrugged and pulled out his computer. "I've done some work and I've come up with this." He turned the screen to face me and I stared at a girl who looked a lot like an animated Wit, only the hair was longer and the skirt was tighter and her top shorter to show her narrow waist without any noticeable muscle definition and scooped low to show off her ample bosom.

"Wow, she's really voluptuous and rocker chick." Apparently, he didn't like cute at all.

I inhaled deeply before I slammed the computer lid closed and stared at it under my shaking fingers. Words trembled on the tip of my tongue about how pathetic and ridiculous he was, how nonsensical his emotional connection to some fantasy he had. Of course, I'd decided to marry someone based on an internet profile and a five-minute video.

I exhaled and leaned over, resting my head on his shoulder while I took deep, even breaths. "I think I get it. Sometimes we need heroes far enough away from us that we can't touch them. It's safe that way, easier."

He put a hand on my shoulder and we sat like that until my skin felt itchy, my scalp tight. I sat up and gave him a wry smile.

"I am so wired from the tiramisu. I'm sorry I'm so weird. Thanks for explaining about Pitch. I think I get you a little bit better now."

I left the room and closed the door, leaning on it heavily while I stared into space. This was the guy I was supposed to marry. I went over to the couch and flopped down, my legs dangling over the end. My body curved in the cushions that had held Drake not long ago, bent over the guitar like he didn't see me. Was he obsessed with someone else, like Pitch? I inhaled deeply while I closed my eyes and smelled a hint of black cherry before Viney walked in, carrying a tray of food.

I didn't feel like talking and neither did Viney. She stabbed a bite of hashbrowns on her fork, perfect late night food.

"Seeing Ian kind of…"

I gave her a wan smile. "If you want to talk about it…"

She shook her head her gaze unfocused before she frowned at me. "We should go."

"Go?"

"Friday nights the Makiss have their volleys and on Saturday night, it's the Chemiss."

"Chemiss?"

"Chemistry club. Do you want to go see the guys wrestle around?"

I hesitated. "It's been kind of a long day. Jean and bra shopping, going on my first date, almost killing the cool redhead with a ball, all that tiramisu not to mention that teeny tiny car ride where the back-seat was so close to the windshield, and Pitch."

I made a face and ripped a bagel apart viciously.

"Pitch?"

I took a deep breath as I glared at the bagel. "Apparently Zach is completely in love with some girl he hasn't even met."

She laughed. "That look on your face, you haven't ever crushed on someone?"

I shook my head slowly. "No. Maybe I should. If I can be in love with someone I can't possibly have, then there's no risk of loving a real person. I should fall in love with someone like that, someone out of reach so he can never break my heart." I bit my lip hard and smiled at her. "So that's the only female he ever liked."

She nodded and rested her elbows on the table, absently tapping her chin. "Zach and Drake were friends pretty much forever. I haven't known Zach that long, really only since last year when he…" She shook her head. "Sometimes I feel sorry for him."

"Zach?"

"Drake." She gave me a flat glance. "He's worshipped so he can't be loved. I only really talked to him last year when he asked me to help Zach." She shrugged and wrapped her arms around her body like she was cold. "He's been around so much lately that I feel like I almost know him and he's nothing like I thought he would be. I thought he'd always be cool and aloof, but he's making you gingerbread houses and doing community service, climbing towers and Pas de freaking Deux with a beginner. If he did that to me I would kick him in the balls. I mean, he's nothing like I thought he'd be and I was desperately in love with him for years. Years. I admit it. My room was plastered with posters of him and I was worse than Zach. I stalked him all the time. I wrote him these sick letters and honestly thought that I knew him." She looked up at me slightly guilty and kind of sad looking.

I stared at her. Viney was obsessed with Drake? But Drake was always flirting with me. Was it her he actually liked and just using me for a decoy? I smiled brightly. "You're really cool, Viney. I think that Drake probably likes you."

She rolled her eyes. "No, he doesn't. The thing is, the more I get to know him, the less my desperate obsession makes any sense. I wanted to be with Ian just so I wouldn't think about Drake, but it didn't even help, not really. I just felt more stupid afterwards."

"But you're still into him?"

She sighed deeply and shot me this weird look, part excited, part guilty. "It's Chemiss, like I…"

Zach came out of his room wearing black soft clothing that looked like pajamas or ninja clothes to me. "Oh, hi. I thought you were going to bed, Penny."

Viney gripped my arm. "We're talking about boys. It's girl talk, so you can be on your way. Good luck. Don't drop dead or anything."

He sneered at her before he spun and left us alone.

"Chemiss," she hissed, turning back to me. "It's the boy's combat team. Once you see Drake compete you'll understand why I am what I am, and maybe you'll…"

"Become a Drake groupie? Well that sounds fun. Then I can throw mashed potatoes at any girl he looks at. What else do groupies do? Are there t-shirts? There should be t-shirts. I want one. I want five. And I want them all to be glow in the dark or scratch and sniff."

She stared at me blankly before she sighed and pushed away from the table. "Come on weird girl. You're going to need a cloak. And some black pants. Don't tell anyone that I let you wear my stuff."

29

WITCH

We sat at the front of the bleachers with little lights illuminating the steps and aisles so no one fell to their death climbing to their seats. Viney leaned forward, gripping the metal railing with her chipped black nails while we waited for the tourney to begin.

I pulled my cloak tighter around me as a chilly breeze picked up and more people crowded into the bleachers. The hood would probably make my hair frizzy. I'd wrapped a black scarf around my lower face, because we were all ninjas. Since the entire school showed up to this thing, you'd think that they'd do it during the day. At least that's what I thought before an explosion of gold showered down as a dragon came to life above us, breathing fire that I could feel on my skin.

I held my breath as the gold beast arched its back and clawed the sky. The sound of embers popping, the heat on my cheeks, and the scent of sandalwood swept away the rest of the audience. I gripped the railing while I stared up as the dragon beat its wings, rising slowly, wind blowing back my hood.

Of course, it wasn't a real dragon.

It seemed to fix its eyes on me before it bent its slender neck and shot a blast of flame. I gasped and flinched back as the flame spread above my head. It didn't burn my skin, but a few fly-away hairs shriveled up around my face that felt like crinkled wire when I pressed my palms against my cheeks.

I turned to Viney who had an arm across her face, guarding it from the flames. Were they using actual fire with their projected holographs? That was risky and unbelievably cool. My heart still pounded as I refocused my attention on the ring below. There was a twenty-foot gap between the bleachers and the platform in the center.

A man seemed to step out of thin air, his lean body covered in what looked like orange liquid metal that covered him from scalp to toe. Body conscious didn't begin to describe it. Every muscle was orange liquid, delineating every bump and bulge. I gasped as he spun around and I saw the full frontal. It was nothing, just a man wearing holographs with a cod piece like a ballerina man, but I really, really wanted to hold up my hand and block out the bits that made my breathing weird.

"That's Oscar. He's not too bad."

I turned to look at Viney and was glad for the ninja mask so no one could see my face on fire from blushing so hard. Oscar cranky pants from study hall was the naked orange man? Not that he was really naked. He must be wearing some kind of skin colored suit filled with light receptors. He wasn't really naked and those weren't really his veins that the orange light flowed through over his body. The orange light flashed brighter and seemed to take a shape, almost like the light was growing out of his skin in tiny scales that expanded until they were quarter sized. It only took a few seconds for the whole process, Oscar sprouting orange light armor, but when he was done he looked really spectacular.

He walked across the stage, but he didn't walk like a geeky student, instead he seemed to float over the platform, like a dancer, moving faster and faster until near the edge he leapt spectacularly high, arm stretched above his head, fingers outstretched to grasp something I couldn't see until he touched it. At that touch, the object flared to life, a two-foot sword that flickered, like it was liquid metal that ran up or down depending how he held the blade.

He came down gracefully to one knee, sword held perpendicular to his body, head bowed. The audience surged to their feet cheering before they settled back down. I glanced over at Viney who met my eyes, but I couldn't read her expression because we were ninjas.

   Another man materialized on the opposite side of the platform, but he didn't come out naked, he already had purple armor that glowed like liquid metal. He came out of thin air holding his fire-metal sword. Orange reflected in a ripple through the purple sword that flickered like fire as he raised his weapon and charged Oscar. I gasped and flinched back as the purple fire wrapped around Oscar, but his sword shifted, spreading out to become an orange shield, flames licking the black platform until I thought I could smell singed wood. Oscar shoved back the purple fighter with his sword/shield and then swung the orange flame sword at the purple warrior. There was a flash of light, orange and purple waves that spread from the epicenter of the clash into the audience. I gasped as waves of purple and orange light lapped around me, like water without temperature.

   I shuddered and wiped my hands on the black skirt Viney had let me have because it was too long for her before I focused once more on the platform. The two fighters danced more than fought, no doubt years of ballet was to blame for those incredible and not very practical leaps by Oscar met by the terrifying spinning ability of the purple warrior.

   "Who is the purple guy?" I hissed at Viney.

   "Pete," she answered without turning her head.

   Pete spun, purple fire from his sword forming a kind of tornado around his body, purple fire flicking, sucking everything into that spinning vortex. My hair escaped from my cloak, strands rippling towards the purple warrior, and I gripped the bar, feeling pressure from behind me as the audience was pulled towards Pete.

   Oliver, struggled to maintain his distance, but he slid over the floor, struggling to stay away from that flame, but Pete kept spinning with his purple flame rising thirty feet into the night sky. My cloak flapped around me until eventually Oscar had no option other than accepting the inevitable. He jumped up and turned towards Pete, forming his orange flame into a shield as he struck the purple column of fire with Pete in the center.

The impact threw me back into the knees of the person sitting behind me while my hands gripped the metal railing, straining my shoulders. I couldn't see anything through the purple and orange flash of light.

When I blinked the world into focus and felt more singed hair hanging around my face, Pete was staggering around on the platform, and Oscar was lying on the ground.

I gripped Viney's arm. "Is he okay?"

She stared at the scene and shook her head slightly. "Pete lost control. It was just lucky that he came out of that without getting decapitated. I'm sure Oscar will be fine."

She covered my hand with hers as guys dressed in black scrambled up to the platform and surrounded Oscar. I waited for them to pick him up, but instead they moved closer, shoulder to shoulder until little white bits of lightning flickered between the guys inside their circle. The crowd murmured while Viney's grip grew painful and I realized that I was holding my breath.

Oscar sat up with a gasp and orange light flickered over his skin, tracing his veins, at least what I could see around the men with the lightning flickers. I stared at those men and barely heard the cheer of the crowd as Oscar staggered to his feet, naked besides orange light that traced his veins.

The circle of men stepped black, lightning vanishing into their hands, tiny flickers of electrical current that stirred a memory I'd buried long ago.

I gasped as I saw a barren field, burnt and smoking, the remains of a black car crumpled in the middle of the field without any tire or skid marks that led to the crash, just the car in the field while I sat there, staring at it. My bare feet poked up to the gray sky, streaked in black and red. I inhaled but I couldn't breathe. I was drowning in my own lungs, metallic taste in my mouth like copper pennies.

"Penny." A dark figure bent over me, his hands spread with miniature lightning dancing between them, lightning that made everything disappear.

"Penny!" Viney's voice came from far away and with effort I blinked her into focus where she bent towards me, eyes bright with excitement while her lower face was still covered in black fabric.

"Is it over?"

The crowd was hushed while she shook her head and turned back to the platform, pointing as the golden dragon came back, erupting in the sky, shooting flame that was still warm on my skin, but it seemed further away. Everything seemed further away, even Viney, pressed to my side and gripping my arm.

I had to go. I had to draw a picture of that scene, the man with lightning, the car in the field. I had to do something before I forgot it again. I shook my head because I couldn't press through the crowd around us, couldn't slip away from the fight unnoticed, not unless I climbed down through the bars in front of me.

The dragon circled tightly as a howl filled the night, a sound that sent a chill running down my spine. Green eyes opened floating on the far side of the platform, enormous eyes, the size of a body, and then the head formed, muzzle, sharp teeth and green fur. The rest of the wolf took shape even as the creature leapt skyward jaws locking around the dragon's throat. They tumbled through the air, curled together like an enormous burning yin yang sign down to the ground and then exploded in tiny gold and green flecks that danced in the air like diamonds. I could see my reflection in the green and golden specks the size of my fingernail. I tried to catch one in my hand, but when I opened it, there wasn't anything in my palm.

Viney snorted at me for trying to catch light then nudged me with her sharp elbow. I looked down in time to see the golden specks swirl and cluster around a figure that took shape, a man who stepped forward dressed in luminescent liquid gold armor but bare skinned from wrist to elbow.

Intricate patterns made of golden light formed on his forearms and the back of his hands. They flared brighter as he brought his hands up in an intricate movement like the Tai Chi Revere performed every morning, but Revere's hands didn't light up so not nearly as cool.

The crowds exploded in hisses, boos, with a smattering of applause and shrieks of pure female appreciation. Viney beside me hissed with a lot of venom which I understood when the guy turned his head, seeming to look directly at me and winked. It was golden-eyed boy from earlier. I slouched in my seat and pulled my hood low.

"So that's what Ian's doing in town. I hope that Drake kills him." Viney's voice trembled with anticipation.

Drums beat slow, while Ian walked the perimeter of the platform, arms outstretched, smirk on his mouth as he waited to be adored. The drums picked up speed and then screeching like guitars and violins in a melody that I could have sworn I knew.

"Isn't that the song Drake was playing on his guitar?"

Viney flashed me a glare before refocusing on the platform, leaning forward, holding her breath, hands white where she gripped the bar.

When the song had reached a screaming pitch, a cloud of green smoke began drifting around the platform, more and more smoke until it began to shake like someone was stirring it up, and then green streaks outlined a body and there was Drake.

He didn't look like Drake, not with his bare chest drawn over with intricate shapes, star patterns like the pattern on his cheek that lit his green eyes. His eyes glowed green as he curled his lips and stalked towards Ian.

His eyes weren't really glowing; they couldn't be. He was wearing some kind of eye protection that would enhance his vision and make his eyes look like that. He wore pants but no shoes. No shoes, no shirt, no service. He moved like silk rippling in the wind, like falling, like ink spilling in water, as effortless as it was inevitable.

I couldn't help leaning forward, studying the movement of his muscles, the clench and fall of his body. My fingers tingled and I tasted black cherry.

"Drake!" Viney's scream shattered the air, the sound of passionate obsession breaking through my own rapture.

I gasped and released the bar, pressing my hands together, digging my nails into my skin until I could feel pain instead of Drake's breath on my cheek, his thighs pressed against mine.

Drake looked over at Viney, his eyebrows lowering into a scowl that made his cheekbones sharper, lips fuller and slightly parted. Viney went crazy, jumping up and down, waving her arms like a complete idiot while I sat there, paralyzed. Everyone around me was on their feet screaming and chanting while I tried to shrink into my own skin.

Drake's expression changed, one eyebrow rising as he seemed to look directly at me before he threw a hand wide and bowed to the crowd.

I'd thought the crowd was already insane, but they jerked and stamped, pressing me forward against the bars while Viney clocked me with one of her wild fists. The crowd began to jump in time with the drum beat, thump, thump, thump until I was sure that the bleachers would crack and we'd all plummet to our deaths.

Drake grinned wickedly for one moment seeming to stare directly at me before he whirled around in time to be engulfed in Ian's golden flames.

My heart pounded as he disappeared for a moment before hissing and sizzling filled the air, like water on hot metal. Drake stepped forward, still surrounded by the golden fire, but he was clearly illuminated in green until with a dull roar like breakers crashing, the flames were extinguished with a wall of green liquid and clouds of roiling steam.

Drake stepped towards Ian, a look of amusement on his face. He raised his hands and gestured, 'bring it on,' or something.

Ian grinned wickedly before he ran towards Drake, a liquid metal sword flowing out of Ian's hands close to Drake's head. Drake bent backwards, beneath the thrust of the sword, then twisted and punched the side of the blade away while he slammed his foot into Ian's chest.

Ian flew away from Drake's mighty kick, a green footprint on his chest, flickering brightly before gold flames bubbled up, eating away the green.

Drake grinned at the audience, like he was sharing a joke with us, and the crowd roared, drowning out the music while Drake threw back his head and howled. Ian ran into him, streaks of gold flickering over his skin as he plowed into Drake, knocking him down to the platform.

The audience gasped and in that moment of almost silence, I could have sworn I heard Drake laugh on the platform in Ian's golden fire embrace. What followed was a series of holds and grips that I couldn't follow. My head was buzzing and the world was getting fuzzy around the edges. I needed a lollipop. I needed to stop staring at Drake while he strained against Ian, body against body, muscles rippling and skin glittering like green diamonds.

I felt like he was straining against me, my hand on his chest, feeling the curve of his muscles beneath my fingers, fingers that burned instead of tingled where I clenched them. I dug my nails into my skin, but the pain seemed far away, everything distant besides Drake, skin illuminated green.

Drake had Ian down against the platform in a headlock, crushing Ian down until Ian twisted and knocked Drake back. They circled each other, both with lips parted, chests rising and falling heavily. Ian pulled his golden flame sword out of the air, and Drake followed suit, arm muscles bunching as he lifted the green liquid metallic instrument in a salute.

The two men leapt at each other, light erupting when their swords clashed with a hissing sound and a cloud of steam. The wave of light lapped against me, my skin tightening against that phantom caress as though Drake's breath brushed my skin. I shuddered and dug my nails deeper.

The swords flashed, clash after clash that rocked through the crowds until I was hyperventilating with every stroke, every lunge and parry until Ian broke away, holding up his hands at Drake to hold him back.

Ian lunged forward and back, familiar movements I'd seen Revere make, but with gold rippling over his skin, much more impressive and I almost managed to get my breathing under control before golden geometric shapes burst out of Ian's hands then sparks of red bounced inside the shapes, stretching them out larger and larger, more and more red sparks until a figure took shape in those shapes, until the golden geometric melted away leaving a crimson Jackson standing on the platform.

He whirled around in a spray of red sparks and ran towards Drake. Drake fell back, kicking Jackson's knee out, throwing off his lunge. Drake's hands moved in this rhythmic motion in time to the music that built and built at the same time he fought off Jackson, using mostly his legs, but sometimes his hands, ducking beneath the swing of the crimson sparks before he shoved his hands forward, a green spear shooting towards Jackson and growing larger, large enough that a man wrapped in blue light could stand inside of the triangle.

Zach looked very different as he burst out of the green lines and stalked towards Jackson in his liquid bodysuit, the blue emphasizing his eyes, or maybe his eyes were glowing like Drake's. I breathed shallowly as Jackson and Zach fought in the center of the platform while Drake and Ian paced the perimeter like two hungry predators who were vying for the lesser creature's carcasses.

Zach and Jackson were not shabby. I tried to watch objectively, tried to take the movement apart instead of being caught up in the audience, the excitement, the obsession. Drake said something low that I couldn't hear, and Zach's head swung around, his eyes meeting Drake's for a second before he grinned brightly, the least Zach-like smile I'd ever seen on him. That smile said wild and fierce, uncontrollable and untamed.

Jackson attacked low and Zach leapt up, flipping backwards in a wide-spread, lazy movement before he landed and whirled, cutting across Jackson's unprotected left before he punched the sword arm hard, then an elbow to his face while twisting Jackson's arm hard enough that Jackson cried out. Wasn't that his broken arm? I winced for Jackson while his spark sword flickered out. Ian came forward, fighting with his golden sword, blowing Zach back with golden flames that laid him out before Drake came forward yelling, green sword in his hand. The final duel was a blur of green and gold. The only thing in focus was Drake's face, his eyes full of raw determination and will that would crush the entire world if it opposed him.

When Ian broke, losing his rhythm, his foot twisting, Drake kicked forward, his stance too wide and his knee cocked out. It could be easily dislocated in that position. Revere had explained it to me when I asked him why he did this, why he did that, why he held his hands out like a birdy, why he kept his knee at that precise angle every time he bent. Drake's knee wasn't perfect.

I blinked and could almost see it objectively, the climax of Ian fighting against Drake's sword, Ian who didn't take advantage of the imperfect knee.

I stood beside Viney and watched them fight, but the audience became a dull roar from far away as I saw another fight, far away where a blue light exploded into the crowd, knocking them back before the mob ripped me apart. I closed my eyes and saw the crowds around me, dark, writhing, chanting as they surged, a scream piercing the rumblings as someone got trampled.

I blinked my eyes open in time to see green fire leap from Drake's hands while he stood in that imperfect stance, green fire that wrapped around Ian until he crumpled, green flames flowing off him onto the platform, leaving the distinct scent of black cherry in the air.

It was perfectly silent for a moment before everyone went wild, screaming, chanting, the crowd swaying while Viney to my left screamed the loudest, her whole soul drawn out in one rapturous cry that made my head hurt. I stood there while the crowd pushed against me, pressing me against the railing until I couldn't take it another moment.

I vaulted over the rail, dropping the ten feet down to the hard-packed earth and began running along the perimeter of the ring. Viney yelled my name, but I couldn't stay there any longer. There had to be an opening that let out of the tournament. Too soon bodies surged around me, heading towards the platform, pushing me as I struggled away from them until finally, I reached a narrow alley between sections that let out into a wide field.

30
WITCH

I ran through the field even though my eyes hadn't adjusted to the darkness. I ran and ran until I stumbled on a dirt clod, fell down on my face and rolled in the dirt.

I lay there panting, my legs tangled in Viney's cloak until my eyes adjusted and I could make out the stars stretched above me. They spread out magnificently, so lovely, so unbelievably far away and perfect. I wanted to be one of those stars, shining brightly in the darkness while nothing touched it, nothing came too close to diminish the bright beauty.

I kept my eyes wide on the stars while tears trickled out the corners, melting the dim lights into one blurry mess. My heart pounded in my chest so hard, too hard. I put a hand on my right side where I was missing pieces of two ribs. Those two pieces were probably lodged in my heart and that's why it hurt so much.

"Bonbons and macaroons, peanut brittle and pink taffy. Cupcakes and pecan pralines, gumballs and ice cream cones."

"That is a terrifying spell. Who are you cursing?"

I gritted my teeth as I lay there, trying to ignore the sultry voice, a voice I'd only heard a few times but already knew far too well. Ian.

I sat up and gripped my skirt with my hands. "It's not a curse but a blessing. You must have never had really good peanut brittle. Is there anything better?" My voice came out clogged and horrible, but I managed a bright smile.

His cheek still had a gold light pattern on it like a sunburst, so I could clearly see him out of my periphery as he sat down about a leg's length away from me. I did not rip off his leg and beat him to death with it. Yay me.

"What's wrong? Did you finally realize that Viney is in love with another?"

I inhaled shakily. "No, I think that I don't like crowds, or violence. I feel sick."

"If you dislike those two things you should definitely stay away from tourneys and Drake Huntsmans."

I closed my eyes tightly. I wanted to be alone. I needed to be alone. This would be a test of endurance like one of the times I was forced to sit on the dining room table for hours and hours without eating while the hired people threw food at me.

I couldn't show my vulnerability because it would only encourage someone like Ian. Telling him to leave me alone would only make him linger. If only I could stomach throwing myself at a guy. "It's not as easy as it sounds, at least the Drake part. I didn't know that he was the guy Viney was obsessed with. Does he know?"

"It would be hard for him not to. Such a cruel mage. She's had a thing for him forever. Too bad Drake doesn't want what's attainable. Too bad for you." He laughed, low and delicious, but the wrong kind of delicious and it just made me ache, like being presented with a piece of lemon meringue pie when all I wanted was black cherry anything. I breathed deeply through my mouth, but the scent of citrus still lingered.

"Too bad." I studied him, the sunburst on his cheek that seemed to be fading out. "What about you? Why do you seduce random girls? Don't you care who you're with?"

"You sound like a romantic. I have the happy fortune of being able to see beauty and charm in anyone. I can appreciate your attributes just like I can admire Viney's, however different they are."

"That seems very strange to me. Letting people close is dangerous."

"Physical closeness is different from emotional. It's easy for a mage to disassociate the body from the heart. It's easy for most witches, but I think that you're right to be cautious. You're not like the rest of them." He leaned back on his elbows, staring up at the sky, his cheekbone throbbing with the golden shimmering pattern. "So, you don't like violence. That's a pity. There is so much violence in the world, it's easier if you can enjoy it."

"Even when you lose?"

He laughed, a sound of pure sensual decadence, but it didn't fill me with anything but nausea, not that I wasn't already nauseous. I needed to be alone, needed to scream into my pillow and feel Señor's little heart thumping against mine. "Especially when I lose. I don't mind losing to Drake. He doesn't like to lose when he's playing a game. I think that's a warning for you, little witch."

"I'm not very little."

He glanced over at me, his eyes golden and gleaming. "That's true. Your hair is very big. How long have you been growing it?"

I shrugged. "Forever. I did cut a little bit off with Viney, but a trim doesn't count, does it?"

He shook his head, lips pursed. "Certainly not. Would you like to stay here all night or are you about ready to go in? I'll need to cast a spell if you don't want to be disturbed by other interested parties."

I frowned at him. "We've met once. Why are you offering to cast spells for me?"

He cocked his head as he stared at me. "You really don't know?" He leaned close and inhaled deeply, like he was smelling me. The scent of citrus bloomed in the night. "You are very lovely." His voice was low, his eyes glowing brighter as he stared at me.

I swallowed and stood up. "Um, thanks. You too. I've never seen anyone with such perfectly symmetrical features." I started in the direction that was probably the school.

He smiled widely as he stood up, brushing off his clothes and followed me. "I am the third most attractive mage in the world."

I glanced over at him. "Really? Only the third? That seems strange to me. I mean if you think that you're in the top three, why not claim first place or at least second?"

He sighed and ran a hand over his short hair. "Drake is the second most attractive mage. I hope you never meet the prettiest mage because after you see him, you'll never be able to look at anyone else."

"Sounds terrifying."

"Oh, Theodore Prince is perfectly terrible, top three most despicable mages in the world, but not the worst."

"That's you?"

He laughed. "Oh, no. I'm number three on both counts. You're practically safe with me. The worst mage is Drake; Prince comes in at a distant second."

"What does that mean, being the worst mage?"

"He has the most vanity, violence, deception, but also determination. When he puts his mind to some nefarious plot, there's no point in struggling against him because he will get what he wants, whatever that is."

I shivered and wrapped my arms around my body. Drake had asked me to a dance but had seemed okay when I'd said no. He'd made me gingerbread and held my hand when I'd been afraid. What part of his wicked scheme was that? He was probably trying to make me fall in love with him so desperately that when he broke my heart I would never feel whole again. I felt like my heart was already broken. Maybe he had to fix my heart before it was any good to break.

"So this other mage, Theodore Prince is the second worst mage? You three all just took a census and when you found out that you three were all so terrible, you decided to have a club, get together and discuss how best to ruin everything in the world?"

He laughed. "Something like that. To be fair, I'm not as awful as I used to be, so maybe Drake and Prince have changed their ways as well. I've been out of the country for a long time. Drake seems slightly altered, more responsible."

I glanced over at him. "Do mages get better? I didn't think that was possible."

He grinned cheerfully. "Oh, we do. Better and better all the time, if we're not getting worse. We're about to be interrupted."

"Ian, that's where you wandered off to. Have you finished here or do you need a few more minutes?"

I stiffened as Drake's voice enveloped me in this mix of longing and anger that made my heart pound and my mouth water. I wanted to hurl myself at him and beat my fists against his chest screaming all the candies in the world. Maybe just wrap my arms around him and cry on his chest. How humiliating.

"Macaroons and bonbons, it's Drake." I crossed my arms as a figure melted out of the shadows, Drake's skin still tinted green and the star shape on his cheek glistening brightly.

"Evening, lollipop girl, except it's morning now. Shouldn't you be safely tucked in bed?" His eyes gleamed at me, glittering green while his lips curled in a dangerous smile.

My breathing hitched and I took a half step closer to Ian. "Yes. I thought it would be fun to watch a tourney, but it turns out that I'm not much for violence."

"Or tourneys," Ian added giving me a slow wink.

Drake smiled and stepped closer to me. "That is bad luck. I don't think you like dating Viney or shopping, either. It's terrible: a Saturday completely wasted. Maybe tomorrow will be better, full of sparkles, rainbows, ponies and pets."

I nodded and edged away from him again, but Ian was right on my other side. "And pizza."

His smile changed, became a little more real instead of furious. How often did he smile mad? A lot. "Give Señor my regards. Ian, shall we go? I'm sure the witch can find her own way to her bed."

Ian raised an eyebrow. "Are you certain that's where she was headed?"

"Yes."

Ian and Drake stared at each other for a long moment like they were communicating all kinds of secret dark messages. It gave me a headache, or maybe that was everything else going on. I needed to get back to my room before I completely forgot the thing, something about a car in a field. Why was that important? I couldn't remember that either.

Drake put a hand on my shoulder. "Viney is looking for you. Do you know how to get back to your dorm? You are walking in the wrong direction."

I froze under his touch while my heart pounded and the scent of black cherry enveloped me. His fingers made my skin beneath the layers of cloak and dress break out into goose bumps.

It took me a minute to get my words together. "Point me in the right direction. I'll go by the light of the stars." His stars on his cheek flickered and I noticed him glancing at the corners of my eyes where I might have traitorous tear streaks. I pulled away from him, his hand falling between us.

Ian coughed. "I suddenly remember an incredibly important thing I left somewhere else. I'll leave you in Drake's capable hands and hope to see you another time." He turned and moved quickly away from me, disappearing into the shadows.

Drake stared at me, his gaze seeming to see way too clearly in spite of the dark. "Why were you crying? Did Ian hurt you?"

I laughed and smoothed my hair back. "I wasn't crying. I was just staring at the stars for too long and my eyes started to water. No. For the third worst mage in the world, he wasn't bad at all. I'm a little bit disappointed."

He exhaled sharply. "If Ian's the third worst, who is the absolute worst?"

"You, but you're only the second most beautiful. I would expect a direct correlation between horribleness and beauty, but apparently not."

He smiled at me and put a hand to his chin. "Ian's more beautiful than me? That's a matter of debate."

"No, Theodore Prince."

Drake's expression became enlightened and he nodded. "That's true. No one is prettier than Teddy. He's vile, though."

"Second worst mage."

Drake glanced over at me. "Ian is too generous giving me that distinction. You really didn't enjoy the tourney, didn't find him impressive? He is very popular with girls before they get to know him better."

I licked my lips. When I thought back on the fight, I could only see Drake dressed in green light, extremely body conscious green liquid light and his movement fierce and ferocious while Ian's were just a tad bland in comparison.

"He stumbled in his second pass going for the showy impact instead of a neater, cleaner and more effective strike."

He half choked, half laughed. "Penny Lane, that's what you noticed? What about me? What do you think about my position as Chemiss captain? Do I deserve it?"

I studied his dark boots, leather that laced over his dark jeans. When my eyes continued the natural progress up his legs I jerked them up to his face. "Your knee wasn't aligned correctly."

He frowned, leaning closer to me. "My knee was out of alignment? Show me."

I stared at him unable to look away from those eyes. "Well, when you take your position, bent leg…"

I trailed off as he took my hand and put it down on his leg right above his knee, the texture of the denim rough under my fingers but I could feel the contours of his thigh beneath the fabric.

"Show me."

I breathed shallowly while I pressed down, putting my hands on his hips to turn them in the right direction, refusing to look at his face, to do anything other than make his knee perfect. It wasn't a big deal, it was just like Pas de Deux.

"If you have your knee cocked it's going to be dislocated if struck from here." I thumped my fist lightly against the inside and his knee buckled. He tumbled over on top of me, knocking the breath out of me, his heavy body pressing me down.

I couldn't breathe, but it took a few seconds to know if it was from his weight and impact or just because I was that stupid about him. He shifted and weight spread through my right ribs.

I gasped and cried out, struggling out from under him. He rolled off me while I curled into a ball for a few agonizing breaths. I forced myself to kneel, sitting up straight while I covered my ribs with my palms then pressed down sharply at just the right angle until they popped back into place.

I smiled at Drake and started giggling.

"Are you all right?"

"My ribs." I gasped but at least I could breathe. The pain had helped clear my head after having Drake on top of me and seeing him fight in the tourney. Viney was right. Seeing Drake like that was completely mind melting. "They're my weakness. I could never be a great wrestler. What was that? I did not hit your knee hard enough to knock you over."

He cleared his throat before he grinned at me, sinking down in a cross-legged position. "I was dizzy from shock at having such helpful critique from my lollipop lover. Do you have any more excellent advice you're holding back? Don't worry, I can take it." The way he said that, leaning forward and staring at me with those glittering green eyes, I had a hard time drawing a steady breath.

I stammered for a moment. "I don't have a lot of critique to offer. It was really well choreographed and the lights were unbelievable."

His grin widened. "You liked my lights and my choreography? Why thank you, Penny Lane. Of course, it wasn't choreographed. That was a real fight, and I won." His voice had a hard edge to it, anger and hunger.

I took a deep breath and stood up. "Of course. I don't know anything about it. I've never seen that kind of thing before. Don't you need to go and celebrate with your enemy?"

He stood smoothly and followed, keeping only a hand's width between us. "Ian is a friend of mine. I've fought with him more times than against him. Why are you letting him close to you? Surely Viney's told you that he's not nice to women."

I crossed my arms and dug in my heels. "And you are?"

He leaned close, brushing my cheek with his, the green light feeling like warm dry water lapping on my skin. "I could be so nice if you'd let me, Penny Lane. I'd rub your feet until you scream and writhe from ticklishness. I'd lick your fingers until I have licked up all the sugar soaked into your skin from years of lollipop experiments." He moved closer until his warmth was against me, filled with this kinetic energy that I ached to devour. "If you want me, all you have to do is say the word."

I opened my mouth and closed it. He was lying. He didn't like people who wanted him. The only reason he was playing this game with me is because I was trying to stay focused on Zach, who I was going to marry even if he was a blue-light-wearing mage who was obsessed with a figment of his imagination.

"Want you for what? I guess you are pretty useful sometimes, like hanging swings and doing laundry and helping with turn-out and helping me not to throw up after car rides. Okay. Yeah, you're kind of the most useful person I've ever met. That's valid. But, I want someone nice. I know it's stupid, because mages aren't nice. I know that, but it's what I want. Not you. Sorry."

"You were not impressed by the show." His voice was flat, emotionless but there may have been a tinge of rage to it that I didn't want to understand.

"Oh, I was. You're the most beautiful thing I've ever imagined much less seen. You're amazingly talented in so many ways, but I can't want the worst mage in the world, or the second worst, or even the third. I'm sorry. We can be friends, okay? I'll see you later. Have fun with Ian. I hope you don't have a bar fight without me. I've never been to a bar fight."

He smiled showing sharp, dangerous teeth. "Wow. Maybe someday you'll meet the perfect mage, one who takes you to bar fights but somehow manages not to hurt anyone at them." He stepped closer to me and I stepped back. I was done holding my ground.

"Good night, Drake."

I turned and ran, but hadn't gotten two steps before he grabbed my arm and swung me around. I stared up at him, his arms around me strong and burning.

"You're going in the wrong direction. That's the way to the woods." He closed his eyes, bent his head, nose against my hair and inhaled deeply. "If you were half as delicious you'd still be irresistible. Run quickly and I'll try not to chase you."

He let me go, pushed me in the right direction and I ran, lifting up my skirt while my cloak and hair billowed behind me.

When he howled, I almost looked over my shoulder, but kept my feet moving away from him, chest aching, body protesting. I wanted those arms around me and I never wanted him to let go. I'd lied. Of course I wanted the worst mage in the world, just like my mother, just like Poppy.

31
WITCH

My room. My bed. My blanket over my head. Señor Mort snuggled into my neck while I closed my eyes tight, ignoring Viney pounding on my door.

"I'm sleeping," I finally yelled and she was quiet after that.

I wasn't though, not really. Who could sleep after their whole insides have been jiggled and dumped out then poured back inside in any random order? I threw my blankets back and sat up. My hands were still shaking from unspent energy, the kind that needed an outlet. I put my bare legs over the side of the bed, sending it rocking. I slid to the floor and pulled my computer out of my bag, sat down at the tea party table, and logged into a site I hadn't been to in almost a year.

The icon blinked showing that I had over eight hundred comments awaiting moderation. That was not what I was in the mood for. I checked the last order that I'd agreed to fill and hadn't. Three finus balls. I double checked the size and went to my trunks. I had all the ingredients to make them, the coloring, the dusting, the flickering flare: the perfect end to a good fight.

First, I had to blow the balls out of the elastic earthen putty, which meant kneading and rolling and beating, which I enjoyed. A lot. It helped to focus my mind and relax my body. I added the colored swirls to the thin membrane before I lit my burner and put in my drops of clear finisher.

Chemistry. If only class was a little more relevant than memorizing some table that didn't even have all the ingredients I used.

By the time I had the balls blown, they were a clear slightly colored swirl of green and pink. I blew five of them then moved to the insides. I filled the injection stick with layers of sparks and ashes with a fine filling of fire before I carefully pricked the balls, injected the filler and then rolled the ball between my heavily gloved fingers, kneading it back into place. It would have to cure for hours before they could be shipped without exploding on the way.

It was already afternoon when I peeled off my gloves and goggles and stared at Señor Mort curled on my pillow. I did not want to sleep. I did not want to think. I turned to my trunks, pulled out some emergency meal bars, ate breakfast and went back to work.

I put on my headphones, listened to Chinese soap opera, and started working on my best-selling beauty products. When I was finally tired, truly tired, I opened my computer, went to the special delivery service, ordered one for the next morning, and then back to that site with all the unread comments and marked the sale, 'delivery scheduled.'

I took a long bath, washed my hair, and went to bed.

I woke up with my phone beeping, my clock showing the time four-thirty a.m. I checked the text and read, 'pickup available for fragile parcel at Northeast loading dock.'

Wherever that was. Northeast at school, that would be two buildings from where I was, towards the polo field. I didn't reply because the text disappeared without leaving a number. I got dressed in my school uniform hastily, my hair once more curly as I carefully picked up the parcels and my bag then opened my door.

Zach was sleeping on the couch, one of his legs on the floor while the video game screen flickered, a control still in his hands. I hesitated and pulled the blanket over his shoulder before I continued on my way out.

I hurried along the empty corridor until I crossed a large driveway then through a covered columned walkway until I reached the

Northeast corner of school. No one was parked anywhere I could see, so I stepped off the walkway and headed down the drive beside the tall brick building. The windows were smaller and closer together the further I walked from the main drive, like smaller quarters were inside the building than in the glorious elevated halls of school. Was this maintenance and housekeeping? I always liked those kinds of people. If Drake were a normal person who could hang a swing and do laundry, I wouldn't be able to resist him.

A building jutted out, like a garage or something, and when I went around it, a brown delivery truck was waiting for me. I stopped walking while I stared at that truck, feeling my heart pound for no reason. It's not like my old crush would actually be here.

"Caramia. Is that Penny Lane? It couldn't be with those strawberry curls."

I searched the shadows between the building and saw the delivery man leaning against the corner, his deep-set eyes mostly hidden beneath the fall of coal black hair.

I dropped my bag and package then ran, my feet pounding on the ground before I threw myself at him.

He didn't fall back at the impact and when I wrapped my arms around him, he hesitated only for a moment before he laughed and wrapped his arms around me, swinging me around like I was still eleven years old.

When he put me down, I stared at him before I pulled back and punched him in the shoulder.

He winced. "Ach, goldie locks still hits like a witch."

I grabbed the lapel of his stained and somewhat unsavory looking jacket. "You just disappeared!" I shook him but he was fairly solid and only tilted his lips slightly.

"Not at all. I went back to Darkside for a wedding and when I returned I had a replacement. It happens in the delivery business."

He shrugged while my heart ached. I yanked his lapel closer, staring into his black beady eyes before I let him go and turned away, crossing my arms over my chest. I was acting like a child. "Congratulations on the marriage."

He laughed and shook his head. "Ah, Caramia, who would marry this ugly face? It was my cousin, a handsome, strapping lad if ever there was one married a girl with the largest dowry I've ever seen." He wiggled his eyebrows.

"Right. That's my job."

His lips twisted. "Ah, the boys at this school, they're your peers, so you must be here hunting for a husband. Have you picked one yet?"

I winced because I'd talked to the delivery man far too much over the years, telling him all about my Grandmama's will before I knew that deliverymen get transferred without informing any of their customers.

He'd slipped into the Italianesque language we'd crafted together, Italian roots but mostly words I'd made up. Poppy hadn't ever approved of my friendship with Signore Ludi. She hated the way he looked at her without blinking, his eyes beneath jutting brows that were cleft and swelling, marked and pocked.

The first time I'd seen him, eight or so, I'd come out to sign for the package and when I took the clipboard, he covered my forearms with his hands, rough, calloused skin and made the hurt less. I'd looked at him and seen the hurt in his face, so I'd put my hands over his cheek and took it out of him. It was only fair.

He cocked his head and I realized I wasn't paying attention to what he was saying, asking about the contents of the package.

I told him that it was a package of finus in green and pink.

"When is your birthday?" he asked in our secret language.

"Not until spring. I have ages to find a peer." I wrinkled my nose. The language felt strange on my tongue. "I don't have anything to give you to drink."

He smiled slightly, the curve of his lips out of place in his deformed face.

I beamed back at him because his smile was beautiful to me. I tugged on his long hair. "You need a trim. And you're out of uniform. Do you remember teaching me to dance? It did absolutely no good. At this school everyone is a ballerina, and a horseman, and a linguist and a genius." I wrapped my arms around him for another hug because I needed one or I would burst into tears or something. I'd forgotten how it felt to have a friend, a real person I didn't have to pretend with.

He patted my back and murmured words I didn't understand but they made me feel better anyway. Finally, he pulled back and studied my face carefully before he said, "You aren't too lonely, though, are you? You have more people to talk to than Señor Mort."

I nodded. "I do have some friends, I think, but it's hard to tell. I keep waiting for someone to light my hair on fire."

He laughed, a growly sound that lacked any of the mesmerizing beauty of Drake's laugh. Of course it did. Drake and Signore Ludi were complete opposites. "There must be someone that you wouldn't mind lighting you on fire."

I pushed away from him and smoothed down my jacket and skirt. "I'm not here for that, literally or figuratively."

He brushed my cheek with his rough fingers. "You are blushing. Is he a peer, an appropriate match for my Caramia?"

I rolled my eyes and crossed my arms. "You are much too anxious to marry me off. I told you that I'm going to marry you."

His smile curled tighter. "My Caramia needs someone young and bold, someone like that gentlemen over there."

He gestured behind me and I whirled around to see Drake in the dim morning light seem to unfold from the shadows.

Signore Ludi called out to him with a wave, speaking in a different language, a guttural tongue full of curled lips and soft hisses. The last time I'd heard that language was the last time I'd seen Signore Ludi.

Drake walked towards us a few steps before he nodded like a regal prince and responded in that same stomach wrenching language.

I'd been sitting in the small enclosed porch, refilling Señore Ludi's glass when Revere had stalked in, his dark eyes like carved pieces of stone, glinting. I'd spilled the golden liquid onto the table and the deliveryman covered my hand with his, righting the bottle.

Whatever Revere said to Signore Ludi I'd never know, but I could smell smoke, dust, and something else, something that reminded me of pain when Revere turned to me with a brittle smile.

"Penny, show your friend your scars. It's bad manners to see someone's exposed wounds and not respond in kind."

I stared at him, my fingers numb beneath the pressure of Signore Ludi. "I've already shown him my ribs. He helped me how to adjust them so they don't ache all the time."

Revere's smile twisted into a peculiarly dangerous shape. "Your back, Penny. Show him your back."

I gasped and blinked in Drake's perfect face, a slightly derisive expression on it. I stepped forward, throwing my arms wide like I could protect Signore Ludi from Drake and the rest of the world.

"What are you doing here? What did you say?"

Signore Ludi cleared his throat behind me before he pulled my arms down and moved me to the side. "I told him I saw him in Darkside as the devil's advocate. It's a kind of errand boy position, isn't that right, young master." Signore swept a bow that seemed mocking with his misshapen shoulder although it looked better than it had the first time I'd seen him, the last time as well.

Drake cleared his throat. "I'm sorry to interrupt. Penny, can I have a word?"

"I need to be on my way. Do you have your parcels for me, Caramia?"

I nodded and went over to my bag and the packages I'd dropped so carelessly. I had a lot of beauty goods to send as well as that one particular package, the one that had brought Signore Ludi. "Can you take these as well?" I asked in our language. "They're only lotions and things."

He nodded with a wide grin. "Of course. Maybe I'll have to order some to make my face pretty enough to catch a bride." He squeezed my hand before he nodded respectfully at Drake and climbed into the brown delivery truck and drove away.

Drake shook his head, a forced smile on his supple lips. My fingers tingled and I edged away from him to pick up my bag and put it over my shoulder.

"Are you all right?"

I frowned at him. "Of course."

He hesitated, glanced after the large truck and back to me. "I thought you made up your delivery man. He's very interesting."

My heart pounded in my chest and my back seemed to burn. Scars. I had enough of them. Drake should have looked normal, ordinary in the light of day, but I could still feel his weight on me in the field beneath the stars, still see him with his bare muscles straining against Ian.

"We're friends, I mean we're barely acquaintances. I need to get to class."

He grabbed my arm as I passed and held out a muffin. I stared at him, his eyes hooded, dark in the early morning light.

"You didn't come out of your room all day yesterday. You have to be careful or you're going to starve to death."

I inhaled shakily before I took the muffin and bit in. It was moist and sweet, with lumps of cherries and chocolate. I chewed slowly while he filled my senses. I grew hot while he leaned closer, the flavor on my tongue so much like I imagined his skin tasted. I leaned closer, feeling the pull towards him as inevitable as falling before I jerked upright.

"Thanks. I am starving. You need to stay back so that I don't accidentally eat you."

He grinned widely and leaned even closer. "You tease but I don't think you're ever going to fulfill your promises."

I held my breath while I edged away. "I need to get to class."

"You said that."

I nodded, shook my head and then spun around, running away from him for the second time in two days.

32
MAGE

I didn't think very much about it, simply stepped into Darkside for a moment then back into Dayside on the road outside of Rosewood that wound down the mountain. I was inside the boundary where shifting of large vehicles through Darkside was forcibly prohibited. Penny's Darksider would have to go through me before he left.

"You're being an idiot," I mumbled, but held my position, legs apart, waiting for the screeching truck and wild-eyed Darksider. The sound of the truck rumbling in the distance grew louder, but not that loud, not even when it followed the curve of the road into view. He slowed down as soon as he saw me and then pulled over in the grass before he shut off the engine.

I had to walk up the road to him while he got out of the truck, his body bulky, mangled, but not too bad considering his origin. He would be considered handsome for a Darksider. Some witches disliked pretty boys like myself and Ian, said we lacked character, strength, virility. I can't say how utterly heartbreaking it was to hear such slurs from the mouths of Darkside witches.

"What can I do for you?" His voice was even, well-modulated, his eyes bright with intelligence and amusement.

Lovely, he found me amusing. "I want to see what packages she had delivered."

He raised his eyebrows and smiled wider. "I guarantee privacy to my clients. I'm sure you understand."

I stared at him. He sounded so sane and rational. I rubbed my chin. "I'm always looking for reliable transporters. Would you be interested in a very well-paying job?"

He barked a laugh, his lips curling over very nice teeth. "I have more work than I can handle. Thanks all the same."

"They come with extremely good benefits."

His eyebrows quirked. "Ah, the irresistible Huntsman offer of sanity in exchange for services. I'm not in the market for sanity just now."

I stared at him. "I can see that. Penny told me about you, all about her exotic deliveryman whom she gave whiskey to in exchange for ghost stories."

His smile faded. "I see."

I struggled not to clench my jaw, to stay calm, rational, at least as sane as this Darksider. "Do you?"

He shook his head. "Penny is…"

I waited, pressing my palms against the sides of my pants, staying very still and calm.

"I can't discuss my clients. You underst…"

I took a step forward, arms swinging up and bringing green flame swords to life in my hands. They sparked and sizzled from the strength of my irritation.

He cocked his head. "You do not wish to fight me."

I raised an eyebrow. "Oh, I do."

He smiled a little bit, a dark smile of near anticipation before he shook his head with regret. "You see, I am her friend. She needs friends. She values relationships with people, witches, mages, even weasels and rabbits. I am not going to hurt you, because you are her friend, and hurting you would hurt her. I do not hurt Penny Lane in any way. Do you understand?"

I gritted my teeth and with a hiss put out the fire swords. "You won't fight me. You'll stand there and let me slaughter you and then Penny will know that I'm a brutal beast. You play dirty, even for a

Darksider."

He laughed, shaking his head like this was extremely amusing to him. "I do," he finally said when his chuckles subsided. "I play very dirty. Did you want anything else? A package delivered, perhaps? The first one is free."

"And subsequent ones? What does Penny pay you for her deliveries? I didn't notice any money changing hands."

His smile became tight. "I do not discuss clients."

I nodded. "Oh, right. I forgot. If I'm your client, will you give me hugs and swing me around, too, because I've always wanted to be petted by a Darksider."

His smile stayed on his ugly face, solid, immovable. "If you would like."

I laughed. "A Darksider with a sense of humor, you must have a very peculiar sense of humor if you like Penny Lane. Maybe you're the one who gave it to her. Do the two of you watch Telenovelas together as well?"

He sighed. "Does she still enjoy those? I don't think those were the exact influence her personality required."

"What influence do you think someone like Penny Lane needs?"

He studied me, walking forward until we were only two feet apart then walked around me, inhaling deeply like he was smelling me. How Darksiders even had a sense of smell after living in Darkside, I had no idea.

He came to stop in front of me and put a hand on my shoulder. His hand was heavy, like it was made of rocks instead of flesh. "Penny Lane requires affection, protection, and imagination. She's…"

"Beautiful."

He cocked his head as though that was strange, pulling his hand off my shoulder and sniffing his fingers. "Ridiculous, infuriating, a monkey that will pull your hair as she rides on your back. Dangerous, so full of craving, aching, needing to be adored that I'm not sure she will ever be satisfied."

"You say that she needs love? A witch?"

He studied me for a long time. "You are not ideal," he finally said, his brows lowering.

"Excuse me? I thought you said that you weren't going to…"

He attacked, a simple strike at my throat that bounced off my shield. Being around Penny I almost forgot that I had one. His other hand swirled a complex pattern that weakened my shield while he struck me again, grabbing my throat in his enormous hand.

I stood there with his hand around my throat. I'm not exactly a pacifist, but he'd brought up a very good point. This Darksider was Penny Lane's friend. She'd told me about him when she'd been rambling on in the grip of the fear, the curse. She hadn't been nearly as sick since then. Maybe it had to do with all the spells I put on her as we drove, maybe she was getting used to it from prolonged exposure, or maybe it had something to do with holding my hand, pulling my energy into her, comfort, taken and given.

I let him choke me until the edges of my vision went dark. Finally, he dropped his hand and crossed his arms over his chest, peering at me. "Avarice, violence, greed, and those eyes, the green in them like the rising of Heliotrope in the East." He studied me for a long while before he finally nodded tersely. "If she chooses you, we'll have to make the most of it. There are advantages to being… green." He said that last with a sly smile before he stepped away from me. He dusted his hands on his pants as thought my immaculate skin might contaminate his Darkside fingers, fingers he'd touched Penny with, sliding them through her golden strands when she didn't notice.

"You don't want her?"

"I'm not a dragon that collects pretty objects. I'm a deliveryman. My business is arranging and fulfilling the needs of others."

I frowned at him. "You do want her."

He continued towards his truck.

I stood there watching him go filled with the strangest mix of anxiety and relief. He wasn't claiming her even though he'd known her longer and she clearly preferred him over me. Why didn't he claim her, take her to Darkside as his bride? If she was an aberration, she was priceless, but perhaps he didn't have the resources to protect her, a witch who could love. Whatever else I was, I had the resources to protect a precious commodity. Whether or not I had the capacity to love her, I couldn't say.

33
WITCH

By the time I got to English class, I was out of breath, and my heart pounded hard in my chest. Signore had picked up my delivery, the first delivery of its kind I'd made in so long. What were the odds of that happening?

I sat through the class in a daze, not hearing the teacher or noticing when class was over until Wit came over and sat on my desk.

"Penny, what did you think of the Chemistry captain on Saturday night? Is Drake finally living up to his reputation?"

She glanced at a straight-haired brunette and they shared malicious smiles although the other girl looked a little bit sick.

"Yeah, he's pretty awesome. I've got to get to class."

I started to stand, but Wit pushed me back down, her arm strong, firm. She leaned back, tossed her hair and pursed her luscious lips. "I feel like you're at a disadvantage from being the new girl and not understanding the history, the dynamic of someone like Drake Huntsman. I think that you're going to take his interest personally instead of for what it really is."

I unwrapped a lollipop and put it in my mouth. "I'm sorry, what personal interest?"

Her smile grew tighter while I stared at her with large, dewy eyes. "Drake's sudden fame in Freshman year was unexpected. We were all surprised. I was dating Ian at the time. We go way back. After we broke up, I went out with Drake, but it turns out he didn't like being with just one girl, in fact, he had girls lined up begging to give him whatever he wanted, so why be with just one girl, even a girl like me?"

She leaned over me, like a vulture about to peck out my face. "Do you know what someone like Drake does with girls?"

My stomach tightened and I gripped the edge of the desk but didn't answer. I didn't like her being so close. I didn't like the look on her face or the way that anger poured off her, anger and something else, something thick and cloying.

I swallowed while nausea swirled in my stomach. I shook my head. "It's none of my business."

She shrugged, her perfectly tailored little jacket over her clearly overwhelming assets. "It wouldn't be anyone's business, except that he likes to publicly objectify the poor things so everyone can be entertained by Drake's special treat. Girls will do anything to prove their love to someone like him."

I bolted out of my chair and barely made it to the garbage can before I threw up. I heard Wit and her friend laughing as they left me to it.

I staggered upright and went straight to my room. This day wasn't going to happen.

When I got to Lilac Stories, Professor Vale was coming out. "Why aren't you in class?"

"I threw up in English. I'm sick. I need to lay down and never ever get out of bed again."

She put her hand on my shoulder and steered me into my room. Once there she checked my temperature, looked in my mouth, eyes, felt my neck, and then shook her head.

"It's not a communicable illness, but you do seem exhausted and dehydrated. I'm going to bring you soup for lunch but try to rest now."

I nodded and waited until she brought me a glass of water. After she left I took off my uniform, put on my robe, and snuggled with Señor Mort.

That's what he was waiting for, me to love him so much that I would do anything for him, publicly, ruining any chance I ever had with a nice mage, if I could find one of those. I groaned and rolled over, burying my face in my pillow.

I woke up to knocking on my door. It wasn't loud but it went on and on and on until I groaned and rolled out of bed. It must be Professor Vale and the soup. I was so hungry, I was going to eat Señor Mort, fur and all if I didn't eat something else. My stomach lurched.

I took a deep breath and swung open the door with a wide smile then froze when I saw Zach holding a tray of soup and breadsticks. I chewed on my lip as I stared at the boy who was in love with a poster, the boy I'd decided to marry before I knew him.

"Penny, are you feeling better?"

I smiled at him sickly and backed up while he came through the door, arranging the tray on my table.

"I am starving. Thanks so much for bringing food. Will you taste it for me?"

He smiled at me, a nice smile that crinkling his eyes while he dipped his fingers in the soup and popped a carrot in his mouth. "Very healthy. Maybe I shouldn't mention it when you're sick, but the other night when I was with Drake and Ian, they knocked over a candy store and I brought back a bunch of stuff for you. You have to watch out for glass though."

He frowned slightly while I sat down and ate. It was finished too soon and then my breadsticks were too.

"Mmm. Wait, what? You knocked over a candy store?"

He shook his head. "I think that Ian threw Drake through the window. While we were there, I thought of you and…"

"You stole candy? That's so sweet if completely wrong."

He shook his head. "Oh, we paid for it along with the rest of the damages. We always pay for it. Drake will split the bill three ways like usual."

Drake. I bent over the table and put my head in the soup bowl moaning.

"Hey, are you really sick?" Zach put his hand on my shoulder and I took my face out of the soup bowl and laid it on his shoulder instead.

"Zach, have you seen what Drake makes girls do in public?"

He stiffened. "Um, what?"

"I hate men. They're so disgusting."

"Did Ian... Did Drake..."

I shook my head vehemently, still buried in his shirt. "No, no, no, no, no!"

He patted my shoulder awkwardly. "Drake was really worried about you yesterday when you didn't come out of your room all day. We all were. If you were sick, you should have told someone so we could bring you soup. Professor Vale insisted that you just needed some time alone."

I lifted my head slowly as I stared at Zach who was pathetic for loving a poster, but probably not as pathetic as me who felt irrationally betrayed by something Drake may or may not have done years ago. That's what the sickness was, me thinking of Drake with other girls even though I already knew that Drake was that kind of person. Drake was the irresistible type who ruined women. Big surprise. Of course, if he was the type to do that, what was going to stop him from informing the school about Signore Ludi, maybe get him in trouble and keep me from seeing him again, just for fun?

I chewed on my lip. "How was your drunken spree, did you have a bar fight? Did someone smash a chair over someone's head? I always wanted to see that."

He smiled slightly as he rubbed my forehead with his finger. "You have soup." He stuck it in his mouth and I saw Drake's teeth, his smile, him sucking on my fingers as he made a scene in public just because he could.

I swallowed and rubbed my forehead with the back of my hand. "Sorry. I think I got it on your shirt."

He smiled and shrugged. "Not a big deal. No, I don't think we smashed any chairs. If you ever come along I'll make sure to smash all the chairs."

I nodded and lay over on the table, head on my arm. "Zach, don't you have classes?"

"It's lunch, and after lunch I'm supposed to be your riding tutor, so I don't have anywhere to be."

I stared at him. "Do you have any easy video games that I could play?"

He grinned widely. "I have my old Nintendo DS and all my old games. They're classics. I'll set it up for you."

I followed him out of my room after putting Señor Mort back in his cage and then realized that I wasn't wearing very much. I grabbed a quilt off the bed all tangled vines and voluptuous roses and wrapped it around the robe that liked to fall off my shoulders before I went out and sat on the couch.

He sat beside me and showed me how the controllers worked, and explained that the goal was to squash mushrooms and collect gold coins. It was fairly straightforward, and he just sat there telling me what to do, gesturing kind of wildly when I was supposed to jump over the abyss then throwing himself back in anguish when I fell to my death.

I giggled because he was as dramatic about Luigi as I was about telenovelas.

I played video games after Zach left me to go to his afternoon classes, and then fell asleep because apparently I really was sick and not just nauseous from the Drake thing. That made me feel slightly better because it was ridiculous for me to care at all, not to mention have a physical reaction like that.

I woke up when Zach took the controller out of my hands.

I stretched and sat up, almost feeling better. I caught Zach's hand. "Thanks, Zach. For a guy in love with a poster, you have a lot of compassion."

He sighed. "Sorry about that. I didn't mean to go on and on about her the other night. I'm such a loser."

I laughed. "She's a cool poster, Zach. No shame! Let your freak flag fly, isn't that it?"

He perched on the edge of the couch and leaned over to me. "Do you really not mind me talking about it? It drives Viney insane."

I shrugged. "I'm already insane."

He licked his lips and leaned closer like he was about to reveal state secrets. "Pitch hasn't been heard of or seen for over a year. She just disappeared without a trace, and her alchemist stopped supplying around that same time, but recently, someone received an order they made with Pitch's supplier so there's a buzz that maybe Pitch is back, or maybe not. I don't want to get all crazy for nothing, but it seems strange that Pitch's alchemist would be working again if Pitch wasn't coming back. What do you think?"

I stared at him while I tried to process this new development. Zach was totally mental. I smiled at him and patted his shoulder. "Wow. That's really exciting. Can you contact the supplier directly to find out if they're still working with Pitch or if she left the country or something?"

He sighed. "It's like a black hole."

"Pitch black."

He gave me a dirty look while I tried not to giggle. "The supplier is incredibly particular about the kinds of hurters he supplies, and the only link we actually have between him and Pitch is that he makes what she uses, and no one else makes hurters exactly like that."

"Oooh, maybe the supplier and Pitch are secret lovers, but there's some kind of obstacle, a curse or a secret, maybe a dead body. They had to go underground to be together but then their love child needs an operation, so the supplier has to have some quick cash. Meanwhile, the mafia is tracking their movements and their only hope is in black market hearts for the baby."

He stared at me flatly before he grinned. He pushed my shoulder, knocking me back into the couch. "That's probably what I sound like to Viney."

I rubbed my shoulder. "Be gentle with me, Zach. You have to remember that you're a blue ninja and must use your super powers for good and not evil."

"I'm sorry." He rubbed my shoulder a little bit before he froze, his arm still on me. "Did Ian really walk with you after the tourney?"

I shifted uncomfortably and patted his hand. "Weird, right? It was weird. It all started with the jeans. And then everything else." Drake in green liquid light. I scowled at the blanket before I took a deep breath. "Classes are over? I don't even know what time it is. Do you know where Drake is?"

"Polo practice."

I winced. "Awesome. When does that end?"

"Let me check my Drake calendar." He rolled his eyes.

Viney slammed in the door, glaring at me. "Are you still sick?"

I shrugged.

Zach pointed at her. "She would know. When does Drake finish with polo practice?"

She narrowed her eyes at him suspiciously. "Five-forty-five. Why?"

He shrugged and pointed at me. "Viney is a walking talking Drake calendar. She stalks Drake like I stalk Pitch. It makes us very empathetic. It's really too bad that you can't obsess with someone untouchable, it would make our threesome complete."

Viney leaned over the couch to peer into my eyes, stopping two inches away from my nose. I stared at her smelling tiramisu on her breath.

"Hi, Viney."

"You want to go see Drake? That's weird." She put her hand on my forehead.

I pushed it off and scooted away from her. "It's not weird. I need to talk to him. I don't want to see him, but I need to. I forgot something this morning, and I have to get it back."

"This morning?" She looked so suspicious.

"I ran into Drake before classes. He gave me a muffin. Maybe the muffin was poisoned and that's why I'm sick."

Zach shook his head. "Drake made the muffins himself and I ate five. Chocolate black cherry?"

I nodded and felt my stomach lurch. Drake shouldn't be making me muffins when he was so vile. Also, if he did make them, he shouldn't give any of them to Zach instead of me.

"Let's play video games until Penny has to go stalk Drake," Viney said, picking up a controller. "What is this? Are you serious?" She made a face, but it didn't keep her from pushing start. They did a two-player game, and Zach was as hilarious to watch as Viney. I sat between them looking from one to the other while they bluffed and blustered, howled and screeched.

Professor Vale came in with more soup. I thanked her and ate while pointing out the dangerous bad guy that Zach clearly saw. It was fun and when I'd finished my soup, Viney turned to me and nodded seriously.

"You need to hurry if you're going to catch him between his shower and dinner. Do you want me to come with you? I can show you where to watch for him."

Zach wacked her shoulder. "Shameless, Viney. You're going to freak her out."

"Already freaked. No thanks, Viney. It will only take a few minutes."

I got dressed in a short skirt and cute pink blouse before I waved goodbye and headed to the polo field. I wasn't really up for it, not the way girls stared at me and whispered not so quietly about 'Pukey Penny'. I smiled and tried to communicate my willingness to go all Penny Pukey on them, which seemed to work rather well, or they thought they'd catch my bug.

Anyway, I made it to the polo field but I felt drained and my hands trembled while I waited by the fence. A guy rode by on his stud, pulled up his horse and whirled it around towards me. I thought he'd trample me, but he pulled up right in front of me, his horse pawing and snorting while he smiled.

"Are you looking for Drake?"

I nodded while my heart pounded and I pressed myself away from the horse. The guy looked familiar, but he only whirled back around on his horse and pounded away into the stable.

I swallowed down nausea and fought the urge to leave. I took five steps away then forced myself back, walked away, and forced myself back. It was pacing and it was perfectly respectable. Drake came up to me on his prancing horse, sliding down beside me before I could run away screaming.

"Penny. Shouldn't you be in bed?"

I stared at him. The last time he'd talked about me being in bed was at night with a star on his face. I swallowed and forced a smile. "Actually, I wondered if I could talk to you."

"Of course. I smell horrible. If you'd like to wait until I shower we can go in to dinner together."

I put up my hands, fending off that idea. My mouth watered at his 'horrible smell' because the scent of dark cherries was stronger than ever and his cheek had a streak of dirt on it. I reached up and rubbed it without thinking. The contact shocked me and him, his eyes widening and showing green while I froze, hand still on his cheek.

"You have some dirt." I pulled my fingers away while he smiled all the way to his eyes.

"I do. A lot. Is that what you wanted to talk about? It's a fascinating topic."

I exhaled and chewed on my lower lip. This was going to be awkward. "This morning you saw me with Signore Ludi."

He nodded. "I remember. He's a friendly acquaintance of yours."

I frowned and nodded. "Drake, I'm not very good at begging or blackmail. Is there anything that you want that I can give you to keep you from talking about what you saw?"

He stepped closer, putting his hand on my forehead and peering in to my eyes. "Say ah."

I pushed him away. "Everyone already did that. This isn't a feverish moment, at least I don't think it is."

"Don't you want to throw up when I touch you?"

I stared at him. "Not any more than usual. Drake, I'm serious. The last time I saw Signore, he had a thing with Revere and I know that he says he went to a wedding, but Revere was always getting rid of anyone I got too close to, anyone I got too friendly with, so I think it's pretty much impossible that Revere wasn't involved with my only friend in the world leaving and not coming back. I know it looked a little bit…"

"Affectionate."

I shrugged and nodded slightly. "It wasn't, though."

"Of course not." He stared into my eyes. "You came all the way here, waiting for me just so you could ask me not to tell your step-father about your delivery man? Hm. And you're offering me something in exchange, only you're not sure what."

"Within reason. Lollipops or foot rubs, nothing like…"

"Go to the dance with me."

I stared at him. "The dance?"

He nodded. "It's getting really irritating. I'll show you."

He led the horse around so I could see its other side and words shaved into it. 'Be my prince and I'll be your princess at the fairy tale Dance, -Corinne Bailey'

"Corinne Bailey, who is she?"

His lips thinned. "She's the girl who broke into the stables and drugged my horse just so she could shave demon without getting mauled. Stupid boy, taking sugar cubes without getting a weasel to taste test them first."

"Señor Mort is not available. What would hurt a horse would kill him."

He shook his head. "Of course not. I'm talking about a different weasel, like Jackson. I'm sorry to offend weasels everywhere. Anyway, will you please agree to go to the dance with me so that my horse isn't shamed again?"

I swallowed and nodded. He held out his hand.

"Shake on it?"

I hesitated, fighting an overwhelming feeling of falling before I put my palm against his. "One dance won't hurt."

He smiled at me, leaning close before I pulled away from him.

"I'm going to go lie down. Thanks, Drake."

34
Mage

Witley cursed Penny. The whole school buzzed with it, the curse that was designed for one purpose, potent and clear: Penny could not have me. Physically her body would rebel at close physical proximity to me.

She'd looked terrible waiting for me by the fence, like a scared little mouse, but she touched me, well, the dirt off my face, but my cheek was quite clearly beneath that dirt. If she could touch me then her protective counter spell was holding up, doing its best to minimize the effects of Witley's curse.

I went in to dinner that night in time to see Viney confront Wit.

"Pathetic, Wit. Can't get a guy on your own, have to take out the competition?" Viney glowered at Wit, her spiked wrists crossed over her chest matching her dark spiked hair. She reminded me of a terrier about to take out a rat.

The rat was sleek and oily, glistening from her eyes to her sharp teeth as she tossed her lustrous black curls. "You care, why? Don't pretend that you like the stupid little tart. You should be grateful to me for putting her in her place."

Jackson edged closer to Witley while Zach backed up Viney, his face stony.

Getting between two witches was extremely stupid. Grinning broadly, I walked directly to the center of the conflict.

"Ladies, ladies, there's more than enough of me to go around."

Viney glowered at me while Wit smiled sharply, lips curving as she glanced up and down my body appreciatively. Sometimes Penny accidentally looked at me and blushed.

"What are you doing, Drake," Viney hissed.

"Being fought over, apparently. Witley, I have to thank you for whatever you did to Penny. She's such a charmingly contrary creature. The more I pursue her, the more she retreats, but after your encouragement, she agreed to attend the dance with me. I'm so delighted, I could kiss you."

Wit's face went pale and Viney smirked. Zach raised an eyebrow and gave me a skeptical glance. Jackson stood beside Wit looking kind of blank and passive. He didn't care. I studied Jackson because we still had unfinished business with the room he'd trashed.

Witley's lips curled. "She'll have a hard time dancing with you while throwing up."

I smiled. "Do you think so? Professor Vale was quite certain that she would be perfectly fine."

She clenched her teeth and glared at Viney. "That's right, you need a dorm mommy to take care of you."

Viney raised an eyebrow and crossed her arms over her skull t-shirt. "I think you need a dorm mother to take care of you if you can't control your cattiness. Maybe Drake would like you if you weren't so desperate."

Witley clenched her fists while I purposefully stepped in front of Viney. I smiled widely at Wit. "I like desperate women. I like all kinds of women. You're welcome to join my harem any time, Wit."

I pulled a green knife out of thin air, the blade curved and delicate, like an over-size scalpel. Wit went pale, her lips twisting into a snarl before she whirled away, slinking out of the room. I put a hand on Jackon's shoulder while I made the knife vanish.

"Did you eat, Jackson? Sit with me. I think we have a lot to discuss."

35
WITCH

The next day was okay until I got into Pas de Deux, and Drake was standing there by the piano, talking to the pianist. I turned around and walked back into the dressing room. I sat on the bench and leaned over my knees. Would he really keep what he knew about Signore to himself? How could I touch him, let him touch me when I kept having an image of girls and him and…

I shook my head. I did not need to think about those things. It wasn't any of my business. I sat there until Madame came and started lecturing me in French about how if I had a headache I should at least do it with good posture and real ladies do not make an entire class wait for them.

I gave her a smile and stood up, forcing myself into the studio. I went to the end of the bar, far away from where Drake was bending and stretching.

He ignored me, but I couldn't help watching him, those muscles beneath the soft fabric, not tights like some of the guys wore shamelessly, but I'd seen him in so much less, felt his body on top of me dislocating my ribs.

When we moved into the center of the room, I waited for Drake to put his hands on my waist like all the other boys were doing, but instead, he stood behind me with his hands on his waist. I waited for a few minutes before I turned around.

"What are you doing?"

"Shh. No talking in ballet class." His words were stern, but there was a glimmer of smile in his eyes.

I turned around and stood there stupidly waiting for another few minutes until he finally put his hands on my waist, firm hands holding onto my sides but instead of lifting, he just kept his hands there. Five minutes we stood there until we moved to the next position, which was him holding my hand while I stood on tiptoe and tried to keep my leg outstretched behind me in a beautiful line.

"Drake, you're killing me. I've been holding my leg in the air for five hours."

"You exaggerate. It's only been two." He glanced at me before he focused once more above my left shoulder.

"What are you…"

"Shhhh! No talking in ballet class!" Madame clapped her hands for emphasis and that was the last time I tried to communicate with my partner. Fine. If he wanted to act weird, I could handle that. I could double that. The next time he took a long time grabbing my leg and lifting me above his head, I grabbed his leg and proceeded to lift it off the ground. Not him though. No. I was not going to get him over my head however irritated I was. He watched me blankly while his foot kept going up and up until it touched his ear then I put it down.

"Aren't you going to lift me?"

I rolled my eyes. He was ridiculously flexible and his feet pointed beautifully.

After class I hurried to change then went into the hall, only brought up short by a girl with mascara streaked down her cheeks.

"Are you really going to the dance with Drake?" she scream/sobbed at me.

I glanced around and the hall was filled with people still as statues, waiting for the outcome. I took a deep breath. Signore. "Yes, I am. We're going as friends."

She started wailing and screaming about the injustice of life while I edged around her. I glanced up and caught Drake's eye where he watched the proceedings with a great deal of satisfaction on his face. Well fine, I was pretty satisfied myself.

After the rest of my classes, including Business which I got through without actually talking to Drake, I stumbled into History to collapse beside Viney.

"Are you okay? Don't puke on me."

I pulled out a lollypop and unwrapped it, cellophane crackling satisfyingly. "No, just tired."

She stared at me. "Are you really going to the dance with Drake?"

I winced. "I guess I am. I think he blackmailed me."

She wrinkled her face up. "I didn't think you'd want to talk to him after that whole thing with Wit, but now you're going to the dance with him? It's weird."

"What thing with Wit?" My stomach tightened and I tasted bile. At least it wasn't black cherry.

"Everyone knows what Wit told you about Drake. It's…"

"Books open, please."

I opened my book and refused to look at Viney for the rest of the class. Afterwards there was homework, lots of it because I'd missed an entire day. I headed to study hall and got to be glared at by Oliver who I kept picturing naked in orange lights.

He paired me with another guy who was remarkably picturesque, all long brown locks and large, soft eyes, with a mouth like genocide. He looked like a telenovela star who wouldn't say much but wouldn't have trouble seducing the entire cast anyway.

He wanted to teach me Italian, which was good because I didn't know real Italian, just Ludi and our secret language. He'd lean forward and give me a definition after licking his lips and looking at me just so beneath his hooded lids.

Finally, it was time to leave. I was nervous when Viney and Zach waited for me at the entrance. What were they doing there?

"Guys, what's going on?"

"We're going with you to do community service." Zach smiled slightly while Viney looked in pain.

"Seriously? I wasn't going to go. I was sick yesterday, so I might still be contagious."

Viney shook her head. "Professor Vale said you're fine. Were you studying with Lester?" She made a face.

"What? He's gorgeous."

She shot me a bewildered look. "What are you talking about? He looks like a wildebeest. All that hair and meat, he's like a…"

"Brooding Heathcliffe. I think he's going to forget that we're speaking Italian and carry me off to some cliff with perpetual lightning storms."

Zach looked at me in confusion. "That's the kind of guy you like? And what's so great about perpetual lightning?"

"Well if I were the bride of Frankenstein, which would be cool, I would be in a constant state of perfect energy and regeneration with all the lightning."

Viney groaned. "So you're saying that Lester is the perfect monster to your monster bride. Now I understand you. Let's go."

She grabbed my arm and hauled me along while Zach gave me a sympathetic smile. After letting her pull me down all those library steps and down the pillared hallways, I pulled away from Viney when I saw Drake's green suburban.

"I don't think…"

"What's wrong, Penny? Are you afraid of me?" Drake stood in the shadows, leaning against the car door with his muscular arms across his chest.

"Should I be?" Yes, yes I should.

He smiled. "I promise to be on my best behavior. I'll play chauffeur while you and Viney ride in the back, and then after we do Community Service, we'll stop at the regular place and eat in our regular booths."

"How is that possible since we'd be four people instead of two?"

He shrugged. "I'll let you work that out. My point is: I'm not a threat."

I mumbled under my breath, 'macaroons and bonbons,' but I climbed in the door he opened for me.

After the ride to the hospital I fell out of the car, eager to get away, but when Drake offered his arm, I stared at it for a moment, knowing what that gesture meant, comfort from my irrational fear of cars. That was sweet. Was there an ulterior motive that I didn't understand? I stared at him for a long time until Viney bumped me.

"Are we going to do something or what?"

We were beautiful princesses by the time the sweet little cancer patients were all done with us. Viney looked at me kind of thoughtfully as I pulled the last of a dozen hair bands out of her hair. She'd looked pretty horrible, like a vampire clown with spots of rouge on her cheeks and red lipstick with her usual black clothing.

"That wasn't too bad," she said softly.

I smiled at her. "I love it."

"That doesn't mean I want to go next week or anything, but I can kind of understand the appeal for someone like you, someone so sweet and innocent she actually believes it when a subterranean like Wit tells her something."

"Subterranean? I knew she was a secret alligator shape shifter. It's in the eyes."

She nudged me kind of hard. "That's not what I'm talking about."

"That's good because who wants to talk about Wit? Not me. Come on, let's see if Zach fainted."

Zach was laughing with Drake about something by the front desk when we came up. He smiled at me, and I beamed back, specifically not looking at Drake, the way he leaned so casually against the desk like he was too cool to be there when he was the one who started this whole thing. I forgot that I wasn't looking at him and smiled instead.

He raised an eyebrow which was close enough to a leer that I had to run away, meaning I grabbed Viney's arm and hustled out of there with her.

"Do you want to sit with me or Drake? Or you could get a separate table with Zach, or a separate table without Zach. So many options."

She didn't understand no matter how many times I explained it until we were actually at the restaurant and the waiter greeted us with bright smiles, two menus, and two tables.

Viney leaned over the table at me. "You sit at separate tables? Why?"

I shrugged. "I don't remember, it just sort of started and now we can't stop. Wait until you've tried the Szechuan chicken. It's incredible. Are you sure you don't want to sit at your own table?"

"I'm sure."

We ordered and then she fixed me with her most steely dark glare. "Drake never did anything with a girl in public as graphic and shocking as you and him with the shake."

I choked on my water, spitting it out all over her. She sighed and rolled her heavily

"Not dinner table conversation, Viney! You're going to kill me. I spend most of my life trying to forget about that moment."

She put her hands on the table, leaning closer. "Wit cursed you so that you wouldn't be able to be with him, but it didn't work, just like all the other curses never stick to you. That's why girls hate you so much. Drake's acting really weird where you're concerned. I know that you came here and Drake's always, 'Penny, let me suck on your fingers, and Penny, let's sing horribly in the bell tower, and Penny, let's go to a dance after you eat this gingerbread house I made from scratch,' but the truth is, he's actually a misogynist who completely hates women. I would suspect him of trying to get close to you just so that he can crush you, but he's exerting way too much effort. His attention span is notoriously short. Why would he go out with you every week and sit in separate booths? What could he possibly get out of that? No one understands. It makes it look as though he actually likes you."

She stared at me while I gazed back blankly.

"Um, fortune cookies?"

She snorted. "You know that's a euphemism, right?" At my blank stare she added helpfully. "You, Drake, a bed..."

I cringed and shook my head which made me dizzy, or the idea of Drake and a bed made me dizzy which was possible. I had way too many issues to keep straight.

"In that case, it's definitely not for the fortune cookies." My cheeks were very hot as I stared at my sesame chicken. It was almost as good as the Szechuan.

She snorted. "When Drake asked us to come with you today so you'd feel pressured to come, I thought he'd corner you somewhere. Do you guys honestly do service, eat separately and then go home? Every week?"

I shrugged and poked my food around. All this talk was making me lose my appetite. "We talk."

"Talk? About what?"

I stabbed a cabbage roll. She sounded a little too interested. "I don't know. Business, Telenovelas, whatever."

She made a disgusted face. "Are you telling me that Drake licking malt off you is the most that you guys have ever done?"

I stuffed the whole cabbage roll in my mouth and shrugged helplessly.

"What's wrong with you? He's willing, isn't he? Is he really just using you to make other girls jealous? That's really cruel of him. But last night, he made it very clear to Wit that her hurting you isn't going to work because the more she pushes you away, the more you want him, whatever curses she uses."

I chewed slowly, but she stared at me until my mouth was empty and I had to answer. "Well, Wit does affect me in horrible ways. I never know what I'm going to say to her."

She narrowed her eyes at me. "Did Drake really blackmail you into going to the dance with him?"

I frowned at her. "I'm not sure. I probably shouldn't try to deal with him when I'm sick. I don't understand him at the best of times."

She shook her head and looked around the room. "You are so strange. You go out with Drake and don't sit and stare at him when you get the chance. I should have sat with him so I could stare at him and he'd try not to notice me staring. This is crazy. I can't stare at him if I want to. Seriously, why would you get a table and not be able to look at Drake? He's perfect, those lips and cheekbones and jaw and hair and eyes and eyebrows and ears and…"

I covered my ears. "Bonbons and macaroons you're as bad as Zach. I'm trying to eat."

She shrugged and then filled her mouth enough that I lowered my hands and ate my own food, but gave her a lot of suspicious glances. After we were finished and left the restaurant, the waiter waved at us enthusiastically, telling us he would see us next week and that my man had paid.

"Your man?" Viney glanced at me while I shrugged.

"He's kind of funny. Did you get your fortune cookie?"

I winced after I'd said it while she gave me an arch look. I hurried away from her and towards Zach and Drake where they sat on the hood, leaning on the windshield, talking about something I couldn't hear. When I got closer I could make out the words, music levels, changing up the rotation, Chemiss stuff.

"I'm going to ride in the back with Zach," Viney announced.

"No," both Drake and I said at the same time then exchanged looks, his amused, mine something a little more terrified.

"No? Fine. I will drive and Zach will ride up front with me while you two ride in the back." She wiggled her eyebrows at me while I stood there feeling like I'd been hit by a truck.

"We haven't gotten malts yet."

"I will buy malts since your man paid for my dinner." Viney held out her hand to Drake until he pulled out his keys and dropped them into her hand, his expression unreadable.

I should have refused, but Drake had already given Viney his keys and was looking at me like he expected me to be afraid of him. "Okay?" I climbed past Drake while he held the back door open for me and slid over when he followed. I stared at him in the dim interior. "I feel like I just got played. I think she's going to crash your car."

He took my hand in his, turning it over and brushing the skin with his thumb. "It's reinforced. I think we'd be fine unless she managed to plummet off a cliff. Even then..."

I slid my fingers in his and squeezed tight. "Not the best conversation. Not the worst, either. That title has to go to Viney."

"I heard that." Viney glanced over at me before she finished adjusting the rearview mirror and the seat to her height.

Drake cleared his throat. "What did you guys talk about?"

I shifted uncomfortably. "Stuff. How about you and Zach?"

"Choreography."

"Nice."

He leaned closer, his lips brushing my cheek as he whispered. "I've changed my mind. I'm not going to tell anyone about your secret mailman lover whether or not you go to the dance with me. I shouldn't use you to keep other girls from going insane. I apologize."

I stared at his hand, strong and firm around mine. "Are you serious?"

He flashed a sharp smile at me. "Yes. I withdraw my offer."

I smoothed my fingertips over his hand. "I don't mind if you tell people you're going with me, and then I can get sick or something at the last minute."

"You'd do that?"

I nodded before I glanced up at him. "Viney was telling me that you're acting really weird about me, that you don't usually hang out with a girl unless there's some kind of fortune cookie involved."

He raised an eyebrow with a slight smile. "I knew I forgot something." He was so close to me, his voice a low murmur that went deliciously with the slight scent of black cherry.

"Fortune cookie is a euphemism for…"

He slid his hand over my mouth, his head still close to mine. "Don't say it. Euphemisms are ruined if you say what they mean."

I giggled and pulled his hand down. "Fair enough."

"Are we okay?"

I stared at him, his smile disconcerting in its softness. What did 'okay' mean when it came to the impossibly irresistible Drake Huntsman? "Of course. Friends?"

"Friends." He tightened his grip while my heart pounded hard in my chest.

36
WITCH

Days passed and I fell into the rhythm of life at Rosewood school for crazy rich kids. The air grew sharper, colder in the mornings, still warm in the afternoons, but dustier, the sun fading down behind the woods in their russet glory.

I leaned against a pillar in front of the library staring at the distant trees, breathing deeply and letting my mind wander. The leaves reminded me of Drake's hair, glistening with sweat, dusty from wrestling with Zach. My fingers twitched, aching to slide through his strands, to bring order to the mess or just enjoy the chaos.

I licked my lips and unwrapped a lollipop. I didn't feel anxious, so it was raspberry, sweet and slightly tart that reminded me of Zach. I walked up the steps slowly, delighted when Oscar glared at me and assigned me to Lars. Oscar shot a dirty look at my lollipop, but didn't tell me that they weren't allowed.

"Have you ever thought about asking Viney out? I think she likes you."

I stuck my lollipop back in my mouth and watched Oscar's face turn interesting colors.

Finally he sputtered, shooing me away from the desk, "Don't get any books sticky."

I sighed and swished my skirt as I headed over to Lars. "Lars, do you have a crush on Pitch?"

His eyes went kind of glassy. "Her ribbon curl is…"

"I take that as a yes. So disappointing. Will you help me pick a topic for my English paper?"

Afterwards, I gave him a lollipop and headed out, aware that Oscar's eyes followed me with a dangerous and deadly glare.

"I only dripped lollipop spit on the five-hundred-year-old book, not the six-hundred-year-old one." I beamed at him. "Just kidding! See you later, Oscar!"

I headed down the hall then at the top of the large marble stairs saw Drake running up. I hesitated before I continued down, determined to act cool and not like seeing him move, so fast, so powerfully didn't get me all stupid and flustered.

He looked up and had wide eyes, like he didn't like what he saw. I paused, but my feet didn't pause, they kept sliding over the marble step while my hand slid off the railing until I was airborn.

I hit Drake, then the edge of a marble step with my thigh, then Drake again, tumbling down the stairs until we stopped, braced by Drake, jamming his foot in a banister and gripping the edge of a step with one hand, his other one behind my head.

I stared at him breathing heavily, my chest pressed against his, and in that moment I wanted to fall down the stairs for the rest of my life, hanging onto Drake and taking all the painful bumps and bruises as long as I got to crash with him.

His eyes burned into mine as I shifted on top of him and then gasped as his leg slid over my bare one. I lost focus of everything while I tightened my grip on the lapel of his suit coat, hanging on for more than dear life.

His lips were so close to mine, slightly parted, soft and supple. I leaned closer to that mouth, inhaling black cherry and something else, something pungent.

"Is that neem oil?"

He raised his eyebrows, his breath cool on my parted lips. "I hope not. Neem will be a nightmare to get out of clothes."

I nodded and my chin bumped his while his leg shifted. I closed my eyes and tried to breathe through the ache in my chest. I needed to touch him, to taste him, to feel his skin against mine.

"Um, Penny? I think my grip is about to fail. I'd love to continue this conversation, maybe in my room?"

I opened my eyes wide and saw his eyes so close, I could make out all the swirls and specks of green and black. His lips were so close to mine. Too close. I rolled off him, hitting my thigh on the marble step beneath. I smoothed down my skirt and winced as I stood up.

"Are you okay?" I bent over to help him, but he stayed there lying on the step in that awkward position.

"I changed my mind. I can hang onto the lip of this step indefinitely. Climb back on top of me."

I sighed and pulled his feet out of the railing and put them down so he could sit up. He grabbed me around the waist and pulled me onto his lap.

"Drake, haven't you learned your lesson about grabbing girls? I'm going to have to bring Señor Mort to keep you in line."

"Are you okay, Penny? I don't think you hit your head, but what about the rest of you? Did you sprain anything?" He ran his hands over my arms and my legs before I could stop him. I inhaled sharply when he got to my thigh, and he actually pushed my skirt up so he could look at my leg.

"Drake!"

I slapped his hands away while he leaned back against the steps to frown at me where I perched on his knees.

"That is going to be an ugly bruise."

"That's what makeup is for."

His scowl deepened. "Someone warned me about the steps being oiled. I almost wasn't here in time."

I shrugged but I felt cold and grabbed his hand. "You could have texted me."

He tangled his fingers in mine and sat up, sliding his other hand over my waist, drawing me closer. "It's probably my fault for telling the world that you're my date for the dance. I think we should call it off."

I bit my lip then lifted my chin. "And I think we should make a big scene where you present me with some seriously adorable dance outfit and make whoever did this sick with jealousy. There it is, that vengeance coming out. Because it's probably all your fault, the fall I mean, would you help me do my laundry tonight?"

He raised his eyebrows. "I will help you do your laundry every night. You know there's nothing I like more than helping a weak, incapable woman who can't load a washing machine." He tightened his grip on me and leaned closer so he was only a breath apart from me.

"What are you doing?"

He smiled slightly before he pulled away. "I thought it looked like you wanted to kiss me before, but it was probably the awkward position you found attractive, not me."

I licked my lips. "Probably. It would be like death by weasel."

He raised his eyebrows. "Kissing me would be like death by weasel?"

I nodded. "Attractive in the unlikelihood. Are you going to help me with my laundry or were you teasing?"

Soon enough, we were once again alone in the laundry room, and every time I glanced at him, he seemed to be looking at me, which was ridiculous, but my whole body buzzed with an awareness of him, every movement he made seemed to be part of me.

Finally, I had a clean and folded basket of laundry, and so did he, and somehow he'd managed to get the nasty Neem oil out of everything.

He caught my fingers outside of the door. "Let me walk you to your room."

I shook my head. "I may not be able to handle a washing machine, but I can walk all by myself."

"Fine." He tightened his grip on my fingers. "Walk me to my room."

I stared at him and in spite of the two laundry baskets between us, I felt like I could feel his chest against mine, his heart pounding rapidly while his pupils dilated. I glanced away and nodded. "I've never been to your room."

We walked slowly, two buildings away from Lilac Stories, but instead of having commons, it was just a wide and elegant hall with a few doors far apart, which made sense when Drake opened his door and let me into his room. It was a suite with a living room area with kitchenette on one side, and then a few steps up was a bedroom and a bath.

"Your bathroom is in your bedroom."

He nodded and passed me to walk up the steps with his laundry. I stood there in his doorway watching him put away his laundry, hanging his suits in a closet with a sliding mirror door. He had a lot of glass along with the black that dripped like oil over everything.

"I have a surprise for you," he said, coming down the steps to me. He took the laundry basket out of my hands and led me over to the couch.

"A surprise? How exciting. I hope it's the good kind of surprise and not the other kind, not the kind with Neem oil. Like the time you threw me a tea party, not the time you held back my hair while I puked."

He grinned showing sharp, white teeth. "Penny, are you nervous? I promise I won't bite you."

I hesitated then let him slowly draw me over to the couch. He grabbed a remote, clicked at the enormous screen hanging over a fireplace and with that flames came to life behind the glass wall at the same time I heard familiar music and saw my favorite characters of all time from the Telenovela, 'Passiones'.

I squealed and actually jumped up and down before throwing my arms around Drake. "It's a good surprise!" I squeezed him tight, burying my face in his neck and inhaling his bewilderingly intoxicating scent before I pulled away, breathing rapidly. "Do you have a blanket? Popcorn? Come on!"

I sat down on the floor in front of the couch while Drake went to get a blanket, black of course, and I wrapped it around myself, covering my nicely bruised leg. I heard popcorn popping, but I was already sucked into Laredo's secret obsession with Marionetta.

"Drake, hurry! He's going through her mail and he's going to see her correspondence and have a knife fight with Antonio! You're going to miss it!"

He laughed and soon settled beside me with a silver bowl of fluffy popcorn. He tugged on the blanket until it covered both of us and I curled beneath his arm against his side. I didn't think about going closer to him, just one moment I was leaning against the couch, and the next I was leaning on Drake. He felt so nice, so right and perfect.

I swallowed and somehow felt less like squealing gleefully. I glanced over at Drake, and he turned his head, smiling at me before I quickly faced front again.

"Viney and Zach should be here."

"You think Viney would like this?"

I shrugged. "She made me watch horror. That means she can watch Telenovelas, doesn't it?"

"Honestly, I think she'd get addicted and that's all you guys would ever do. It's better this way, trust me."

I leaned my head on his shoulder then sat upright because what was I doing, getting closer to him.

"Are you all right? Uncomfortable?"

I turned my head to stare at him, shook my head, and then turned back to the screen. For some reason, everything made me think of Drake, lying on his body on the steps. I could practically see Marionetta in such a position with her brother-in-law, Hester, because they were always accidentally getting into those kinds of positions. She wouldn't snuggle under a blanket with him, though. That wasn't an accident. What was I doing so close to Drake when it wasn't an accident? I couldn't be so close to him, not when my body was so stupid about him, not when my mind shut off when he brushed his fingers over my skin.

Finally, the show ended and I shot up, grabbing my laundry basket. "That was so amazing! I can't believe you let me watch that. You're so sweet. I've got to get to bed. See you tomorrow, buddy!"

He grinned at me while he stood, folding the blanket into neat thirds before draping it over the black couch. "I'll walk back with you."

"That's silly. I just walked here with you, if you walk back with me, then I'll have to walk back with you, and then you'll have to walk back with me, and it could take all night."

He tugged the laundry basket. I held on for a second but then let go when the laundry bounced alarmingly. I would hate to fold it all over again. "Do you have a lotion for bruises that I could put on my back? I hit it on the stairs."

I sighed. "Oh. Of course. That's a good idea."

We walked back, but I walked fast that time, like hounds were chasing me. Finally, we got back to my room and I did my code and hand scan then let Drake in with my laundry basket. I rummaged around for the right lotion and then turned back to Drake. I held it out to him, but instead he grabbed the hem of his shirt and pulled it up, over his rippling abdominals, rounded pectorals, sharp collarbones, and over his head.

I stared at him while my mouth watered and I almost dropped the lotion out of my limp fingers.

"Can you put it on me?" He gave me what may have passed for a demure smile on anyone else then turned and showed me his back. I hissed when I saw the raised welt that ran down his left trapezius. I unscrewed the lid and smoothed the lotion on, barely noticing the soft skin, the silk covering rock hard muscles, starting at his shoulder blade and working down to his hip. I rubbed and rubbed, way more than was necessary, but I couldn't seem to stop touching him, stop stroking and sliding my hands up and down his back until he turned around, pulling the lotion out of my hands.

"My turn." He nudged me into a chair with the elaborate rose carvings, and then started on my leg, at the knee, smoothing lotion over the skin in circular patterns, working with his thumbs over the tight muscles, up, and up, until he was at the edge of my skirt. My breath caught while he hesitated at that flimsy barrier until he slid his thumbs beneath the edge and worked up my outer thigh to my hip. His hands smoothed and caressed, until my whole body was tight and trembling. He pulled away, stood up, and carefully screwed the cap back on, the movement flexing his naked pectorals.

I exhaled in a rush before I ran a hand through my hair. "You're going to give me a stroke."

"I thought I did give you a stroke, several in fact. Do you need more?"

I whacked his leg. "None of that. Get to bed unless you have more excuses to keep you here."

He stared at me for a long time before he closed his eyes, nodded slowly and turned away. He put on his shirt, his muscles disappearing beneath the fabric.

At my door, he turned and gave me a long, slow look before he nodded, flicked his eyebrows, and turned, closing the door firmly behind him.

37 WITCH

I spent all night dreaming about Drake. The things my dream self was capable of on stairs with Drake were shocking. I woke up in the morning fuzzy and cranky. When I came out of my room, Zach was sitting on the couch. He stood up when he saw me.

"I'll walk with you to breakfast."

I gave him the brightest smile I was capable of. "Sounds good."

"Are you okay? I heard what happened on the steps. You're lucky Drake was there to break your fall."

I stopped walking for a minute, frowning at the students in the corridor ahead of us, heading towards the Dining room or classes. "I don't need Drake to break my fall. How does it make sense for both of us to fall down the stairs instead of just one of us? Am I more breakable than Drake?"

He nodded, his eyes wide and sincere. "Drake is really tough. No offense, Penny, but you're not."

I punched his shoulder and he shook his head.

"Was that supposed to hurt?"

I lifted both of my fists and crouched down before I sighed and straightened up. "Of course it wasn't supposed to hurt. Why would I hurt you? You're the only one who likes all the flavors of my lollipops."

With that, I gave him a handful of lime, which he tucked into his bag with a wide smile. "Last night after you guys hung out in your room, he came in my room and kept me up for hours."

"What did you talk about?" Not like I cared. That much.

Zach smiled slightly. "Different things, whether he should stop flirting with you so people stopped bugging you, or if that would make things worse in the long run, who should compete in the next Chemiss tourney, the best way to take Neem oil out of wool, he just kept talking until I finally kicked him out. I think he really liked falling down the stairs with you. You guys could go to the dance as Jack and Jill."

I stared at him. I couldn't let Zach think that I was going to the dance with Drake, that I was serious about him or he would never marry me. "We're not actually going to the dance. I agreed to let him tell people that so girls wouldn't get so crazy about him."

He stopped suddenly, his eyes narrowing. "You're not actually going to the dance with him?" He nodded slowly and resumed walking. "That makes sense. He's really annoying."

I laughed and shook my head. "That's true. What is with the howling? I think he's a wannabe werewolf."

Zach snorted. "It's his spirit animal. Also, most girls really like it."

"Does he do it to make girls like him?"

Zach shook his head. "Naw, he's always run around howling. I don't know why. Maybe he is a werewolf."

I snickered. "He has such big eyes."

"And sharp teeth,"

"And big ears..."

"I heard that."

I gasped and turned around to see Drake leaning against a pillar in the early morning light, his arms bare in spite of the chill. "We were talking about..."

Zach interrupted me. "The fairy tale dance. You guys could go as the Big Bad Wolf and Little Red Riding Hood."

Drake cleared his throat, and held out a brown paper bag to me. I took it gingerly, half expecting a wolf to jump out at me, but of course a wolf wouldn't fit, but an extremely short skirted dirndl did. I held up the green and pink thing, the white blouse with way too wide neck, the black shoes and white knee high socks, it was all so adorable.

"This is cute!" I whirled around and the skirt spun with me because it was about fifty layers of lace and chiffon.

"You said you wanted vengeance, right?" Drake murmured, moving close to put a hand on my arm.

I inhaled deeply before I beamed up at him. "I only hope all my bruises are healed because I don't think this skirt is going to cover very much thigh."

"That's what makeup is for." He stepped closer, his knee brushing mine while my chest tightened.

Zach cleared his throat. "So, Jack and Jill?"

"Hansel and Gretel." I whirled to him. "Isn't it fabulous? Drake is going to wear Lederhosen and we are going to look so great!"

Zach blinked at me then gave Drake a sidelong glance. "Hansel and Gretel are siblings."

Drake shrugged. "Our hair is complementary."

Zach cleared his throat. "Sounds pretty taboo, if you ask me."

I rolled my eyes. "Like a wolf and a girl together are worse than a brother and sister, or the girl and the creepy old man who wants her baby, or the unconscious girl and the prince, or the other unconscious girl and the prince, or the prince dressed as a bear, never mind that one is really hot. Anyway, Hansel and Gretel were probably switched at birth or something."

Drake cleared his throat. "Yeah, and the guy's actually a changeling elven prince who can give the girl bliss through endless nights of shared immortality."

I glanced over at Drake, swallowing as he smiled at me seductively. I cleared my throat and projected my voice so everyone could hear us who wanted to, or didn't want to. "Right. Anyway, thanks so much for this super adorable Gretel costume, Drake, because now I'll be so cute and fabulous at the dance that I'm going to with you. It was so thoughtful and caring and brilliant for you to get us matching costumes."

Zach winced. "That was loud."

Drake smiled slightly. "I think that does it."

I hesitated before I launched myself at him, forcefully enough that he should have fallen back a step, but he only braced himself and slid his hands over my lower back, holding me closer to his body. Oh dear. "I can't wait to dance in your arms all. Night. Long."

I surged up to my tiptoes, hesitated a breath away from his lips then turned away, a hand on my forehead while I looked faint from being close to so much Drake. Okay. I was faint from being close to him, but he would naturally think it was my fabulous acting skills.

He fought back a laugh as he let me go, struggling to keep a dangerous and seductive look on his face. "I'll see you later, sister."

Zach winced while I held onto my manic smile until he was out of range.

"That was really sad." Zach shook his head. "It would be better if he went as the wolf. As Hansel he'll just confuse people."

Friday came, and it was the night before the dance. I went in to dinner with Viney, ignoring the stares of envy and hatred. I should just let them rip Drake apart like a pack of wolves. Wolves. My mouth watered for some reason and it probably wasn't the extremely beautiful lasagna sitting on its white plate in front of me. We were at the little table in the corner Drake usually sat at, but he wasn't there at dinner. I could have asked Viney where he was, but I liked pretending not to be interested.

"Drake's at polo practice."

"Mmm hmm. That's nice. Are you going to the dance?"

She snorted. "To watch you and Drake try to dance? I've heard stories about your lethal ballet maneuvers. Honestly, it will probably be hilarious. I'll think about it. Have you ever thought about having a make-out party?"

She leaned forward, staring at me over her chicken cacciatore with the gaze of a hungry predator.

I swallowed the bite of lasagna I'd just put in my mouth and gave her my least freaked out freaked out stare. "Make-up party? That is such a great idea!"

She rolled her eyes and leaned closer, keeping her voice low. "Make-out. You know, kind of a mash-up of people all kissing at the same time."

I leaned forward until we were only inches apart. "How would that even be physically possible?"

She shrugged and stabbed a piece of chicken. "It could be a not big deal, just Zach and Drake..."

I giggled and pointed my fork at her. "You're trying to make out with Drake. Very subtle, Viney. I don't think it sounds very fun. I'd probably end up sitting there in super uncomfortable jeans watching two guys fight over you again. I know, we could have telenovelas on so I have something to do." Of course I was not about to go anywhere near the making out of Drake. If I kissed him, I wouldn't ever be able to stop. Just look at how ridiculous I'd been on the stairs, hovering over certain death but not caring even a little bit because Drake was beneath me and his leg...

She sighed and wrinkled her nose at me. "The idea of Zach and Drake making out with me is nauseating. No, you'd have to keep Zach occupied."

I rolled my eyes. "All I have to do is dress up in a black bodysuit and paint my hair black and my face white."

"With black lips."

"Tons of kohl. It would help if I was two dimensional."

She smiled slightly as she eyed me. "You are so flat you're practically one dimensional."

"Ha, very funny, shorty. Are you going to be around tonight?"

She shook her head. "I'll be busy with the Makiss."

I nodded. "I'll probably get sucked into playing video games with Zach, although it would be way better if I could trick him into watching telenovelas with me. Maybe I can think of an actor who looks like Pitch."

"Good luck with that." We got up, put our plates away and separated, me heading for my room and her to her nocturnal fighting band or whatever.

I stopped suddenly as Wit stepped out of the shadows, her hair not quite as perfect as usual, wearing jeans and heels. If I'd looked anywhere near as perfectly seductive as she did, I should have had guys absolutely crawling over me.

"Why did you do this? What did I ever do to you?" Her voice was thick with tears as her eyes widened and grew moist and dewy. Where had she learned to cry on demand? She held up a long, silk, red dress and cloak that shimmered in her hands.

I had no idea, but I could pretend. "I think in a past life you cut me off on the freeway. I think I blame my horrible driving on you."

Her eyes narrowed as she shook the fabric in my face. "Someone heard you telling Viney that it would be funny if someone cut up my costume, and now it is. You did it, admit it!"

I stared at her then down at the silk. Had I said something about cutting up a costume? I couldn't remember. I stared at the silk, transfixed by the swirl of blood red fabric before I looked up at her. "Witley, you don't know me very well, but I would never hurt red silk. I'd sooner go slasher on her." I pointed at the brunette standing at Witley's shoulder. I forced a sympathetic smile. "If you need help fixing your dress, I'd love to. I'm sure we can get it ready before the dance."

She stiffened and curled her lips. "I'm not wearing some patched dress that you ruined. Maybe you didn't cut it up, but you gave someone the idea, and are still guilty of the crime."

I sighed. "What do you want me to do about it if you don't want me to fix it?"

She smirked and lifted her chin like she'd won. "Give me your costume and take this trash in exchange."

I stared at her. "You want to go as Gretel?" Oh seriously, she wanted to match Drake? I was torn between wanting to scratch her eyes out and wanting to light her face on fire.

I bit my bottom lip while I struggled with the visceral rage. Witley touching something Drake had given me? Never. I'd sooner burn it and dance in the ashes. I opened my mouth then stopped. It was all very well to pretend to go to a dance with Drake to irritate girls like Wit, but every day I got closer to Drake, closer to losing my mind, my heart. Drake was my enemy. I couldn't forget that. He would be furious if he saw Witley in the beautiful dirndl, maybe so angry that he'd leave me alone and stop being so sweet that I couldn't help but want to nibble on him.

I inhaled deeply and gave her a sweet smile through gritted teeth while my heart ached. "Sure, Witley. We'll trade costumes although they probably won't fit exactly. I'm a little bit taller than you, but if that would make you feel better about the cruel prank someone played on you, I'd love to help. Come to my room and I'll get it for you."

She looked surprised for a moment before she smiled victoriously and followed me with her band of troubled beauty queens to Lilac Stories. Witley stayed in the doorway to the commons, not quite coming in while I went to fetch the dress I'd hung up on my wall over the kiss or kill tapestry. It was an adorable dress, so cute, so perfectly woodland to go with my bedroom theme. It even had little deer cut-outs along the hem. I hesitated, considering putting itching powder inside it, but that would hurt the dress.

It was for the best. I couldn't hang onto Drake or anything he gave me. Taking a deep breath, I grabbed it and carried it out. I tried to smile, but instead felt sick when she grabbed it with her claw-like fingers, not really, sensible nails actually.

"Maybe next time you'll think before you wish harm on somebody else." She shoved the clouds of red silk into my arms and turned to dance out, so graceful and lovely while I groaned and threw the silk across the room. It spooled out in a long swirl, truly gorgeous fabric that would have looked incredible on Wit, blood red with her dark hair and pale skin, like Snow White or something.

I sighed and went to Zach's door, knocking on it hesitantly. Maybe he was sleeping or gone, or playing video games, or something... He opened his door and smiled at me. I let out a relieved sigh when I saw that he had a shirt on.

"Hey, Penny. What's up?"

I wrinkled my nose. "I'm such a lawn chair. Wit confronted me and I folded like a bad poker hand. You know what I need? Video games. Will you play with me?"

He smiled and nodded, grabbing his box of old games and system. He slid on the silk as he walked across the room. "What's with the red?"

I sighed and curled up in the corner of the couch while he hooked up the cords. "Do you think that Wit's legs are as good as mine?"

He glanced up from his position kneeling in front of the screen. "Hold on. Let me see if I can guess what Wit wanted. She took the costume Drake gave you and traded it for her little Red Riding hood, right?"

I nodded glumly. "I wasn't going to the dance with Drake anyway, but I really liked that dress. I thought I could use it for a tea party some time."

He nodded like that made sense then flopped beside me and

handed me a controller. "Your legs are much better. I'm not sure the two of you have the same kind of..." He waved his hands around in an hourglass shape and I rolled my eyes, pushing Zach over.

"The silk is gorgeous even if red isn't really my color. Maybe if I have the right lipstick..."

Zach shrugged. "There will be hundreds of red riding hoods. Because Drake's the big bad wolf."

The silk was gorgeous. I had a lot of black dye and a lot of experience dying things black. I could wear black for one day, right? What was I thinking about? I wasn't going to the dance with Drake, but maybe I could go with Zach and find his whole heart key in the process. Did I still want to marry Zach even though he was in love with a poster? I liked him much better than anyone else at school, so that was a yes.

I swallowed. "What are dances here like?"

He shrugged. "I guess they're like people dancing."

I nudged him over again, his shoulder against mine. Kind of a lot of body contact, but he didn't seem to mind, just nudged me back.

"Do you have a live band, a disco ball, fancy refreshments, or a dance show?"

He frowned at me. "You've never been to a dance?"

I shrugged and shook my head. "Isn't that sad?"

"So, why aren't you going with Drake?"

"He makes me nervous." I tangled my fingers together. "Also other girls make me nervous when I'm with him. Also dancing with him is always a disaster."

He nudged me. "We could go and hang out for a little while tomorrow, if you'd like. Not like together, just going there as friends to see the decorations and watch the dancing, and maybe if you're brave, a dance or two."

I bit my bottom lip before I gave him my most sincere smile. "Really? I think you'd have to be the brave one to dance with me. Are you sure?"

He grinned and turned back to the video game.

"What's going on?" Drake's voice filled the room and me, bringing back my most recent weird stairs dream.

I couldn't think of anything to say that wasn't about the dance that I didn't want to talk about other than, "Viney wants to have a make-out party."

Zach swung around to stare at me while I blushed and refused to look at Drake. Drake did not make it easy because he leaned on the arm of the couch directly over Zach's head to stare at me.

"When?"

I stared at him and forgot to breathe. "When?"

Zach shoved him away. "You know that Viney would be making out with you. We have zero chemistry and you're the Chemistry captain."

Drake glowered at Zach. "Well maybe I'd start out with Viney, but eventually..." His head swung to me and I held up my hands, squeezing back into the corner of the couch.

"Not me. I was going to watch Telenovelas while you three got it on. I mean, I'd watch you guys for a little while, but it would probably get boring, you know? No dialogue."

Zach snorted. "You think it would work to have a make-out party with only three people? It may as well be me and Drake making out. I think that I'm more attracted to Drake than Viney, but it's a toss-up."

Drake smacked Zach across the chest. "Don't give Lollipop ideas."

"Too late. Would you guys really make out?"

Drake turned to look at me, his eyes narrow. "Of course. If the stakes were right, I'd do anything."

"What kind of stakes do you need?"

He smiled sharply. "Come on, Zach. Let's do this."

"Wait, I don't actually want to see that. Really. And I'm not being tied to any stakes."

Drake stood up and gestured for Zach who rose slower, glancing at the controls regretfully. Drake grabbed Zach's shoulders and pulled him roughly close, but it was more like martial arts practice than anything romantic.

I went over and took Drake's hand, tugging it off Zach's shoulder.

Drake raised an eyebrow. "You think the hip is a better hold? You're right." He pulled his hand out of mine and put it on Zach's hip instead.

I shook my head and stepped away, crossing my arms over my chest. "Drake, I was joking. Really, really, really joking."

Zach looked over at me and grinned while he put a hand on Drake's back. "Penny, you really blush well."

I turned away with my eyes squinched closed. "If you insist on doing this, you should do it right. Zach, your other hand should be tangled in Drake's hair."

"Give us the count, Penny," Drake said.

"Count?" I looked up at the two guys and they immediately lunged towards each other. Drake snapped at Zach's face, sharp teeth flashing while Zach twisted his fingers in Drake's hair, jerking his head back. I stared with wide eyes for a second before they went down on the ground, twisting and struggling to kill each other.

"Um, guys, I don't think that's making out."

"Sure it is," Drake said, coming up with Zach in an uncomfortable looking hold. "Feel free to join in at any time."

Zach kicked up and knocked Drake over into the little side table. It cracked and shattered impressively.

I took a step away from the struggling pile of testosterone. "Definitely isn't making out. This is bar fighting without the bar, I'm almost sure of it."

I perched on the back of the couch to stay out of the way while they rolled around. Professor Vale came in with a bunch of groceries and I waved at her while she wrinkled her nose at the two boys but didn't say anything as she went into her room and closed the door with a thud.

When they were directly behind the couch, I put my feet on them like a rocking, violent footrest. For some reason this violence didn't bother me at all.

"Weirdly enough, I am kind of tempted to join you guys, but I think you would pull my hair."

Drake lifted his head and grinned at me, holding Zach's face against floor with his arms crossed behind him. "You could put it up like in ballet."

I pursed my lips and shook my head. "I am just going to enjoy the show. I'm so glad you guys aren't actually making out."

"We are making out, right Zach?"

He grinned at Zach who gave him that wild smile, the crazy one I'd only seen a few times. Zach bit Drake hard and deep in his arm. Drake howled and punched Zach in the face.

"What was that, Zach?"

I leaned forward to put a hand on Drake's chest to hold him away from Zach. "Biting is completely normal in making out," I said. "Usually not the kind of bite that leaves teeth marks, but he didn't break the skin. Good job, Zach. Is your face okay?"

Drake's chest rose and fell beneath my hand, damp from sweat and smelling so strongly of black cherry that my mouth watered.

Drake said, "His face is fine. It was a love tap."

I raised my eyebrow and turned to Zach, but Drake covered my hand, pinning it in place. "Drake, I'm checking Zach's injury."

"You need to demonstrate to me exactly how biting is acceptable in making out. I think Zach's disqualified."

His voice was low, rough while his breathing hard and heavy, heart beating beneath my palm. I stared at Drake then bent down and put my teeth on the side of his hand, the one over mine. I meant to kind of shock him into letting me go, but instead I tasted him and I didn't want to stop.

I sank my teeth slowly into his skin, scraping it while I slid my tongue over his flesh. I bit down a little bit harder, feeling his skin stretch taut between my teeth before I sucked on his skin and tasted black cherry.

Zach's hand on my shoulder broke me out of my reverie and I pushed away from Drake, blinking up at him while my tongue tingled and lips trembled.

Drake's eyes were wide, pupils dilated as he stared at me, his chest still rising and falling rapidly. He bit his bottom lip and I bit mine, hallucinating his teeth on the soft pad.

Drake inhaled deeply and grinned at me. "You win. Biting is absolutely allowed. Zach just isn't very good at it."

Zach snorted. "I must need more practice. Come here, Drake, let me practice on your leg."

I laughed and edged away from them, my eyes straying to Drake, the way he cradled his hand to his chest and stared at me like he knew what I was thinking and wanted.

38
WITCH

The red silk was indeed slashed to pieces. The bodice was rather skimpy with spaghetti straps, but the skirt was full and flowing while the red cloak had five times as much fabric as it needed. It would be beautiful in a spin.

After I'd dyed the entire thing a rich and perfect pitch black, I deepened the bodice slashes and inserted panels of cream silk in gathers that gave the top a bit more breadth than I would naturally have. Instead of patching, I put in more slashes, more inserts of cream silk, dramatic against the black.

I finished in time to make a little aphrodisiac perfume to wear with Zach. I did my makeup carefully, darkly smudged eyeliner, and almost black lips with a purple tint, like black cherry. I winced and pushed the thought away. It wasn't black cherry but almost indigo or maroon, burgundy, merlot, anything besides Black Cherry.

I stood in front of the mirror and didn't want to look away. I hadn't worn black in such a long time. Even if my hair was in neat strawberry blond ringlets, I still looked dramatic, dark, dangerous and moody with my makeup and the dress that clung to me, like midnight slashed with moonlight. I closed my eyes tight and felt Drake's arms come around me as he danced with me, clothed in darkness and anger that matched my heart.

I opened my eyes wide, smiled brightly at my reflection—a fairly terrifying sight—and whirled around to the door.

"Zach?" I said as I closed the door behind me then stopped when he looked at me from his position on the couch in jeans and a t-shirt.

His eyes widened as he sat up, staring at me with a weird look on his face. "Penny? I thought you were going as Red Riding Hood."

I shrugged. "I had some dye. Do you like it?" I swished the skirt and it swirled around my ankles like black water, delicious against my legs.

He coughed. "It's nice, but what are you?"

"I'm the wicked witch, of course. Either that or the woods in the moonlight. I'm not sure if Rosewood is ready for that much subtlety."

He stood up and smoothed down his shirt then glanced down like he just realized what he was wearing. "I'm not dressed."

"It's okay. I just like getting dressed up, so if you don't want to, we'll just hide under a table, steal some punch and come back here for video games."

He laughed and shook his head. "No, I will definitely get dressed. Give me a second, actually fifteen minutes. I'll shower. Okay?"

He vaulted over the couch and left me standing there feeling kind of, suddenly so excited that I had to spin around, and the dress spun so gloriously, and the cloak, and if black lipstick was all it took to make Zach look at me like that, then everything would be okay.

When Zach came out, he was wearing leather pants, no-nonsense boots that laced over his calves, and a jacket as sharp as the edge of a katana.

"That jacket is beautiful." I went to him and ran my fingers over the fabric, the extremely fine wool. I looked up and realized how close I was to him. I cleared my throat and backed up. "Sorry. I am kind of into fabric, and jackets, and really handsome boys wearing jackets in great fabric."

He grinned widely. "That's good because I'm a sucker for a girl who has a thing for fabric. You smell really good."

"It's an aphrodisiac." I blinked at him while his smile grew wider.

"Really? Are you trying to seduce me?"

I shook my head laughing while I knew my face was pink. "I was just trying to get in the mood, you know, dancing and dresses and stuff." I bent close to his neck and inhaled deeply while he stood stock still. I pulled away and looked up at him going for sultry. "You smell incredible. Is your base musk with a hint of jasmine and a tone of cinnamon? I want to make Zach flavored lollipops."

He pressed his lips together and held out his arm. "Wow, Penny. You should wear that dress more often because I think it brings out your…"

I raised an eyebrow as I slid my hand on his jacket sleeve. "My what?"

"Temptress."

I shrugged. "That makes sense. It was Wit's dress."

He scoffed. "That dress never belonged to anyone besides Penny Lane. I am honored to be your guide on tonight's adventure."

That's what I wanted, a companion on life's adventure, a little more than friends and a little less than something too much. Maybe after tonight we would be over that line and I wouldn't have to worry about Drake stirring up my insides like an overdue volcano.

We walked down the wide corridors lined with pillars, and I felt like a princess in my enormous skirt beside a handsome prince. When I looked at Zach, he met my gaze and smiled, his blue eyes slightly mischievous.

"I can't get over how different you look. I feel a little bit nervous."

I gave him a demure smile, gazing at him beneath my eyelashes. "I'm still the same lollipop girl, but I am kind of excited to pretend to be something else for a little while. You look like a prince charming. What would the wicked witch do with one of those?"

He scowled darkly, startling me before he flashed a smile and resorting once again to his glower. "I am a huntsman. Can't you tell? Leather pants."

"But the jacket..." At his renewed glower I pressed my lips together. "Yes. Definitely a huntsman. The lack of axe threw me off for a second." I gripped his arm tighter and leaned into him. "I'm not sure if the wicked witch and the huntsman should be seen together, no, the huntsman did go around and collect hearts for the witch or something. That's disgusting."

He shrugged. "Anything for my queen."

"Oh, that's right, that was the evil queen who was also a witch. Wasn't she the most beautiful woman in the world?"

He glanced at me, and something about his expression made me nervous. "You'll hold your own against the other evil queens that will be there tonight."

We climbed the stairs lined with men dressed in black like the men who had climbed the platform with the lightning in their hands. I pressed closer to Zach as we passed them, their eyes directed forward as though we were invisible.

I lifted my skirts high in my hand that didn't hold Zach's arm so I didn't trip on them. "It's like Cinderella."

He laughed. "Now you're Cinderella?"

I shrugged. "I don't have a curfew and I didn't come in a pumpkin."

We stepped out on the balcony at the top of the stairs and I paused because spread out below us was a crowd of swirling dancers dressed in elaborate gowns and dancing intricate steps. The music was a waltz, but these people waltzed like they'd been doing it their whole lives.

"What do you want to do first, Penny?"

I blinked while I walked forward, leaning against the balcony instead of walking down the steps on either side immediately into the dancing. Instead of cheesy cut-outs dangling from the ceiling with pompoms and balloons, it was like the woods had spilled into the room, mist curling along the ground between dancers, silver trees stretching long arms above, dripping with leaves that glowed and sparkled. A moon hung from the ceiling, and stars twinkled in the distance. A breeze rushed past my cheek that smelled like grass and dew and fallen leaves. Two walls were glass doors, open to let in the night.

I spun around to grip Zach's hands. "Thank you. This is more beautiful than I imagined. If you want to go back, I've already had my fill of perfection."

He smiled widely and shook his head. "No, you haven't tasted the bubbling cider or coconut silk. Come on, there is so much to taste."

Zach held my hand as he led me running down the stairs to the left, and I laughed as my slippers barely touched the marble steps, my silk gown rippling around me until I felt like I was flying.

Long tables in thick white tablecloths were laden with a bewildering assortment of delicacies. There was a goat with its horns still attached with other animals cooked inside it including a duck, beak and all.

I was staring at that when Zach pressed something cloudlike to my lips. I parted and yes, clouds and also coconut with chocolate and something darker, something richer that made me tremble and slide my hands down my bodice over the black silk.

"It's called pleasure, which I'm sure you understand. Would you like another?"

I smiled and with that he had another of the cloud confections against my lips. I laughed and ate, then floated along with him as he went to the next incredible thing I had to try. Everything was beautiful, delicious, incredible, and the bubbling cider actually bubbled, like cold bubbles that continued bursting in my champagne flute as I held it to my lips and it tickled my nose.

I was laughing from the bubbling cider when I noticed people staring at me. I stopped laughing and moved closer to Zach. I wasn't sure why, but I felt more vulnerable in black, like I was without my macaroon armor to keep all the hatred and anger at bay.

"What's wrong?" He cocked his head and I smiled tremulously.

"I'm feeling a little weird. Maybe we should call it a night."

He put his hand on my waist and pulled me against him in a smooth movement straight out of a dream. The clouds beneath my feet made me feel like I was in a dream, and Zach looked like a handsome prince, sweeping me across the floor with his firm yet gentle grip.

I didn't stumble, didn't get nervous and elbow him in the head, just floated across the floor, staring into his blue eyes as if he was the only person in the world. My heart accelerated just the right amount while he pulled me closer, his scent a tantalizing, comforting smell, like baked bread or cookies.

"Zach, you smell so nice," I murmured as I rested my cheek on his shoulder, the collar of his jacket rough on my sensitive skin.

He tightened his hand on my waist and we spun, dizzying, deliriously fast. I laughed, breathless as I stared at him and he stared down at me, his eyes locked on mine, the blue deepening, darkening as he leaned down, his nose brushing mine, our lips so close I could taste his breath, the flavor of pleasure.

A scream ripped through the melodic violins and cellos, silencing the room. Zach turned us towards the balcony where the scream had come from. I stared at a spike haired girl who perched on the edge of the balustrade then froze and felt my heart crack as she jumped. She didn't fall forward to be skewered on the Waiting Soldier, but landed lightly on the marble floor like she'd fallen a foot, not fifteen. She glared at us as she came, moving faster and faster until she was a blur of black while I clung to Zach under.

"Get away from him! He belongs to me!"

Her voice cracked through the air like a whip and Zach jerked like the lash had landed on his skin. I looked up at Zach and he met my eyes for a moment when I was certain he would bend his lips and finish the kiss we'd almost started, but instead he blinked, smiled slightly and let me go.

I stood there alone while the dancers around me came into suddenly sharp focus. So many girls in blood red sneered at me, their eyes full of poison words I didn't want to hear.

I turned to Viney in time to see her grip Zach's arm, her hand strong and unyielding. "Viney, I didn't think you were coming to the dance. Where is your dress?"

She didn't look at me, just dragged Zach away, putting his hand on her waist as they fell into the steps of the waltz that wasn't playing. I stared after them, my heart pounding until the music began again, the fog swirling around their feet. Viney moved beautifully, like a glorious fey creature in the arms of her handsome prince, hers, not mine.

My hands were shaking as I gripped the edges of my cloak, pulling it around me as though that would keep anyone from seeing me standing deserted and pathetic, unwanted in the middle of the dance floor.

This was not how the fairy tale was supposed to go. No, it was, because I hadn't come as the princess but the witch. I was supposed to come after they hadn't invited me and curse them all. My fingers ached while my stomach twisted with nausea. A pair of dancers knocked into me, then another, and another until I felt like I was a leaf spinning in rapids, the dancers spinning around and around until a strong hand slid around my waist and he pulled me against his chest, a boulder unmovable against the onslaught of all the forces in the world.

I stared at his chest, unblinking at the wolf eye in a golden circle at his throat. "You're not wearing lederhosen."

"And you let Wit have your dress." He turned so I could see Wit wearing my dirndl. It shouldn't have fit her, but she must have had it altered. She looked beautiful and enchanting, walking through the woods in search of something edible, something like Drake, all long legs impossibly slender cinched waist and bosom perched precariously in a bed of snowy linen.

I turned so I was once more facing his chest and stared at that wolf eye for a long time before I could lift my eyes to his. He looked fierce, green sparks in his eyes, russet hair, his lips in a thin line of disapproval.

I'd had enough disapproval for one night. I tried to step away from him, but he didn't let me go. "Drake, I'm tired. Please."

He pulled me harder against him until I could feel the contours of his bare chest through my silk gown. "I don't want to. I don't want Wit to see you humiliated."

I pulled my lips back to snarl at him. "That's what you care about, what Wit thinks? She's a nothing, a purposeless viper that strangles herself in her own coils. Do you have any idea how meaningless humiliation is? Humiliation is a gift that reminds me of the price of love. Do you want me to dance with you, to show Witley?"

I stepped forward into him while he stepped back then I slid my hands up his chest, my nails pressing into his skin, but not cutting. I wrapped my hands around his neck over the heavy chain and pulled him down to me while I rose into him, sliding my silk encased body against him, arching while I pulled his head down until his lips touched my throat.

Fire came to life in my veins as my heart thrummed and he inhaled, so deep, like he would drown in my skin. He moved against me, somehow with the music although it was not a waltz. I ran my hand up to his hair, tangling, tugging while I shifted against him with so little separating us.

The music came to a stop and I froze, my arms wrapped around him, my forehead pressed against his cheek while his chest rose and fell against mine, every inhale sending a frisson of desire through me.

I wanted him. I trembled to take him, to make him mine, to

declare it to the world the way Viney had Zach. I wanted him with an uncontrollable roaring that magnified a thousand times as I rested against him, the scent of dark cherries, dark forests, night wind rustling through me and bringing my whole soul to life. Another song began, this one modern and throbbing, the lights seeming to lower, the room darkening until I no longer felt on display, but worse, secluded in a room of anonymous bodies.

"Penny," he whispered, his voice sweet and low. "I care about you, not anyone else, certainly not Witley. I want you to dance with me because it's what you want, and you're not afraid to take what you want."

I shuddered while his hands seemed to soften on me, gentle and persuasive instead of hard and unyielding. His body nudged me backwards, his legs brushing mine through the silk. What I wanted. I wanted so much to sway against him and for a moment I did, looping my arms around his neck while he cradled me against his chest, our legs tangling as we moved. His hand slid up my back until he reached the bare skin of my shoulder blades beneath my cloak. He spread his hand and brushed lightly while I trembled and clung to him. His hands urged me closer and closer to him until I found myself staring into his eyes, the tip of his nose brushing my cheek as he bent down, his breath dark, sweet, heady.

I closed my eyes and tilted my head back, every nerve extended but in that moment, instead of focusing on the slight copper tinge to Drake's scent, I heard Witley's laugh, her amused voice.

"It looks like Drake has another toy to play with."

It was enough to pull me away from the sheer drop of absolutely lost. I twisted out of his arms, and slid through the dancers, my body once more mine, heart pounding, mind focused on one purpose, escape, as quickly and completely as possible.

I fled through the silver trees and through the open glass doors over the patio that gleamed silver in the moonlight, down the steps and over the grass as I ran towards the woods, deep and dark that beckoned like waters, waves I could drown in.

39
Witch

I ran through the trees, feeling steadier the further I went from the ball. Ball, not dance. That whole experience had been surreal, completely bizarre in absolutely every way. It seemed like I'd hallucinated the Viney thing. Why would she do that? It made no sense, not when she'd said over and over that her and Zach were not dating, that they had no chemistry, etc. etc.

Was there any way to salvage my plans with Zach? I couldn't marry someone who would leave me in the middle of a pack of wolves the second Viney called him. I needed someone like Revere was to my mother, someone reliable and cold, someone who I could think around. I also needed someone who would marry me that wasn't in love with a poster.

I stumbled over an exposed root and caught my balance on the tree trunk. I stood there, panting from my run. I slid down the trunk and pulled the cloak around my shoulders, fiddling with the cord. I inhaled deeply, filling my body, my head with the night, the sharp cry of crickets, the scent of dusty leaves, the cool wind that brushed my skin, rustling in my hair.

"Penny."

I stiffened as Drake took shape from the shadows. He stared at me for a long time before he sat down, across from me at the base of another tree, his arms as bare as his chest.

My voice came out nearly emotionless. "You were not very well dressed for the ball."

"I didn't know that you wanted a prince."

"A huntsman. At least someone with a shirt."

He cleared his throat. "You are dressed perfectly. I hadn't pictured you in that kind of dress, but it suits you."

I shifted. We were not complimenting each other. "I'm glad you came so you can help me find my way back to my room. I'm so helpless and stupid. Shall we get going?"

I stood up and started walking back the way we'd come.

"Where did you get the dress?"

"Witley gave it to me."

"Witley wouldn't fit in that dress."

I glanced at him then away, pulling the cloak tighter around me. "I dyed the red silk and made it more interesting. I'm sure Witley didn't realize the potential of the slashed dress in my hands, but I'm used to working with raw and ruined materials. She looked beautiful in my dress. It was a really great dress, Drake. Don't you think that you should stop being stubborn and fall in love with her?"

He laughed, but it was short and not amused. "I'll do that as soon as you fall for Jackson. Of the two, I'd rather fall for him."

"Do you think Jackson would like me?" I tugged on the cord and felt it slide through the channel of fabric.

He exhaled sharply. "No. I think that he would like to ruin you, but that's not the same thing."

"Isn't it? All the boys here are so confusing. It must be because I'm so stupid and naïve that I can't tell the difference between a guy who likes me and a guy who doesn't. Can I tell you a secret? I thought that Zach almost liked me for a minute when we were dancing, but he wouldn't have left me like that if he'd even liked me a little bit, at all, even as friends."

He grunted. "It wasn't his best moment, but it wasn't really his..."

"And Viney coming in like that, after we went bra shopping together. It's like she was trying really, really hard to make me trust her just so she could go insane on me in the middle of the ball. Not like I mind that, but what's with you, coming up to me without a shirt after that whole thing when you knew I was vulnerable and weak? Not that I don't expect it, but how could you possibly pretend that you care, come out here all, 'Penny, don't get lost in the woods, let me help you find your way even though everyone knows that I'm the big bad wolf, and I'll howl at you if you show any signs of forgetting.' Don't worry, Drake. I remember. I think that the trouble is that I'm genetically predisposed to prefer wolves over regular people."

He put his hand on my shoulder, pulling me to a stop. "Penny, you don't have to pretend that you're fine. I'm not fine. I'm incredibly frustrated by what should have been the perfect night with you. It should have been me feeding you pleasure and spinning you through clouds."

I laughed. "Drake feeding me pleasure, yes, I'm sure that's just what I need, more pleasure, more desire, more weakness for you." I yanked hard on the cord of my cloak and it came out while I wrapped it around my hand.

"You say that as though you want me."

I spun around to face him, a dark and irresistible shadow that watched and waited for my final mistake. "Are you so desperate to be wanted?"

He stepped closer. "So desperate, yes. I never knew what this felt like before, wanting someone always a little bit out of reach, wanting so desperately that I forget my pride. Is that what you fear, losing your pride, your independence? I try to give you space, when you flinch away from me with fear in your eyes I want to hurt someone, but I'm trying. Tonight was my fault. When I saw you with Zach I lost control. I would have hurt him very badly if Viney hadn't stepped in."

I closed my eyes for a moment, silk cloak swirling around my ankles before I stepped closer to him. "It's so easy for you to hurt people. You say what you want so regularly, you must be used to getting it.

How lucky to be Drake the wolf. How lucky that your humility comes at no real price."

"What do you want, Penny? I'll do everything in my power to give it to you."

I swallowed hard while I twisted the cord in my hand. It was too much. I twisted the cord into a very specific knot and slid it over his hand while I gazed at him, holding his attention so he wouldn't see what my hands were doing, would only feel me clinging to his fingers as I pressed him against the trunk of the tree.

I let go of his hand only for a moment to toss the end of the cord around the tree, caught and knotted by my other hand then slid over his wrist. I brushed against him, staring into his dark eyes as I tightened the rope slowly so that he didn't notice, his eyes so full of his own desire he was blind to my rage.

He would notice soon enough.

I twisted the cord and pulled it high rising on my tiptoes, his hands jerking behind him. His eyes widened and he gasped while I felt a flicker of satisfaction. What did I want? I wanted Drake to feel helpless, completely, terrifyingly helpless in my hands. I stretched up, securing the cord around the tree while I brushed his cheek with my lips until I pulled back, my fingertips on his naked shoulders. I cocked my head and studied him.

"Penny..."

"Shhh." I pressed my fingers to his lips, and he kissed them. I pulled away, frowning. "You don't seem to know how this works. I have you tied to a tree."

"You think that I mind?"

I raked my nails down his chest, cutting through his silky pale skin. He gasped and I smiled at him. "I think you should. You think that I'm different because I've worked so hard to resist you, but I'm as pathetic and weak as all the other girls who want you."

"You want me?" He smiled, his teeth glittering as he stood, arms stretched back, eyes gleaming with anticipation.

"Oh, I do, Drake. You have no idea how I tremble, aching for your touch, but always more, always the one I can't have. I want to lose myself inside of you until I never remember a shred of pain again. I want you to scream my name until your lips are branded and you never say another name again. I want..."

He gasped as I danced my fingers over his chest. His breathing came hard and heavy, like he was running while he strained against the cord, arms flexing. I nipped his arm right above his shoulder, tasting the sweetness of his skin. Pleasure was tasting Drake, hearing him whisper my name. I didn't want whispers, I wanted screams.

I bit his shoulder hard, sinking through the skin while he shuddered. I bit down until I tasted blood. I sucked and nibbled while his body jerked chest rising faster and faster. He was my Hansel and I was going to gobble him all up. I laughed and slid up him to tangle my hands in his hair and press my lips, teeth to his throat. I pressed against him harder, scraping his sides with my nails while I devoured him.

I touched and tasted his body from chin to belt, but the more I tasted, the more I wanted. He was like that magical candy that you couldn't stop craving once you'd tasted and all of this would only leave me more desperate in the long run.

Anger flooded my veins, that he would dare make me want him, that he would destroy my plan to do the right thing, to marry a nice boy and save my mother who I hated, that he would stand there, lips parted, eyes closed and revel in my torment.

"Didn't I say that I wanted you to scream? Scream, Drake!"

I dug my nails into his chest while anger and frustration bubbled out of me. His voice was sharp, but not the scream I wanted but a gasping moan that echoed inside me.

I pulled away to stare at him, his eyes unfocused as he gazed at me, soft, like his lips that I ached to touch. I trailed my fingertips over his mouth then blinked at the red I left behind. I gasped and stepped back, staring at his body, no longer pale and perfectly untouched, but shredded and torn, like I felt, like my heart when I thought of Poppy.

My breath trembled as I reached out, carefully, running my fingertips over the words I'd carved into his chest, 'Property of Penny Lane.'

I held my breath and stared at his face, stepping forward, close to cup his face in my hands, smooth up his jaw and cheeks but everywhere I touched left a trail of red. I stared into his eyes, dark in the shadows that gazed at me unblinking, unafraid, a challenge in them to own what I'd done, what I wanted, to own him.

I shook my head and stumbled away. My shoulders were bare. One of my straps had snapped without me noticing. My cloak spilled across the ground, an oil spill shot through with light. I was that cloak, all black except for the tiny flickers of light I tried to capture, but I'd failed. I'd tried so hard to be someone Zach could really like, fun, happy, cute, but I couldn't keep that up forever, not when I wasn't that person. I didn't want to be a person, I wanted to be busy with work that never ended and kept me focused away from the pain, the fear.

I pulled the cloak around my shoulders, settling it in place before I looked at Drake one last time.

He stared at me, willing me with his eyes to touch him, to hold him, to love him as though I had love inside of my broken heart to give.

"Penny..."

40 WITCH

When I got to Lilac Stories, I stopped short when I heard the voices of Zach and Viney arguing.

Viney's voice was shrill. "He talked to Jackson. He knows who broke into Penny's room. He was going to confront you with it. If he hadn't gone to your room before going to the ball, I wouldn't have gotten there in time and you..."

"Do you think I'm afraid of Drake?" Zach's low growl made my stomach lurch. He sounded like a wolf.

I leaned against the wall outside of the Lilac Commons while my heart pounded.

Viney hissed. "You should be. He wants her."

Zach barked a short laugh. "I know. I can't blame him, but if you think I'm going to stand by and let my friend throw his life away on a witch who knows how to be precisely the poison he craves... He actually likes it, the tea parties, the community service, somehow she figured out exactly what he couldn't resist and then put on that whole act, not wanting him so that he'd find her even more irresistible."

"You're full of it! I saw you dancing with her. That wasn't you helping out a friend, it was you stealing your friend's girl. You were going to kiss her."

"Yes, and then I was going to take her and..."

I walked in the room because I didn't want to listen anymore. They turned quickly to stare at me while I ran my fingers over the edges of the cloak.

Viney glared at me before whirling away, heading towards her room.

Zach's jaw tightened while he stared at me, his eyes alight with wild energy as he studied me. "Penny. I thought you'd be with Drake longer."

I tried to beam brightly, but my face was numb. "Did you?"

His eyes narrowed as he took a step towards me. "Did you hear that?"

"All I hear is the drone of disaffected arrogance." I walked towards him, well, towards my door which was behind him, but when I veered to walk past him, he side-stepped, blocking me.

I stared at his chest, the beautiful jacket mocking me.

"You heard that I'm the one who trashed your room?"

I flinched before I shook my head. "No. I've already heard too much today. My ears are full. I will have to hear that tomorrow."

"You hacked into my limo, my room. That would have been enough, but the way you seduced Drake…"

I looked up at his face, shock breaking through. "You're mental. Seriously deranged. Move, Zach, I'm going to bed now."

He grabbed my shoulders, his fingers biting into my skin, but not painfully, just firm. "No. Since I'm deranged, you understand that I'm not letting you go until you explain how you knew how to seduce Drake, using me and Viney in your whole plan."

I blinked at him. "Well it started when I was eight. I saw my first telenovela and realized that my life's mission was seducing arrogant rich jerks who had nothing better to do than run around hurting people and playing polo, while hurting people. When I saw Drake's photo on the Rosewood page I thought to myself, 'that looks like the kind of guy that Marionetta would try to seduce,' so naturally, I packed all the clothing that he would like, you know, because I thought a complete and absolute ass like Drake Huntsman would be helplessly drawn to someone sweet and fun, cute and kind. Because that makes sense. And then I got a room here, with you and Viney, not because I also saw you on that Rosewood page and thought that you looked nice and kind of fun, but because you were old friends with Drake, which I knew because you don't have any pictures together, and the only interaction I saw was of him kicking the crap out of you after he tried to hang you. So, obviously me being roommates with Drake's friend Zach would totally make him fall in love with me, but to make sure, I had to draw it out. Separate booths at the restaurant? My diabolical way of giving him a sample of Szechuan bliss without getting the whole fortune cookie." I stared at him and shook my head. "You are a complete imbecile. I thought you had sort of a brain floating beneath that hard head, but turns out, not even a flicker."

His eyes flared bright blue and he gripped my shoulders harder while he turned me, pushing me against my door, knocking my head back against the wood. I stared at him, waiting for more violence, but he only stared back.

"You expect me to think that you're actually this sweet little bonbon? That you really care about children and animals?"

I swallowed hard and struggled not to cry. I'd worked so freaking hard to make him like me. All this time wasted, all this effort... I'd actually thought he was my friend, maybe a little bit more, maybe enough that I wouldn't be miserable with him.

"I guess I did. But I'm kind of stupid too. I thought you were actually a nice guy. Instead you're just a jerk who knows how to pretend to be something else. I used to wear black clothes, though. You nailed that part. I also didn't smile, but I didn't really have anyone to smile at, so maybe that was part of it."

He pushed me against the door again, his face close to mine, as close as it had been when I'd thought he was going to kiss me, but he looked like he was about to bite my face. "Are you going to stand here and let me push you around?"

I frowned at him. "You want me to fight you? En garde."

He brushed my cheek with his lips. "Penny, I'm going to hold you like this, touch you until you finally break, finally curse me."

I sighed and closed my eyes, leaning my head back against the door. "Psychotic. You want me to curse you? All right. Bon-bons and ho-hos, I turn you into a toad, oops, you're already a slimy newt. I'll have to work on it."

He gripped my shoulders, digging his fingers into my skin until it really did hurt. "I'm going to hurt you."

"So, hurt me. I can't cast a spell on you because I don't have magic. If I had magic, I wouldn't have picked a roommate who I thought was as picked on and hated as I was certain I'd be at this pisshole school. Make me feel like my eyeballs are going to explode, fill me with your mage fire until my skin threatens to melt off my bones. Drown me in your pain until my brain shuts down. It doesn't matter anymore. That kind of pain doesn't bother me. Have fun with it. Enjoy yourself."

His blue eyes burned brighter. "If you don't mind me hurting you, then you won't mind if I check you, see for myself."

"Wait! No, please don't..."

But he'd already started the spell, muttering syllables that made my skin prickle and then the horrible sensation of having my insides sucked out of me and my whole body filled up with radioactive melted marshmallows, sticky, cloying, sickening while he searched me for the magic that I'd never had.

I went limp until only his grasp on my shoulders held me upright, my head bobbing forward until it hit his shoulder, the perfect suit coat beneath my cheek the integral reverse of my own wrecked insides.

He pushed away from me, holding me up against the door while my own legs seemed to belong to someone else. The pink shoes beneath the black skirt didn't match. I stared at those shoes, then the hallucination of toes that flickered into my vision, toes covered in blood with a field past them. I blinked slowly and the floor beneath my shoes came into focus, a swirling purple carpet that was about to be thrown up on.

Yep.

I closed my eyes tight, tears leaking out the corners anyway. From puke getting in my hair. I wasn't crying because after everything I'd done, all the effort I'd put into being a lovely nice girl any boy would love, I was being tortured by some imbecile who thought I was trying to seduce Drake. Drake who I'd left tied to a tree in the woods with my name carved in his chest.

Black flickered in my vision as darkness stirred in my heart. Impotent fury? Just because I didn't have magic didn't mean that I couldn't hurt him. I raised my head until I could see Zach's face.

He looked like someone had just chopped off his leg and stolen it, leaving him to hop after it pathetically. No, like someone who just heard that their favorite barbecue machine was used to capture a skunk. No, like he'd just realized what a complete and total asinine imbecile he truly was. That was always a shock.

"You're going to have to clean up the puke. It's in my hair." My voice came out low, terse as my throat tightened and my stomach hardened.

He mumbled a word and immediately the pile of vomit on both of our shoes decomposed along with the bits in my hair, until it was nothing but black compost. That was incredibly useful. Most magic I'd seen was from Poppy when she showed me how weak and disgusting, pathetic and worthless I was without the power she held over me.

She liked to torment me until I broke. It took a lot to break me, much more than potatoes in my hair or groups of catty girls publicly humiliating me. I'd spent my entire life learning how to control the demons, the darkness. They never helped, only hurt. I stared at Zach and when I looked at him, I still saw my friend, the idiot who was in love with a poster, the loser who brought me soup and played easy video games with me, the guy who liked all the flavors of my lollipops.

I didn't want to hurt him. I straightened my legs and stared at him, chin lifted. "Is that all you've got? I can do this all day."

He stepped away from me, clenching his fists until they were white. "You have no magic? How is that possible?"

I was against my door. I turned around, moving so very slowly as I hit in the code and pressed my palm against the reader.

"Penny, I..."

"Don't care." I stepped into my room and slammed the door behind me, locking the device in every possible way, including pushing the big red button in the middle that armed it with magic spells that would be impossible to undo. Magic in machinery was as close as I got to magic, well that and hurters.

I leaned against the inside door while I tried to breathe, to figure out a new strategy, a new plan, but I couldn't untangle my thoughts. I walked over to the mirror and stared at my reflection.

My face was red, chapped from rubbing against Drake's skin, my lipstick long gone and my eyes bloodshot while my shoulders were red from Zach's fingerprints. A glance down at my hands showed red, which should be red because I'd slashed Drake to pieces, and he'd still looked at me like he wanted me no matter what I did to him. I spun away from the mirror and went in the bathroom, ran a bath and sat on the edge, sliding black silk through my fingers while I tried not to think of Zach or Drake.

I slid the single strap off my shoulder and the dress pooled to the ground like an oil slick. So beautiful. I washed my face, scrubbing until my skin was raw all over instead of just around my mouth, then worked on my hands and nails until I didn't have a speck of Drake's skin beneath them.

I sank under the water and stayed there, holding my breath until

I had an image come into my head of Drake standing there, bleeding, blood filling the air while wolves gathered around, wolves from the woods and him helpless.

I burst from the water and clambered out of the tub. I squeezed water out of my hair as quickly as I could before I wrapped a pink and white polka dot towel around my body. I left wet footprints across the floor while I hurried to my bag where I'd left it on my bed.

I climbed up and sat cross-legged, phone in my hand. I checked my contacts and there was Poppy's number. I enlarged her picture for a minute, staring into that wide smile. She was a lot like Zach, my friend who couldn't help hurting me. It was his nature like it had been hers. My nature? Did I have one? I was a nothing, a mess of nothings. Still, I couldn't leave Drake defenseless. If he hadn't gotten out of my rope, I would have to tell Viney to go rescue him.

I pushed the button with his name and stared at the empty box waiting for a text message. 'Hey Drake, just wondered if wolves have ripped out your liver yet,' or 'had so much fun tonight, did you happen to see a cloak cord, I seem to have misplaced it,' or 'Surprise! I'm psycho!'

I shook my head and put a question mark in the box. I hesitated and then sent it. I sat there, rivulets of water running down my shoulders and onto the bed, the rose quilt Drake had gotten for me. I traced the swirls of vines while I waited.

My phone beeped and I stared at his message.

?

He'd responded with a question mark? What was that supposed to mean? It meant that his hands were free so he could text. That's what it meant. That's all I cared about. I was done pretending to be nice, pretending to like anything about him or any other person in this world.

Done being Penny Macaroon Lane.

41

Mage

I stood tied to the tree for a long time.

"She's not coming back, Drake. You should probably untie your arms before you're permanently numb." My voice trembled. And I was talking to myself. "She might come back."

I shook my head because I could still see her face, the shock when she realized exactly what she'd done. Probably, it was good that she didn't want to be the sort of witch who took whatever she wanted, but why resist when I wanted it even more than she did?

I shivered as a ghost touch of her fingers brushed over my skin. I had to capture those touches, memorialize them and I couldn't do that tied to a tree. I twisted my wrists and ran my fingers over the complicated pattern of knots that I wasn't familiar with. Darkside knots. I could have broken the cord, dissolved it, but she'd made the effort to tie the knots. I should at least put in as much effort in escaping them.

It took me fifteen minutes before I could untangle the knots. Me and my genius fingers. Genius numb fingers. By the time I felt the cord give, I'd come to a conclusion about something. The next time Penny Lane tied me to a tree, I would step into Darkside then back into Dayside, so I could retrieve the cord with knots intact. Such resolve and decision.

I stood in that clearing while I wrapped the cord around my wrist. I wanted to stay in the woods, to close my eyes and feel the breeze whisper across the gashes in my chest and pretend it was her, but there were things to do. If I didn't put something on those gashes, they would heal without a scar.

With a sigh, I stepped into Darkside then back into Dayside, in my room. I walked towards the bed, pressed my palm on the compartment above it and then took out the red top hat when the door opened. I dumped the contents of the hat on the bed and added the cord to them.

A lollipop stick, a hot-pink hairband, a handful of receipts from the Chinese Restaurant, and a folded bag with a weasel applique. I ran my hand above the objects, sending green sparks from my palm. Images formed in sparks, her face with the teasing smile that lit her eyes, thoughtful, afraid, emotions so close to the surface she could barely restrain them.

She kept the witch deeply buried. I'd unearthed it tenaciously. I'd been pushing her from the first time I saw her, wanting to know more, to see beneath the rich and decadent frosting. Tonight, I'd finally tasted her anger, her possession, her darkness and it was delicious, but no more than her sweetness. I wanted more. I wanted everything.

I smiled when my phone beeped and I saw her name, the image of her in profile, curls swirling around her face.

?

What next?

I responded.

?

I don't know, but I can't wait to find out.

Made in the USA
Columbia, SC
08 January 2019